Keys in the Dust

Vivian Catfield

CATFIELD
PRESS

Keys in the Dust

By Vivian Catfield

Published by Vivian Catfield on her imprint, Catfield Press

2692 Madison Rd.

Ste. N1-354

Cincinnati, OH 45208

www.viviancatfield.com

www.catfieldpress.com

First Edition, Published 2025

eBook ISBN: 9798992771510

Paperback ISBN: 9798992771503

Printed in the United States of America

For Linda,
Who taught me to always pick up the key

Contents

Book One

Into the Otherworld

Chapter One

M y silver key unlocks every door.

I found it on the day Stephen and I hiked the Nantahala Wilderness Overlook Trail. In Cherokee, the word Nantahala means land of the noonday sun, which is ironic because that's where I discovered a door to the moon.

The first day of August was blazing because I live in the South. Heat shimmered off the asphalt as we wound our way up the snaky mountain roads to the Overlook. As usual, Stephen was almost an hour late picking me up at my dad's house in Oak Ridge. He blamed it on the traffic coming from Nashville, but Stephen's always late. He also forgot to bring his water bottle. I had a spare ready for him. That was the way our relationship worked. At least, it had been until that day, when I'd already decided to break up with him. Choosing the day to dump your high school boyfriend is a delicate operation, especially when you've known each other forever, like Stephen and me. And when he's a super sweet guy, just not *the* guy. That hurts the most.

I'd calculated when to drop the news as if I were working on a mathematical equation. First, I divided by not responding to my acceptance from Vanderbilt because I knew that I couldn't afford the student loans. Then slowly I subtracted my presence from Stephen's life while he was busy with early admission summer classes and fraternity rush. The only quotient could be a breakup blamed on distance. Hopefully, the remainder would be friendship. Still, I was never good at math. I hadn't figured out the rest. We'll get to that later.

Perhaps I should tell you about Stephen and me first. Stephen Thornton and I met at camp when we were ten. His parents sent him because they thought he spent too much time in front of the television. Mine sent me because summer camp was a good place to park kids while their parents got a divorce. It was an ordinary sleepover camp: archery, canoeing, and a ropes course where you're supposed to learn to trust other kids. The whole nine. Not a big deal for me, since I practically lived in what most kids would call summer camp year-round. It was groundbreaking for Stephen, though. The dude who, to this day, has never done his own laundry and burns grilled cheese. But he's hilarious and cute, in a blue-eyed, sandy-haired way, which gets guys most places they need to go in America, especially if their parents are loaded.

My dad, Oliver Todd, was a geological engineer who worked for one of the labs at Oak Ridge, where we lived in a legit log cabin. It was pretty deluxe for a cabin, even though my mom didn't think so, and massive. The whole top floor was nothing but my dad's office. We had a game room, a pool, and a huge kitchen that my mom, Darla, never used except for the wine fridge. The view from the pool deck out back was spectacular. My room was in the back of the house and looked out over it. Miles and miles of rolling green hills as far as I could see.

I never remember wanting for anything, but I was never a kid who collected stuff either, other than geodes and crystals. Most of those were from my Dad, who brought them home from his travels around the world. I loved hearing his tales about all the faraway places he'd been. I dreamed of going with him someday. If I've ever been anything, it's a girl who's never content to sit still. Growing up, I spent most of my days rambling around in the woods, talking to the animals; my corgi, Luna, plus all the untamed ones—deer, squirrels, rabbits, wild turkeys, you name it. We had some excellent conversations back then when we were still speaking different languages, but I could understand them just the same. Now, I know why.

Poor Stephen, on the other hand, grew up in Belle Meade, which is the fancy part of Nashville. He went to one of those expensive private schools where parents could pull a Karen and get a teacher fired for not giving their kid straight A's, whether they'd earned them or not. As a result, Stephen was dumb as a post when we first met. He was scared of everything too, especially germs. Stephen just about died the first time Luna slobbered all over him. To cover the fact that he was terrified of the world in general, Stephen cracked jokes all the time. That was what drew me to him in the first place, I guess. I love being around people who talk too much because it relieves me of the burden of coming up with things to say on the fly just to keep the conversation rolling. I'm friendly enough, but it's a quiet kind of friendly. If I like you, I keep showing up and doing things for you. That's more my jam.

Most of the kids at my high school were geniuses, even though Oak Ridge schools are public. Not a shocker, considering all their parents were like Oliver—scientists of one kind or another. I'm just barely a genius. My IQ is only 153, so I'm kind of a disappointment. Being intelligent is a viral thing. If a girl is around other people who are curious and want to learn, chances are she'll catch that spirit too. That's what happened to me. I was always a *why* kid. Everything from *Why were the Appalachians smoother than the Rockies?* to *Why did the course of true love never run smooth?* as Shakespeare mused. Mom would throw up her hands, but Dad was always patient with me. He never just gave me the answers. He made me guess first, amazed at my wild imagination.

People like Stephen's parents never ask why. They think that because they're rich and control the questions, then they should already know the answers. This is probably why so few of their kids hang onto their dough through multiple generations. They lack imagination.

Imagination has gotten me out of a lot of scrapes. Like that time I was in Algebra class and I couldn't work problems. I scrambled around on my calculator until I found numbers that fit the solution. Then in the space where I was supposed to show my work, I drew a wizard, waving his magic wand, with a little trail of stars leading up to it, and captioned it *Eureka!* My teacher was so knocked out that she gave me partial credit because I ended up with the correct solution. Whatever works.

The flipside of imagination—curiosity—is what brought me to the story I'm about to tell you here. About how I found a silver key in the dust that changed my life forever.

Stephen and I were strolling along the trail when, out of the blue, he asked me the question that I'd been dodging all summer. Had I confirmed my enrollment at Vanderbilt?

What could I have told him? That Oliver had lost his job at Oak Ridge because the grant for his research project ran out and wouldn't be refunded? And that the only solid job offer that he'd had since then was for doing surveys as a consultant for some random offshore oil drilling company? Which meant that I knew I'd have to take one of the full rides I'd been offered by half a dozen other out-of-state schools instead because I couldn't afford anything else. Or that Oliver was, on that very day, meeting with a realtor to sign over the house where we'd lived since I was in kindergarten, and we had thirty days to get out?

Latin was mandatory at Stephen's fancy high school in Belle Meade. He spoke some French too, because his family "summered" there, but financial hardship was not a language Stephen Thornton was fluent in. Still, he wasn't the sort of guy who would reconsider being with his girlfriend because of such things. However, I was the kind of girl who was ashamed to admit that they'd happened. So, I didn't.

Instead, I did what I've always done when something upsets me. I took off to the woods.

"Wait!" Stephen cried as I bounded away from him playfully. "Where are you going?"

"I think I saw something. Maybe a bear. Gonna try to get a picture." Not a total lie. There are black bears in the woods of North Carolina and Tennessee, but probably not the best lie to tell if your boyfriend thinks every grass spider he sees is a brown recluse. In my defense, though, if I had seen a black bear, I would have taken a picture. They're pretty rare.

Was it wicked of me to keep running without answering Stephen? Maybe. Was it my fault he was a former wrestler with bad knees already at nineteen, which made me able to outrun him in the first place? I think not. We all make our own choices. Choices have consequences. And those consequences turned out excellently for Stephen. But yeah... I probably shouldn't have told him I was running toward a bear in the middle of the wilderness. That was questionable.

However, that's one thing you should know about me if we're going to be completely truthful with one another. That is, I'm a bolter. Whenever someone gets too close, or something gets too hard for me to deal with, I run. Any decent therapist who knows their stuff would chalk it up to trust and attachment issues that started when my mom left. She was a bolter too. It's probably the biggest trait we have in common and my worst character flaw. But the bolting instinct has also saved me from a lot of bad situations. Make of that what you will.

Regardless, once I was over the ridge and far enough away from Stephen that I could hear him but not see him, I came to another pathway. It was rocky at first, and narrower than the main touristy trail up to the Overlook. As I slowed to a walk, the path became like a pig trail through the woods, only a few inches wide. I was panting in the heat but intended to keep walking until I'd come up with a truthful answer to give Stephen. Honestly, if I hadn't found the key, I might still be walking.

Yet, there it was, about half a mile down this little narrow path that dipped and twisted its way through the forest. A silver key in the dust. I stooped down to pick it up without hesitation. It was a bit longer than an average key, about three inches, and so brightly polished it sparkled in the sun when I turned it over in my palm. The bottom had square teeth like an old-fashioned skeleton key, but the top was delicately scrolled into an ornate letter *W*.

W for Willow, I puzzled, like a child who'd just recognized their name for the first time. My name is Willow Todd.

Odd, but it could have been a coincidence. That's when the first really weird thing happened. As I stood examining the key, it slowly rotated around in my hand. By itself. Then, it began to pull me forward, tip first, further down the trail toward what looked like a solid wall of kudzu vines. If you've ever held a pair of copper dowsing rods and felt the tug of a magnetic field with them, that's what it felt like. Holding the key tightly by pressing my thumb against the large *W* at the top, I allowed the key to lead me, parting the vines as I passed through.

On the other side of the vines was a long, straight driveway covered with tiny white pea gravel. The drive was shaded on each side by at least a dozen gigantic live oak trees. Their lush, green branches formed a canopy that blocked out the sun. Turning back, all I could see behind me was the tall wall of kudzu and nothing beyond. With the key urging me on, I followed.

At the end of the driveway, I came to a clearing with a circular drive. In the center of the circle was a pentagram. Each leg of the pentagram was filled with flowers of different colors: white at the top, with blue, red, green, and yellow finishing out the clockwise rotation. They looked like dahlias or maybe zinnias, but they were as large as a person's head. Some of the colors were like nothing I'd ever seen before. Walking cautiously around the figure, I continued to follow the key up to the double front doors of a five-sided tower with turrets at the end of each point. It looked like a castle.

The doors were made of wrought iron over heavy planks of wood. The tower itself was five stories tall, solid brick, and the bricks looked very old—uneven and likely handmade. I could tell the doors were set into a nook between two long wings of the same height and material. The carving in the arched rock mantel over it spelled out *Rookes College* in letters two feet tall. Staring at them closely and then comparing them with the key in my hand, they were inscribed with the same ornately scrolled, delicate font. Also above the mantel was another pentagram. This one was almost as tall as me. The tip of each point was punctuated by a round silver coin an inch wide.

Just as I began to wonder what kind of coins they were or why someone would embed them into the mortar, the key jerked my arm out straight. Pulling me like a fish on a line, the magnetic energy emanating from the key felt alive. The silver key pressed itself into the lock on the door and turned.

Chapter Two

The lock clicked. A cascade of tumblers moved unseen inside. The doors swung open.

I hesitated, scanning down the sides of the long brick corridors that flanked the entryway. Then, I let go of the key and took a step back to stare again at the inscription on the mantel. *Rookes College.* Having just finished applying to practically every college within a hundred miles of Oak Ridge, the name wasn't one I recognized. Upon closer inspection, there were weathered stone birds about three feet high perched atop each side of the entryway, wings folded to their sides. With their heads cocked inward as if they were examining all who entered, they reminded me of Poe's raven.

Peering into the darkness with my sun-blinded eyes, the cool air beckoned me on that steamy afternoon. My t-shirt clung sticky to my back with sweat. Somewhere I had dropped my water bottle. I was thirsty. Yet, I hesitated on the threshold.

I must have been gone for at least twenty or thirty minutes, and I knew Stephen would be worried sick. Pulling my cell phone out of my back pocket to check the time, I found my screen blank. Although I'd had a full charge when we began the hike, my cell was completely dead. *I should turn around*, I thought.

Then, I could smell it. The warm, seductive scent of sage smoke and something more. I sniffed the air again, like a dog on the doorstep. I've always had a crazy strong sense of smell. Stephen used to make fun of me about it. How I could smell everything, including trouble, for miles. *Maybe I could just see what was inside*, I rationalized, *then go back*.

This scent was far from trouble. It was comforting. Roasted chicken. Maybe some sweet potatoes dusted with cinnamon and brown sugar. Then my favorite, summer squash casserole with the buttery cracker crumb crust like Oliver used to make on Thanksgiving for the lab's potluck supper. He always made a double pan for me, and I would eat on it for days. In the end, more cinnamon with sweet caramel and apples. Like the pies at the barbecue joint Oliver used to take me to when I was a kid.

Perhaps it was because I'd skipped lunch, or perhaps it was because I thought that a place smelling that amazing couldn't be dangerous, but I allowed the scent to pull me inside. Stepping over the threshold, I took the silver key from the lock and slipped it into the pocket of my crossbody bag.

The wooden double doors swung shut behind me, but I didn't panic. The air inside was cool and still, like in a sanctuary. Oliver had no use for church, but Mom took me every once in a while, when she was still around, to Downtown Presbyterian in Nashville. Inside, it looked like something out of that old Elizabeth Taylor movie, *Cleopatra*, I used to watch on TCM. Only this place didn't look Egyptian, not in the least. It had the same reverence, but the Great Hall of Rookes College was something else entirely. Padding down the corridor, I felt thankful the soft rubber soles of my hiking boots made almost no sound. I didn't want to spoil the silence.

Looking up, I traced the limestone columns skyward, where they ended in a glass-domed halo of golden light. Rings of balconies framed the interior, with more stone ravens alighted on the banisters identical to those outside. Only these ravens had their wings fully outstretched, spanning nearly the length of each hallway section. Five rows of long, highly polished dark wooden tables and high, carved-back chairs were arranged in a radiating star pattern on the main floor. The end of each row pointed down another long, unlit hallway. As my eyes adjusted from the brightness of the late summer day I'd just left to the dim glow inside what appeared to be the castle's Great Hall, I could tell this massive room was also shaped like a pentagram. Each of the corridors leading off into the darkness were its legs, leading to a tower at the end. On the tables, twelve silver place settings had been laid out on starched black linen napkins that matched the velvet seats of the chairs.

In the middle stood a five-cornered table atop a stone slab pedestal, laden with an abundance of food arranged on silver chargers. Towering over the feast was a silver candelabra the height of a small apple tree. Each tier of its arms had five branches, with unlit candles of each color, the same as I had seen outside in the flower garden. Glancing around the perimeter, I could see that there were other similar five-armed candelabras at each point of the five-sided hall on every level, punctuating the wingspans of the stone ravens, straight up to the top. The floors were natural gray slate, and the coffered walls were dark burling walnut. The whole place looked empty, but it vibrated with anticipatory energy.

"By the stars, you're quick," came a voice from a hallway near the top of the pentagram. I must have leaped about a foot in the air, for her comment was followed by a musical peal of laughter like chimes. "I wasn't expecting you yet, or I would have lit the candles already." She snapped her fingers.

In an instant, every candle I could see flared to life, setting the Great Hall ablaze. This new illumination revealed even more intricacies. Garlands of silver chains swagged from the banisters with the weight of cascading crystal droplets. Some were shaped like oak leaves and others like little prismatic acorns. All projected endless layers of rainbows where moments ago had been shadows. Within the walls, what I thought to be the ordinary whorls of walnut wood became intricately carved faces of people and beasts, both real and fantastical. Princesses rode great winged birds or led unicorns on silver bridles.

"Won't you sit down? The others will be arriving soon," the voice continued. It was an older woman's voice, crackling with the surety that can only come with years. Still, I could not tell exactly where the voice came from. Carefully, I walked around the table. On the other side, in the arched entryway leading down a white hallway, I saw her.

Her skin glowed in the candlelight with a porcelain incandescence. Soft black curls piled high on top of her head with one thick tendril falling over her left shoulder. Her deep-set eyes glittered like coals in her pale face. She was about the same height as me, but her dress made her appear taller. It fell in thick folds of black velvet to the floor around a V-shaped satin brocade bodice with a low neckline trimmed in lace that displayed the tops of her milk-white chest. I wanted to ask her name, but from the way she stood appraising me, I felt as if I should already know. My lips trembled, unable to form the question.

"On second thought, why don't you go upstairs, dear, and put on your gown? I know you must be bursting with questions, but I prefer to address everyone at once. Gregor can lead you while I wait to greet everyone as they arrive down here. It's not far, and we won't be long."

Pulling a thin silver whistle the length of a drinking straw from among the many folds of her dress, she placed her fingers over the holes and blew lightly a few notes of melody. Crooking her right arm, she held it up to almost shoulder level. From somewhere high in the rafters, I heard the cawing of a large bird. Then, I watched as the bird spiraled gracefully down to light on her outstretched arm.

"Gregor, dear. Could you be so kind as to show Willow to her room?" The bird blinked once and brushed his beak against her cheek softly. His feathers shone like highly polished obsidian in the candlelight. Swooping into the air once more, Gregor flew around me. My gaze following him, I could see two curved staircases on either side of the white hallway leading up to the second floor. Landing once more on the walnut banister right above me, Gregor cawed again. Then, he tipped his head to the side to stare at the first open door on the right. Knowing what he meant, I climbed the stairs.

The room was laid out like a suite, with a study area in front and a bedroom behind, each about a dozen feet square. The study portion was ringed floor to ceiling with built-in bookcases. They were filled with neatly dusted shelves of old-fashioned, leather-bound books and a variety of other curiosities that I longed to touch and explore but decided to wait. The seating area held a small table and a pair of chairs on one side and a large desk with a single chair on the other. All the furniture, like the paneled walls downstairs, was burling walnut. The tops of each piece were carved with flowers, and the legs ended in clawed feet. The little tea table grasped four glass balls in its talons as it balanced on a weathered Persian rug covering the slate floor.

Heavy black velvet curtains divided the study from the bedroom. Parting the curtains, I walked through. The bedroom contained a large metal canopy bed that was sculpted to look like a tree, its branches twining into ends tipped with silver and crystal leaves. A little footstool with two steps to help the sleeper climb on top of the high mattress was beside it. The frame was swathed in white mosquito netting. Beside the bed on the wall closest to the curtain was a vanity with a cheval glass mirror and a little scrolled bench seat. The opposite wall was inset with a series of peaked windows and a padded bench beneath, which looked like it would be cozy to sit on and read. The wall to my right adjoined the walkway around the Great Hall, but the interior wall was all cabinets and drawers.

Opening the double doors of the central cabinet, I found a series of gowns, similar to the one the lady downstairs wore, but in a dazzling array of different colors. How would I know which one to choose?

As I stood pondering the rack, Gregor came hopping into the bedroom and squawked. "Of course," I replied, turning to him. "Black."

Laying the black gown out across the bed, I noticed my feet. Hoping that there were suitable shoes in one of the drawers, I began to slide them open one by one. Finding a pair of pointed-toe slippers encrusted with intricate beading and a low kitten heel, I tried them on. They fit perfectly. Putting on the new shoes pulled me back into reality.

How long has it been since I ran away from Stephen? I wondered. My mind swam as I remembered my original intention had been just to have a look behind the door and then turn back. *What in the world was going on? Why was I up here getting dressed for this strange dinner with people I'd never met? Did I just pick out a dress because a bird told me to?* A small pulse of panic shot through my synapses, making the hairs rise on my arms. I tried to cut through the fog of my thoughts. It was as if I had been enchanted by the woman downstairs to do what I was told. Yet, I didn't even know her name.

Through the curtain, I heard the melody of her whistle sound again. Quick as a wink, Gregor flew out the door to answer. I followed him.

Chapter Three

He was standing in the hallway the first time we met, watching Gregor sail away into the Great Hall beyond the balcony. Looking half-dressed like an actor caught changing costumes for a play, he wore normal sneakers and jeans on the bottom and a tunic-length white shirt with a stiff collar covered by a silver-trimmed black velvet vest on top. The shirt was undone from the top few buttons, and a wrinkled length of black silk hung down on each side. Catching sight of me, his gray eyes lit up.

"Oi! You don't know how to tie one of these, do you?" he asked bluntly, not introducing himself at all. His accent was rough British working class, which seemed out of place in the lush surroundings. Frustration twitched in every muscle of his face. He snaked the offending piece of silk off from around his neck and held it out to me, eager to be free of it.

I took it from him and tried to smooth it out. "I'll try. I can tie a normal tie, but this one looks different."

"Of course it is!" he snapped, furrowing his thick eyebrows. The muscles of his jaw clenched, and I noticed that he was unshaven. A shadow of stubble crept along a jawline so sharp that it could cut glass. I tried not to notice. Guys who looked that good couldn't be trusted. Yet, the quick change in his tone when he saw how his hostile attitude affected me made my usual bolting instinct switch off.

He softened, speaking in a loud whisper. "Here now, I'm sorry. I'm just having trouble putting this blasted getup on. If you have any idea at all how to tie this tie without strangling me, I'd appreciate your having a go at it." He smoothed the ruffled mop of his dark, curly hair back with both hands, and one lock sprang back immediately into his face. A cute little natural Superman type of curl. He blew at it, exasperated.

"Damn! I'll have to wet it down." He stalked back into the room across the hall and motioned for me to follow.

"Willow," I said, hoping he'd catch how rude he'd been not to introduce himself, especially under those bizarre circumstances. He didn't.

Instead, he rolled his eyes and stepped to the side of the door, sweeping his hand mockingly over the entryway. "Elliott."

Smiling without teeth, I entered, pulling the door shut behind me.

The furnishings in Elliott's room were the same as mine, but they were strewn with stacks of books and discarded clothes. On top of the pile, under which there must have been a tea table because all I could see were its little glass ball feet, was a long black coat and a pair of short velvet pants. "I'm not putting those damn things on until the last minute," said Elliott, pointing at the offending coat. "I'll roast in this heat."

He plopped down in the claw-footed desk chair and scooted it around to face me. Elliott was hard to look at; his face was so beautiful. I was relieved when he closed his eyes, squinching them together like a man facing execution. "Alright," he said, slapping his hands down the knees of his jeans and grasping them firmly. "Do your worst."

Giggling, I stretched out the black silk in my hands and glanced over at the short pants lying rumpled on the table. "I think I get it. This is supposed to be sort of colonial style, right?"

Elliott snorted. "Genius. What gave you the clue? The name of the college, or did you think I went parading around like an American grammar school boy at Samhain all year?"

I tossed the tie back in his lap and stepped away from him, fuming. "I don't have any clue where I am or what you're talking about. Half an hour ago, I was walking in the woods, and now here I am being insulted by you in this crazy bird house while I try to tie your stupid tie. So if you have any clues, I'd appreciate hearing them."

Elliott opened his eyes. "You don't know?" From the shocked expression on his face, I could tell that this time, he wasn't mocking me.

I shook my head, no. "All the lady downstairs told me was to follow that raven up here and put on my gown. That she would explain everything else after the others arrived."

"Crikey... that makes more sense then. Nobody's told you," he replied, swiping in vain at his hair again. "That bird—Gregor—isn't a raven. He's a rook. Different kinds of blackbirds. The lady downstairs is Mary Rookes. She's the founder. This is Rookes College." Here, he paused, as if that should be enough explanation. When I shrugged, he continued. "Rookes is a college for female witches."

"Witches?" I replied, incredulous. "There must be some mistake. I don't think I'm supposed to be here. I'm not a witch."

Elliott sighed. "Yes, you are, or you wouldn't be here at all. You picked up a silver key somewhere, right? It had your first initial on the top, and it led you here?"

I nodded, yes.

"Then congratulations, you're a witch," Elliott said with finality. "That wouldn't have happened if it weren't so. Mary never makes mistakes. She watches people too long for that to happen before she leaves them a key. Besides, there's a glamor around this place that normal people can't see through. If you weren't a witch, and somehow you'd accidentally picked up the key, you'd have had no idea what it was for. It wouldn't have brought you here."

Still, I didn't totally believe him. Elliott was the kind of guy who gave off an aura of enjoying messing with people. And that he knew he was good-looking enough to get away with it. "Didn't you say that this was college for female witches? If that's the case, then why are you here?" I asked.

Elliott looked away, seeming to study the bookshelf intently. "Because I'm not welcome at the other colleges. I was supposed to go to one in Britain, but none of those would take me after what happened. Mary offered me a chance to come here on account of my mum."

He closed his eyes, halting abruptly. "You ask too many questions. Mary can explain the rest. I'm sure that's part of the plan anyway, in making you wait until the other girls are here and forcing us to wear all this nonsense. She wants to make a big ceremonial announcement. Are you going to help me tie this tie or not?"

Stunned at his quick turn in conversation, I said no more. I did the best I could with Elliott's tie and then returned to my room.

The formal gown I'd laid out on the bed was much easier to put on than his tie, once I'd figured out I had to loosen the laces to be able to fit, then retighten them. The bodice was tight and stiff. Not so suffocating that I couldn't breathe, but nearly so. The skirt was so long and full that it completely covered my feet. Glancing in the cheval glass over the vanity,

I thought that with my tight top and voluminous bottom, I looked like a very somber ice cream cone turned upside down.

Outside my door at intervals, I could hear Gregor cawing and flapping as who I imagined must be the mysterious other girls were led upstairs to change as well. Figuring I had some time, I began exploring around my suite. Pulling back the curtains in the bedroom, I could see a long expanse of thick lawn leading down a gently sloping hill, and beyond that, the sandy shore of a beach. *How did I get here from the mountains?* I thought, watching the waves lap against the coastline. Opening the windows, I leaned out as far as I could to try to catch a glimpse of the wall of vines through which I remembered walking. Nothing even close. All I could see were the other wings of the castle I was in, the lawn leading down to the shore, and several outbuildings constructed of the same rough-hewn stone.

In the drawers of the vanity table, I found a heavy, silver-handled hairbrush and a small container of bobby pins, also silver. I put my hair up in a French twist, with a few strands left out to frame my face, and felt better about how that looked in correlation with my gown. Then, I went out into the study area and began examining the names on the spines that filled the bookcases. One shelf, just above the desk, had self-explanatory, one-word titles, like "Prognostication" or "Spellcraft." All of those were bound in the same green leather and were roughly the same size. If I were to accept what Elliott had told me, I figured those must be textbooks. However, many more shelves were filled with books that were of all different shapes and sizes, and none of them had names printed on the spines. Some looked very old, as if they would fall apart at the slightest touch.

Not wanting to destroy anything, I scanned the shelves for one that looked sturdy enough to at least withstand its pages being turned. I've always had this weird habit, when I was in a library and couldn't decide what to read, of just closing my eyes and running my fingers along the spines of the books until I found one that felt right somehow. Holding my skirt up with one hand so that I wouldn't trip over it and closing my eyes, I skimmed the shelf in front of me lightly with the other. Seizing upon a volume almost as thick as the width of my palm, I wrapped my fingers around it and pulled. It was so heavy that I almost dropped it. I had to use both hands to carry it to the table.

The cover had a dry, papery texture like parchment. I knew it to be vellum because my high school art teacher had been in one of those Societies for Creative Anachronism, where people dressed up like it was medieval times, pretended to have jousts, and ate turkey legs. One of our projects was how to make sheets of paper and sew them together in a binding. This book seemed to be of somewhat similar construction, although it was ten times as large as my sad little booklet had been and a million times fancier. Holding the top and bottom corners delicately, I opened the cover. Despite my effort to be careful, I could hear the spine cracking as I turned to the first page.

The handwriting inside was so embellished with swirls and flourishes that it took me a moment to decipher. "The Grimoire of Alice Grey," I read aloud from the yellowed paper.

Grimoire? I wondered. This must have been someone's book of spells. I looked back up at the full shelves surrounding me. Not all of them were as old as this one, or as large. *Was every one of them some witch's spellbook?* I thought. Curious, I wanted to read on, but I was terrified to turn another page. What if it crumbled to dust in my hands? How would I explain it? As I weighed the decision, I noticed there wasn't a clock in the room. Or a television. There hadn't been any in Elliott's room either, or downstairs, that I could recall.

Just then, there was a knock on the door. It was Elliott. He was wearing the entire outfit that I'd previously seen piled on top of the laundry stack in his room. If he'd taken the time to iron out the wrinkles, he'd have looked like a movie star.

"Everyone's arrived and dressed. We should go," he said curtly, apparently intending not to mention how he'd concluded our previous encounter. Although he didn't look at me directly, I could sense he was subtly appraising my changed appearance in the long black gown. A shiver of excitement tickled its way over the back of my neck and down my spine through the tips of my fingers.

"What time is it?" I asked him, trying to ignore how his hair was now slicked back almost perfectly, with only the one wet, rebellious curl out of place. I played with the loose strands from my French twist, hoping to appear chill instead of nervous.

He shrugged. "I have no idea. Besides, it doesn't matter."

"Time always matters," I said, impatient with his elusive answer. "I don't think I can stay for the whole thing. Or I at least need to call Stephen and tell him not to worry. I must have been gone for hours already. Do you have a phone? Mine's not working."

He winced, almost imperceptibly, then leaned over to whisper in my ear. "I think Stephen will survive. Time isn't the same here in the Otherworld. You'll see."

Chapter Four

Standing on the interior balcony, I couldn't believe how much the Great Hall had changed in the short time since I'd last seen it. Decorative sheaves of multicolored corn, grains, and sunflowers ringed the perimeter of the room, obscuring the carved wooden panels. Baskets of cornbread and sunflower bread with pots of honey and butter were set out on each table between the place settings, along with large, frosty pitchers of apple cider. The garlands over the banisters and candles had changed colors to shades of gold and copper. To the right of each place setting was a rough chunk of yellow crystal that I supposed to be citrine, and to the left, a basket filled with unshucked ears of corn. Most importantly, a dozen other women in black gowns identical to mine milled about, chatting with one another.

Glancing over to where Elliott and I now stood at the foot of the stairs, the lady whom I'd seen when I entered the castle picked up a brass bell near her place and jingled it brightly. "Have a seat, everyone! I have a few announcements before we begin the Lammas Feast and our other activities for the evening."

Seeing the other women file into their places but having no idea where to sit myself, I looked at Elliott. He nodded at the four place settings on the table, pointing down the white hallway toward our rooms. I sat down opposite Elliott. A petite woman with light brown hair and gray eyes pulled out a chair beside me, closest to the table filled with food. She regarded me with a quick, warm smile, unfolded her black linen napkin into her lap, and sat waiting patiently.

"My name is Mary Rookes," the lady whom I'd met first stated. She made her way around the central table, curtseying to each woman present. Her greeting phrase, "Merry Meet," which the older ladies echoed, was unlike any I'd heard. Her accent was unusual too. British, to be sure, but with some other sort of undertone that I couldn't quite place.

"You may call me Mary or Professor Rookes, whichever level of formality feels most appropriate to you," she said, stepping back again to address the whole room. "Many, many years ago, I founded Rookes College as a haven for young witches to spend their traditional year and a day not only learning the Craft but also gaining an understanding of their gifts, which are of tremendous value to humanity. Each of you here tonight may rest assured that you have been chosen specially, not just by me, but also by your Mentors because we have found you to be young women of great promise and ability, as well as intellectual curiosity and creativity."

Here, the brown-haired lady seated beside me patted my hand reassuringly, as Mary continued. "Tonight, I am delighted to welcome you to our Lammas Celebration. This night, also called Lughnasadh to honor Lugh, the Celtic god of sun and light, represents the first in our series of three harvest sabbats, followed by Mabon and Samhain, that mark the turning of our Wheel of the Year from the growing season of summer to the harvest season of autumn. On this table," Mary motioned to the feast spread out on top of the five-sided dais in the center of the Hall, "and decorating this Great Hall are symbols of Lammas. Corn and other grains remind us of the rewards of harvest for our labors so far. Along with sunflowers, so that we may reap and remember that the Wheel in its infinite motion gives us the seeds to sow for the next season, even as we savor the bounty of this one. The gods and goddesses have been especially kind to us this year, so you'll see some early cider and pies as well, although apples are not always enjoyed so early before Mabon. Let us accept this gift as a sign that our time together this year will be fruitful and filled with fortunate surprises."

Here Mary paused, as the five older women in the circle clapped softly. It was then I noticed that the younger women in the circle, of whom there were only four besides me, looked almost as confused as I felt. Yet, each of us had the same half-smile of bewildered anticipation, as if saying silently, *I have no idea where this is going, but I can't wait to see what happens next.*

Pouring a glass of cider for Elliott and herself and then handing the pitcher for our table to the brown-haired woman sitting beside me, Mary announced that we should each stand and introduce ourselves, beginning with Elliott. Mumbling with the humbleness I wasn't aware he possessed based on our brief acquaintance, Elliott said his last name was Welles and that he was born in Somerset, England. Then, he almost missed his chair because he was in such a hurry to sit down.

Mary regarded him with an amused expression, and Elliott's face flushed crimson. She calmly sliced a piece of sunflower bread and placed it on his plate. "Last names are not required at Rookes until when and if you choose to disclose one," she announced. "Although I will say I'm pleased that Elliott has decided to tell us, since it allows me to compliment his mother. Gwendolyn Welles was one of the finest young witches I've taught, and I'm greatly looking forward to mentoring her son as well. Thank you, Elliott, for joining us this year."

Elliott's face blushed even deeper, from crimson to almost purple. His long eyelashes fluttered adorably as he muttered something like, "Thank you, Mum. That's very kind." All of us clapped politely.

The brown-haired lady seated beside me also spoke with a British accent. Hers had a sort of breathy, bouncing, musical cadence to it, much different from either Mary's unusual half-Americanized one or Elliott's, which the more I thought about it, sounded like some of the downstairs characters that I'd heard on BBC. Introducing herself simply as Alice, she said that she was from Lancashire, and she'd be teaching spellcraft. "I'm so glad to work with you in developing your talents, Willow. And with all of you," she concluded, addressing me and then the rest of the room. "Places like Rookes did not exist in England when I was your age, which was a pity. I certainly could have used a Mentor." The older women in the room applauded loudly at this last remark, which I didn't quite understand, even though I had the feeling that I would soon.

I introduced myself quickly to the room as Willow Todd from Oak Ridge. Although I was nervous, I managed to resettle myself into my chair safely. Still, my concern about how long the introduction process was taking and how urgently I needed to get word back to Stephen that I was okay must have been obvious. Alice leaned over and whispered into my ear as she put a slice of sunflower bread on my plate. "Do not worry, dear. Time in the Otherworld passes much more elliptically. A month here at Rookes could seem like a minute at your home in a more natural chronology. Mary will make sure everyone is notified properly."

"How did you know I was thinking about that?" I whispered back. Alice simply placed a finger to her lips, indicating that I should be quiet, and mouthed the word *later*, as the rest of the women continued around the circle, announcing themselves.

Despite my anxiety over how long it seemed to be taking, for I felt certain that Stephen would have gone into full panic mode by then, I found the introductions of the other women intriguing. They seemed to be from all sorts of backgrounds. One girl, Hana, was Korean but had been adopted by a family from Boston as an infant. I thought it was interesting she told us right off the bat. She dyed her hair lavender and seemed very friendly. I liked her right away. Tayen, another girl who was more aloof, said she was from California, but her family lived in Texas. Model-tall and drop-dead gorgeous, Tayen had that perfectly sun-kissed look about her that screamed money. However, I had a feeling from the way she sort of snarled when she said Texas that her home life probably wasn't exactly sunshine and roses. Imani was from Columbus, and she said that her dad Rick Griffin coached football at Ohio State. Which made sense, because she looked athletic. Her arm definition was visible through the sleeves of her gown, and she wore that very intense, focused look that reminded me of the Williams sisters. The last of the girls my age, Miranda from Florida, was very shy and quiet, with hazel eyes and long, curly, reddish-brown hair. Her skin was very tan, like Tayen's, but I couldn't tell what ethnicity either of them were. My guess was perhaps Latina. The more certain impression I got from Miranda, as I watched her glance nervously around the room, was that she was one of those girls who was super-smart but never let on because they were ashamed about it for some reason.

The remaining Mentors were an even more randomly assorted bunch. It seemed their only similarity, other than being witches, was that they had the same odd style of blended colonial accent as Mary—European with a flavor of something else. Katerina, who would teach prognostication, said she was born in Germany and then immigrated to Rhode Island. Her violet eyes were piercing, as if they could see right through to your soul when she spoke, and her swirling red curls were like a blaze of wildfire. I found her mildly terrifying. Katerina's intimidating presence didn't seem to faze Hana, her mentee, at all. Hana seemed energized. The professor who taught healing, Candy, was of African descent but had lived in Barbados first, then Salem, Massachusetts. The rolling lilt of her voice was as comforting as a wave. She and Imani, her mentee, seemed well-matched. Both had a calm aura of capability that inspired confidence. Grace, a statuesque red-haired woman with bright green eyes, said she was from Virginia and would be teaching ecology. At the end of her introduction, she moved around the table to hug her mentee, Miranda, who didn't look like she knew how to respond to this small gesture of welcome. The final Mentor to speak, Cora, didn't mention her origins at all, only that she would be teaching us sorcery. Her ice-blonde hair was waist-length and stick-straight, and her skin was pale as death. Speaking without any warmth or inflection at all, Cora was the only one who did not welcome her mentee. Instead, she simply regarded Tayen's presence with a blink of her cool blue gaze. A fact that did not go unnoticed by Tayen. She scowled.

Mary Rookes, however, did notice. "Thank you, Cora, for your willingness to share your time with us this year. I am certain that Tayen will benefit from your presence, as will we all. There is much more to share this evening, but let us dine before we go out to the Rookery." From somewhere high in the rafters, Gregor floated down to perch upon her shoulder. He nibbled at her ear with the tip of his beak. Mary broke off a small piece of sunflower bread and offered it to the rook, who swallowed it whole. She laughed again, that tinkling, musical laugh. "It simply won't do to keep hungry birds waiting."

The feast was an astonishing array of dishes, even for twelve people. From the murmuring of the others, as we filled our plates, I could tell that I wasn't the only one there whose favorite food was served randomly alongside the main meal. It turned out the main course I'd first thought was chicken was roasted pheasants, which I had never tasted before, but I probably could have guessed if I'd paid attention to the plumes of tail feathers sticking out of the table arrangements. They were plump and juicy, with crisped rosemary skin. The flavor reminded me a little bit of duck—wilder than chicken. The potatoes were those cute little multicolored fingerlings and came with rainbow carrots and corn too, all basted in herb butter. There was also a fall salad, with kale and other dark greens, feta cheese, apples, pears, sweet potatoes, honeyed pecans, and crumbled bacon. I didn't realize how hungry I was until I began eating, but I snarfed down my entire plate, leaving nothing behind but bones.

Debating on whether or not I would look like a total pig going back for seconds, I turned back to the center table. There, a dozen white paper boxes hovered in the air, circling the table. Large spoons and serving forks danced back and forth, filling them with unseen hands, and I watched what must have been my amazement mirrored in the eyes of the other girls. The aerial clearing ballet concluded with each white box neatly folding itself and coming to rest by our cider mugs.

"Not to rush anyone," Mary said, snapping her fingers twice, as our empty plates floated away to what I later found out was the kitchen. Dishes of hot apple pie and ice cream topped with caramel sauce sailed in to replace them. "But it is almost sunset. Let's have a few bites of sweets and then be off, shall we? There's something I'd like for all of us to see together while there's still light out."

Gobbling down the last bites of my pie and ice cream as everyone rose to leave the Great Hall, I overheard Tayen talking to Cora.

"My mom would have an absolute meltdown if she'd seen how much food I just ate," Tayen said. "All those carbs and that much sugar in the same meal?" She shook her head.

"Well, aren't we fortunate she wasn't here to witness it then?" Cora replied.

"I'm always fortunate when she's not around," Tayen smirked approvingly.

"Haven't I seen you somewhere before?" Hana asked Tayen as she fell into step with us.

"Probably," Tayen shrugged. "Did it look something like this?" Tayen stopped abruptly just in front of the doorway and struck an exaggerated pose with one leg popped out and her opposite arm extended as if she were holding a large handbag.

"Yes!" Hana exclaimed, clapping her hands together and making a little hop of excited recognition. "Last year's Hermes campaign! You had that alligator Kelly bag, and it was like in some steamy jungle scene."

Tayen relaxed back into her natural, half-amused expression. "Pretty good eye, but it was in Florida, and the bag was actually crocodile. You could tell if you looked closely because their scales are bigger. Although maybe not, with that damned fog machine. I couldn't see my hand in front of my face. Almost choked me to death."

"You're a model?" Miranda asked, looking awestruck.

"Unfortunately," Tayen replied, yawning. "You're not? What are you?"

Miranda looked flustered, not sure whether to take the return question as a compliment or a challenge. She settled for the safest answer. "I'm from Florida. My dad's a minister. Pastor Ian Flanagan. He's on television. LifeSpark Church."

"I'm sorry," Tayen replied, sarcastically. Miranda's hopeful expression fell.

"That was salty," said Imani, pulling a face. Then, to Miranda, "Ignite Your Passion for the Lord or something, isn't that the LifeSpark slogan?"

"Yeah, how did you know?" Miranda asked, perking up again.

"My grandma watches a lot of those inspirational shows," Imani shrugged. "She's a big fan of Pastor Flanagan. Kind of ironic that you ended up here then, isn't it? Chosen for a witch college?"

"Actually," said Grace, "I can speak to that. The two aren't mutually exclusive. It is possible both to possess and practice magick while still holding onto the beliefs of another faith."

Imani and Miranda both stared at her questioningly.

"It's true," Candy added, in her ocean soft voice. "Although since before even my time, there have always been those who try to impose their beliefs and force a witch to choose, rest assured that no such pressure will ever come from us. You may choose to use your power in conjunction with any other beliefs you may hold, or you may choose not to use it at all. That decision is up to you."

"But you must ever mind the Rule of Drei," Katerina cautioned, holding up three fingers as she used her native German word for the number. "For whatever purpose you may use your powers shall always come back to you three times. It's what we call the Threefold Law."

"Most of the time," Alice concluded. Catching my eye, she winked at me. "There is only one law that guides us, and that is the Rede." Then, in a lyrical voice, she recited, "Eight words ye Rede fulfill; an' harm ye none, do what ye will."

Mary motioned for us to reassemble into a semicircle in front of the open double doors of the college. Gregor fluttered down to sit once again on her shoulder. "Sisters, that was the perfect transition into my story; thank you." She glanced up at the pentagram set into the rocks above the entrance. The silver coins that marked each point gleamed brightly as the last beams of evening sun shone through the five-colored panels of stained glass, casting their shape onto the stone floor inside as Mary told her tale.

"Over three centuries ago, two men accused me of witchcraft. One claimed that I could raise great storms of wind as wild as hurricanes and conjure frightful apparitions from firelight. Another alleged that I had bewitched his wife because after spending time in my company, she found her tongue to speak out against him. Both said also that they had seen me consorting with animal familiars and spirits and most egregious of all, that I had learned such ways from the Native tribes in the area. I denied these charges and was awarded five shillings from one man for slander, and a single shilling from the other." Mary paused, pulling a silver shilling from a pocket in her dress and holding it up. The shilling began to glow. As she let go of it to point up at the five-pointed star over the door, the shilling flew into the air, following her direction like the tip of a laser. She smiled as we watched and listened, enchanted.

"The twist in this tale was that I lied. Nevertheless, admission to a charge of witchcraft during my natural lifetime meant certain death for any person unlucky enough to be accused. Most of those who were brought to trial were women. Men in positions of power, particularly wealthy ones, have always been afraid of women who spoke their minds. They felt threatened by the possibility of women who were beyond their control. Yet, once I managed to free myself from their clutches, I vowed to build a place to train young women to embrace that sort of independence. To learn to wield their powers with principles and conviction." Here, the five silver points of the star above the door began to glow.

Mary stared directly at Elliott, who had hung back, closest to the doorway. "Over the years I have learned that it is essential for men of thought and kindness to be brought into our circle as allies. Thus, now and again, I have extended an invitation to such ones who manifest an interest and empathy. For we have much to learn from one another." Elliott said nothing, but he did not look away as Mary continued.

"I sold the land that my poor departed husband had left to me, and which they were trying to take, for that was the true reason for their accusations. With that money, I built this college around the five disciplines that you will learn as you grow into your understanding of the Old Ways. At Rookes, you are protected from the disappointments of the outside world, and you may always return for safety and comfort. Shielded by our glamor and the mutual protections of the Otherworld, you need never worry about the wearing down of life. Here, you shall never grow old." Outlining the points of the star as she spoke, each flashed brightly as Mary named it.

"We will begin each week's lessons with sorcery, the energy resonant in all things, learning how to harness and channel it to the paths we direct. Next, ecology, how that energy manifests itself in the world around us, as part of every plant, animal, and stone. Then, prognostication, or the prediction of what shall be, is based on the communicated interdependence of all that we understand. After that, healing is the art of calming and curing the ailments of humanity and animals as they relate to the Earth. And finally, spellcraft, the summoning of energy from within ourselves, for the betterment of all. Along our journey into this new world of knowledge, you will find that some powers are stronger than others, but that all resonate within each of you, waiting just beyond the doors of perception. For all souls present here possess a key that will unlock any door. I have merely offered you the opportunity to recognize and learn to utilize its existence."

By this time, the sun had fully set. Yet, the star above the door still gleamed with an otherworldly light. "Wise women," Mary glanced back to Elliott, whose gaze had not left her this entire time. "And wise man. I applaud you for finding knowledge like so many keys in the dust. We are honored to have you step inside our magick circle. May we all find mutual protection within it."

Here, Mary snapped her fingers, and the original silver coin slipped back into her palm. Raising her hand high over her head, she caught a beam of light from the star that still shone over the doorway. It gathered above her outstretched fingers like a ball. Bringing her arm forward, she cast the orb before her, where it flew to a resting place just in front of a large stone barn.

Over the barn's mantel, in the same place where the school door said *Rookes College*, was carved into the stone one word: *Rookery*.

"Now," Mary said, starting down the illuminated path. "Let us go and meet our messengers."

Chapter Five

With a wave of her arm from left to right, Mary opened the rough-hewn wooden doors to the Rookery without touching them. I glanced around, trying to catch the expressions on the other girls' faces as we stepped inside, not surprised that they remained as mesmerized as I was. Rolling her arm up toward the roof, Mary directed her orb to shine down on us from above the building, then closed her fingers together, as if grasping a tennis ball. The light dimmed.

In its soft, golden glow, I saw dozens of birds stirring in their large nesting boxes. Looking at them more closely, I noticed the difference between rooks and ravens or crows. Although all three species had shiny black feathers, the rooks each had a pale, featherless patch around their chins, which made their beaks look much larger than they were.

"Gregor," Mary said to the bird on her shoulder, who cocked his head to listen. "Tell Parliament to circle, will you? It's time to begin their selection." Obediently, Gregor flew from perch to perch in front of each nest, cawing at his compatriots. I snorted, trying not to laugh, at the cranky-sounding clucks and squawks of their responses. We were interfering with their naptime.

"Perhaps this will liven them up," Mary said. With another wave of her hand, she unlatched the lid of a bin beside the double doors. The rooks perked up at the sound and stopped squawking. Hopping onto their perches, all the rooks stood at attention, with their sharp eyes trained on Mary's every movement. In a series of additional waves, Mary directed a small straw basket with a rounded handle to hover in front of the bin as she filled it with acorns and then relatched the lid. Summoning the basket to her side, Mary allowed it to float there as she explained.

"Rooks are very special birds. They can move between worlds—the normal terrestrial world, from which you have so recently arrived, and the magickal world, wherein you will spend your year and a day of training among us. As such, the rook is not merely an obvious mascot for our college, but an important bridge as you each learn to navigate your paths within the Craft, and to negotiate your chosen terms of existence between the two worlds of which you are now a citizen. In human time, a rook lives approximately seven years. Thus, the bird who chooses you tonight will remain your companion throughout that tenure, serving as a messenger and advisor by proxy, should you seek my counsel or the counsel of your Mentors after we are away from one another. Then, at the end of that seven-year term, you and your rook will return briefly to the College, where he or she will be allowed to retire peacefully here among their old companions at the Rookery or to follow his or her instincts elsewhere within the magickal Otherworld."

Wiggling her hand slightly, Mary caused the basket of acorns to shake. The rooks clicked their beaks approvingly as she continued. "Acorns are to rooks what cookies are to children. They love their crunchy sweetness and will squirrel them away in their nests if they aren't hungry. Each of you should take a handful of acorns as the basket comes around."

Mary made a swirling motion in the air with her first finger extended, and the basket hovering at her side began to move past each of us. I took my handful of acorns, which were all sorts of sizes, shapes, and colors. I wondered how many different types of oak trees they'd come from and from how far away, as Mary concluded her instructions.

"Rooks are naturally very friendly and sociable birds. Most likely, every one of them will accept an acorn from you if you offer it. However, the bird that returns when your acorns are all gone is the one who belongs with you. That is how they make their selections. So, let us all go back outside and allow the rooks to make their decisions, shall we? Whoever is last out, please leave the doors open so that the birds can move freely."

We all filed out and followed Mary around to the far side of the Rookery closest to the shoreline. Being last, I didn't shut the doors behind me.

"Willow, I understand you have quite the rapport with animals," Mary said as I rejoined the group. "Why don't you have the first go? Just stand out there, towards the point. Hold as many acorns as you can without dropping them in your open palms, with your arms fully extended. Try not to let them drop down close to your sides. They wouldn't flog you intentionally. Our birds are too well-mannered for that. However, a rook's wingspan is quite broad, and getting slapped in the face by one isn't pleasant, I assure you."

I nodded and shuffle-jogged out to the spot Mary indicated as the others looked on. Thankfully, the tall grass concealed my clumsiness moving in the long skirt. I took a moment to peer over the crest of the hill as it sloped down to the beach. As I turned around from this vantage point, I could see that not only was the main college castle shaped like a giant pentagram, but the entire island also.

"Ready!" I called, facing them with my arms fully extended, hands full of acorns.

Mary nodded back and pulled her long, thin silver flute from among the folds of her dress. As she played a happy gig of a tune, filled with tumbling runs, I could hear them coming. Cawing and flapping excitedly, the parliament swirled like a fast-gathering storm around the Rookery and sailed towards me. Then, one by one, they swooped in, gingerly taking an acorn from my hands, as easily as long-tamed parrots picked up sunflower seeds for treats.

Just like Mary said, after each bird picked up his or her acorn, they settled into a spot on the grass and began to crack it open, never once glancing again in my direction. As more of them landed, I noticed that the pattern in which they positioned themselves around me was a perfect circle. I stood empty-handed, marveling at how close they were when it dawned on me. They were all eating but not coming back. What would happen if none of them returned to me?

As I began to worry, I heard a rustling of feathers when a single bird took flight again. Watching as she flapped and floated, eyeing me closely the entire time, I could tell that she was interested. "What do I do now? Do I need your whistle?" I cried out to Mary, who didn't answer.

"No, just call to her. Use her name!" Alice replied instead.

Call her name? I thought, frantically. I didn't even know what kind of bird a rook was until a few hours ago. They all looked the same! How in the world could I possibly guess what this one's name might be, or what she would respond to? So, I just yelled out the first name that came to my mind. It was in a line from an old Tennessee Williams play that I'd been in during high school. "Stella!" I exclaimed. "Stella for a star!"

The bird stopped circling as abruptly as if she had run into an invisible wall in the air. Then, she opened her wings to their fullest extent and floated down to perch on my shoulder. Refolding her wings again, she rubbed her shiny head against my cheek. She even made a few whistling and clicking sounds, as if she had been my pet bird for ages.

"Well, it appears Willow has been chosen," Mary said. "How exciting too that your intuition was strong enough to catch her name on the first try! You should trust yourself more often. Come, stand beside me, and feed her a few more acorns for being such a smart girl. Oh, and I will need the number on her tag, please. We always keep a log of which birds are out with whom so that we'll know where they came from if they arrived without a message."

Looking at Stella's feet, which were firmly clamped to my shoulder, I could see the tag on her right one. As if she could hear me wondering how I might read it without disturbing her, Stella stuck out her right leg, balancing only on her left. I resisted the urge to wince—her talons were sharp—and looked at the tag. "Nine," I read aloud to Mary. Pulling a small notepad covered in gold metallic leather from among what I was beginning to realize was the most amazing series of hidden pockets in a skirt that I'd ever encountered, Mary jotted down my name, Stella's new name, and the number.

"I think I've got this," said Tayen, striding out to the spot on the point unbidden. The rooks flocked to her, just as they had to me before. However, when all her acorns were gone, no birds returned immediately. Tayen rolled her eyes and stood with her arms folded as if to say, *Now what?*

"You can't expect a bird to come to you if you're not doing anything to welcome it," Cora called to her. "Just waiting for it to happen isn't enough. You have to make at least some small overture of friendship. They can sense who truly wants to communicate and who doesn't. Put your arm out and hold it there."

Tayen rolled her eyes again but stuck her arm out. Right away, a rook larger than mine with a balder beak that made it look older flew over to land on her hand. He was too heavy for Tayen to hold up with her long, skinny arm. The bird promptly flopped off onto the ground, making pathetic cries as if he'd hurt himself. Now genuinely concerned, Tayen crouched down beside the bird and felt along his wings for a break. Then, as she picked him up, the rook responded by rolling over in her arms, snuggling into the side of her neck. I know it sounds ludicrous, but I swear the rook had an almost smug look on his face. Tayen noticed it too. Mary looked at her expectantly, waiting for a name and number.

"Number twenty-one, and Darcy. Because he made me wait forever." Tayen replied, walking back to the group holding the bird. Darcy was still making little soft cooing moans as he fluffed and rearranged his feathers, unharmed except for his pride. "Such a drama queen," she said, half to my bird and half to me. "Stella," Tayen mocked, "this bird's nearly as bad as you."

"Darcy?" I asked, shading her back. "Like from *Pride and Prejudice*? I wouldn't have pegged you for a Jane Austen girl."

"Whaaaat?" Tayen returned, exaggerating her surprise. "I read!"

"Ooohhh, twenty-one is a lucky number. Me next!" Hana bounced into position, interrupting her. I began to realize that Hana's energy level was like a live-action version of Tigger from Winnie-the-Pooh. Hana had the opposite problem of Tayen. The birds wouldn't leave her alone, even after the acorns were gone. They swarmed and sparred amongst each other in midair for so long that Hana became nervous and started waving her arms, trying to get their attention.

"Don't flail about like a falling fairy!" Katerina snapped, her German accent growing thicker with impatience. "You'll only make them more confused. Focus your energy on just the one you want, then call it."

Subdued, Hana dropped her arms. She closed her eyes, and I could almost see the wheels turning in her mind because she was thinking so hard. Then, her eyes popped open. "Joan!" she exclaimed. The frantic cloud of fighting birds parted and resettled back into their circle in the grass as a young, smallish rook alighted on Hana's shoulder.

She examined the tag on the bird's foot. "Eight," Hana said, resuming her place beside me. "We're neighbors." Our birds tapped beaks with one another, which looked like the rook equivalent of a high five.

"Well done, Hana!" Mary congratulated her, jotting down their names and the bird's number. "Was that Joan in honor of Joan of Arc? She was a very powerful sorceress."

"No," Hana replied, her face flushing a bit. "I'm afraid it wasn't that serious. I chose Joan because of Joan Rivers. I used to watch reruns of her old show on the Style Channel. She could lay the smacketh down on anybody."

I couldn't help laughing at that one. Here we were, in the middle of what seemed to be the wonders of a whole other world. Then there was Hana, quoting The Rock and referencing old-school gossip-show TV. Tayen elbowed me in the ribs and snorted too, which started Elliott going. He'd been so quiet that I'd forgotten he was even there.

"Decorum, please," Mary sighed wearily. "There will be other times for merriment, but the rooks' selections are a serious business. Imani, you're the sensible one. Why don't you go next and silence the cackling crowd over there?" Imani raised an eyebrow at us, which had the desired effect. Still, I was careful not to look at Tayen, Elliott, or Hana. I get tickled easily, especially when I'm nervous, and I knew one smirk could set me off again.

With more solemnity than I thought was truly necessary, Imani assumed her place. She stood still as a stone, arms perfectly shoulder-level, as the rooks circled her, nipping their acorns from her open palms. As they landed back in their circle on the grass around her, Imani closed her eyes and remained motionless. Seconds ticked past, marked by no movement or sound except our breathing and the wind. I could see the tension beginning to ripple through Imani's body from her calves up to her neck, as I could sense her trying to decide whether to speak a name. "Hecate," she said in a tone that sounded like an invocation. Yet not a bird stirred. "Hecate," Imani repeated. Again, no response.

"Perhaps try another name, dear," Candy told her. "Sometimes it is possible to be receiving energy from more than one life force at once, and that Goddess is very powerful."

The muscles of Imani's jaw clenched and relaxed as she methodically began naming off one goddess after another. Diana. Nothing. Aphrodite. Nothing. Bastet. Nothing. I wondered how she could think of that many goddesses right on the spot. She must have studied them.

"Try Isaac," Miranda whispered loudly. Mary and Candy both shot Miranda stern looks, but Imani heard her anyway.

"Isaac?" Imani ventured, her voice uncertain. Obediently, one of the larger rooks broke the circle and flew over to alight on her patiently outstretched arm. Imani pulled the bird close. He put his head over her shoulder and then encircled her with his wings. She checked the tag on its foot and then pressed her face against his neck. Imani began to shake, and I could see that she was crying. Mary and Candy walked over to her, and they conversed quietly. Eventually, Imani followed them back to where we stood.

"I was only trying to help," Miranda whispered nervously to Grace.

"I know, dear. Everything is okay. It was just a shock, that's all," Grace replied.

"What happened?" I asked Candy.

"Isaac Griffin was the name of Imani's brother who passed away," Candy answered. "He was an athlete. Football. His number was twenty-six. The number that was attached to the rook whom Imani summoned."

Hana put her hand over her mouth. I didn't know much about professional sports, but considering that Hana was a walking Wikipedia of popular culture, I knew that she must and she recognized the name.

"I appreciate your restraint, Hana, for not discussing the matter further," Mary said. "The rest of the story is Imani's to tell, if and when she chooses to do so. We will respect her privacy. However, now is a good time to mention a couple of things that are relevant to what we've witnessed here. First, that intellect alone is not the only part of a witch's education that must be cultivated. Emotions must be considered too. We must learn to listen and respect the will and wisdom of the universe, even when it tells us what we do not wish to hear. Imani confided in me moments ago that she had heard the name Isaac even before Miranda's suggestion but chose to ignore that voice in favor of a choice that, to her, seemed more logical and less triggering. Magickal forces are mercurial, yet we must be willing to follow their directions and hear them out, no matter how painful or illogical they might seem when we are certain that they are speaking to us clearly and honestly. Regardless of whether we are ready to accept it at the time, the universe always unfolds as it should. That being said, accepting the advice and counsel of one's coven can be of great help when we struggle with interpretation. So, thank you, Miranda, for offering your sister guidance when you were able to recognize what she needed to hear but could not. We must learn to attune ourselves to the music of the spheres to live in harmony with Nature."

Then, Mary turned to Miranda, who recognized it was her turn.

"If I know which one it is already," Miranda asked, "do I still have to go out there in front of everyone? By myself?"

"I'm afraid so," Mary replied. "It's part of the tradition."

"Go on, it'll be good for you," Grace encouraged, giving Miranda a little pat on the back and a tiny shove, like a chaperone pushing a wallflower out onto the dance floor.

Miranda walked out to the point. The rooks began to follow her closely, hopping along behind her in a little trail. When she stopped and turned around, Miranda knelt and held a single acorn out to each of them individually. Yet, even after they had taken one, they remained clustered around her feet, causing the last birds to have to wing one another out of the way like kindergarteners elbowing to the front of a crowd surrounding a favorite teacher.

"Hello, Puck," Miranda said, as a tiny rook, still somewhat gray in his feathers, hopped into her hand. She stroked the little bird's head as she walked back to us, the line of older birds waddling along in her wake. Miranda checked the tag on his foot. "Eighteen," she told Mary.

"Kindness is perhaps the most important gift of all that witches are given," Mary said, noting Puck's number in her book. "Animals can always sense it, and in time, Nature will always reward it. Thank you, Miranda."

Knowing that he was the only one left, Elliott began walking out to the point.

"No, no, dear," Mary stopped him. Elliott paused, looking at her quizzically. "Rook messengers are for the young ladies only, according to the method established here at the college, to allow for a gentler transition back into non-magickal life. I will be training you separately, Elliott, to assume your familiar form before the wheel of the year concludes its turn, as per the traditional English custom, so that you will not be behind your peers upon your return. Although I'm sure it will be of no great mystery to either of us what that form will be. Something of equine nature, no doubt, given your lineage. We shall save that for later."

Mary motioned for all of us to gather closer to hear. "That will be all for the evening. We should rest, as I know it has been a long and unusual day. I appreciate the trust that you have placed in me and your Mentors, and the patience you have demonstrated tonight. For your first lessons in sorcery with Cora, please assemble in the Great Hall in your red robes after breakfast, which is served at sunrise." Once more, Mary pulled the thin, silver flute from her pocket and sounded several low, legato tones. In reply, the rooks sailed back into their nesting boxes. Mary closed the doors behind them.

Walking back to the main castle of the college, Hana nudged me. "What does she mean by familiar form?"

"Witches often have animal spirits who are connected to them in some meaningful way. They can be trained to work together with the witch, and/or the witch can sometimes transform into a form that resembles that type of animal," Imani replied, overhearing Hana's question. Being able to give a solid answer to something she knew steadied her, I could tell.

"How do you know so much about witches?" Tayen asked.

Imani shrugged. "How do you not know?" Tayen bristled as Imani continued. "My mother and grandmother both had some of the gifts. Grandma's gift was never as strong as Mary's, but she helped a lot of people. Mom, well... I'll just say that she would never have picked up the key."

"That's quite an assumption," Tayen scoffed.

Miranda, who seemed as bored as I was already with Tayen and Imani's bickering, whispered, "Why don't you ask them if we can train early with our familiars too? Like Elliott."

My whole life, I've had this problem. People who are usually smarter than me, prodding me to be the dumb one who asks all the questions so that they don't have to appear stupid. It's super awkward because most of the time I'd rather figure things out for myself rather than ask. Still, I must give off some kind of vibe to the contrary because people keep pulling me into their games of telephone unwillingly. Stephen used to do it all the time when we were growing up.

Stephen, I paused. His name grounded me back into reality in these surreal circumstances. I had other questions that needed answering, which to me were far more pressing than whether I'd be able to shapeshift sooner rather than later.

"Why don't you ask?" I said to Miranda, mildly irritated.

"Because I'm not someone who asks questions," Miranda replied, in a tone so cowed that I felt ashamed of myself, so I caved.

Alice happened to be walking on my other side, and I asked her. "Why does Elliott get to practice with his familiar form before we do?"

"Oh, it's an English thing," Alice replied, the highland lilt in her voice growing stronger the faster she explained. "To incorporate all the advanced magickal techniques into the first year of training. It has a long history, back to when many of the covens decided that all witches, no matter how young, needed to know how to disguise and protect themselves by any means as soon as possible. America has always had a longer post-education period of witchy adolescence, if you will. However, Mary, the other Mentors, and I have been discussing the possibility of speeding things up a bit, in the English manner, considering our current circumstances."

Alice's allusion intrigued me. Miranda thought the same. I could tell she was hanging onto every eavesdropped word of the question that she'd asked through me as a proxy. "What circumstances?" Miranda and I asked in unison.

"Circumstances that you will be informed of as soon as a decision is reached," Mary answered, also overhearing behind us. "And that I would appreciate Ms. Grey not elaborating on until we are all unanimous regarding the matter."

Alice stopped and stared at Mary indignantly. "I thought we weren't using last names until we were ready to reveal them individually?"

"*I was ready*," Mary replied, with a tone of icy finality, as she swept her arm to open the doors of the college over which her name was engraved. "And I am Mary Rookes."

Chapter Six

Back in my room, I collapsed into a heap on the seat beneath my window. Staring up at the moon, I supposed it was about midnight but wished that I knew the real time. I never realized how much my life revolved around the ordered spacing of hours until there was no such thing. Slowly, I realized that the bodice of my dress had grown even tighter after my enormous dinner. Loosening the ties, I took a deep breath and once again began to prowl the cupboards.

"Nightgowns?" I said in disbelief, shaking the folds out of a long, soft white cotton bundle of fluffy tiers that tied in front and at the cuffs with pink ribbons. It looked like something from a children's storybook, or a pen-and-ink illustrated volume of a Dickens novel. I half-expected to find a cap with a long tassel too, but I didn't see one. There were many other different types of clothes—more gowns, the robes Mary had mentioned, and surprisingly even a few pants outfits. Although they looked like something straight out of a vintage Ralph Lauren ad, or the kinds of things Elizabeth II might have worn to ride horses before she became the Queen. Some underwear, slightly more modern and silky, but still white and full coverage, but nothing else to sleep in. Just the drawer full of nightgowns and a long silvery gray robe that I supposed went over it. I put them on and pulled back the velvet curtains, feeling as if I were the first actor onstage in some sort of period drama.

Then, I remembered the book on the desk. It was still open to the first page. *The Grimoire of Alice Grey*, it read. Carefully, I turned the crackling overleaf, holding it with both hands as I had the cover. I'd expected there would be some sort of table of contents, but there wasn't. Instead, in large, loopy cursive so ornate it was difficult to read, were the words *Spells of Attraction and Persuasion*. However, just as I began trying to decipher the instructions below the heading, I heard something rustling behind me. Someone had slipped a piece of paper under my door. The end was crumpled from being scooted through the narrow space.

Awake? It asked. And beneath that, *I saw your lights. Can't sleep.*

I knew who it must be by the handwriting, which was a typical staccato boy's scrawl. Each printed letter was pressed heavily into the creamy white paper. *How did he see my lights, though?* I wondered, glancing around the room at the various wall sconces and candelabra. They'd been lit already for my return that evening. By Mary, I'd assumed, in the same way she'd lit the ones downstairs, with a snap of her fingers. There were no interior windows to the hallways, just rows of coffered walnut paneling. The only way to know that my candles were lit would have been to stand outside my exterior window. Nevertheless, I unlatched the door.

"What are you reading?" Elliott asked, noting the book open at my desk.

"No, hello? No, sorry to barge in late at night?" I asked.

"I told you I couldn't sleep," Elliott replied as if he thought that was enough explanation. I gave him my most obvious, *How is this my problem?* shrug. Impossible to ignore. It worked. "I was walking around outside after everyone else went to bed. Done it for almost three weeks now. The only way to keep myself from going absolutely mental from not having any tv or internet to fall asleep with at night. Plus, I've been simply mad for someone to talk to who isn't about three hundred years old. Anything would be better than that or total silence."

"Glad to know my company is preferable to nothing," I said, trying to hint at the balance of emotions I felt between mildly insulted and somewhat relieved also to have a companion in this strangeness. If he caught on, Elliott showed no signs of it, so I changed the subject. "I've been reading *The Grimoire of Alice Grey*. I suppose she's the same Alice Grey from tonight. Ever heard of it? Is there a copy in your room?"

"Hmm..." he said, walking over to the book. I noticed that he had on a long, old-fashioned nightshirt. I tried not to notice that he had gorgeous legs. Perfect muscle definition. The kind that my girlfriends and I called soccer legs, because all of the hot guys back home in Tennessee who played soccer had them. The kinds of guys whose shapely legs carried them right past rows of nerdy girls like me and onto their real sickeningly stunning girlfriends. I began to wonder if he was wearing boxers under the nightshirt.

Stop it, I warned myself silently. *This is absolutely pointless. He's not interested in you. And you still have a boyfriend. Just look away.* Then, he ruffled his hair, and I looked. The same little unruly looking Superman curl flopped down over his forehead, just like before. Knowing that I couldn't help but want to run my hands through his hair if kept staring at him, I forced myself to turn around and face the bookcase.

"No, I don't recall one, but that's not surprising. I imagine they're all one of a kind. Perhaps two of a kind at most, if they're still living, like Alice. They'd probably keep the original and leave a copy here." Elliott gestured to the wall of bookcases.

I scanned the shelves again, relieved to have something to talk about that didn't require gazing into his eyes. "So, you think all of these are spellbooks of different random witches through the years? Why are they all here? Basically, in some girl's dorm room?"

"Because nothing about any of this place is random," Elliott said, settling into my desk chair and flipping the fragile first pages of the book so carelessly I winced. He chuckled. "Don't worry, silly. I'm not going to break it. And if I did, Alice could just magick it back together again or whatever. These aren't like the First Folio of Shakespeare at the Bodleian, you know. Old and rare, yes, but they're working reference books. They're meant to be used. Although I'm the same as you, I haven't started any official lessons. I imagine they're here for us to review and compare techniques that have been used on similar spells as we come up with our own. All magick is individual, you know. No two spells are precisely alike. They have the same general intention and basic ingredients but are personalized for every witch who works them. That is, they should be if they're going to work properly."

"No, I'm afraid I don't know. Anything," I sighed, getting anxious despite how tired I was. "Other than what you told me before we went down to dinner about the keys and what Mary and the others said out there tonight, I don't have the foggiest idea why I'm here or what we're doing. All I know is that this afternoon, or yesterday afternoon—I don't even know what day it is now because there aren't any clocks—I ran away from my boyfriend in the woods, and then I found this key that led me here. So, I wish someone would just start from the beginning and tell me what's going on."

"Why were you running away from your boyfriend?" Elliott's piercing gray eyes clouded with concern. Half of me was thrilled the question hinted that he cared about me. The other half already hated how he redirected everything I said to him with a completely different question. I never like to be the person getting questioned. It's much better to be the person asking questions.

"Why does that matter?"

"Because I want to know. Stuff like that's important."

I studied his expression. He was serious and more worried than I thought he should be, although I didn't know why. My bolting tendency caught up with my attraction, as I realized my breathing stopped when he spoke. I needed to slow things down a bit. Create a distraction and give myself time to assess the situation. Since there's no better distraction than getting other people to talk about themselves, I said, "I'll tell you all about it if you'll tell me what you know about this place and how you know it."

"That's fair," Elliott replied, ruffling his hands through his hair again as he got up to pace around the room. Then, he sat down in one of the carved wooden chairs by the tea table. "You'd better have a seat. This is going to take a while." I sat down, leaning forward expectantly as Elliott began to explain.

"I know so much about Rookes College and the Craft because my mother went to school here. My parents were witches. Both of them. But Mum's..." He paused, shook his head, and nibbled at his nails. "There's no other way to say it, and you'll find out at some point anyway. Everyone does. It's why I'm here. My mum's dead because my dad killed her. He didn't mean to. It was an accident. They were arguing on the staircase. He said something she didn't like, so she slapped him. Then, he slapped her back, and she fell. Many different people might tell you all kinds of other dramatic stories about it, but that's how it happened. There was no magick involved. They fought constantly, like two cats, but that time it just went too far. I was there and I saw it. Dad didn't know that I did at the time. I blamed him for her death, of course, but I blamed him more for what he did afterward. He couldn't face it. He just ran."

"Oh, I'm so sorry," I said, shocked. I wasn't expecting a deep confession. "I... don't know what to... where did he go?"

"Here, America," Elliott replied. "And it's okay. I mean, it's not, really... But I've learned to cope with it. Dad knew that in the magickal world, it isn't as easy to get away with killing your wife as it is in the regular human world. Even though his family, the Capells, were rich and Mum's people weren't. Justice still works here. Most of the time. Anyway, afterward, my mum's parents, my grandparents, the Welleses, took me in and raised me. They're witches too, which is how I know so much about the Craft, even though I can't work many spells yet. Pop and Nan respected the traditions and decided not to teach me any magick before I came of age—which is nineteen. I'm sure you'll hear all about those sorts of things as we go along. Rookes is very thorough with the history and traditions of the Craft. Nan told me that it was part of Mary's philosophy to keep to the Old Ways as much as possible. For better or for worse. Hence," he waved at both of our outfits, "all this. The clothes are hand-sewn from natural fibers, with no electronics. It's supposed to ground us, being in closer contact with the school's foundations. The Earth, animals, plants, and the elements—all of that. Mary wants us to be able to concentrate on magick alone, without interference from the world outside."

Everything that Elliott said sparked a dozen different questions in my mind. There was so much to unpack. "Okay, one thing at a time. First, if the magickal world is so much better at finding justice, then why was your dad just allowed to come to America and get away with..." I couldn't say it... "What he did."

Elliott took a breath. "That's why I said most of the time. Witches try not to interfere with the human world except in cases of extreme catastrophe. Since the beginning of recorded history, it has only caused trouble for the magickal world. The death of one human or one witch isn't enough. It has to be a situation so desperate that hundreds or thousands of people would die, or the future of an entire country or even the planet could be in jeopardy before the Grand Council would act. They're sort of like Parliament and the court system rolled into one for our kind. Regardless, one of the most severe punishments in the magickal world is to be stripped of one's powers and cast out of the company of other witches and all covens. To be banished from the Otherworld forever. That's where the term warlock comes from—the act of being locked out and permanently at war with the magickal world. If a witch kills another witch and tries to remain in the magickal Otherworld, the punishment is death. However, if the murderer voluntarily relinquishes most of his powers and flees to the human world permanently, then he is allowed to live as a warlock, barred from ever returning. That's what my father did. That's why he left me with my grandparents and never came back."

"I understand," I said, beginning to piece the logic together. "So, is that also why you can't go to school in England? If so, that doesn't seem fair. You didn't do anything wrong."

Elliott bit his lower lip and nodded. "That's one of the parts of the Old Ways that are for the worse, I'm afraid. The sins of the father and mother follow the children. In all of Britain, and most of the schools in America, if one or both of a child's parents is a warlock, then he or she is forbidden entry to any program of training in the Craft. Their blood is considered poisoned. I'm sure something will be said about it in ecology or healing, perhaps even prognostication. Certain crimes reverberate with negative energy through the generations until they echo back amplified threefold or more. Or so the more absolute adherents to the Old Ways would have us believe."

"But Mary must feel differently, right?" I asked. "Otherwise, why would you be here? She wouldn't have set a key out for you to find. Especially from so far away."

Elliott smiled. "Mrs. Mary Rookes has always prided herself on being different, even among witches. According to Nan, she founded this college as the very first for female witches in America, partly because of what she mentioned tonight—to empower women—but also to thumb her nose at some of the things she thought were wrong about the witch colleges in Britain. For example, their preference for admitting only legacy witches, especially those from wealthy families that might shell out the pounds, even when their children had no magickal aptitude."

I was kind of shocked by this, although, in hindsight, I shouldn't have been. "So, Nepo Babies are just as alive and well in the magickal collegiate world as they are among plain folk at ordinary universities. That's comforting. Not."

"Too right, you are!"

We both chuckled, which helped ease the tension. Talking about Elliott's past was difficult for both of us, him in the telling and me in the understanding. Still, he continued.

"As I said though, Rookes is different. That whole business of picking up the key in the dust has nothing to do with any tradition other than Mary's own. She came up with it as a test because she believes the two most important traits that a potential young witch can possess are curiosity and imagination. All the rest—source work and spellcraft—she feels can be taught if a person is willing to learn. For her, lineage, wealth, or status means nothing. There are dozens of rumors as to why, although no one knows for sure. Other than the fact that Mary was born and trained in England and then later showed up in America where she pissed off a few buggers badly enough that they called her out for misusing her Craft, every account of her origins is different. She does seem to hate rich people especially though, so there's something there."

Elliott paused to rub his jaw. "She hated my dad right off the bat, Nan told me. My Mum was a special pet student of Mary's. She despised that Albert turned Gwendolyn's head with money and promises of all the big things he said that he was going to do."

I hesitated. "If you don't mind my asking, what happened after your father came to America? Do you know?"

Elliott snorted. "You know, in some ways, it's okay that we don't get the news here. Otherwise, you'd already know. Kind of nice to control my narrative for a change. Have you ever heard of Albion Coal & Oil? My dad is the President, Albert Capell. His company's planning to start offshore drilling operations under that new law that just passed allowing it on the East Coast."

"Seems familiar, but not exactly," I replied. "My dad Oliver was supposed to start a new gig soon as a geological consultant for some oil company or other, but I'm not sure which one."

"Probably for the best. Otherwise, if it were Dad's, you might hate me. From what I saw on the BBC before I came here, seems like all the regular people here in the Outer Banks and the rest of the Carolinas hate what Albert's doing. That's part of the reason I use Mum's name. Welles. It's got Mary all in a tizzy, that's for sure. She's even petitioned the Grand Council over in Glastonbury about it as a potential cause for intervention. I overheard Mary complaining to the other Mentors as they arrived, trying to win them over to the idea of joining her petition. Mary thinks that where they're going to place the first round of rigs could potentially endanger the College because the island is directly downstream. And she's correct. If there's a spill of any kind, this place would be right in the current. Total oil slick waiting to happen."

"That's awful!" I exclaimed, wrinkling my nose. "Do you think this Grand Council will do anything to stop it? I mean, according to what you just told me, potentially ruining an entire ecosystem should provide enough cause for intervention, don't you think?"

"It's iffy," Elliott said. "They'd be concerned about the possible negative environmental impact, for sure. However, according to Nan, Mary's never been a favorite of the Grand Council, for the reasons I just told you. And, as you can probably tell from how few students are here this year, Rookes College isn't exactly thriving. Only six students in a college built for five hundred? I've heard Mary and the others complaining about it. They're seeing just as many young witches with potential. The problem is simply that no one is picking up keys anymore. They keep putting them out, but people just walk on by, glued to their mobiles. It's the main reason Mary hates electronics and has even put a glamor around the island so that they won't work. She thinks being plugged in all the time kills creativity and curiosity. Regardless, from what I understand, the Grand Council is sort of sitting back and watching. They're hoping that the American government or some non-magickal activist group will step in so they don't have to. They prefer to act only as a last resort. Too much risk of exposure."

"Ugh, politics. Even in the magickal world," I said, yawning. "One more question, because everything you're saying is fascinating, but I'm starting to fade." Which was true. If the chair hadn't been so hard and straight, I would have been asleep. "Did you say we're in the Outer Banks of North Carolina? Whereabouts?"

"Eh," Elliott replied, mirroring my yawn. "My American geography isn't great, but a bit southwest of Ocracoke, as near as I can tell. The glamor around the island makes it look deserted. Ships tend to steer clear because of the coral reefs. However, if you're interested, you should ask Cora. She's from the next island up. Hatteras, I think? Although, on second thought, maybe not. Cora gets spitting mad talking about it. There's just as much bad blood and backstory there too, as with Mary, so good luck getting it out of her. Still, I would have thought you'd know more than I. Given the accent, I'd assumed you might be another local or close to it."

"Nope, Tennessee," I said, unwinding myself from the chair in which I'd had my legs tucked up under me. Sensing that I was ready for him to go, Elliott rose too.

At the door, he stopped. "You don't play fair."

"Why is that?" I asked.

"You made me spill my guts, and I still don't know a thing about you."

"You know that I'm from Tennessee and that I don't like politics."

Elliott yawned again. "I mean, anything that matters. Can't I ask one question?"

"One," I said. "Then, really... go!"

"Same one that I started with. Why were you running away from Stephen?"

Elliott grinned, and I hated it. Because if I didn't tell him, I'd seem evasive, and he'd think I liked him. But if I told him the truth... ugh. He would be right either way, but still. I always despise the moment when a guy who looks like he's been told he was cute all his life practically forces you to admit it.

"Because Stephen asked me a question I didn't want to answer."

Elliott's grin got wider. "Because you knew he wouldn't like the answer."

"No," I replied, "Because I didn't like it."

Then, I shut the door. I couldn't stand looking at his stupidly beautiful face anymore.

Chapter Seven

The next morning, after I'd showered and put on my red robe as instructed, I trotted downstairs to breakfast. Instead of the massive spread from the night before, I found a short stack of pancakes with fresh blueberries and whipped cream on top, sitting at my place. Beside it was a mug of coffee—black, just as I liked it. The coffee had an inviting hazelnut flavor. All my favorites. Glancing around the Great Hall, I noticed that everyone's breakfast looked amazing but was completely different.

Elliott caught me staring. "It's like this every day that isn't a sabbat," he said through a mouthful of bacon. "Those all have special foods we're supposed to eat together. Before they set out keys, Mary and the Mentors observed us for years. They take good notes because every meal is like this. Kind of a twist on something we like, but not the same every day. More balanced out. Healthy-like."

"Which is good in that one's case," remarked Alice, sitting down beside me to her plateful of eggs benedict. "He eats so much bacon, you'd think it was a fifth food group."

"It should be," Elliott countered, slurping the last bits of pulp out of his glass of fresh-squeezed orange juice. "It's even better when it's covered in chocolate."

Just then, bright peals of bells echoed around the Great Hall. When they stopped, Cora announced that when we finished, she'd be waiting outside by the entryway to the red hallway, which was called the Fire corridor. Not wanting to be the last one lagging, I quickly stuffed my face with as many blueberries and pancakes as I could.

As I passed down the Fire corridor, I noticed that it was lined on both sides with a long series of doors, just like the ones in the hallway Elliott and I shared. Also, the tapers in the brass candelabra lining the walls were red and decorated with large, crimson crystals. The candles in our corridor were all white, and the crystals cascading down from them were clear. Filing that comparison away in my mind to ask about later, I hurried outside.

When I arrived, Cora was telling everyone to remove their shoes and follow her into a grassy clearing that ran about a hundred yards down toward a natural fence of sea oats, beyond which I knew must be the ocean. Morning dew tickled my feet as I tried to remember the last time I'd walked barefoot in the grass. Probably never. The ground in Tennessee is filled with sharp rocks, just waiting to stab holes in the soles of your feet, which doesn't make for the most comfortable barefoot outdoorsy experience. However, the earth here was soft and cool. I had a feeling that if the island had ever been rocky, such hazards would have been removed long ago.

Overhead, the sky was dark and ominous. Tiers of voluminous gray clouds churned constantly. The wind whipped around us, causing our red robes to fly out like flags as the storm pushed inland. The air had the unmistakably salty flavor of coastal rain.

Cora motioned for us to come closer and for Tayen to stand beside her. "For our first sorcery lesson, we are fortunate to have a day in which the elements have chosen to cooperate. To elaborate on what Mary mentioned last night, sorcery is the art of catching, holding, and controlling energy from a source outside the realm of one's being or making. One of Nature's purest forms of energy is lightning. Lightning has a cleansing power that burns white-hot through the atmosphere. In this untainted air, it is easier for spirits to open portals through which they can move by conduction energy. I know, because I frequently employ the practice myself. Once, knowing how to work with lightning saved my life. Fire witches are especially adept at it, which is why I have chosen Tayen to join me here in the demonstration."

Tayen watched her closely, without what I had begun to realize was her usual skepticism. Reaching into a long, slim leather pouch beneath her robe, Cora pulled out two wands. They looked almost identical, both a dark, grayish brown. She handed the shinier one to Tayen, who turned it over in her hand, examining it closely. As they stood together, I noticed how similar their hair was. Even though Tayen's was black and Cora's was white-blond, the length, cut, and texture were the same.

"I will give the rest of your wands out at the end of today's lesson so that you can practice after lunch," Cora said. She pointed to Tayen's wand and then her own with her free hand. "In Rookes' tradition, the proper wood for one's wand corresponds with when their birthday falls in the Celtic tree calendar. There are thirteen signs in the tree zodiac, and since my birthday is December 12th and Tayen's is the 13th, we should both use elder wood wands."

"But I thought that the zodiac only had twelve signs?" Imani asked.

"That is true of the most common Western zodiac," Cora explained. "However, we must remember that the entire universe, whether terrestrial or magickal, does not revolve solely around Western traditions. Many cultures all over this world and the next have different zodiacs. There are Eastern zodiacs dating back to ancient times, such as the Egyptians. The most commonly used today is the Chinese. Even within the Western world, there are variations. Celtic Britain was in the Western Hemisphere, and theirs is the main one we use here at Rookes. Were any of you aware of these other zodiac traditions?"

Elliott nodded, but the rest of us shook our heads.

"For homework, why don't each of you jot down a thousand words or so giving us the basics of the origins, signs, and dates of a different zodiac besides the Western one we all know?" Cora instructed. "Elliott, since you probably know most of the basics already, just go ahead and do the Celtic, but see if you can add a bit more detail. Then, the rest of you can choose amongst yourselves so that everyone selects a different one. We don't want to be repetitive. Could we have that completed by next Monday's lesson, perhaps?"

We all murmured yeses, because what else was there to say? None of us knew if it was possible to fail at completing a magickal homework assignment.

"Wonderful!" Cora said. "Now, back to what I was saying about wands. The purpose of a wand is to better direct and redirect energy. As you grow stronger and more adept in the Craft, you will be able to do as I will here in a few moments. To control raw energy—even fire—with your bare hands. Until then, it is safer to catch and release any energy you are attempting to transfer from source to destination using a wand. Gives you better focus."

Cora stepped away from Tayen about twenty feet and pointed her wand at the ground. "Wands are also essential instruments in casting circles to create spiritually safe spaces in which a witch may work." As she explained, Cora traced the outline of an invisible circle on the ground. She snapped her fingers, and the previously unseen circle began to glow with a shimmering iridescence. "Your wands may be used to draw circles of protection any time you need a workspace. I've illuminated this one so that you can see it. They are also excellent for shielding you against any malevolent forces that might be near. Once you have finished your work, or when the threat has passed, you may simply reopen the circle and step outside of its protection."

Here, Cora slowly rotated back around in the opposite direction, again with her wand trained on the ground. The circle disappeared.

"We will see how effective circle casting can be against all kinds of energies, both internal and external," Cora said. "I will summon a bundle of straw that we will need for our next demonstration." Pointing her wand across the meadow at a small barn, the doors of it swung open. Giving her wand a little dip of a wave and then slowly drawing the tip toward her, Cora guided a sheaf of straw from the barn to an area just about five or ten feet outside where she had cast the circle. The way she moved looked like someone who was fishing. First setting the hook and then gradually reeling in the fish so they didn't jerk it out of the animal's mouth.

Spinning quickly around in the center, Cora cast the circle once more. Without saying another word, she attempted to pull the straw across the illuminated boundary of its circumference. Yet, as the straw touched the circle, it crackled and began to burn. Cora held it there for a second, as we all watched the tips just barely touching the circle singed black. Giving a little whip of her wand that reminded me of a conductor's cutoff, Cora set the sheaf down outside the circle, which continued to glow softly.

"As you can see, even I cannot break a circle that I have cast with other magick of my own." Cora looked at Tayen. "Now, it's your turn. Try to push the bundle of straw into my circle."

Snapping out of the trance that all of us had been under watching Cora's demonstration, a look of panic crossed Tayen's face. "I... I don't think I know how."

Cora smiled. "Of course you do. If you can move an object with your hands, then you can move it with your wand. You just need clarity of focus. Think of your wand as an extension of your index finger. Concentrate all the energy you think it would take to push that bundle of straw over into your wand. Sometimes it helps to close your eyes. Feel it moving through your body, down your arm, and out the tip of the wand. Just a little push is all it takes."

Tayen closed her eyes and raised her wand. Nothing happened. She shrugged. "Guess I'm not doing it right."

"You're not committing to the intention," Cora said, slightly impatient this time. "Of all the different types of magick, fire magick and sorcery require the most passion and the most vulnerability. You can't be, as young people say nowadays, just whatever about it. You have to open yourself to allow the energy of the universe to flow through you. Catch hold of it and push as hard as you can. Have you ever wanted anything, Tayen, that you've never gotten? Truly wanted it?"

Nodding reluctantly, Tayen was careful not to make eye contact with anyone, as if we could read her thoughts by doing so.

"Good," Cora acknowledged. "Think about that unattainable thing, Tayen. Get angry, if you need to, at the reasons why you can't have it. Then, when you can feel the desire for it burning inside you, grab onto it and push it away. Push it toward this sheaf of straw with everything you have. Now, try it again."

Tayen switched her wand over to her left hand, planted her left foot firmly in front of her right, and clamped her eyes tightly shut. Sure enough, after a moment or two, the sheaf of straw began to quiver, then tilt slightly toward the circle.

"You're doing it!" Cora encouraged her. "Keep going. Get angry. You can't hurt anyone, so just let it out. Push!"

Suddenly, the sheaf flipped over and rammed into the circle. The ties holding the bundle together broke, and the straw burst into flame. Tayen opened her copper-colored eyes and stared at the pile of burning straw, amazed.

"Well done, Tayen!" Cora said, quickly breaking her circle and extinguishing the blaze with a sharp downdraft of wind, like an unseen giant blowing out a candle.

"What were you thinking about to make it move like that?" Hana asked. Tayen stammered for a second, her face flushed.

"As with all personal stories and attachments to magick," Cora responded. "That is Tayen's to share only if and when she is ready to do so. Now that we've finished warming up a bit, let's move on to the main task at hand."

Just as she had before, Cora summoned two more bundles of straw with her wand. She set them down at the very edge of the meadow, in front of the line of sea oats framing the shoreline. "We've witnessed how energy can be sourced from within us to affect the world surrounding us," Cora announced. "What I want you to see now is how witches may also source energy from outside our bodies and redirect it to other things. An internal versus external comparison."

Cora motioned for all of us except Tayen to move further back, closer to the walls of the castle. Then, she told Tayen to move to a spot across from her so that they were both in direct alignment with the two new sheaves of straw. She pulled up the hood of her robe and instructed everyone else to do the same. All around us, the wind began to pick up. "I am about to call a storm, from which I can summon lightning. I intend to catch the energy of that lightning with my wand and then redirect it into that bundle of straw. Watch me carefully, Tayen, and remember that sensation you had a moment ago when you pushed the other bundle. You will need to reverse that energy, make yourself vulnerable and receptive, to call the lightning to you. Then turn all your anger, all your energy against it. Do you understand?"

Tayen replied yes and repositioned herself with her left wand-hand forward toward the coastline. She didn't look afraid as she had the first time—now more determined.

"Excellent," Cora responded. "Then prepare yourself, Tayen. From this moment on, you will know what it's like to hold the power of lightning in your hand."

Immediately, Cora thrust her arm into the air, waved her wand in a broad circle, and pulled. Her back bowed as if she'd just snagged a giant marlin. A deafening crack of thunder reverberated around the meadow as the storm clouds rushed forward. I clutched my robe around me as a wall of rain hit us. Peering out from under my hood, I saw a white-hot bolt of lightning streak straight down from the sky toward Cora. When it connected with her wand, the air tensed and popped as the muscles in her arm quivered. Then, with a cry, Cora brought her wand arm down hard to waist level. The redirected lightning flew out the end of her wand and hit the bundle of straw. It burnt to a sizzling crisp and collapsed into a smoking pyre.

Sensing it was her turn, Tayen repeated Cora's casting motion, then pulled back. When it hit her wand, the lightning bolt she pulled from the cloud was wild. Tayen's whole body shook with strain as she tried to pull it under control.

"Don't show it any fear!" Cora screamed. "Hate it if you have to, but commit to it!"

Slapping her right hand over her left, Tayen brought both arms down like an ax. Whipping back onto itself in a curl, the lightning lashed out in front of her. Striking the straw, it incinerated instantly, just as Cora's had done. The two of them stood grinning and exhilarated as their long, straight hair stood out from their heads in auroras of crackling static electricity.

"Once more!" Cora yelled, cackling ecstatically. Throwing her wand arm back skyward, the lightning that Cora drew down this time was vibrantly red. Holding it steady with her wand, Cora crouched low to the ground, sprang into the air, and then disappeared.

"Sweet Jesus, help us!" Miranda exclaimed. "Where did she go?"

A low rumble of thunder sounded as the rain began to slack off. Near the end of it, what sounded like Cora's voice reverberated through the echoes. "Tayen," the voice said. "Call me."

Using the same motion as she had before, Tayen summoned the lightning again, this time straight down into the grass. After the red streak flashed and dissipated, Cora stood there. Alone and unharmed in the meadow, her long white hair still like a nimbus framing her face.

"Woo!" Cora exhaled, panting as she walked toward us. "I'd almost forgotten what it was like to ride the lightning." Cora stopped in front of Tayen. "Marvelous work for your first go. A few weeks of practice, and I have no doubt you'll be up there too."

"How did you learn to do that?" Tayen asked. The rain had evaporated to a mere drizzle, and we lowered our hoods.

"That," Cora replied, still catching her breath. "It is somewhat of a long story, best told over a break for lunch, I think. Why don't we go inside for some dry clothes and give our hair a bit of time to calm down? Then, I'll tell you."

Perhaps it was because we'd had our hoods on the entire time, but I hadn't noticed until that moment that my hair, like everyone else's, was standing straight up.

Chapter Eight

Back inside the castle, I hurried through the bathroom to towel dry my hair. Then, I changed into one of the mid-century-styled riding pants outfits and a crisp white blouse, leaving my red robe out to dry too. Although I hadn't stopped to think about it before, it occurred to me then that the door on the opposite side of the bathroom must lead to another student's suite. *Why were there so few of us?* I wondered, pulling on flat-soled riding boots and putting my hair up in a ponytail. It had gone limp as usual in the rain and wind. Finding a pad and pencil in one of the desk drawers, I made a note to myself to look up hair spells that evening. Then, I headed downstairs.

The other girls, Elliott, and the Mentors were already seated. Lunch was lighter—a sandwich—but even so, it was my favorite type. Turkey, avocado, and bacon on toasted pumpernickel bread, paired with passion fruit herbal tea and salt and vinegar kettle chips. Sitting down across from Elliott, I noticed that he had a Reuben with sauerkraut on rye and the same chips. I know it sounds weird, but that made me feel a little more confident about liking him as a person, not just because he was beautiful. Only excellent people love salt and vinegar. It's like a clue that they're just the right amount of adventurous. Elliott didn't seem to notice our similar taste in chips. He kept mindlessly stuffing big bites into his mouth as he listened to Cora and Tayen.

They sat in the middle of the room, in two chairs pulled up to the round table on which the feast had been laid out the night before. Cora had what looked like a small chicken pot pie sitting in front of her that she hadn't touched, but Tayen had no food. Just a tall glass of water. Taking a bite of my sandwich and trying not to make too much noise chewing, I listened as Cora told her story.

"It was the autumn of 1723," Cora began. Her voice had a musical cadence to it that I recognized as soon as she named it. "Before America was even a country. I had just left Boston with my baby boy. My husband had died, and his family wanted me to take Noah back to England. Or rather... they wanted to take Noah, as his heir, and leave me. They weren't too keen on Henry's choice of bride: an Irish girl who'd only been brought over as a lady's maid. After I got that letter from London, saying as much, I sold out Henry's holdings in the joint stock company and ran. Henry's lawyer took pity on me and handled the deal. The Lord had seen fit to take Henry with a fever, but nothing was going to take my Noah from me. The money didn't matter. Noah was all I had left on this side of the world."

"What made you choose Hatteras?" Tayen asked. "It seems so random."

"That was the point," Cora replied. "Henry's lawyer told me that if I intended to stay in the New World, I'd best establish myself in a place fewer people would want to take from me. I know it sounds foolish, but I'm a Galway girl. I wanted a place where I could look straight out across the ocean and feel as if I saw home, even if it were a thousand miles away. So, I contacted an agent and went to Hatteras. Bought myself a piece of land and ordered a little cottage built in the style of what we'd had back home; stone with a shingle roof, little beveled glass windows, and a view of the ocean. None of the fuss we'd had in the city. I couldn't stand it with Henry gone. My father was a fisherman, so I'd never had such growing up. 'Twas more comfortable to make something like what I was used to. Mind, I never intended to stay forever. Just long enough for Henry's family to think we'd died and leave us alone. We had plenty of money, so I had no need for work. Noah was such a delightful boy. He was easy to keep. I was happy to be home with him, just growing my garden and advising folks here and there whenever I was needed."

"How did all of it begin?" said Tayen. "What made them come after you?"

"Oh, a woman alone with control of her own money and land back then was reason enough," Cora scoffed. "But yes, there were other reasons too. My mum was a midwife, and when Da was gone, she'd help ladies, you know? That's where I started learning it. The Craft. Through watching my mum help them. All the powers are intertwined. You'll learn that as you go along. Eventually, though, I came to realize that I could do other things. That I could call the wind, the rain, and the lightning—which is very useful for sailors, you know, most of the time. It would have been more useful if I'd learned it before the storm that sunk Da, but then I wouldn't be here, talking to you. It did save me though, in the end."

Taking a second before going on, Cora dipped a spoon into her pot pie and mashed it around, mixing it up for a few seconds. "You've nothing to eat," she said to Tayen. "Are you sure I couldn't make you anything? You're a fair girl, but you're so wan..."

"Me? No... I," Tayen paused, eyeing Cora's food. "I never eat lunch. Or dinner. Only breakfast. It's easier to burn off the calories that way."

"You'll waste away at that," Cora replied, taking a bite of her pie and chewing thoughtfully before she continued. "Anyway, when I got to Hatteras, there weren't many settlers. Mostly Croatoans, the natives of the area. I know that you might have heard otherwise, but they were quite friendly to me. Perhaps because I was alone with just Noah, I didn't seem threatening. It was a long wait between ships from England on the trade routes. The Croatoans allowed me to barter for everything I needed. They helped me with growing corn, squash, and beans. When I told them I had some knowledge of herbs and was interested in learning what remedies they might have, they were only too happy to share. That's where I picked up the rest of it. It was a happy time until Captain Blood showed up."

"And this Captain Blood was the one who started all the trouble?" Tayen prompted. "Even his name sounds sinister."

"Aye, it does," Cora said. "Although the natives were very kind to me, the locals were less so. I was the only woman living alone there with a child, which made me suspect. None of them were used to a woman who could provide for herself without a man in sight. They hated my cat too. A big black tom that Noah took to right away. Came bounding through the weeds a meowing one day out of the blue and looking half-starved, kind of like you."

Tayen flushed, just like she had when we'd been outside. Cora stared pointedly at her spoon and then met Tayen's gaze. Tayen picked up the spoon, dug it into the pie, and took a bite.

Pleased to see Tayen eating, Cora continued. "This Blood fellow, he called himself a Captain, but no one knew truly what he was. Given his reading habits and all that Cotton Mather nonsense, he seemed more of a half-baked Bible scholar to me. He came in on this ship, the Susan G, that had been half-wrecked in a storm. As I said, the ships were slow to arrive, so it was a few months before Blood had what he needed to repair it. Strange winter that year, colder and longer than usual. During it, a man's body washed up onshore with the number 666 carved into his forehead. The rigor had taken hold of him. His body was all drawn up, and his hands were clasped together as if he were praying. My best guess? He was some poor sailor that his mates had gotten the notion was bad luck or something, so they put him off. Seafaring men were superstitious in those days. Being a girl from a coastal town, that certainly wasn't the first strange body I'd seen wash up onshore. At any rate, some townie women had been out walking, looking for the wreckage that might have washed up that morning, and they spied him. Of course, I was blamed for the footprints they left in the sand, even though I'd never been on that beach in the morning. Having a little one at home needing to be nursed, I was never out and about until the sun was well up."

Tayen thought for a second. "How did Captain Blood get the idea you were a witch then?"

Cora cackled, making Tayen jump. Me too, even though her back was turned to me. "How did any man get such a notion in their heads? Because they read too much, assumed too much, and had way too much time on their hands. Blood found a handful of people whom I'd tried to help and couldn't, and who were still angry about it. They had something of a trial, which was a farce of all the usual ways practiced then. They ducked me and tried to cut my hair. Then, they made up some nonsense that Blood probably picked up from a pirate about pricking me and mixing my blood in a bowl. After all of that, they found me guilty of being a witch. Which of course I was, even though I'd never done them any harm."

Cora rolled her eyes, and Tayen took another small bite of her pot pie. Cora pushed it over to her as she finished the story. "They tied Noah and me to an old, gnarled oak tree. The poor black tomcat that was so fond of Noah heard him crying and ran up the tree to see what was amiss. Then, the crowd started screaming something about me turning Noah into the cat, and that pushed them over the edge. They set the tree on fire!" Cora slapped her hands down on the table and cackled again. "It was pure insanity!"

Tayen's copper eyes were wide as the spoon hung out of her mouth. "How did you get away?"

"The same way I showed you this morning," Cora finished. "I'd had a lot of time to spend alone in nature working with my Craft, although I was never formally trained as you will be here at Rookes. Through blending what I knew from my mother in Galway, what I'd picked up from the Croatoans, and a lot of trial and error on my own, I'd learned that I could capture energy and redirect it. Also, I could allow that same energy to take hold of me. When the time came that they tied Noah and me to that tree and set it on fire, I knew that there was only one way out." Cora pointed skyward. "Here. To the magickal Otherworld where I belonged."

"Imagine my surprise when she popped out of a cloud, right over there in that meadow," said Mary, as she stopped by to refill my glass with passion fruit tea.

"But that's crazy!" Tayen exclaimed, dropping her spoon. "Hatteras is what... Twenty miles from here? How did you..."

Cora interrupted her. "That's what I intend to teach you during our time together, Tayen. All travel is not completely linear. Some of it involves other worlds. But I think you know that already, don't you? From your own experiences? That was what drew me to you. We are alike in that way. Different in the methods, I suppose, but essentially the same, as all Fire witches are."

Cora's pale blue eyes linked with Tayen's copper ones, which grew round with recognition, as words passed between them unspoken. Sensing the conversation slow to a halt, the rest of the room grew quiet as well.

"Cora, did you give everyone their wands this morning?" Grace asked, breaking the awkward silence. "I've got a full morning planned for us tomorrow in ecology. I'm sure they'll need to practice what you covered this afternoon."

"Oh yes, I almost forgot," Cora replied, reaching into the leather pouch concealed by her robe. Rising from the table, she pulled the wands out and brought them around to us.

"Willow, your birthday is December 31st, so Birch," Cora said, thinking aloud. She set the wand down beside my place as nonchalantly as if she were laying out extra cutlery. "Tayen has her Elder already for December 13th. Hana... February 1st. Here's Rowan for you. Such a lucky girl, to be born at Imbolc! We'll have to make an extra special offering to Brigid this year."

Hana looked puzzled, and Katerina leaned across the table to whisper something into her ear. Cora continued. "And Miranda, another lucky girl, on March 17th. But I suppose everyone knows about St. Patrick," Miranda nodded as Cora set out her wand. "Ash for you. Then Imani is August 17th, so Hazel. Do you have a black cat, dear?"

"No, I don't have any pets," Imani answered.

"You should, given your birthday is on the Black Cat's Day," Candy said. "We'll have to make sure to create some opportunities. It's better for both if the cat selects you."

"Quite right," Cora seconded. "Especially since she's a Leo."

"Doesn't that seem a bit cliché, though?" Imani scoffed. "I mean, a witch with a black cat? Come on! How obvious do I have to be?"

Cora looked a bit huffy, but Candy intervened. "It isn't a cliché if the stars willed it. Such a clear sign can hardly be ignored. You *were* born on August 17th." Candy continued to whisper to Imani as Cora finished up with the last wand.

"She's right, you know. Such a shame we never found Noah's old cat. He might have taken a shine to you too." Cora shrugged. "And finally, the Reed for Elliott. November 23rd."

Elliott frowned as he looked down at the slim, light brown wand by his plate. "Seems fragile. Isn't there an alternative material that's a bit stouter?"

"I beg your pardon," Mary said, pulling her own nearly identical wand from a pocket beneath her robe. She held it under Elliott's nose. "Flexibility implies resilience, not weakness. Plus an eloquence that you do not quite yet possess. I should know. I am a Reed wielder, and with it I built this castle." Elliott watched her, sheepishly. "Perhaps we should partner together this afternoon and I can enlighten you as to a Reed wand's better qualities." Mary's steely gaze glittered with challenge.

"Actually," interceded Alice. "Shouldn't we cleanse and charge their wands first? 'Twill make their energy transfer clearer from the start."

"Alice, you are quite right," Mary said, turning her gaze away from Elliott. He let out a relieved sigh. Then, to Tayen and Cora, "Are you finished? If so, I can clear these away and fetch a cauldron to hold the salt water."

Tayen scooped one more large spoonful of pot pie into her mouth and then motioned for Mary to take it away. She did, with the slightest wave of her wand, all the while still eyeing Elliott haughtily. Then, with a much larger sweep, Mary caused the doors to the hall beneath the balcony connecting my and Elliott's rooms to open, and an enormous, shiny black cast-iron cauldron floated out.

"Oh," Mary said with mock surprise. "I forgot to fill it. Silly me. Elliott, could you hold this for a moment with your wand whilst I retrieve some water and salt?" Mary steered the cauldron over next to the dais. Looking back at Elliott, she asked in a voice sweet as honey. "Again, dear boy, could you hold this for me?"

Elliott looked down at the table. "I don't know how, Mum."

"Excuse me," Mary continued, in a sickeningly sweet tone. "What was that?"

"Oh Mary, come down off your high horse!" Alice interjected. "He didn't mean you any slight by it. Even I thought that Reed was a sort of wimpish wood to start. He's just learning. Here," Alice flicked her wand toward the cauldron, which had begun to sag in the air as Mary spoke. It rose several inches. "If anyone should be offended this afternoon, it's me. You allowed Cora to steal my thunder when everyone knows the spellcraft Mentor is the witch who traditionally bestows wands."

Cora cackled, as Tayen groaned, both catching the reference. Steal my thunder about a witch who... sigh. It was a terrible pun. Dad-joke level, for sure. I rolled my eyes at Alice.

"Besides," Alice added, winking at me. "We all know Birch is the strongest wood here."

Mary was about to clap back when Grace stepped between them. "Ladies! Wouldn't this be better settled outside, as an educational demonstration for the girls, and Elliott?" She added, hastily including him. "Regarding the various strengths and weaknesses of all different types of wand woods, or better still, how they all might be used together?"

Grace's suggestion seemed to diffuse the situation, as I noticed the dynamics of our Mentors' relationships. Alice seemed to truly enjoy messing with Mary's authority, while Grace often intervened as a peacemaker between the two. As they finished filling the cauldron and showing us how to properly cleanse our wands, I wondered how long they'd been like that. Probably forever.

After lunch, most of us headed back outdoors to charge our wands in the sunlight before beginning afternoon practice with the demonstration. Elliott remained indoors near the central dais with Mary. Before we walked out, Mary also explained the colors of the hallways and turrets in the castle corresponded with the five elements: red for Fire, green for Earth, yellow for Air, blue for Water, and white for Spirit. She instructed us to leave the exterior doors open at the ends. Then, at her signal, to direct the full force of our energies through our wands toward the lightning rods on top of each turret.

"What signal are we waiting for?" I asked Alice as we stopped outside of the Spirit hallway. Shielding my eyes from the glare emanating from the windows, I looked up at the dome on top of the central tower as Alice motioned toward it. Just as I spoke, a blinding column of silver light exploded through the top, brighter than a lighthouse beacon. I couldn't see a thing, except for the flashing echoes that still pierced my tightly shut eyelids. A metallic boom shook the ground. Stumbling backward, I felt something raise my wand hand as Alice called to me. *Push back!*

Instinctively, the muscles in my arm tensed. My energy surged, rippling down the length of my arm like an electric current. The shock of its release forced my eyes open. I could see the two stronger beams of white light coming from our wands. Mine was trained straight on the lightning rod atop the turret of the white hallway. Alice's bolt snaked in a wild arc, connecting the beam from my lightning rod to the top of the silver column that Mary raised from the center. As my eyes adjusted, I could see from the other four corners a different colored pair of ethereal beams cutting a blinding prism through the afternoon sky: red, yellow, blue, and green.

Then, as suddenly as it had sprung to life, the prism vanished. My arm was numb as if it were asleep; I collapsed hard onto the ground. Sweating with exertion, Alice flopped down beside me.

"What was that?" I asked her.

"It's what happens when witches representing all the elements direct their energies toward a common source," Alice said. "The Cone of Power. An almost unstoppable force we can only raise when we work together. I guess that's Mary's way of ending the argument. She never could just let a point go easily." Alice put her palms down flat on the grass. "Ground yourself like this. Contact with the Earth will restore you faster than any-thing else."

Laying my wand across my lap as I pulled myself up to sit, I spread my fingers wide in the grass on either side of me. A soft tingle, like someone was tickling me, spread up my arms. When it reached my biceps, the muscles twitched for a moment, then continued upward, across my shoulders and along the length of my spine to my scalp and my tailbone at the same time. Once the sensation subsided, I massaged the spot just above my nose, at the inner tip of each eyebrow, where all my worst headaches began. All the soreness was gone.

"Woohoo!" a pair of voices whooped as I opened my eyes to see Cora and Tayen walking toward us, their faces flush. The detached scowl Tayen slouched around with after dinner the night before was gone. Something had changed for her, I could tell. I wondered if I looked different too.

"Young Mister Welles," Mary asked, as she and Elliott emerged from the white hallway. "What do you think of your Reed wand now? Is it equal to the others?"

Elliott's eyebrows pushed together as his eyes darted toward me mischievously. "Better."

"Not better than Birch," I replied, struggling to stand as Alice offered me a hand up. "Everyone knows it's the strongest."

Grace threw up her hands. "Why can we only get along until the Cone goes down?"

"Maybe we could work some of it out," Miranda shrugged, as everyone looked at her. "I'd like to see how Cora illuminated that circle again."

"You taught them to cast circles too!" Alice moaned. "What's left for me?"

"The world," Mary replied, snippily. "Miranda is correct. You should be practicing, not bickering. The right to argue about nothing only accrues with time."

"How long?" Elliott asked.

"About three hundred years," Mary frowned at him.

The rest of the afternoon we spent learning to summon sheaves of straw from the barn and calling down the lightning. By dinnertime, when all the straw was burnt to ashes and we were soaked to the bone once again from a half dozen tiny thunderstorms, Cora showed us the opposite command: how to bring the sun back to the sky by pushing clouds away.

Basking in the glow of the evening sun in my newly dried clothes while lying on my robe spread out over the grass, my mind drifted to what Elliott told me the night before. About how Cora allegedly never spoke about her human life. If she'd always been so secretive with other witches before, I could understand if she'd chosen to tell Tayen privately. She was Cora's protégée. But why the rest of us, all at once, in the middle of lunch? That seemed inconsistent.

I pushed myself up onto one elbow and studied the other witches relaxing in the southeastern meadow. The way everyone was sitting so far apart felt lonely. It reminded me of an Andrew Wyeth painting that I'd seen once in a museum on a school trip to New York. *Christina's World*, I think it was called. The story behind it was very sad. Something about this girl who couldn't walk, so she would crawl everywhere. Then, I couldn't figure out why I thought of such a melancholy painting after an exhilarating day, but now I do.

An Atropos can always sense an ending coming.

Chapter Nine

That evening, I changed back into one of my silly, frilly nightgowns and studied my hair in the gilded mirror over the white marble vanity in the bathroom. It was hopelessly flat. Since there wasn't any electricity, and thus no dryer or curling iron, let alone hair products, I decided that I would try to pin-curl it. I'd been in a play once that was set in the forties, and that seemed to give me decent enough waves and body. I remembered my resolution to look up hair spells from earlier in the day and walked back into the study area of my room. *The Grimoire of Alice Gray* still sat propped up on the reading easel where I'd left it. Although I know it's superficial of me to be thinking about my sad hair, I reasoned that such a small spell might be something good to try out on my own. Plus, I was curious to know what Elliott's reaction would be if I fancied up a little. Maybe it might get him to open up again. I regretted shutting the door in his face the first night that he'd tried to get to know me, and he'd been quieter toward me since then.

Besides, what harm could come of it? Alice's hair was excellent. It still looked great even after we were out all day in the wind and rain. Surely, some kind of magic was involved. Setting a handful of bobby pins down on the desk, I took a deep breath and carefully turned the page.

Then, I heard a tap-tap-tap coming from the window in my bedroom. I'd left the curtains between it and the study pushed back, so I could see what was making the noise. It was a rook, somewhat smaller than many of the others that I had seen. When I opened the window, the bird hopped inside and held out its right leg patiently. There was a note tied to it, which I removed. The rook ducked its head under my hand for pets as I read the bubbly-lettered handwriting:

Hey, it's Hana. Tayen, Elliott, and I are out here in the Rookery. Come join us and bring Joan back with you. We need to talk.

Do any words in the English language universally scare people more than the phrase *We need to talk*? I don't think so. They never suggest anything good. It was running away from that very type of dreaded conversation that prompted me to flee into the woods, away from Stephen.

Stephen. I sighed, feeling a pang of guilt. The Mentors reassured me several times that they'd gotten word to him that I was okay and I'd just been called away suddenly to somewhere with bad cell service. Even so, the thought of sweet Stephen out there on the trail, wandering around and calling my name kind of broke my heart. Mostly because I dreaded what I knew I'd have to say to him when I did go back at last. That it was all over between us. *At least now*, I thought, as Joan the rook hopped up onto my shoulder, and I put my outdoor clothes back on, *I'd have plenty of time to think about what to say to let him down easily.*

Padding down the stairs as quietly as I could, I left through the back door of the white, northernmost hallway, thankful that the door didn't creak as I shut it. The meadow air was still, probably worn out after its day of microstorms, and the stars were clear and bright as snowflakes on windows. The air smelled of the sea and white gardenias that encircled the pathways around the white Spirit point's turret as I hurried out to the Rookery.

"See, I told you Joan could do it!" Hana beamed as she saw me open the door. Joan, the littlest rook, swooped in after me, chattering happily, and resettled herself on Hana's shoulder. She stroked the bird's head. "Such a smart girl!"

"So, you've figured out the mystery of how the rooks work," I said, wanting to know the worst if there was any to find out upfront. "What's all this about needing to talk? Where are Imani and Miranda?"

"Probably still snoring," Tayen replied, her familiar scowl returned. "I'd already sent Darcy out twice, but he didn't come back with anyone. Figured I was doing something wrong or that my bird was just dumb. Hana was confident Joan could do it. Guess she was right... Ow!" Tayen exclaimed as Darcy, nipped at her ear. "What was that for?"

Elliott shrugged. "Rooks are sensitive birds. Darcy didn't like you saying you thought he was dumb."

Darcy cocked his head to the side at Tayen, looking like some sort of meme for *See, I told you so*. My rook, Stella, gave him a haughty look and floated down to rest on a bale of hay near me. She made soft, satisfied clicking noises as I stroked the smooth top of her head and down her back.

"Anyway…" Hana interceded, twirling a wisp of her lavender hair around her finger. "I was up reading, and I saw Tayen in the meadow. Wondered what was up, so I followed her."

"And I was out here because I'd seen Elliott going into the Rookery, which I thought was weird because he doesn't have a bird," Tayen added.

"I couldn't sleep, you know," he said, glancing in my direction. Both Hana and Tayen stared at me, quizzically, as Elliott continued. "Although I don't have a rook of my own, I've been hoping that Nan will send her falcon, Freyja, back to me with a reply to the letter I'd sent her. About what I'd found out from Mary and the rest."

"About what you overheard," Tayen corrected. Elliott frowned at her. "Sorry, can't have Willow thinking you've got some kind of inside track on top-secret info that makes you special. Plus, I just think it's funny when dudes eavesdrop. Way to break stereotypes, man!"

"Thanks," Elliott replied sarcastically. "Isn't the message more important than the situation here?" Tayen shrugged as Elliott continued. "I sent Nan a letter a week ago telling her what I've already told you. How Mary is worried sick with Dad's oil company. Mary wanted to know whether Nan heard if anything had come of that petition to Glastonbury for an intervention. Nan still has some connections with the Grand Council because she clerked there for several years before she married Pop. Mary thought Nan might have some inside scoop if the Grand Council were planning to revoke the Charter and close Rookes College before they issued an official proclamation in *The Augur* or *Old B.*"

The rest of us had no idea what he was talking about, so Elliott clarified. "Those are the two witches' newspapers. *The Augur* is the paper that always tells the worst of whatever news has happened during the day. *Old B*, or the *Old Bulletin*, tries to paint current events with lighter, more optimistic strokes. Pop calls *Old B* "Old Blighty" because everything they report has this sort of nostalgic haze about the golden days of witchcraft, whenever the hell those were supposed to be. Some new editors came in a few years ago and tried to spice things up with the *New Bulletin*, but it didn't last. Witches who want to bore down to the hard facts and issues read *The Augur*. Those who read *Old B* do it for the same reasons that regular humans read whatever optimistic local rags are available. It's like a cauldron full of chicken soup."

"Gotcha," I said, marveling again at how the magickal world contin-ued to surprise me with how similar it was to the plain, boring one we took for granted. "What did Nan say? Any news?"

"Not a peep yet," Elliott replied. "Which probably means one of two things. Possibly, the Grand Council hasn't decided anything on Mary's petition because they're waiting to see whether there's any real danger involved. If so, that would be typical of their style. Magickal bureaucracy tends to sit back and hope one of the terrestrial governments will act so that it doesn't have to whenever its interests collide with non-magickal life. Alternatively, it could signify more swiftly moving bad news."

"Meaning the Grand Council plans to shut down the Rookes College anyway after the end of this year, and they don't want to spoil it for us if we're the last ones," Hana blurted out. "Don't you think that's awful? That they just don't care to respond until they're ready!"

"They don't care what happens to Rookes College, you mean," Tayen said. "But according to Elliott, they should care anyway, right? About the potential slow-rolling environmental disaster that his dad's stupid oil company could create for this part of the coast?"

"They should," I agreed. "However, from what Elliott told me before, they are pretty bureaucratic, so it makes sense if they plan to do both of the things we're afraid of. To shut down Rookes College and look the other way about Albion Oil's new enterprise. If neither is likely to be a popular stance, then why would they be in a rush to put anything in the papers? *The Augur* would drill down into the sore issues of their inaction, and *Old B* would just moan and groan. No one would be happy. Am I right?" I asked, directing the last question to Elliott.

"As rain," he answered.

"Yet, I still think we can read the tea leaves, so to speak, from the way that the Mentors have been behaving," Tayen added, extending a cautious fingertip to stroke Darcy's wing. The bird turned his back to her. Tayen shut her eyes and took a breath. "For example, Cora told all of us her life story this afternoon. According to Elliott, that never happens." Elliott nodded in agreement. "Then, after practice today, Cora shared more things with me—things I doubt she would have shared so readily with a new witch if she weren't afraid that time was running out faster than expected."

"What kinds of things did she tell you?" I asked.

"Well, to begin with, Cora told me how I was found and why Mary and the rest began tracking me," Tayen said. "According to Sleepless by the Shore over here," Tayen inclined her head toward Elliott. "The mystery of why each of us was chosen isn't usually revealed until later in the year when we younger witches are better able to comprehend the significance of our actions and choices without the burdens of the past looming over us."

Hana glanced over at me pointedly but said nothing. I could tell she was holding back so that Tayen's story could unfold more organically. Possibly to gauge my reactions to it in comparison to her own, as Tayen resumed her tale.

"Cora told me Mary began watching me when I was a very little girl because of something that happened in the woods. Growing up, my dad Nyles's main house was in Palo Alto because of his business." Tayen shrugged, assuming I'd know which business she meant. I didn't. "He used to take us on these trips up the coast when he wanted to unplug and recharge, as he called it, which I thought was a weird way of putting it. The year I turned ten was the first time Mom refused to go. My mom Bly always hated the fact that Dad wanted to spend what few days off he had each year out in the middle of nowhere, talking to no one. Lyle, my little brother, had a cold, so he stayed home with Mom. I went with Dad alone to Humboldt County. Although Nyles planned to stay off the computer if not completely off the grid for a week, on the second day he got a call from back in Palo Alto that was supposed to be urgent. So he kind of ditched our plans for a peaceful hiking trip and spent the next couple days putting out fires online. Nyles did that a lot back then before he and Mom divorced. He just totally checked out of life for days at a time whenever something at work needed him."

Tayen shrugged again as if she didn't care, but I could tell that she did more than she let on. "Anyway, I got bored, so I packed my backpack and headed out toward one of the trails we were supposed to hike. I didn't have a phone signal, so no GPS. Naturally, I got lost. Around dusk, I came to this clearing on top of a hill with what appeared to be an old homesite. Ancient redwoods were all in a perfect circle around it, and the falling remains of an old cabin were in the center. Beside it was an abandoned well that had been boarded up. Pretty creepy overall. The kind of place that pops up in horror movies. I sat down on the edge of the well, waving my phone around and trying to get a better signal so I could call Dad. That was when I saw it."

Hana squeaked with anticipation. I realized Tayen must have already told this story to her and Elliott before I arrived. "Saw what?" I asked.

Tayen took a breath and scanned my face for signs of skepticism. "A big, hairy, human-like thing came out from the forest into the clearing. It didn't see me at first, and I ducked down behind the well and peeped over. It was just shuffling along, all hunched over like some tall people are, around the edge of the circle. Then, it stopped to sniff the air and started walking over in my direction. I didn't know what to do, so I panicked and ran. As I took off, I hadn't gotten more than a few steps before I felt my feet lose contact with the ground. Turning in the air, I could see that the creature had lifted its hands or paws or whatever. The higher he moved them, the higher I rose too."

"Oh my god!" I exclaimed. "That must have been terrifying, although not much more..."

Tayen interrupted me, smiling. "Not much scarier than today with the lightning, right?"

I thought for a moment about how calm Tayen seemed that morning when Cora told her to focus on something she wanted and to get angry about it to move the straw. Tayen seemed skeptical to start, that she could do it at all. However, once she tried, it happened easily.

"Is that how you got away from it?" I asked. "By focusing and getting angry?"

"I guess so," Tayen replied, "even though I didn't realize it at the time. I've always been a pretty angry person, even as a kid. Especially whenever anyone tries to act like they can control me." Tayen shrugged again. I realized that gesture was just as much a part of Tayen as her disdainful scowl. "Because they can't. I screamed bloody murder, and whatever it was dropped me. I was pretty high up because I sprained my ankle in the fall. As I lay there, crying over my throbbing ankle, I saw the creature disappear right before my eyes. It took me hours to hobble back to the cabin. When I told my dad what happened, he immediately thought I was in shock and suffering from PTSD after being assaulted in some way. Nyles called the cops. They checked me out but found nothing physically wrong. When we got home, Mom lost it. Blamed Dad for letting something happen to me in a place I never should have been. Sent me to half a dozen shrinks, who all diagnosed me with something different because I kept telling them the same story that I've told you. No one believed me."

I was puzzled. "How does that square up with Mary and Cora finding out? Were they listening in on the psychiatrists?" Pulling a face, I put my hand up, mimicking holding a phone. I tried to imitate Mary's proper voice in a ridiculous dialect that she would never use. "Whaddup, chicka? Yeah, I know our girl is seeing Sasquatches. What's the 411? Enrollment's down, so I thought she might be a crazy enough girl to attend my school."

Tayen snorted. "Pretty good, but no. Seriously, I'm getting to that. After Mom calmed down and figured out there was nothing seriously wrong, she took an interest in me for once. Booked a trip to a spa up north of Moab for both of us. Bly's always going to some granola girl spa or other. You know the type—I call them JC-IDs—Juice Cleanses in the Desert. To find herself and get in some girl time with her friends." Tayen made air quotes with her fingers. "That turned out to be not much different than my trip with Dad. Mom spent most of her time with girls her age—tech widows from Palo Alto—and I was alone again."

I was beginning to get the sense that Tayen, despite being gorgeous, spent a lot of time by herself growing up. That kind of thing always floors me when I realize it. Beautiful people can be lonely too.

"One night, after lights out in the yurts—don't ask..." Elliott wrinkled his upper lip and started to say something snide, but Tayen waved him off. "I got bored again and wandered out into the desert. Nothing too crazy happened that night, except I saw the lights for the first time. Bright, glowing orbs out in the distance flying fast. They were fascinating, the way they would bank and turn." Tayen made sharp, swirling gestures with her hands to indicate their movements.

"I sat down to watch and must have gotten very still because I started to see all these coyotes come out slowly. One at a time at first, then in pairs and small groups of mothers with cubs. They paid no attention to me, even though they were doing the same thing I was doing. Curling up and just staring at the orbs flying back and forth over the stillness of the desert. We sat that way until the first rays of sunlight started peeping over the horizon. Then, the coyotes left, and I did too. Went back to the yurt with Mom. Fell asleep off and on through meditation sessions all day, which Bly chalked up to me finally relaxing and reuniting with my true self," Tayen used the air quotes again. "Which, maybe I was, after all. The next night, the same thing. After we went home from our weekend, I told Mom how much I'd enjoyed the trip. It wasn't a lie. There was something... I don't know how to explain it really... warm and homey feeling about it, you know? About the cool, stillness of the desert, and sitting just watching those lights, with the other coyotes around me."

"Other coyotes?" I asked. It was hard to wrap my tongue around the words, as if Tayen's story had pulled me into some kind of trance.

"That was what Cora told me," Tayen finished. "About how she and Mary found out where I was and what made them decide to reach out to me. The coyotes told them."

"Coyotes talk? How is that possible?" I asked.

Hana couldn't contain herself any longer. "Cora told Tayen the animals tipped them off. The ones that are theirs—ours—are familiars. They have some kind of telepathic network, where they can sense humans who are kindred spirits. Mary is going to start training us on Saturday to communicate with them and to..." Hana searched for the right word. "To start learning how to convert into their forms. For our safety."

Elliott rolled his eyes. "The correct term is transmogrify. The shifting from one's human physical form into another animal form by use of magick. Otherwise known as transformation or shapeshifting, in the common vernacular." He sighed heavily, clearly tired of having to explain what he thought we should already know. "Tayen was seeing signs of extraterrestrial life. The coyotes in the desert noticed it and felt a familiarity with her because they could see such things too. They reported it along through their network, so to speak," Elliott repeated Tayen's air quotes, "and eventually word got to Mary, who then began scrying to watch Tayen for other signs that she later displayed. This observation proved over time that Mary should leave a key out for Tayen. Then, Mary also began contacting likely Mentors who were Fire witches and who might be interested in working with her. It's an unusual method of finding students, but Mary Rookes has never been a common witch. If there ever was such a thing."

"Okay," I breathed, taking it all in. "So that explains the secret of why we were brought here. But I'm still not following how that secret connects with what they don't want us to know about the future of the college."

"We," Hana gestured around to Tayen and Elliott, "think Cora told Tayen about how she was discovered and about her familiar animal spirit because the Mentors don't know how much time we have left to train as witches. They aren't sure whether we will have the full year and a day, or if something will happen to interrupt that."

"Specifically, they're worried about my dad's new venture with his oil company," Elliott added. "Like we discussed the other night, Mary wants us to have this one year of our lives to focus on magick alone. There seems to be some kind of concern—whether based on real prognostications or just plain fear, we don't know—that Rookes College and the whole of the Outer Banks are doomed. Something terrible is going to happen because Albion Oil has been allowed to start offshore drilling operations. Like a major oil spill. Mary seems to have warned the rest of the Mentors not to talk about it, because she's concerned that it will distract from our training."

As Elliott mentioned our previous conversation, Tayen's eyebrows went up. I could read her mind from the way she looked at me. She was wondering why Elliott and I were up talking at night by ourselves. I shot her what I considered my best *don't you dare ask* stare. One side of her mouth curled into a half smile, but she didn't pry further.

Instead, she said, "That would explain why Cora told me what she did, as early as she did. If the Mentors are nervous that we might not be able to complete our year and a day of study in the regular order before some kind of disaster happens, then it makes sense that they would try to tip us off to as many things as possible before then in subtle ways. So that we are mentally prepared enough to help them combat it, even if they get no assistance from the Grand Council."

"They trust us that much?" I said, incredulously. "They don't even know us."

"They've been watching me since I was ten," Tayen replied. "Cora knew me well enough to decide that I was another Fire witch and to agree to be my Mentor. I know it sounds hokey, but they've put a lot of thought into it." Tayen's copper eyes flashed at mine, and I knew what she meant. They've cared enough to pay attention all this time. They've seen us, and they know what we're capable of. That's more concern than most of our parents take with us.

A million questions zoomed through my mind. Some of them were self-serving—part of my curiosity. *How did they discover me? What is my familiar animal?* Others were less so.

"We should tell Imani and Miranda," I said.

"I tried," Tayen replied. "After we talked it over, I sent Darcy out to them right away, but they didn't respond." Tayen and the bird exchanged looks.

"I don't think that he screwed it up now. I think they either didn't hear him or chose not to listen." Darcy, who had been on the far end of his perch ever since she'd attempted to pet him, fluttered down closer to Tayen. It seemed to be the bird's way of saying she was forgiven.

"We can tell them in person tomorrow," Hana said. "What I want to do now is read some cards to give us a little clarity on what to expect." She pulled a deck of tarot cards from beneath her cloak and slid them out of the box to begin shuffling.

"Do you just run around with those on you all the time?" I asked as both Tayen and Elliott tried not to smirk. It seemed way too stereotypical, all things considered.

"What?" Hana replied. "When I was called by the key, I was in the middle of a sorority rush event at Harvard. We were doing this part where they put us out in the woods and we had to decipher clues that our possible future sisters left for us to find our way back. When I found the key, I thought it was just another clue. Turns out, it brought me here. I've read tarot cards for years. Brought them along in my pocket just in case I needed, you know, a little boost of intuition."

Hana began shuffling the cards against her lap. I wasn't surprised that she had been in a sorority rush event when she found her key. From what I'd seen from Hana at that point, it was a perfect fit. But tarot? I wondered where she picked that up from. Still, I was curious as we pulled up bales of hay to sit near her in the Rookery, what else I would learn about the others as she read. Stella flew over to sit in my lap, bumping her head under my hand like a cat seeking pets.

"I'm just going to pull one for each of you to give some general guidance," Hana said. "Rather than a full reading. So much has happened, and we all have too many questions. It would be confusing to try to answer everything all at once, with so many different energies in the air."

Without much ceremony, Hana shuffled the cards again and handed one to each of us face down. "I'm going to turn mine first," she said, slowly flipping the card over.

"The Lovers," she breathed as if relieved. "That fits. How I connect with other people is changing, and I need to learn to be more true to myself. Also, it signifies how I might be living life in two halves, one that is expected of me and another that is who I am. Generally, I should be more open and honest if I want to gain confidence and make real connections."

Hana placed the card back in the deck and continued. "Okay. It asked for honesty, so here goes. I've had a rough year so far. I wanted to go to an art school like RISD, but the folks weren't supportive because they thought I had the grades to do better. Plus, they're Atwaters, and the Atwater family always goes to Harvard." Hana shook her head. "I've always felt like a disappointment to my parents. They're both college professors. Dad's at MIT in Neuroscience, and Mom is at Wellesley in Biochemistry. They couldn't have kids, so they adopted me from Korea. They've never been so rude as to say it to my face, but I've overheard them talking about it to their friends how they got the only Asian kid in the world who isn't great at STEM. It sucks, but it has to be okay, you know? I mean, they chose me for some reason, right?"

I didn't know what to say to this. My dad Oliver would be tickled to death if I finally decided to go to college anywhere. He'd started late at the University of Edinburgh after taking a gap year. Mom had only managed one year at the University of Tennessee before dropping out. I knew both of Elliott's parents went to Rookes, but nothing about Tayen's folks. Sensing that none of us had an answer, Hana motioned for me to turn over my card.

"The Magician," she read. "You have all the right tools, but you need to manifest clearly what you want out of life and why. Focus your attention, and it will appear to you. Ring any bells?" Hana asked.

I stared at the card. The Magician with his white robe and red cloak, hand held aloft to infinity. "I know that I should, but nothing in particular comes to mind, other than the fact that I need to make up my mind soon, about a lot of things. Not just here, but back home."

Hana nodded. "You'll know when you see it. Tayen, would you like to go next?"

Tayen flipped over her card. "Really?" She held it up. "Can I draw again?"

"No," Hana replied, taking the card from Tayen's hand. "The Fool. What don't you like about it? New beginnings, opportunities, and untapped potential. Those are all good."

Tayen snorted and pointed at the card. "Until the Fool falls off the cliff that he can't see."

"Perhaps that's why we're all here," Hana responded, nonchalantly. "To catch you. Last?"

Elliott flipped over his card.

"The Hanged Man, reversed," Hana read.

"You don't need to tell me," Elliott said. "It's like that old song. Oftentimes it happens that we live our lives in chains and never even know we have the key."

"Seriously?" I said. "The best insight, Mister I-know-everything can come up with is quoting Eagles lyrics like some old Boomer?"

"Duuuude," he mocked, in a terrible California accent. "Why do you hate the Eagles?"

"I don't hate the Eagles, but I do hate *The Big Lebowski*," I countered. "And I'm not so sure about any of this either," I said, motioning at the cards. "I mean—the Lovers, the Magician, the Fool, and the Hanged Man? It's so vague; how can we be sure what any of it means? We all need to be open to rethinking our entire lives because the whole world has just flipped upside down. How is that not just retelling us everything we already know?"

"It isn't," said a soft, firm voice from behind us. I jumped as Grace walked into the circle. "But that doesn't mean that the cards are inaccurate. I applaud your interest, Hana. It takes a long time to learn the meanings of tarot. However, you should be more precise in directing your questioning. Otherwise, they will merely interpret the present for you in ways that make it easier to comprehend, rather than forecasting the future."

Grace picked up each of our cards, placed them back in the deck, and slid the deck into its box. She handed it back to Hana. "I'm sure you will hear all you care to know about how to gain precision in your interpretation of tarot and other methods of prognostication from Katerina this year. Tonight, however, I would prefer if you would return to bed. My ecology lesson tomorrow will require everyone's full engagement. Considering Miranda has already demonstrated that she is leaps ahead of the rest of you in magickal intuition, I'm expecting your best attention will be required to keep up." Grace made a shooing motion with her hands. Our rooks fluttered back to their nests, and she shut the door behind us.

Back in my room, I changed again into my voluminous nightgown. Remembering the grimoire on my desk, but too tired to look anything up in it, I resolved to wake early in the morning. Then, I remembered there were no clocks, and thus no way to set an alarm.

As I puzzled over a way to wake up without one, I heard a tapping on my window. It sounded just like when Hana's rook had arrived with her message.

What now? I thought crankily as I went to the window. When I opened it, Stella hopped in and came to rest on the end of my canopy bed. Sticking out one foot, in a way that I realized they must all be trained, I removed the note tied to it.

Write to your father, the note read. The swirly cursive handwriting was so elaborate it was almost unreadable. *Tell him everything.* I sat down on the window seat, examining the note. The handwriting seemed familiar, but I couldn't place it.

Stella cawed loudly at me and flew from the end of the bed past the parted velvet curtains and into the study area of my room. Perching on my desk near Alice's grimoire, the rook cawed again. Understanding what the bird must mean, I walked over and held the note next to the grimoire. The handwriting matched perfectly.

"Good girl," I said, rubbing Stella underneath her chin as the rook preened. Grace must have told Alice how she'd found us out in the Rookery. What I couldn't comprehend, though, was why Alice wanted me to tell Oliver everything. What would be gained by his knowledge?

Still, I decided it was best not to ask questions. Shuffling around in the drawers of my desk, I found paper, a pencil, and string. As succinctly as possible, I wrote down the highlights, including what Elliott told me about Albion Oil. Also, I included a message for Dad to relay to Stephen, reassuring him once more that I was okay and would be in touch soon. I tied the note to Stella's foot. Seeming to know what to do, the bird hopped over to the window and sat looking at me expectantly.

Thinking it was not likely that birds could tell one zip code from another, I explained from what I knew about how the landscape would look between the College and Oak Ridge. Then, I told Stella as many unusual details as I could think of to make Dad's house immediately distinguishable from a multitude of other similar cabins in the area. Hopping impatiently from one foot to the other, Stella took flight immediately after I finished giving her the directions.

For the next hour after Stella left, I lay awake trying to mentally calculate how far she would have to fly and how long it might take before it finally dawned on me. The usual time and distance calculations probably didn't apply to magickal animals coming and going through the Otherworld. As I fell asleep at last, I realized that this new life was going to take more than a little while to get used to.

Chapter Ten

"**N**ot that one dear," Grace said to me the next morning, as she examined the gray stone in my palm. "You'll want one with a larger hole in the center. At least big enough that you can string a cord through it to wear or carry." She held the stone up to her bright emerald eye and peered at me through the pencil eraser-sized hole in it. "Remember, you need to be able to see clearly through the center too if you want to use it for divination."

Grace handed the stone back to me. I skipped it out across the waves and trained my eyes on the sand, searching for another. It was a beautiful morning, balmy and not too hot. We'd been out on the beach for almost an hour since breakfast, dressed like a bunch of coastal grandmas. Light, natural linen outfits over the tops of bathing suits, along with our green robes for the day open and fluttering in the breeze. Together, we combed the dunes for what Grace had initially referred to as "hag stones," until Imani challenged her to call them by another name, saying that the term was ageist. Grace merely nodded and acknowledged Imani's correction by referring to them as "witch's stones" during the remainder of her explanation about their uses. I thought that spoke volumes about Grace's temperament. Without any sort of confrontation at all, she simply changed her wording. Legions of people who've passed through my life before and since that day could learn a lot from Grace's reaction.

"What about this one?" Miranda called from further down the beach. She held up a white stone, flat as a coaster and about the size of a tennis ball with a hole the size of a golf ball in it.

"Oh my, that one is excellent, yes!" Grace exclaimed, gathering up the ends of her long green robe as she hurried over to Miranda. "Girls! Pause where you are for a moment and look at what Miranda has turned up. I want to show you something."

Once we'd all gathered around her, Grace held Miranda's stone up for everyone to see. "This is exactly the kind of stone you want. Worn smooth and even, with no cracks on the surface, and a perfect oculus for viewing. Your eyes are indeed sharp as an eagle's, my dear, to have found such a lucky piece."

Grace smiled approvingly at Miranda, who blushed as Grace returned the stone. "As I mentioned before, holey stones can be used for a variety of purposes. They can be worn for protection during travel, especially over the sea, to ward off storms. Also, they can be incorporated into a witch's ladder, with a series of knots and feathers, for spellcasting. To call the winds and such. We will practice those techniques in a few moments. However, what I would like to show you now is perhaps my favorite use of witches' stones." Grace paused and swept her arm broadly. "To see beyond the farthest horizon."

Hana raised her hand, "Isn't that technically prognostication? Which is tomorrow's class? I thought today was ecology."

"Sharp," Grace replied, glancing over at Imani, who'd been looking slightly smug ever since her subtle correction earlier. "You are correct on all counts. Scrying with a holey stone is a form of prognostication, but it also involves all elements of the Great Circle that is life. A holey stone is born, as all stones are, from deep within the fires of the Earth. Then, it is worn smooth by water and bored through by a mollusk. All of this before someone picks it up and breathes life into it. This is why, Hana, I have chosen to include them as part of our first lesson in ecology, one that serves as a bridge between what you learned yesterday with Cora when you used sorcery to draw lightning down from a storm, and what you will study tomorrow with Katerina in prognostication. The Craft, like Nature herself, is similar to a ball of yarn without any end. Constantly encircling itself into a larger and larger sphere. As you grow stronger within the Craft, you will learn how to pick up that thread and to weave your path through this magickal life."

Grace turned back to Miranda. "The air that we breathe has been shared by every living thing since the dawn of time. To use a holey stone for scrying, you must complete that circle. That way, it can begin again, with your sight becoming part of the all-seeing whole. Cup the stone in your hands so that you can breathe through it, and so that air circulates back into your eyes. Then, hold the stone up and look through the hole out there," Grace pointed across the waves, "and tell us what you see."

Miranda cupped the stone to her face and took a deep breath. Exhaling slowly, she held the hole in the stone to her eye, as if she were looking through a telescope. "I see..." she said softly. "I think I see an island, but it's very steep."

"Look more closely dear," Grace suggested. "If you've ever used a spyglass, or a..." she turned her head to the side, searching for the modern word.

"Telescope?" Hana offered.

"Telescope," Grace added. "Thank you, Hana. It's similar to that, only there are no lenses. Let your mind relax and then focus more closely on what you're seeing. Sometimes the mechanical sensation of turning the stone or squinting helps to release the connection between physical sight and second sight. Try that, and your vision may clear up a bit."

Turning the stone and squinting, Miranda eventually switched eyes, holding the stone up to her left instead of her right. "Oh!" she exclaimed, immediately. "Yes, I can see it now. It's not an island at all. It's more like a boat, but square." Miranda tucked her soft, red-brown curls behind her ears as she peered through the hole in the stone again. "Some men are standing around on top of it, and it's raised above the surface of the water. Kind of like a bridge or..."

Elliott interrupted her. "Like a platform." He looked toward the ocean, shading his eyes in the sun. "That would probably be one of the rigs they're building for Albion Oil. Didn't know they'd gotten so far along yet. I thought they were still in the surveying and testing stage."

"I've heard about that," I seconded, noticing that Elliott had referred to the company only by name, without mentioning his father's attachment to it.

"I didn't know oil rigs were permitted off the East Coast," Imani frowned.

"They're not supposed to be, but times are changing," Grace answered. From the tension on her face, I could tell she had hoped Miranda would see something different. Hurriedly, Grace changed the subject. "Okay, now that we know how remote viewing works with the stones, let's move on to how they might be utilized in making witches' ladders and the like."

Awkward, Tayen mouthed at me once Grace's back was turned. I nodded, then caught Miranda looking at Tayen and me with a pained expression.

Tayen saw it too. "I wasn't talking about you, goofball," she said, sticking out her tongue and crossing her eyes. Then, Tayen grabbed Miranda's hand and swung it exaggeratedly into the air, skipping ahead and pulling her forward. Miranda giggled, blushing again.

Ahem, Hana cleared her throat and nudged me with her elbow.

I raised an eyebrow in return as if to say, *Yeah, I know.*

We followed Grace along the beach, to a boathouse off the north-western shore of the island facing inland. There, several sloops floated in the water, tied to a small pier. "Who among you knows how to sail?" Grace asked.

"Oh, I do!" Hana replied, waving her hand in the air again. "I rowed crew in high school and lettered on the swim team."

"Not surprised you'd feel at home on the water Hana, given your sign," Grace said. "Would you mind partnering with Tayen?" Hana bounced over to stand beside her, making tiny, excited claps. Miranda dropped Tayen's hand quickly as Grace kept assigning partners. "Elliott, I've seen you manage one of these sloops single-handedly before, so I think you should be fine sailing one alone with Willow."

"Deadweight," Elliott whispered in my ear. I kicked him in the side of the leg, a little too hard. He winced, and Grace gave us a stern look before proceeding. "Imani, you can come with Miranda and me. The sloop can hold three easily. Do you sail?" Imani shook her head. "That is no problem. I'm sure you'll pick it up quickly once I show you the ropes. I may ask you just to hold it steady for a few moments while I swim down to cut some seaweed with Miranda."

"Wait... swim?" Miranda's voice jumped about an octave higher than usual as she took a step back. Everyone stared at her. "I can't... I mean, I've never..."

"Really?" Grace asked, slightly incredulous. "My apologies, I assumed being from Florida you would swim like a fish. Why ever would you not?"

"Dad didn't want me to," Miranda explained, staring down at the sand. "He allowed my older brothers, but not me. He thought all the swimsuits for my age were too revealing."

"Jesus! I know he's a preacher but that's like, some special kind of puritanical idiocy." Tayen rolled her eyes. "Don't let him see my modeling portfolio. He'd die of shock."

"Don't call her an idiot!" Imani snapped back, crossing her arms and casting Tayen some serious side-eye. Miranda winced, as Grace stepped between them.

"Girls! I am sure Tayen didn't mean to call Miranda an idiot, did she?" Grace glanced over to Tayen, who blinked slowly once and whispered *no*.

"Good," Grace replied. "Imani, if you don't mind, we'll have you exchange places with Miranda so you can swim out and harvest some seaweed first. I will direct you on how and what to look for. Then, we can all take turns. Afterward, I will demonstrate how to dry it quickly, and braid it into a ladder for spellcasting with knotted cords, ribbons, and feathers. It may even be used to direct the winds for sailing. Which is the goal of today's lesson. And Miranda!"

Miranda jumped. "Yes, ma'am?" she mumbled.

"We absolutely must teach you how to swim as soon as possible," Grace finished. "It saved my life once, and it may save yours at some point. I understand modesty and discretion, but a grown woman not knowing how to swim, or at least float, is extremely dangerous. Remind me to explain more at dinnertime. For now, here."

Grace reached into the straw beach bag that she'd kept slung over her shoulder all morning. She pulled out a sickle-shaped knife with a white handle and gave it to Imani. "That is called a boline. It is a ritual knife used to cut herbs and such. We will be using it every day we meet for ecology, so be sure to bring it with you." Grace handed another boline to each of us.

"Today, we will use them to harvest seaweed. Imani, you will sail out with me as I said before. Pilots," Grace indicated to Hana and Elliott, "Follow me out to the point. I'll show you how to do the harvesting. We'll return to the pier to do the drying and tying with Miranda."

Sensing she was about to be left behind, Miranda started to protest, but Grace stopped her. "Miranda can view us through her stone. We're at a much closer range, so there should be plenty of detail. I am not taking any risks of losing a novice swimmer in a riptide."

As we separated into our boats, I could tell Grace was slightly exasperated. Miranda felt abandoned, and the rest of the group was oddly quiet. I hated that. Being around silent, unhappy people always makes me anxious.

Like I have to try to do something to fix it. I know it's mostly because of my mom Darla. She's like that Prince song. Never satisfied. Being a fixer is a bad habit. However, I can't help it. I'm not a big talker, but I like to clear the air. Even if sometimes it means playing slightly dumb.

Scanning around for something meaningful to talk about, some shapes painted on the bows of the sailboats caught my attention. "Those eyes painted on the fronts of the boats have some kind of significance, but I'm not sure what," I said to Grace, loudly enough so that everyone else could hear. "Could you tell me?"

It was as if by asking that one simple question, I had turned the tuning knob just right to bring all six strings of our interaction back into accord. Elliott scoffed at my saying fronts and boats instead of bows and sloops. Then, Imani, always a fountain of information about pretty much anything that's ever had a book written about it, launched into a lengthy digression about ancient Egypt and the Eye of Horus, to which Hana and Grace also chimed in. Even Tayen made a joke about how she thought Horus always looked like he had on too much eyeliner, which was terrible but cool at the same time because it meant she wasn't still miffed. Too bad my talent for restoring group harmony doesn't extend to real music. If I weren't completely tone-deaf, I could be the next Adele.

The seaweed harvesting task was slimy, but kind of satisfying in the way digging the guts out of a pumpkin is satisfying. When my turn came, I was happy my boline had a little leather loop tied around the handle so that I could cinch it around my wrist to keep me from dropping it. The water was super murky from all of us swimming around and hacking at seaweed, so I didn't even try to open my eyes while I was submerged. I just felt for a stalk that seemed as if it were thick enough and the right length and sawed away. Once Grace examined our harvests and deemed that we'd collected plenty, we toweled off, redressed, and sailed back to the pier.

"Could you hear them out there too?" Miranda asked as we tied up the sailboats.

"Hear what?" I asked, stepping onto the pier.

"The voices who were singing," she replied. Her face was red and blotchy as if she'd been crying while we were gone. The other girls and I looked at one another, puzzled.

Then, Elliott said, "I wouldn't know for sure without hearing them for myself, but they might have been Merfolk." He directed his next question to Grace, "I've never heard any here though. Do they live on this side of the pond?"

"Oh, they certainly do," Grace replied. "We just don't notice them because Americans are often in too much of a hurry to take account of anything that isn't blatantly obvious. Miranda, can you recall any of the songs?"

"Not really," Miranda replied. "I remember the melody, but the words were in language I'd never heard before, or at least I didn't recognize. Here, I can hum a bit for you." Miranda proceeded to hum a melody that was about the same tempo and meter as "Greensleeves," but in a more haunting minor key.

"Oh!" Grace exclaimed, clearly recognizing the tune. "Yes, I've heard that one. I believe who you heard, Miranda, were indeed Merfolk. My question, though, is why they would wait to communicate with you alone, after we'd gone and when..."

Tayen interrupted Grace, still a bit salty from before, "...when you can't even swim."

"Enough!" Grace countered, shooting Tayen a warning look. "Clearly because your hands have been idle for a few moments, your minds have drifted." Grace dug around in her shoulder bag again and pulled out a sage-colored velvet drawstring pouch. When she opened it, I could see it was filled with seagull feathers. She carefully counted out nine feathers at a time and handed them to each of us. Reaching back into the bag, she pulled out several large spools of ribbon in different colors, along with a bigger bundle of hemp rope. "What we are going to perform now is a little knot magic. Making a witches' ladder from natural elements, which we can use to generate, summon, or calm winds for sailing."

Grace fished her boline out of the same bag and rolled out an arm's length of hemp rope three times, then cut it into equal pieces. She did the same with one piece of each of the colored ribbons, then placed them side by side, across the planking of the pier. "Since this is a sea spell, we want to be sure to use something from the sea itself." Grace gestured to the mesh bags hanging off the side of each sailboat, filled with seaweed. "Pull out three goodly strands for each of you, and then spread them out, like this." She straightened and flattened three long tendrils of seaweed against the deck. Then, Grace rolled them together, so that they looked like strands of thick, wet yarn.

"Did each of you bring your wands?" Grace asked, producing hers from beneath her robe. We nodded in unison. "Good. If you recall your lesson with Cora yesterday, this will be slightly less dramatic. We are going to draw down a bit of the sunlight and concentrate it to dry out this seaweed. That will allow us to braid it more easily into our witches' ladders. Just watch me, and concentrate." Grace reached skyward and almost instantly, the tip of her wand lit up, like one of those soft white miniature string lights at Christmastime. Bringing her wand down, she guided the tip over the yard-long pieces of seaweed, which shriveled to green-black instantly.

"So that's how it's done," Grace said simply, picking up the strands along with the cord and ribbon to demonstrate as she spoke. "You'll start by taking all nine pieces and tying them so that there is a kind of looped handle at the top. Next, put a piece of seaweed to the back of each length of cord, and a length of ribbon to the front. Braid them together. At about every fifth plait or so, tie in a feather to the side. After that, tie a knot in the whole apparatus. Try to alternate sides. It's more aesthetically pleasing. Perhaps if you find a nice piece of sea glass or a particularly pretty shell as you continue to search for holey stones this afternoon, you can add those in too. Anything to increase the natural connection between you, the ladder, and the sea. Save tying the end until you've found just the right holey stone because it's the most important piece." As quickly as she'd explained this, Grace finished braiding her ladder. She reached out to Miranda to ask whether she could borrow her holey stone. Once it was attached, Grace tied nine knots in the braided cord and began to swing it in a circle over her head.

"What you want to do," Grace said, "is to concentrate on calling the wind up by becoming one with the sensations of Nature herself." Grace continued to twirl the ladder over her head as she closed her eyes. Softly, a light breeze began to blow. "Elliott, since you and Hana are the handiest with the boats, could the two of you please take one back out and follow the winds as I turn them, please?"

Hearing Grace's instructions, Elliott and Hana assumed their positions in the fore and aft of the sloop. No sooner than they had done so, Grace held up her other hand. Motioning as if she were pushing something forward, Grace kept swirling the ladder in a circle above her like a lasso. Rotating her body slowly counterclockwise, Grace turned toward the ocean with her palm facing out. As the breeze picked up, the surface of the water began to ripple. The sailboat glided in a graceful arc around the pier.

"You can also stop it," Grace announced, flaring her fingers like a conductor making an orchestra hold a fermata note, and then closing them. The sailboat came to a full stop, with the water surrounding it unnaturally still.

"Now, it's your turn. Miranda?" Grace asked, catching the end of the witch's ladder with the holey stone and handing it over. "Would you like to try?"

Being left-handed, Miranda took the ladder in her opposite hand and directed the sailboat with her right. Otherwise, she repeated Grace's motions perfectly. "Well done!" Grace acknowledged, patting Miranda on the back. Calling Elliott and Hana to bring the sailboat in once more, Grace dismissed us to have lunch, saying that we would return that afternoon to finish foraging stones and braiding our ladders.

"I'll give you twenty pounds if you'll do mine up for me and not tell anyone," Elliott whispered, as we walked back to the castle. "I'm all thumbs with that sort of thing."

"Why me?"

"Because you won't tell anyone." He flashed a sly grin. "It can be our secret."

"Boys are incapable of keeping secrets," Tayen countered, overhearing us as she passed.

"What's it to her?" Elliott sneered. "Why's she been so catty all day?"

As I watched Tayen from behind, I couldn't help but notice how she walked when she was alone and thought no one was looking. Not the hot girl strut, as I'd always thought of it, slinky and feline—even though I felt certain that she could affect one when she needed to for her modeling work. Instead, Tayen's natural gait was a sort of quick, small-stepped shuffle. Like her ankles were chained together, kicking little pea-gravel pebbles along with every step.

"She probably has her reasons," I shrugged. "Besides, you don't know her. None of us here know anything about anyone, which is part of the point. It's kind of beautiful. Having no basis for judgment other than what we see and what they choose to share with us. Given what you've told me, I'd think you of all people would appreciate that."

"Yeah," Elliott sighed, flipping open his green robe and stuffing his hands in his pockets. "I guess you're right. It is a relief in a lot of ways." He stared up at the castle, lost in thought.

"Hey," I elbowed him, "I'd be happy to help you braid your ladder. Just keep the money. Friends don't need that sort of thing."

"Friends," Elliott huffed and picked up his pace. "No, I guess they don't."

Chapter Eleven

That afternoon, when we'd finished combing the beach for shells and sea glass, I helped Elliott braid his witch's ladder. Growing up in a landlocked state, I'd not considered the possibility that the tide going out (ebbing, as he corrected me) would reveal better possibilities, but he thought of it right away. Leading the group of us down to a little cove that he'd spotted that morning when we were out in our sailboats, we found a whole little treasure trove of holey stones. Most of them were sort of gray with black or white speckles.

Sitting down in the sand, I wove the pieces of Elliott's ladder together far enough to tie in two feathers and a shell, then handed it back to him. Although he watched me closely, Elliott still couldn't seem to get the hang of it, even after I put my hands over his and guided him to finish the rest. It was as bad as with his tie, only this time he didn't seem so frustrated. As I got to the end and secured the holey stone piece, I could feel him staring at me, but he said nothing.

His silence continued through dinner. It was unusual enough that Alice commented about it. Some kind of quirky inside joke about a fox catching his tongue, that I supposed was the magickal world's version of a cat getting someone's tongue. Not wanting to appear stupid, I pretended to get the joke and chuckled, which in turn made Elliott almost jump away from our table with an excuse to flee to the bathroom. When he returned, he wouldn't even look at me, let alone speak. Otherwise, dinner was quite similar to the previous evening, only with a different pair sitting at the center table. Once she started, the story Grace told made me forget about Elliott's weirdness.

"My troubles began like many women who were accused of witchcraft back then," Grace said. She cleared her plate off to the kitchen with a flick of her wand and patted the corners of her mouth with a napkin. "The women of the town were jealous because I was independent, and their husbands took notice. They considered me desirable and witty, I suppose, because of my frank manner of speaking. My husband, James Senior, passed in 1701, leaving me and our three sons a farm of about two hundred acres. The boys were still young and had to be supervised to stay on task in the fields. My skirt was always getting caught up in things, so I took to wearing James's old pants." Grace motioned around the room to indicate the linen trousers that we'd all worn on the beach that day. "Which simply wasn't done, as they used to say. It was considered immodest because women in pants were thought to attract the wrong kind of attention from men." Grace took a sip of her after-dinner coffee and raised an eyebrow at Miranda over the rim. "A concern to which I am sure you can relate, given your father's conservative views on women's swimming attire."

Miranda closed her eyes and nodded slowly as Grace continued. "Nevertheless, more offensive than my clothing was my practice of herbal healing. I'd worked as a midwife for many years, even before James died. Most children were born at home in those days. Often there simply wasn't time for a doctor to get out to a village as small as Pungo, especially if there wasn't much money to be paid for their troubles. My mother had done the same. She taught me the art of growing and gathering plants and herbs for all sorts of purposes. What teas to mix for nausea, what poultices to use to put down coughs and fevers, and what herbs to compound for pain. Mother taught me all of it. After we came to the Virginia Colony, she added more from what we learned from the natives about the remedies they used. Our family was fortunate to always be well-off financially, so we never asked for payment."

"It seems like they should have been happy to have your assistance, especially if you were offering it for free." Miranda said, taking a bite of her grouper. It had pineapple salsa on it and smelled amazing, even from across the room. My barbecued salmon had been good, but I kind of wanted to try the pineapple. Alice must have thought so too, because a few moments later a little dish of it with two serving spoons floated over to our table.

"Never underestimate the ability of envy to overcome kindness or good sense," Grace replied. "Even when people of upper social classes attempt to be charitable, there are some who will always say they aren't doing enough. Who will look with eyes directed at scrutinizing the faults of their benefactors, simply because they are more privileged, pretty, and self-assured.

Those types of ungrateful people will twist and misuse religious beliefs to direct attention away from their cowardice and to act out their immoral desires. An ugly, lecherous woman is often the first to call a beautiful, chaste woman a whore, because it is she who desires to act out lusts that she cannot fulfill. And so the case was with me. I was tried for witchcraft by men trying to steal my late husband's land, yes, but it was their wives who accused me."

"I'm sure owning that black cat didn't help either," Cora smirked. She spirited pieces of pineapple upside-down cake around to each of our places. I hadn't been the only one enticed by the tropical aroma. "What was it that one woman accused you of? Jumping over her bed and whipping her, then transforming into a cat and slipping through the keyhole? I have to hand it to her, she had some imagination," Cora cackled.

Grace sighed. "That cat belonged to my boys, just as yours belonged to Noah. Hell's Bells! For all I know it could have been the same cat, or at least from the same litter. I've had black cats that lived fifteen years or more. It would have been easy for the little fellow to jump on a ship in Virginia and hop off again at Cape Hatteras. They're on the same trade route." The pair of witches stared wide-eyed at one another realizing the possible connection.

"I'm just happy you maintained the presence of mind to bring a case to court over it," Mary interjected. "At least the courts in Virginia and the Carolinas were willing to listen to some kind of reason, unlike those savages in Massachusetts."

"Aye," Candy agreed. "There was nothing that Tituba or any of us could have said that would have proven our innocence in Salem. To tell the truth—that we were witches but meant no harm—meant death. The only thing those zealots understood were lies. Tituba and I figured that out right away. We made up the most sensational nonsense we could think of. However, I was luckier than Tituba. Mrs. Hawkes was willing to vouch for me because she'd been accused too, and to bribe the Court to have the charges dropped for us both."

"Yes," Grace sighed. "Bribery seems to be a universal language that guides the enforcement of law in many cases. Still, some are just..." Grace wrinkled her nose. "Perverted. I was accused and released twice with just a small fine. Even countersued for defamation once but lost. Yet, they kept coming. That last row with Elizabeth Hill in 1706 was the worst. I should have known when I saw that other old rabble-rouser Elizabeth Barnes was the forewoman of the jury that it was going to be the worst one."

"I still think the whole thing was about Barnes's self-hatred," Alice said, chewing a bite of pineapple cake thoughtfully. "I mean, the woman had a dream about you leaping over her bed. She jumped at the chance to run her hands all over your naked body, allegedly searching for a witches' tit. To me, that's just anger from repressed sexual desire. Barnes wanted you, and she wanted to be you. When she couldn't have either one, she tried to destroy you."

"They hate us 'cause they ain't us," Tayen added, a little too loudly. "I get that one all the time. Churchy women are the worst about it. All super sexually repressed."

Miranda glanced back and forth from Alice to Tayen to Grace. "Those women were Christians?" she asked in disbelief.

"They claimed to be, yes," Grace said, taking another sip of coffee. "But there were few Christian virtues to be found among them, I can assure you. The last time, when I was tried, it was because Hill had accused me of being a witch and making her miscarry. She'd had several miscarriages at that point, mostly because she wasn't eating enough of the proper foods to nourish her pregnancies. Of course, I couldn't say I was a witch—that would have meant certain death—so I told them I was a healer. They didn't believe me and formed a jury who searched my house for poppets. Not finding any, Barnes led another jury of a dozen women old enough to know better as they stripped off my clothes and examined me for a possible Devil's Mark, such as an odd mole or maybe third nipple, that they claimed could be used to suckle a demon. Not finding anything definitive enough, the judge, sheriff, and church elders decided a trial by water might offer better proof, so they bound me for dunking."

Grace leaned over in her chair to demonstrate the pose. "They tied both thumbs to the opposite big toes, stripped me again, tied a thirteen-pound Bible around my neck, stuffed me in a sack, and threw me into the Lynnhaven River. They reasoned that if I sank, I was an innocent Christian woman, and they would allow me a proper burial. However, if I floated, which I did, then I was a witch and should be jailed as a danger to the colony."

"So there was no possibility for justice to be done by you either way," Imani shook her head. "That's crazy. I mean, you were a rich white woman! Didn't that come with privileges?"

"You're right, Imani," Grace said. "Things have always been worse for women of color who stand accused of anything. I'm sure we'll hear more about that on Thursday." Grace exchanged glances with Candy across the room. "However, just being a woman of any kind at any time, especially one who is willing to stand up for herself, made many men feel threatened. Their wives too. And so they had to humiliate her, to make her a pariah, on whatever dubious grounds they could devise."

"But we're not all like that!" Elliott protested, breaking his silence at last. "There are some men who would stand up and fight for a woman whom they knew was falsely accused. I would never..."

Mary interrupted him. "Yes, Elliott, I am sure that you, as a well-educated young man of feeling in the twenty-first century, would not engage in or allow such behavior. Yet, you must realize that today, even hundreds of years later, many men choose to remain in the Dark Ages. Because they are insecure, strong intelligent women scare them. They use money and social standing to try to disempower them. Which makes it all the more important that young men such as yourself feel welcome to work with us. We need you."

Here Mary paused. "I don't think that can ever be said enough. Women have to speak loudly to assert our worth because we want to be equals to men. For that to happen, we need good men to realize that and agree to support us. That is part of the reason I invited you here, Elliott. Not just because you needed a school to learn your Craft, but because I feel that it is important for the girls—and all of us—to learn from you too. I hope you understand that."

Until that moment, I hadn't realized Mary was paying close enough attention to Elliott to observe how quiet he'd been all evening. I should have known that almost nothing escaped the sharp eyes of Mary Rookes.

Chapter Twelve

That night in my room, I read through Alice Grey's grimoire cover to cover. I know it sounds basic, with all the other possibilities of more impressive magick I could try, but I was still looking for something to curl my hair in the absence of a curling iron or electricity. In my defense, I did note the page numbers and descriptions of each spell. It was a productive activity because indexing the spells would save time later on.

Although Alice's grimoire was filled with hundreds of spells, on everything from levitation to finding lost sheep, there wasn't a single thing to fix flat hair. One of the closest spells that I could find was for growing more hair. I was scared to try because I didn't want to mess up and give myself a beard. Others involved different variations of a glamor spell that would make people think my hair was beautiful and perfect, even though it stayed the same. However, the most convincingly written one of those had to be performed under the light of the full moon.

Checking out the window, I could see the moon was some type of crescent, but I couldn't tell whether it was waxing or waning. I've always been bad at remembering things that involve left versus right correlations. When I was about seven, my dad used to kid me about being so slow to learn which hand was which. He almost resorted to writing an *L* and an *R* on the backs of my hands with a waterproof marker. Fortunately, or unfortunately, around that time I fell off a trampoline in the back yard and sprained my left wrist. He used the opportunity to write *LEFT* in all caps on the brace instead. Looking at it for eight weeks turned out to be enough. After that, I always associated my left side as being my sprained side. I guess everything in life happens for a reason.

Regardless, I was just about to head back to the bookshelf and look for something that had a chart of moon phases, so I could make an approximation of how long I'd have until I could try a glamor spell to make my hair fluffier, when I noticed someone walking out toward the pier. They were wearing the green robes we'd all had on that day during our ecology lesson. Since they had their hood up, I couldn't tell who it was. Picking up my holey stone from the lesson that day and opening the window for a closer view, I looked through it. Although I still couldn't see their face, I could see the wind blowing a few loose strands of long reddish curly hair. Which meant that it had to be one of two people: Grace or Miranda.

As I sat by the open window hoping they would turn around so I could see for sure, I heard it. The soft strains of that same song Miranda hummed for us that afternoon. I didn't hesitate any longer. I might not always remember my moon phases, but my grasp of Homer's *Odyssey* was solid. Although I knew that sirens and mermaids were completely different supernatural creatures, I didn't like what I saw. Super rule-following, non-swimming Miranda walking out to the pier late at night following a Merfolk song.

Throwing on my green robe, I hurried down the back stairs and out past the gardenia circle toward the path leading to the pier. Along the way, I made sure to run in the grass. Partly so that Miranda didn't hear me, and also partly so that I could continue listening to the song of the Merfolk. It seemed to get louder as I approached. Stopping at the last boundary of seagrass, I crouched down and peered over a dune as I watched Miranda walk out to the end of the pier. Holding my breath, I wished that she would stop. I'd never had to save a drowning person before. Miranda was a good three or four inches taller than me. I wasn't sure if I could do it.

However, I shouldn't have been so worried. At the end of the pier, Miranda simply sat down with her feet dangling over the edge. The soft breeze pushed back her hood, and the wind tousled her perfect curls as she remained motionless, entranced by the mermaids' song. One by one, the Merfolk began to break the surface of the water. Their skin sparkled with a rainbow of iridescence that glowed across their tanned bellies and voluptuous breasts. Leaping out of the sea, the countless mermaids arrayed themselves on the tiers of rocks at the end of the point, just past where we'd gathered seaweed earlier that day. Stroking their long hair, which changed colors in the moonlight through a shimmering spectrum of silver, aquamarine, turquoise, and amethyst, they posed and preened. Their harmonies pulled achingly tighter and stronger.

Gradually, the dune I was leaning against began to shake. I became aware of a slow, rhythmic boom like a hundred bass drums being struck in unison. Growing louder and closer, dozens of mermen crashed to the surface. All at once the singing and drumming stopped. Fierce-faced and impossibly muscular, they encircled the mermaids, a bronzed wall of Greek warrior statues. Waves crested white against the shoreline as the mermen raised their conch shells like a line of trumpets and blew. The sound reverberated back off the walls of the castle and died into a ripple of echoes in the distance. Through all of it, Miranda remained motionless, transfixed by the mermaids. She hardly noticed the mermen's arrival at all.

"Look at the way Miranda watches the mermaids," a voice whispered behind me. Fortunately, I recognized her, or I would have been startled and revealed myself.

"I thought I noticed it today when I grabbed her hand. Now I'm pretty sure," Tayen said.

"Do you think she knows?" I asked.

"Maybe, but probably not," Tayen replied, nonchalantly. "Girl doesn't even know how to swim because her preacher pop wouldn't allow her to own a swimsuit. I'm guessing any ideas she has about sexuality are kind of theoretical at present. I heard her parents think she's on some kind of spiritual retreat out here, which isn't quite a lie."

Tayen spread out her robe against what was left of the dune and reclined onto it. "She'll figure it out eventually. Who she is, I mean. Just not with me, poor thing. I hate everybody equally. Men, women, they all want you to be something you can't be sooner or later. Some idealized version of whoever they've decided you're supposed to be, which usually has about zero correlation with who you truly are."

"Elliott will be sad to hear that," I said, laying my robe next to hers and rolling over onto my back.

Tayen snorted. "Wow, you are so blind."

"For your information, I have a boyfriend," I replied defensively.

"Yeah?" Tayen challenged. "Spill. What's he like? I'll tell you whether you should break up with him or not and make a play for Elliott."

"That's a little presumptuous," I countered. "Thinking you can assess someone's entire relationship from one conversation."

"People have been evaluating me, what I look like, and who I should be with literally before I could walk," Tayen said. I must have looked skeptical because she added. "For real! Bly, my stupid mom, rented me out as a prop baby for television. You know how they're only allowed to use a baby for a certain number of hours? Well, I was the baby body double for a lot of the celebrity kids' babies listed in the screen credits. Bly got triple-paid for it. My money, her money for being a secondary baby wrangler on set, and whatever extra bit part that she could finagle her way into. That was how she supported herself for a while after Nyles kicked her out of the house. She refused to have me paternity tested for like, the first year after I was born. Eventually, she caved. Too bad for Nyles, I was his. Knowing what I know now, I thought she should have walked out. However, they had a prenup, so Bly had to go back to Nyles or continue her exciting career as a second-shift baby wrangler."

"Wow. Sounds like your folks were an even more fantastic match than mine," I replied. "Remind me to tell you sometime about how Darla wrecked her so-called country music career by being such a mean drunk, among other brilliant things."

"I thought that was the whole point of country music? To be a big enough drunk redneck that you pull all the other wannabes into your orbit like some kind of sad-ass dying star," Tayen scoffed.

"Even Nashville has its limits... for some people. If they stop selling tickets," I quipped.

"Hey, girls! I didn't know you were out here too," Miranda said, still in half of a dreamy trance from the Merfolk's song. "Did you see the mermaids? Weren't they wonderful?"

Tayen wiggled her shoulders and tossed her hair over her shoulder, winking at me. "They were real, and they were spectacular."

"Really?" I asked. "The Teri Hatcher episode of *Seinfeld*?"

"Nyles has the reruns on a non-stop Netflix loop in the waiting room at his home office," Tayen said.

"Your dad has a waiting room in his office at home?" I crossed my arms at her.

"Well, ever since we moved to Austin, the house compound and the office compound have sort of grown together. It makes sense if you think about it." How Tayen could say such things with a straight face freaked me out. It's always weird when you think a really rich person is relatable for about half a second. Then they burst the illusion bubble with something like that. Miranda wasn't fazed though.

"Oh, I get it," Miranda seconded. "We live right off the main church campus. Members of the congregation or even random people off the street used to just wander in whenever. When Dad built the new pastor's residence, he added a reception area in the foyer. It's staffed until nine in the evening. After that, the secretary locks up and puts the camera on."

Compound? Foyer? Receptionist? I thought. This was getting out of hand. "Doesn't anybody here live in a regular house?"

"Hana told me her parents lived in a brownstone in Cambridge," Tayen shrugged, catching my drift. "Across the street from Wellesley. Her mom's a professor there and her dad's at MIT. Academics usually aren't super wealthy, unless they're big-time football coaches or something like Imani's dad. Dunno what kind of house they have, but Coach Griffin's probably loaded. Collegiate athletics is like a different world. Nyles hires loads of regular broke professors for consulting work. They always jump at the chance to make some extra dough."

"Great," I sighed, letting Tayen's explanation sink in. For the first time, it registered for me that I was the only not-rich girl there. I hadn't thought about it before. When I did, the potential consequences of it made me feel kind of sick. Amazing coincidences align all the time for rich kids to have fantastical things happen. For them, it seemed like the stars hovered, waiting for their chance to fall in line. However, for someone from a background like mine, with a dad who lost his job and had to sell our home, great opportunities just didn't happen every day, if ever. There would be a lot of explaining to do if anyone noticed my magickal good fortune.

When I got back to the castle, I stopped to knock on Elliott's door. He answered it wearing just his pajama pants and no shirt. His abs were ridiculous. I almost knew without asking what kind of answer he'd give, but I asked anyway. "Where does your dad Albert live?"

Ruffling his hair, Elliott scowled. He looked like an angry swimsuit model. "That's a helluva thing to roust a fellow out of bed to ask. Manhattan most of the time, but he still owns the country house in Ireland too. The one he inherited before he founded Albion Oil."

"Did it have a name?" I asked sarcastically.

"Desmond Manor. It's near Shanagolden. Why?"

"Never mind," I said and tried to shut the door. Elliott stopped it with his foot.

"Hey now, what's all this about?" he asked. "A chap finally gets to sleep after two days, and then here you come pounding on the door to ask some nonsense like that?"

"Forget it," I replied over my shoulder, crossing the hallway to open my door. "I just thought we could be friends."

Elliott narrowed his eyes and crossed his arms over his too-perfect chest. "Fine. I never wanted to be your *friend*." He sneered the last word and slammed the door.

Chapter Thirteen

The next morning, I awoke to the soft pattering of rain. It hadn't rained without someone calling the clouds since I'd arrived, so it was the first morning I hadn't woken automatically with the sunrise streaming in through the windows. I didn't know what time it was, but I sensed it was much later than usual. I dressed quickly and took my blue robe from the closet because it was Wednesday. As I opened the door of my room, a note fell out.

Bring your globe and wand to the Water tower, it read in heavy, down-slanted script.

I scanned my rooms, seeing nothing that even remotely resembled a globe. Turning the drawers out in my study didn't reveal anything promising either. Then, sitting on one of the bookshelves, I noticed a large, square wooden box. Opening the lid, I found a midnight blue velvet bag with something roughly the size and weight of a bowling ball inside. When I untied the cords, I realized that I'd misread the note. It wasn't a globe with countries printed on it that I'd been looking for; it was a crystal one. Cursing myself for not understanding the message sooner—it was Wednesday, after all, our first prognostication lesson—I re-tied the bag, grabbed my wand from the box on my desktop where I'd put it the night before, and left.

"I'm delighted that you've finally decided to join us, Willow," Katerina announced, pronouncing my name with a hard *V* rather than a *W* in her chilly German accent, as I attempted without success to open the door of the tower without making it creak. Sheepishly, I sat down in one of the chairs encircling her. I placed the blue velvet bag carefully on the small table in front of me, bracing it with my arms so that it didn't roll off. Everyone else already had their globes out and resting on little wooden pedestals. Imani nudged me and pointed to the row of cabinets lining the opposite wall. As Katerina and every other person in the room watched me expectantly, I rose, retrieved a pedestal, and slid my globe out to rest on top of it. I wanted to apologize for being late because it was clear that I had disturbed everyone, but the silence was so complete in the room that I couldn't speak.

"As I was saying," Katerina resumed, addressing Hana, who sat across the table from her, in front of a crystal orb that looked identical to mine. "Amethyst or smoky quartz may also be used, even ordinary glass if it is flawless. However, those are liable to give viewpoints that are attuned to specific thoughts. Clear quartz is the most openly receptive and least biased material. Thus, it is the best on which to learn prognostication. Regardless, the technique is the same. You must concentrate your gaze intensely on the elliptical point in the center of the sphere and then relax your eyes. Place your hands on the globe and think of the question that you would like to have answered. Eventually, an image or a phrase will come to you. Hana, do you have your question in mind?"

"Yes," Hana whispered. I'd never noticed her so quiet and still before.

"Then focus your gaze and relax," Katerina said calmly. "Whenever you are ready, tell us what you see."

Hana's normally perky expression turned serious. She squinted hard at the globe. Her shiny lavender hair fell around her face like a curtain as, slowly, the pupils of her dark brown eyes began to dilate. She placed her hands delicately on the surface of the sphere and exhaled a long breath as all tension relaxed in her shoulders.

"I see a young man," Hana said softly. "He's short. Sandy-haired. It flips up at the ends of his bangs. Kind of preppy. I don't think he likes it." She blew at her nonexistent bangs.

Like Stephen's, I remembered reflexively. My boyfriend had hair like that. I used to kid him about it. Having the generic haircut of preppy Southern boys everywhere. He hated it and was always blowing his bangs out of his eyes.

"He's cute but has kind of a dad bod. I think he drinks a lot of beer." Hana continued. "And he's wearing a t-shirt with some kind of writing on it. Can't tell what it says, but it's dark blue and the letters are gold colored. His skin is red. He looks sunburned."

That's funny; Stephen could just look at the sun and turn into a lobster. I thought but said nothing. *And he's wearing Vanderbilt colors. Like where Stephen's going to college.*

"Do you recognize this young man at all?" Katerina asked.

Hana shook her head, no. She looked a little upset.

"That is all right," Katerina reassured her. "Focus your gaze a little closer, if possible. See if you can get something that will be easier to identify."

Hana nodded to indicate that she understood. "He's with a bunch of other guys. They're getting in like..." She narrowed her eyes again. "Some kind of Jeep. But it's an old one. The kind with those wood-paneled sides."

"Wagoneer," I said, without meaning to. Stephen's vehicle. Imani shushed me.

"Quiet please," Katerina said absently, her attention zeroed in on Hana. "Any other details? Describe everything you can see."

"It's like I'm looking over his shoulder now. Out the front window. There's a little hula girl on the dashboard. He's driving. I can see his hands on the wheel. He's wearing a watch with Snoopy in a spacesuit on it."

I couldn't hold it in any longer. "That's Stephen!" I exclaimed.

Her concentration broken; Hana whipped around to look at me as Katerina slapped her hands down on the table.

"Miss Todd!" I thought I told you to remain silent!"

Hana ignored her. "Who's Stephen?" Her eyes were wide with anticipation.

"My boyfriend," I said.

"But that can't..." Hana replied, confused.

"Yes, it most certainly can," Katerina interrupted, visibly upset the session had been irretrievably broken. "Crystal gazing shows you only what may be in the future, not what is currently true. Hana, could you please tell us what question you asked of the crystal?"

"I..." Hana glanced furtively back and forth between Katerina and me. "I asked it to show me my future boyfriend. There was this guy I met last week during summer school at Harvard before I came here. We hit it off. I thought *he* would be the guy I'd see. At least, I was hoping so. He'd already asked me out before I came here, but we hadn't gone yet. You told me to think of a positive question to ask, so that was the first one I thought of. I don't know why I saw Willow's..." Hana looked at me, slightly panicked.

"...boyfriend. I swear I've never met him before in my life. Please don't be mad at me!"

"I'm... I'm not," I sputtered.

"Well, that answers one of last night's questions," Tayen remarked, sliding down in her chair. She glanced over at Elliott and raised an eyebrow.

"Girls!" Katerina stood up from the table. "Please, calm yourselves. This is an excellent opportunity for interpretation. As I mentioned before Willow arrived, prognostication shows us only what may be most likely to happen, given the current trajectory of all circumstances. Relationships, especially among young people, are very mercurial. It is highly possible that, as new acquaintances materialize, the type of affection that one person has for another will change into something different, even if they care for one another deeply. Since Willow and Hana will probably continue their friendship after they leave Rookes College, it is also possible that Willow and..."

Katerina motioned to me, trying to recall Stephen's name, so I said it again. "Stephen, thank you. Stephen's relationship will change, and she could at some point introduce him to Hana. Love is perhaps the most random of emotions. The slightest change in circumstances can alter it at any time. Thus, what Hana saw may or may not come true. However, it is likely that if she and Stephen were to meet, then there would be an attraction. Whether it would evolve into a relationship is impossible to determine from just one vision."

I could feel everyone looking at me, but I didn't know what to say. Fortunately, Katerina called a recess for lunch. We ate differently than usual at our tables in the Water tower. Afterward, Katerina called us back to order and asked Hana to sit again at the table in the front of the room. Opening the cabinets beside the one from which I'd retrieved my pedestal, she pulled out a stack of small brass bowls and sticks, which she distributed to each of us. Then, she took out a large abalone shell that she sat on the table and a bundle of incense. She lit it by just snapping her fingers.

"Lavender and rosemary," Katerina explained. She blew softly on the bundle, making the vibrant flame soften to a smoldering gray, as she proceeded to walk around the room, enveloping us in swirls of smoke. "Wonderful combination for awakening second sight. We will explore many types of incense and incantations vis year, as we determine which works best for each of you."

Katerina set the incense bundle down in the shell and picked up one of the bowls. "The vibrations produced by sound and music are also very powerful aids to prognostication, as they can help induce a comfortable, trance-like state. These are known as singing bowls, and this is called a *puja*." Katerina held up one of the sticks and began rubbing it around the outer edges of the bowl. Gradually, the bowl began to hum, a warm metallic sound, like a trumpeter playing pedal tones. She set the bowl back down on the table. The ringing stopped. "What I would like for each of you to do is use your bowl to raise a song in unison, as I ask Hana to focus on another question. The power of our harmony will strengthen the clarity of what she sees on the globe. Everyone ready?"

Katerina glanced back to Hana, who already had her hands on the crystal sphere. Her eyes locked on its invisible center. "*Puja* in your dominant hand, bowl in the opposite. Begin whenever you are ready."

Picking up the *puja*, I began to run it carefully around the bowl. Slowly, as I felt the vibrations rising from its surface, a tone began to sound. As the others joined in, the room began to resonate in unison with a vibrant, metallic hum.

"Hana," Katerina said. "I would like for you to focus on the question of your future here at Rookes College. When a vision comes to you, tell us what you see."

Just as before, Hana squinted intently at the crystal sphere, then relaxed. "I see the castle in a storm," she said dreamily. "The wind is very strong. It has blown down the trees in the orchard." She blinked very deliberately and gazed deep into the crystal again. "I'm looking at the shore now. Not sure which side of the island I am on. I can't see the pier. But the water... oh!" Hana caught her breath. "There is something wrong with the water. It's black." She wrinkled her nose. "And the smell! Like something rotten that's burning. Ugh!"

"Can you see the source of the fire? Look around you," Katerina urged.

Hana shook her head and peered closer into the sphere. "Not really. The edge of the horizon is bright yellow orange. Kind of glowing... but I can't tell whether I'm just facing west into the sunset or..." She jumped back, jerking her hands away as the crystal ball flashed white-hot. Hana sat staring in disbelief at her hands. Katerina rushed forward and grabbed her wrists. "Did you burn yourself? Let me see."

Tears began to rise in Hana's eyes as Katerina examined her hands. "Elliott! Run down to the Earth tower and fetch Candy. Tell her to bring her bag and the special aloe salve that she makes. If she can get Hana bandaged with it quickly, perhaps we can keep the blisters down." Katerina hugged Hana, who was shaking because she was crying so hard.

"What was that?" I asked Imani.

"It looked like there was an explosion," Imani replied.

"The platform," Miranda added. "The one that I saw yesterday through my stone. Didn't Elliott say it was an oil rig? Maybe that's what the Merfolk have been so upset about. Last night, when..."

We never heard what Miranda thought the Merfolk were worried about. At that moment, Candy burst into the room with Mary and Alice right behind her. Taking Hana's hands in her own, Candy examined them. Quickly, she pulled out a small pot of salve and a roll of gauze from the basket she carried.

"How could you be so irresponsible!" Mary yelled at Katerina.

"How was I supposed to know that was the vision she would see!" Katerina snapped back. "All I asked was that she try to see her future at Rookes. I made no insinuation that..."

"There is no need to make an insinuation," Mary snarled. "When it is so clear this is the future for all of us here. It is no longer a question of if, but a question of when. Of all people, Katerina, you should be aware of that! It was you who first told me about the vision you had of the hurricane. You've always been able to predict them accurately, for over three hundred years!"

"Mary, please..." Candy said, motioning to the rest of us. "Not in front of the students. We agreed not to argue or discuss anything about it until we heard from the Grand Council."

"It's too late for that now," Alice jabbed her finger into the air toward Mary. "I told you that it would come out anyway, no matter how much we tried to cover it up. They aren't children, and I'm sure they've already been getting hints of it anyway. They deserve to know the truth, or what credibility will we have as their Mentors when they learn it?"

"Alice is right," Candy seconded, still holding Hana's bandaged hands. "Grace and Cora told me it came up in their lessons already as well. It just wasn't this obvious. I know you wanted to protect them, Mary, to not allow it to affect the development of their magick, but look around you.

There are only twelve of us left in this entire college. If they know that they could be the last class, it might make everything that we do here more meaningful."

Mary seethed as she met the eyes of everyone in the room, one at a time. "Tonight," she said at last, quietly. "But let them see something else this afternoon if they can, first. Something hopeful. Otherwise, the world outside can wait just a few hours longer. Whatever you think is best, Katerina. My apologies."

Saying not another word, Mary left the tower, with Alice close behind her.

Chapter Fourteen

I've never been able to stand an awkward silence in a room. You know that person who always has to make some random comment about the weather on an elevator? Not a long, protracted conversation, just something to break the tension? That's me. Chronic people pleaser.

"Katerina," I ventured after I'd been quiet as long as I could. "Why don't we all try that first question Hana asked? After all," I winked at Hana, willing her to understand that I was joking. "I've gotta see if she's going to steal my boyfriend, right?" Hana smiled at me with her eyes, but I could tell that her hands were still painful. Candy held them securely through the bandages, palm to palm.

Relieved that someone had volunteered anything else to talk about, Katerina quickly motioned me up to the table at the front of the room. I set my crystal ball on the pedestal and tried to focus as I had seen Hana do before, but no vision came. Try as I might, all I saw in the depths of the orb were reflections of glass. Katerina asked if I'd ever had any trouble with my vision. I told her that when I was a child, I had a lazy eye. She patted me on the shoulder and told me that might be the problem. Apparently, witches with lazy eyes are more adept at seeing through dreams or other self-generated visions. Their eyesight is not suited to scrying. "Or..." Katerina finished. "For some people, there truly is no one."

Hana and Miranda gasped like this was the worst tragedy in the world, but Tayen was unfazed. I totally understood where she was coming from. Watching my parents circle each other like wary animals for the last few months before they separated had given me the early impression that sometimes being really alone is better than feeling alone with someone else.

"So, it's like one of those Magic Eye things then?" Tayen asked. "Let me have a try. I used to be pretty good at those." However, when Tayen took her crystal ball to the table and attempted to see someone in it, all she got was a bright, white light. Not the searing blaze that Hana's had been, but just a steady, pulsating orb within an orb.

"What's wrong with it?" Tayen scowled. "Is mine, like, defective or something?"

"No, I don't believe so," Katerina replied, peering over her shoulder. "I think what you are seeing is just the pure spirit form of the being who is meant for you. It is possible that the entity who is your destiny, Tayen, is not someone from this world."

"That explains a lot," Tayen said, removing her hands from the sphere and motioning for Miranda to come up to the table.

Miranda's vision came clearly and effortlessly, like all her magic. "I see the Merfolk," she said. "All gathered out by the point as they were last night."

"Do any of them stand out to you in particular, my dear?" Katerina asked.

Miranda's eyes grew wide and soft, then her face clouded. "No, not really."

"Liar," Tayen whispered into my ear. "Hundred bucks says she knows exactly who."

"Miss Kennerly, do you have thoughts that you would like to share?" Katerina asked, slightly perturbed.

Tayen leaned back in her chair. "I thought the rule was that we weren't using last names until that person gave permission?" Tayen looked slightly stunned.

"Perhaps you should consider that occasionally there are exceptions," Imani interceded. "May I try, Katerina?" Relieved not to have to explain her vision further, Miranda gladly exchanged places with Imani.

When Imani placed her sphere on the pedestal, the vision was so plain and perfect that all of us could see it from across the room. A tall, gorgeous young Black man appeared, with shoulder-length locks. He wore baggy jeans and a thin t-shirt that showed off his ripped pecs. His caramel-colored eyes twinkled, and he laughed at an unheard joke told wherever he was in the world. Tapping his baton on the podium, he counted off a musical downbeat. He smiled and swayed as he directed an unseen ensemble, feeling music that we could not hear playing. Watching him, Imani glowed with a radiance of sheer bliss.

"Where... who is he?" Imani whispered, not wanting to disturb her vision of this mysterious conductor.

Katerina shook her head. "If you haven't met him yet, then there's no way to know. Once you've seen him, however, there should be no mistake. That's one of the chief advantages that prognostication offers. Even if the vision seems uncertain at the time you receive it, when you meet the person who is the subject of it, you will know. That can be a great comfort in times of distress. It certainly was to me when I first saw my husband."

"You met your husband after you'd seen him in a vision?" Imani asked, incredulous.

"Yes," Katerina said. "Given the situation, I think it best to break with custom and tell our story now. I feel certain Mary will have other things to share with you tonight at dinner. Hana?" Katerina called to her. "How are your hands?"

"Better," Hana offered. "Still a little sore."

"That is to be expected. I just wanted to check. My apologies... I didn't know that..."

"It's okay," Hana reassured her. "Tell us about your husband."

Katerina nodded and began her story.

"It was the winter of 1738. I was nineteen. I'd married Walter not long before we set sail. He wasn't a bad man. It's just that, well... being a young second wife was difficult when the first died having their child. All the man's love and hopes are still tied up in that initial life. The one that they chose was the first woman they would have preferred to live it with. Walter had never recovered from Selena's death, but he needed a wife to go with him for the new life he'd planned. Someone young and stout, which was why I suppose he chose me." Katerina straightened to her full height, which I could tell must have been over six feet.

"I wasn't considered a beauty. I towered over him, which intimidated the boys I grew up with. I think, in some ways, that reassured Walter. His Serena was just a pretty slip of a girl, blonde and delicate. He loved her beyond death, and he kept her portrait at his bedside always. As for me, well... I was like marrying a mountain. Walter did not worry for me. Or love me, as he did Serena. In the end, it was just as well." Katerina glanced down and then back to Imani and Hana before continuing.

"Our ship, the *Princess Augusta*, was the last out for the season bound for America. Most of the passengers were from the same part of Germany as we were, a region called the Palatine. Walter booked a separate cabin for me. He said out of deference for not wanting to make me pregnant while we were on the trip over. Truly, it was that he wasn't ready to share a bed with anyone, not even a decade after Serena's death. The sight of me naked beside him was a torment, I could tell. He compared every part of me negatively to her. My red hair to her gold, my big hands and feet to her delicate ones. He wasn't unkind about it, but I could tell that he perceived the differences. Although I don't know how it could have ended otherwise, I think it was best that he died as he did. The fever took him quickly, in a matter of days. At least they didn't have to be apart anymore." Katerina ran her hands through her hair as if massaging out the memory.

"Nevertheless, on the evening that Walter passed, I was standing on the deck and gazing out into the water, trying to compose in my mind the letters that I would write back to our families in Germany. I wondered whether my father would panic and demand that I come back home. They thought that a young lady surely could not survive in the colonies alone. Then, out there on the waves, I saw a vision of him. My Kobe, plain as the moon in the midnight sky. He was standing at the counter of a shop, showing cases of silver flatware to customers. I couldn't tell what he was saying, only that he was handsome and self-assured. At first, I thought I was merely remembering some merchant. Perhaps one I'd seen in Amsterdam. There were many men from Africa there."

"1738," Imani mused. "Kobe must have been enslaved or recently freed. Where in America were you going?"

"Our original destination was Philadelphia," Katerina continued. "But several storms at sea had blown us off course. When we finally landed, it was at Block Island. At that time, Rhode Island housed one of the largest ports trading in enslaved people in the Americas. The rocky shoreline was not hospitable for farming. The locals were completely dependent on the shipping industry for their livelihood. That Christmas, when we made landfall, the villagers were desperate. They had turned to wrecking ships. Purposefully misleading them so they'd run aground and they could claim the cargo for their own as salvage."

Katerina's eyes took on a faraway glaze as she finished her tale. "I will always believe that Captain Andrew Brook, who took over when our original captain passed from the same fever that took Walter, was complicit in it. Captain Brook had some kind of agreement to share any wealth stolen from us with the villagers. Regardless, after our ship ran onto the rocks off the coast of Block Island, the locals immediately began pillaging everything they could grab. I took every piece of jewelry I carried with me and put it on. Then, I stuffed all the money Walter had brought in gold coins into every pocket and bag I could find. I strapped those to my body, around my chest, and under my skirts. The nor'easter that hit us was a massive storm. Snow and sleet were blinding from the moment I stepped outside the cabin. Then, the ship began to break apart. I took Walter's pistol and made my way out to the very end of the bowsprit. Then, I froze. I could swim, but I knew that if I jumped, the gold would weigh me down and I would drown. I felt trapped. I stood and screamed for any honest man to save me. And that if he did, I would marry him."

"That was how you met your husband?" Hana gasped. "Was he the one who answered?"

"Yes," Katerina replied. "Kobe dove into those freezing waves and swam out to rescue me. We survived. It was only after we'd made it to the shore that I was relieved enough from my panic to notice his face. And what do you know? Kobe was the man from my vision."

"That's wild!" Tayen interjected. "He just dove in, not knowing who you were?"

"His actions were no accident," Katerina replied. "Afterward, Kobe told me that he had visions about me too. Visions echoing the way his mother perished after she was accused of witchcraft and put off the slave ship that carried them to America. Kobe's mother, Sika, was a healer in Africa. A shaman's daughter. Sika taught him all the magickal ways of their people before they were kidnapped. It was Kobe who awakened the witch in me. Kobe helped me know who I was and the power that I possessed. There were no schools of witchcraft in America when I arrived. It was simply too dangerous. One was either fortunate enough to find a kindred spirit and learn the ways of the Craft from them, or they were not. Thus, many witches, particularly women, never realized how powerful they were."

"But, as a person of African descent at that time, wouldn't Kobe have been enslaved?" Imani insisted. "How was he able to marry you?"

"Normally yes," Katerina acknowledged. "A Black man of his time would have been a slave. However, Kobe's original master, the Reverend Donovan Dodge, who kept him as a valet, allowed him to buy his freedom. Later, they became partners in the silverware business."

"American history is so complicated," I sighed.

"You think so?" Tayen rolled her eyes at me. "Try being half-Navajo and half-white. A world of infuriating complexities awaits." Then, to Katerina, she added, "Still, though, that's super cool about you and Kobe. Kudos, girlfriend! Love wins... sometimes."

Katerina laughed. "Sometimes, it does." She turned to Elliott. "Just one left. Would you like to..."

"No," Elliott said abruptly. "No offense, but I'd rather not dabble around in pedestrian love magic. Nothing good ever comes of it anyway. Especially when there are so many other things to worry about."

I watched Tayen observing Elliott. She was almost willing for him to look at me as he spoke, but he didn't. Elliott kept staring straight at the wall.

Katerina took it in stride. "Suit yourself. By the sun, I'd say it's about dinnertime anyway. Why don't we call it a day and go see what Mary has to say to us?"

Chapter Fifteen

That third night, after the usual presentation of the dinner and dialogue, Mary finally told us the whole truth about the college's future. It was honorable of her, all things considered.

"For many years," Mary said, "our numbers at Rookes College have been dwindling. The strength of young witches' power burnt just as brightly. That was never the problem. It's more heartbreaking, at least to me." Mary glanced around. "It's that they were no longer listening. To themselves or their intuition. To Mother Earth and Father Sky. To the God and the Goddess. To anyone or anything. Rookes has always been a college in which intellectual curiosity was rewarded. Yet, what are we to do when so few are curious anymore? When we place key after key for them to find, and no one picks them up?"

"What do you believe was the source of it?" Hana asked from her place on the Great Hall's central dais.

Mary shook her head. "There are so many things. Fear, I believe, is the first and foremost cause. No one feels confident nowadays to assert their position on anything. Inattention is another enemy. The distractions of life for young witches are innumerable. With so many paths available, why would anyone choose the way of the Craft? When it is so uncertain and has no monetary reward after requiring so much? Lastly, I believe there is a growing disconnect between humanity and the natural world. How many humans today go from cradle to grave without ever having grown or raised a single thing they've eaten? Lived in a home built completely through the efforts of others, in which they've never raised so much as a hammer or paintbrush? Instead, we have divorced ourselves as a society from the Earth, our communities, and one another. And this is the result. It is not even possible to give away the things one would experience at a college like Rookes, simply because no one is willing to take the time to accept such gifts."

"Where does that leave the state of the Craft?" Imani asked. "I thought Rookes was the only college in America that accepted students of promise regardless of their background or their ability to pay for an education?"

Mary looked at her, "It leaves us in the very position that I have been trying to avoid for three hundred years. A world in which the rich control not only all aspects of magickal education but the essence of magick itself. Without schools like Rookes, there would be no one to question the acts of witches who come into the Craft from positions of extreme privilege. Those who will never know or even be able to relate to the hardships suffered by previous generations who've suffered for their Craft, having only entered it during prosperous and accepting times. That is why we tell you all our stories. So that at least one more year's worth of young witches will remember and be influenced by the gravity and lessons of history."

"Do you know what the Grand Council has decided?" I asked.

"Not officially, no," Mary replied. "As you are already aware, I have petitioned them regarding the inevitable disaster with Albion Oil's endeavors in the area. However, I have received no response." Mary closed her eyes and lowered her voice. "Which I take to mean that we are alone together in our desire not only to save Rookes College but the entire Carolina coastal region in which we reside."

"It just doesn't seem logical, let alone fair," Miranda said. "For an organization that professes to draw all its power from the Earth to completely disregard a credible threat to it? Even if they aren't worried about Rookes College closing because they prefer witches from more affluent and hereditary backgrounds, then surely they could be made to understand the importance to all of us of preserving the Earth, from which all of our power is derived?"

Mary smirked. "You'd be amazed at what the Grand Council can choose to overlook when they have the mind and monetary motivation to."

"Where does that leave us then?" Tayen asked. "Will we even be able to finish out our education? The year and a day that we've been brought here for?"

"I will do everything possible in my power to assure that," Mary replied.

"So will I," Katerina seconded, and the rest of the Mentors agreed.

Elliott pushed his chair back from the table. "There must be something we can do to help. I know my father is not likely to change his mind regarding the opening of Albion's new drilling operation, but can't we reach out to him? Let him know what we have foreseen? Even if Albert isn't concerned about preserving the natural environment, I feel certain he would be interested in preventing an expensive disaster that would shut down operations. It would cost him a ton of money. If we speak in financial language, I think even he will listen."

"You're quite right," Alice said to Elliott. "That's why we have to communicate with someone who will listen both to our story and to reasons Albert Capell will understand." Alice turned to me. "For that, we will need Willow to speak to her father."

"Oliver!" I exclaimed. "What does he have to do with any of it?"

"Surely you recall where he was going for his next position?" Alice said.

"To do a geologic survey for an oil company on the coast," I said, forcing myself to accept the suspicion I had initially dismissed. "So, Albion Oil *is* the company Oliver is working for?" It seemed too coincidental to be believed.

Mary nodded. "It would be most beneficial if, when your rook returns, you continue your correspondence with your father. Subtly urge him to look into the aspects of the drilling operation that are likely to pose the greatest environmental threats. Perhaps that's all it will take to prevent such a disaster. For you to alert Oliver as the surveyor. Then, for Oliver to awaken in Albert the sense that the entire enterprise is faulty in its present state and could place him in great monetary jeopardy." Mary paused for a moment, studying me. "Will you do this, Willow? Do you feel comfortable?"

"Yes," I whispered. "Of course."

Even though I agreed, it was a lie. The idea of going to see my dad to try to convince him to call out his boss after all the second-guessing and self-convincing I knew he must have gone through before selling out to take a job with an oil company felt terrible. It triggered all kinds of bad memories about the fights he and Darla used to have about his work. Nothing he was capable of doing with his career ever seemed to earn enough money or prestige to please her. Oliver was always so down on himself for years afterward, even a little kid could see it. So, I became Little Miss Overachiever to cheer him up. And on most levels, it worked.

Subconsciously though, it was exhausting. That feeling of always having to be the light-bringer of emotional support for the number one male figure in my life. Looking back, I think that was a big part of how I fell into this thing I have about bolting. When my feelings about a relationship start to get too intense, I'm afraid of having to be responsible for anyone else again. Fortunately, my Rookes sisters didn't give me much time then to dwell on the idea.

"If Willow can get through to her father and Elliott to Mr. Capell," Hana added, "would that save the college?"

"I'm not sure," Mary replied. "It couldn't hurt. We all have our time in the sun and must gracefully surrender our dreams when the time is right. Yet, if we can prevent this disaster and persuade the Grand Council that Rookes is worth fighting for, no matter how small our numbers are, then we might have a chance at survival. Of proving that Rookes and its methods are worth preserving."

The remainder of our meal was somber. Hana tried to lighten the mood by praising Candy's skills at healing her burned hands. In turn, Candy attempted to awaken some excitement regarding her first lesson in healing for the next day. Neither of their efforts succeeded completely. By the time Mary dismissed us for the evening, almost every bit of the camaraderie that we'd built over the past few days had dissipated like an early morning fog at sunrise.

I'd not been in my room for more than a few moments when the knock came at my door. I could tell it was Elliott even before I answered.

Dressed in his old-fashioned nightshirt, Elliott settled into one of the chairs in my study. Knowing what the content of our conversation would likely be, I waited for him to begin. When he did, it was not in any way I'd anticipated.

"Do you hate your family?" Elliott asked abruptly.

"No," I replied. "Oliver's a solid dad, if oblivious at times. But his heart's in the right place."

"What about your mum?" Elliott pressed. "You've not mentioned her."

"They're divorced," I said simply. "Darla... Mom," I corrected myself. "Never really wanted children. I was sort of an accident. The year I was born, she was supposed to go back out on tour with her band. She was working on a new album."

"So, she was a singer then," Oliver affirmed. "Anything I've ever heard of?"

"Probably not," I answered, wincing slightly. I've always hated talking about Darla. "When her management company found out she was pregnant, they decided to postpone the tour. Then, the album took longer than expected too. By the time it was finished, a couple of years had gone by. Darla didn't look as good as she had before me. At least, according to how the country music execs thought female singers were supposed to look. She'd gained a lot of baby weight and never lost it. Plus, after I was born, her drinking problem escalated to the point that she became crazily unreliable. Her reputation for picking fights with her band members and cancelling small shows in the clubs around town made all the good musicians refuse to work with her. Then, her label dropped her. Darla tried to get a new contract, went to rehab, had liposuction, lip injections, the whole nine, but it didn't work—unless you count starting an affair with Kurt, her plastic surgeon. That seemed to turn out just fine. Darla and Plastic Kurt have a big house together in Brentwood now."

"Do you ever visit her?" Elliott asked, with a slight huff of amusement at the nickname I'd given my stepfather.

"No," I said. "Darla always seemed to think it's better for her second marriage that way," I half-laughed, self-consciously. "Honestly, I have no opinion of my mom's new husband at all. I've never even met Kurt face-to-face. When Darla wants to see me, she comes to Dad's cabin in Oak Ridge. Or she did, until he sold it to keep from getting behind on his payments."

"Which explains why your dad took the job for mine," Elliott stated matter-of-factly. "When most other geologists wouldn't touch the project."

"Yep," I replied, forcing myself to look up from the grimoire I'd been thumbing through just to avoid his gaze.

"Do you think Oliver is a good man?" Elliott continued. "That he would care if he found out the work he was involved in might do irreparable harm to the environment? Even if it meant he wouldn't be able to make his living because of it?"

I blinked slowly. "Oliver Todd is the kind of man who named the trees around our house and had regular conversations with them. It sounds crazy unless you've seen it. Dad can get sort of absent-minded at times, but the outdoors are his whole life. Since he was a boy in England, he's always loved rocks, plants, and animals. Oliver always said that he chose geology because it was the most secure career path in the sciences at the time he went to school. He was too much of a softie to watch animals suffer as a vet. So, yeah... I feel confident that, if I can make Oliver believe what is inevitably going to happen according to the visions we've seen, he'll try to do something to stop it. Or at least slow it down long enough so that someone else can."

"Must be nice," Elliott shrugged, getting up from his chair and walking over to the door. "To have a parent that you're so confident in to do the right thing."

I could sense what he was hinting at. "I know that your dad was a hard guy to care about, but from everything I've heard, I'm sure that your mother Gwendolyn was a wonderful person."

"Gwendolyn," Elliott said, nodding. "Gwendolyn was... my mother. And we'll leave it at that." Elliott looked away toward the window, staring vacantly at the clouded sky. Saying nothing more, he slipped out into the hallway from my suite. He did not return for the rest of the night.

Chapter Sixteen

"Breathe deeply," Candy intoned the next morning, as we lay on light blankets in the grass surrounding the courtyard of the Earth tower. Her warm, gentle voice made me think of a hammock swaying in a soft island breeze. "Let your lungs fill completely as I count to eight. Then exhale evenly as I repeat the countdown. Try to feel not only the air but also the light of life energy rising from the grasses around you. Allow it to move through every part of your body until you radiate with it. Learning to calm one's own body and mind is the first step in making a witch ready to heal others."

As we cycled through several eight counts of breaths, Candy paced among our blankets. Carefully, she placed pillars of clear quartz crystal above us, just touching the tops of our heads. "This is the *Sahasrara* or crown, the seat of mindfulness and spiritual connection to a higher power. If it is blocked, you will feel disconnected with yourself and your memories."

Candy followed with other crystals for each chakra. I'd heard of that kind of thing before, balancing one's energies. Yet, I didn't pay close enough attention to know what it meant. Imani studied it, though, as she had everything else. Candy let her explain the basics, adding details as she went along.

"Lapis lazuli is for the *Ajna* chakra. It opens the third eye," Imani began. "It helps you gain wisdom and a deeper understanding of situations beyond the superficial."

"Blockage of the *Ajna* chakra also tends to lead people into skepticism," Candy said, patting Tayen lightly on the shoulder. "They only believe what they can physically see. It often results when someone has a lack of trust in the world after being hurt. We'll work on that."

Tayen turned her head to the side to look at me. The expression on her face read, *Is it that obvious?* Wordlessly, I blinked back. *Yep.*

As Candy carefully balanced a turquoise stone on each of our necks, she put a finger to her lips to remind us to be quiet and lie still.

Imani continued, "The throat chakra, or *Vishudda*, controls the voice. Not just the physical voice, but the urge to proclaim opinions to the world."

"Never allow your true self to be silenced, my dear," Candy said, as she laid a piece of polished turquoise on Miranda's throat. "Know that what you have to say deserves to be heard."

"*Anahata*, or the heart chakra," Imani went on, "is controlled by love and compassion. It can be blocked if a person closes themselves off because being lonely is better than being hurt."

"You are safe here," Candy said, setting a piece of green agate on Elliot's chest. He opened his eyes and looked at her. Candy winked. "I think you know that already."

Imani finished out the remainder of her recitation. When Candy placed a citrine on each of our upper stomachs, she said, "The *Manipura*, or solar plexus chakra, has to do with power and independence. Needing the validation of others and the anxiety of having no belief in your self-worth are signs that it is blocked." Turning her face slightly, Imani looked at Hana, who was lying on the blanket beside her. "I'll show you how to do the Breath of Fire. It really works."

Candy beamed. "Imani, your knowledge and eagerness to study are commendable. Please relax for a moment, as I would like to finish up." Putting an orange carnelian stone just below each of our navels, she explained. "Knowledge is a beautiful thing. However, in our quest for it, we must not forget what it means to feel, to intuit, and to be sensual beings. Imani, you are an incredibly beautiful young woman and very intelligent. But it is *perfectly* permissible," Candy drew out the word. "Every once in a while, to let go from all things intellectual and to allow the serendipity of love to flow in. You would do well to listen closely to what the *Svadhishthana* chakra has to say to you."

Imani smiled softly and closed her eyes, at last relaxing back into the grass as Candy completed her discussion—most of which was directed at me. "Willow, you should always be mindful of your root chakra. The *Muladhara*. Those who lack the support of home, have survived family trauma, and who have encountered financial troubles may need some work in this area. Life is more manageable when your feet are planted firmly on the ground. It gives you more confidence to reach for the stars."

Hearing her words, I sunk deeper into the grass. Through the thin blanket, I could feel the soil supporting the bones of my spine. Candy stopped at my feet. She rested the palms of her hands against my soles for a few seconds. I could feel the warmth of her energy circling through my body. Then, she left a piece of red coral between my ankles as she stood to speak to all of us.

"You will notice," Candy began. "I have selected for each of you the area in which to improve your overall energy. It is essential for any individual who chooses to practice true healing to be aware of their health, both physical and spiritual. We will continue to work through healing exercises that are personal to each of your experiences. Thus, you can improve not only your own life but also extend your gifts of learned healing to others. As any of you who have experienced such things know, there is far more to healing a person than just the performance of a procedure. To be truly successful, one must believe they are cured of whatever sickened them. That takes confidence. The most difficult of mental states to reproduce, unless it is real. Genuine confidence flows naturally, like a river to the sea."

I know I was supposed to keep my eyes closed the entire time, but what can I say? I'm a naturally nosy individual. As Candy lay down in her space within our circle, she positioned her crystals, leaving the clear quartz of her crown for last. "The *Sahasrara* chakra is the most difficult to heal and make useful. When I was quite young, my crown chakra was damaged. As a result, for many, many years I felt isolated and disconnected from the life that I have always known."

Imani started to say something. Candy whispered that we should remain quiet for a few more minutes, focusing on our breathing and following her instructions. Starting with root, Candy asked us to envision a wheel of light spinning clockwise that was the same color as the crystal associated with that chakra. When I did so, I felt the soles of my feet become hot and tingly. In my mind's eye, the red wheel spun faster and faster. Finally, it slowed and cooled, expanding like an exploding star in a supernova. Candy's warm, motherly voice guided us through the remainder of the chakras. Her Caribbean accent was like a lullaby. To be quite honest, I think I fell asleep. Maybe that was part of the point, for the meditation to cause us to completely relax. If so, it worked. By the end, I felt as if I had melted into the ground.

"Now," Candy said, rising slowly and helping Imani up as well. "We are more open and clear-headed. I would like to show you a very simple healing spell that can be used in many ways. Imani?" Candy motioned for her to approach. "You suffer from frequent migraines, do you not?"

Imani nodded, still slightly dazed as the rest of us were from the energy work.

"Are you feeling one currently?" Candy asked.

"They never really go away," Imani answered. "Sometimes they're so bad, it moves my head when they hit. My vision goes all sideways. I have to sit down because I get so dizzy. My dad thinks they're from all the eyestrain. That I read too much. My chiropractor thinks it has to do with my posture. That I have a tech neck from bending over the laptop."

"They may both be correct," Candy mused. "Any over-exercise of the physical or mental facilities must be recharged spiritually with rest." She reached into the large shoulder bag that she'd brought and pulled out a wooden stick, a bundle of prickly grass twigs bound tightly with cotton twine, and a box of matches. Candy then asked Imani to sit down on the grass in front of her again. This time cross-legged, and to close her eyes once more.

"This is sandalwood," Candy said, lighting the stick and balancing it on a rock. She reached to retrieve the bundle and lit it. "And this is rosemary." Candy blew lightly on the burning ends, which softened down to smoking embers. "The aromas of incense and essential oils help to make the body calm and receptive to healing energy. Breathe deeply, my dear," she said. Candy walked around Imani barefoot, waving the burning sandalwood and rosemary gracefully, as if in a dance. When Imani was completely encircled with a light ring of smoke, Candy stepped inside the circle and sat down beside her. She crossed her legs and set the incense stick and herb bundle aside.

As we watched, Candy reached for Imani's right hand and placed it on her forehead. Then, Candy placed the palm of her right hand on Imani's forehead and her left hand on the ground. Gradually, their breathing became unison. I realized I was inhaling and exhaling in precisely the same rhythm too, even though I wasn't trying. After several minutes, Candy and Imani dropped their hands to their laps and opened their eyes.

"How do you feel?" Candy asked.

Imani blinked a few times and rotated her neck to the left and right. "It's gone. How did you do that?"

Candy answered loudly enough so that all of us could hear. "What you've just seen is called drawing out pain. It can be used for any type of discomfort. However, one must be careful. the more severe and long-lasting the discomfort is, the more of a toll it takes on the drawer to physically pull it out. Also, drawers should always be mindful of channeling the painful energy into a non-reactive surface so that it can be grounded and slowly ebb away." Candy patted the grass on either side of her. "Mother Earth herself has the greatest ability to ground and dissolve pain. It is often best practice for a drawer to ground himself or herself with one hand to the Earth and contact their patient with the other. An ungrounded drawer simply carries the pain of her patient with her until some other release is found."

Turning back to Imani, Candy said, "Healers must always be aware of their limitations and not try to carry the burdens of their patients' worlds without release. Otherwise, they will simply break under the strain and pressure."

"Is that why so many doctors become drunks?" Tayen asked randomly. Imani frowned at her.

Candy laughed, "Partly, yes. But also, most of today's medical doctors go about their practice all wrong. Healing is perhaps the most physically taxing of the magickal arts. It requires the greatest amount of time to prepare oneself for the next patient. Yet, how many times have any of you been in a hospital and seen a surgeon go immediately from one patient to the next, stopping only to wash his hands? He pays no attention to the necessity of cleansing himself spiritually as well. To prepare to give his full energy to his next patient by discharging the negative, painful energy from his previous one?"

"Like, never..." Hana interjected. "My dad's a neurosurgeon. He's constantly complaining about how many patients his hospital churns through. That he doesn't even have time to close their wounds himself. His PA does it instead. Dad never eats all day either. He just comes home and plops down in his recliner and moans about how slow the delivery driver is until the food arrives. He pounces on it like a starving animal and falls asleep watching TV, without saying a word to anyone. Day after day." Hana shook her head. "And he wonders why I'm not interested in medicine. I like people too much."

Candy nodded. "Perfect example. Hana, I am certain that your father would be a much better doctor, not to mention a more pleasant person to be around, if he were just permitted time to recuperate between cases. To speak with his patients and reassure them of his methods and prognosis for recovery. Unfortunately," Candy sighed. "Modern medicine does not operate in any fashion that is conducive to real healing. That is why it fails to cure so many. It has become too impersonal and too..."

I couldn't help butting in. "Greedy. They're just damn greedy. Sapping a patient's insurance for every dime. And if people don't have insurance, they get kicked to the curb."

"The whole damn world is about money," Elliott rolled his eyes. "At least Britain has the NHS. I've always felt bad for Americans with all they have to go through. It's ridiculous."

"I agree," Candy replied. "A true healer views his or her work as a calling. A gift to share with humanity. They do not seek to profit from others' illnesses. Instead, they only accept what payment is truly necessary for time and supplies. To behave otherwise would be like..."

"Like stealing from the collection plate at church," Miranda said. "When the money is meant to be a gift to help those in need."

"I see that we are all in accord on this sentiment. It seems to have brought us around full circle, as all healthy discussions do, to what's next." Candy rose, picking up the bundle of rosemary and stick of sandalwood. "Do any others among you suffer from migraines?"

Tayen's hand shot up.

"I thought so," Candy said. "Your *Ajna* chakra felt very out of balance to me. Please, come over here and sit with Imani, as you saw me do. I will recleanse both of you with these." Candy waved the still-smoking embers in her hands. "Then, Imani, you will repeat my motions. Right palm on Tayen's forehead to draw the negative energy out. Left hand on the Earth, to ground and release it. Envision the blue spinning wheel within your third eye, just as you did when we meditated before. Wait for your positive energy to pull Tayen's negative out. You will know it when you see it. It will be pale and faded, spinning very slowly. When it contacts you, Imani, I want you to push your positive, healing energy, spinning as fast as you can, toward Tayen, as if you are pushing off a boat with your mind. The sea and human consciousness behave very similarly. Tayen, you will place your right palm on Imani's forehead to allow a channel for your negative, painful energy to ebb away. Allow Imani's positive energy to flow into you. Again, you will know it when you feel it. Try to be as open and receptive as possible."

Tayen and Imani both eyed Candy suspiciously, refusing to look at each other.

"I know it may seem difficult," Candy said. "In healing, we have to learn to trust one another and to trust the energy that ebbs and flows through us from Mother Earth." Candy patted Tayen on the shoulder again, just as she had done when she placed the lapis lazuli on her forehead. "You have to open up to heal, Tayen. It's going to hurt, but only for a little while. Pain lessens when you share it. Imani, you could benefit from understanding where Tayen's distrustfulness is coming from too. You will feel it as you draw the discomfort from her. Hopefully, both of you will walk away not only migraine-free but with a better appreciation for one another."

We watched as Candy swirled the veil of smoke in rings around the two of them. Imani and Tayen carried through the same procedure as before. I couldn't help but think about how Candy noticed Imani and Tayen didn't like each other from the very beginning. I had a feeling that was why she'd chosen this healing activity for our first lesson. To show them how much they had in common.

It worked in two senses of the word. Not only was Tayen relieved of her constant migraine pain as well, but they stopped sniping at each other for several days afterward. I never knew what they saw in each other's pain and never asked. It must have been *something*.

Chapter Seventeen

S ince nobody else had migraine issues for us to practice on, we spent
the rest of the afternoon inside. Candy showed us how to make the
salve that she had applied to Hana's burned hands to make them heal so
quickly after the incident in prognostication. It was a very involved process,
which included mixing honey, freshly harvested from the hives on Rookes
College grounds, with aloe vera and coconut oil. We ground seeds from sea
buckthorn with a mortar and pestle to extract their oil and simmered fresh
rose petals in a wood-fired cauldron to make rosewater. Last, we whisked
those together with the rest. Once again, I had the feeling that Candy's
choice of spell was intended to have multiple purposes: to teach us how
to make natural burn salve and to demonstrate how to properly utilize the
other implements as well. With the added benefit of keeping us busy long
enough to tell her story, which she did while we were preparing the salve.

"I was born on the West Coast of Africa," Candy began. "In what is now
Ghana. Like Katerina's husband, Kobe, I passed through the *Door of No
Return*. My sisters told me later that it was because some people from a
nearby village betrayed us. A family of women mostly near childbearing
age living alone without a man to protect them was worth a lot of money,
and many people were starving. Although, I hardly remember it because I
was so young. Just barely walking. I was my parents' late-in-life baby girl,
which probably saved me. My mother and older sisters were not so lucky.
They were tall and beautiful, and so they caught the eyes of the colonial
governor and his men." Candy closed her eyes. "I do not like to think about
what happened to them, but it made them hard. That is what I remember
most. So hard that when we finally came to Barbados, and the guard took
me from my mother's arms, she shed no tears. There were none left."

Candy turned her back to us and pretended to stir the cauldron for a
few moments, then continued. "I was bought at first by a family to train

as their daughter's maid. They wanted a small child who was still young enough to learn proper English and good manners so that she could grow up as a companion to the girl. Providence, her name was. A sweet girl, but not well. She celebrated her birthday as mine too, since I did not know when mine was. To this day, I still count Providence's birthday as my own. Originally, Providence had a twin sister who died already. Her name was Plenty. Their parents were young and had hoped that naming their first daughters as such would increase their luck with the new sugar plantation. Although the plantation prospered, Providence did not. She died when we were almost twelve. Her father, Mr. Eaves, was not a particularly cruel man to his slaves, but he was very frugal. He did not beat us because he said injuries would cost him money. Perhaps that was why his plantation prospered? Regardless, since their third child was a boy, the family thought it more proper to buy a male companion as his servant. I was sold so they could reinvest the money."

"That must have been terrible. Did you ever see your family again?" Imani asked.

"No," Candy replied. "Strangely, losing them was less dreadful than Providence's death from the yellow fever. I hadn't seen my mother or sisters since the auction in which Mr. Eaves bought me. It is hard to long for those whom you don't even remember. But I will always miss Providence. She was the one who named me. As Providence was learning to speak, for some reason she would look at me and say *Candy* as if I were a sweet. Since I had not arrived at their plantation in Barbados with a name, that was what the Eaves family called me. I have been Candy ever since."

"Was that how you came to America?" Imani wanted to know. "Through a sale by Mr. Eaves?"

"Yes," Candy answered. "Mr. Eaves knew that I was not fit for field or kitchen work, as I had been trained to become a lady's maid. So, he sold me to a company looking to buy up domestics for families in New England who had not brought their servants from England. Being almost thirteen then, but looking and acting older, I was purchased to be the maid for a woman named Margaret Hawkes. Her husband was in the lumber business in Salem, and they were wealthy. The Hawkes family was from old money. They intended to make much more from America, where the need for lumber was great. However, Mrs. Hawkes was very particular in the ways that she wanted everything just so. In the beginning, there were certain rooms in their house that I was not allowed to enter, although I soon learned why."

Pausing a moment to peer over into the cauldron, Candy announced that the salve was ready to ladle over into our jars. Otherwise, it wouldn't set properly. Once that task was completed, Candy finished her story.

"One day, after Mrs. Hawkes had been bustling in and out of the forbidden rooms all morning, I noticed a strange smell and smoke seeping out from under the door. Worried that it might be a fire, I took a chance at disobeying her and opened the door. Sure enough, a cauldron just like this one had something scorching within it. I screamed for Mrs. Hawkes, and I grabbed a bucket of sand to throw over it and put out the flames. She came running back up the stairs and, seeing me standing there by the smoking cauldron, slammed the door. It was only then that I started looking around the room. It was filled with drying herbs, crystals, and dolls that I came to know were poppets, along with stacks of old leather-bound books. Some of which," Candy glanced at Imani, "I have placed in your room. You are welcome to look through them any time you like. I hope you find something useful. They are meant to be read, not gather dust."

"I will," Imani said. It took her longer than usual to say more. "That must have been how you found out she was a witch too, then?"

"A witch, *yes*, but not a witch *too*," Candy corrected. "At least, not yet. It was Margaret Hawkes who taught me the Craft. That was one true part of my testimony at the trials in Salem. Much of it, though, Margaret and I just made up to save our necks." Candy smiled, "For as you have heard, I speak and understand perfectly sound English. I just pretended not to be able to understand or express myself so that I wouldn't slip accidentally and give testimony contradictory to what Margaret said. We agreed that Margaret could most likely buy her way out of the accusations, which she did. However, things could have gone very differently for me if I had let on that I was intelligent enough to understand the ways of magick. Enslaved people weren't even supposed to be allowed to read in the American colonies. Some feared that knowledge would cause rebellion. A correct assumption, I suppose. Once any person becomes awakened to how poorly they have been treated, it is only natural that they should want to fight back against their oppressors."

"Then, your confession at the Salem Witch Trials, before Judge Hathorne, was a lie?" Imani asked in disbelief. I glanced at her quizzically.

The name sounded familiar, but I couldn't place it. Elliott recognized it right way.

"Judge Hathorne was one of the main judges in Salem," Elliott explained. "Some of them later changed their minds, but not him. His great-great-grandson was so ashamed of it that he altered the spelling of his name to distance himself during his writing career. Nathaniel Hawthorne. Probably every school kid in America has read his most famous novel."

"The Scarlet Letter!" Tayen exclaimed. Imani shushed her. "Told you I read," Tayen mouthed silently, as Imani nodded at Candy to continue.

"Part of my confession was true," Candy acknowledged. "The part about signing my name in the Devil's Book was a lie though. The Devil doesn't have any such books because he doesn't exist. Every real witch knows that," Candy replied, with a dismissive wave of her hand. "I played up the dumb act by feigning the broken English that I'd heard from many slaves who'd been captured as adults and never given a chance to learn the language properly. Margaret manipulated the judges' prejudice. They believed an enslaved woman was too stupid to learn or work magick. Margaret thought if we pretended I had been tricked into doing so by a devious master, it would save me, even if I confessed. Turns out she was right. Margaret and I both walked free, even though she had been doing a little knot and poppet magic to annoy those women who accused us. They hated Margaret because she was attractive even in middle age. Furthermore, she was rich enough to pay the minister double tithe and thereby avoided having to attend church meetings, which she found boring and tedious. If only she and the others accused in Salem had minded the Rule of Three..."

Imani broke in. "Wait... so you're telling me all of the people accused of witchcraft at Salem were real witches?"

"Oh, no dear!" Candy exclaimed. "Not all. But quite a few, yes. It all started as harmless prankstering. Witches love a good prank because we're all a little childish at heart. Margaret only meant to make those women have kinks in their backs that would pain them as they sat on the hard benches of the meeting house all prim and proper, judging everyone. Pinching the poppets was just supposed to make the girls yell and jump during church so that it would embarrass their mothers. Margaret was always like that. She liked to see overly precise people get their comeuppance. And it was quite entertaining while we were doing it. Watching them in Margaret's crystal ball as they arched their backs and yowled like cats. Every time the minister looked at them, Margaret would pull another knot tight, or I'd pinch a doll, and *Yeet!*"

Candy giggled as she threw her arms in the air, mimicking the women. Then, she grew more somber. "However, the joke wasn't worth it. Any time a witch does magick, even in fun, she must be mindful of the Rule of Three. That whatever they do will come back threefold. It caused a lot of us a great deal of trouble. Some even lost their lives, as I'm sure you know from all the accounts through the centuries. After we were let out of jail, things were never the same between Margaret and Mr. Hawkes. Giving the payoff money in secret was only part of it. Mr. Hawkes was too embarrassed. Having people know that Margaret was his wife and I her servant was destroying his business. Neither of them believed in divorce. They decided that she should go back to England and take me with her. After a year or two, Mr. Hawkes pretended that Margaret died so that he could remarry. We spent the rest of our natural lives at their ancestral estate. It wasn't terrible. Hawkes Manor was a much finer place than her American home, but Margaret always felt taken down a peg or two by the whole incident. She's still there today, behind the veil of our Otherworld, of course."

Elliott thought he recognized the name of Hawkes Manor. He and Candy got into a whole side discussion about English geography and the histories of witching families that none of the rest of us knew anything about, not being British ourselves. They promised to explain it to us, which they did, but I'm still not sure I followed most of it. I jotted down many names to look up afterward in our books, though.

After dinner we all went around to each other's rooms, examining book-cases and sharing what we'd found so far. I was not surprised to find out that Imani spent every night since our arrival pouring over volume after volume. No wonder she had migraines from all that studying!

That night, I fell asleep thinking about how odd it was that the Salem Witch Trials began, at least in some cases, with real witches simply playing harmless pranks on hypocritical people. How many other times in American history have such disastrous consequences resulted from something so small as a careless word or harmless action?

Chapter Eighteen

T he last day of our first week at Rookes College found us at the northernmost shore of the island, our white robes flapping in a stiff breeze, as Alice gave her spellcraft lesson. Unlike the rest, Alice did not gather us together in the Spirit tower until after dinner, when darkness had fallen.

Handing out dagger-like knives with black handles to each of us, she explained their significance. "This," Alice held up her knife, "is called an athame. On Monday, Cora taught all of you how to cast a circle with your new wands and to draw down lightning to you, representing the element of fire. An athame can be used for the same purpose as a wand. However, it is thought by some to create an even stronger circle of protection if you also use a blade to call the corners. That allows the spirits attendant to each element to hear and join their magick with your own. Today, we will focus on the proper method for doing so. How to channel the energy from within a circle of protection. This will enable you to perform the three most common types of actions that witches might engage in to protect themselves if threatened. Can any of you tell me what those are?"

Not surprisingly, Imani's hand shot into the air. "Banishment, disappearance, and flight."

"Quite right," Alice nodded. "Although both the wand and athame can be used to cast circles, the wand is preferred for circles into which you intend to draw down energy and then redirect it outward again. Those circles are considered to be more porous. The athame is preferable if a witch does not want any external energy to penetrate the circle of protection at all. Instead, it is used primarily to project the energy that she summons from her powers outward, from her internal connections to the spiritual realm. Thus, when cast correctly, with enough force and strength of spirit, a circle drawn by an athame can be impermeable. Observe."

Alice spun swiftly around clockwise with her athame pointed toward the ground. A blue flame sprouted from the ground in its wake. Standing in her white robe in the center of it, with her dark curly hair flowing, Alice looked like the pupil burning at the center of an intensely blue eye. "Once you've drawn the perimeter of the circle," she announced over the crackling flame. "You must then call the corners. I like to begin with the element of Air in the East, symbolic of sunrise and new beginnings. Then, I move south to activate the element of Fire that kindles passion. Next, I engage the self-reflective element of Water from the West, and I end in the North with the grounding element of Earth. Last, I channel all these energies inward to strengthen my spirit so that the center of the circle can hold firm. You may use an incantation if you choose. The one I will recite is contained in my old Book of Shadows. It is in Willow's room if any of you care to adopt it."

Alice rolled her head from side to side and took a deep breath, then began her recitation:

Spirits of Air, I summon thee. Lash all who seek to lash me.
Spirits of Fire, I summon thee. Burn all who seek to burn me.
Spirits of Water, I summon thee. Drown all who seek to drown me.
Spirits of Earth, I summon thee. Crush all who seek to crush me.
Ever as I mind the Rule of Three, I invoke all of you to set me free.

As Alice spoke, she directed the tip of her athame toward each direction's corresponding element. By the end of it, a five-cornered star burned brightly blue inside the circle, completing the pentacle. The flames leaped almost to shoulder height around her. Alice's pale face seemed to float above them.

"Since it is very dangerous to summon an evil spirit, I would wholeheartedly discourage you from ever doing so. It is destructive magick. You will simply have to trust me that the circle of protection I have raised would shield me from one." Alice turned to me. "Nevertheless, we will demonstrate the first method of protection, banishment, visually by recalling again your lesson from Monday. Willow, would you be so kind as to draw down some lightning? I know we are all still working on directions, but try to make it strike as closely to me as possible. Here in the center of the circle." Alice raised her athame skyward and grounded her feet shoulder-width apart. "Whenever you're ready."

Calling the lightning just as I had earlier that week, Alice caught it with her athame. Rather than rechanneling it and pulling herself up into the sky as Cora had done, Alice stopped it about twenty feet above the circle that she had cast. Then, grasping both hands around the black handle of her athame, Alice closed her eyes. The blue flames of the circle covered her completely in a dome of azure fire. The lightning bolt fractured and ran over its surface, like veins of static over an electric globe.

"As you can see," Alice called from inside the orb, causing rays to crackle outward. "I am now completely encased in the heat and static energy that was the lightning. This effect is produced any time an external energy force attempts to break through the circle. I can banish it with a single word or thought, or allow it to continue to resonate around me as an additional barrier layer. One word is usually sufficient. I recommend this one. It's the most powerful."

No! Alice exclaimed. Instantly, the blue orb flew away over the bay and hit the surface of the water like a comet. The water sizzled and boiled behind her, slowly dissipating. White-capped waves rolled into the shore as Alice continued. "The next method of protection, disappearance, is best demonstrated outside the circle. That way, you can sense me moving about among you. All three spells can be conducted inside as well." Just as swiftly as she had drawn it, the blue flame vanished under Alice's hand as she rotated again, counterclockwise.

"For this part, I will need your assistance again, Willow," Alice began. "I want you to hit me with a quick banishing spell. The words are yours to choose. Any words can be magickal so long as the witch puts her true life force behind them. Something monosyllabic and quick is best. Then, if you are ever caught by surprise, it will come to you without thinking. You're a strong witch when you choose to be, so just enough to push me down, please. Envision yourself doing that, with your athame raised and aimed. Then, everyone should observe my reaction." Alice braced herself once more, one foot in front of the other, her athame raised at a slant in front of her like a shield.

Pointing my athame at Alice, I screamed "No!" as loudly as I could, shoving forward with both hands. As the blast of energy hit her, she caught it with her knife and turned it to the ground. It hit with a thump like a large stone. The impact rocked her backward. Stumbling, Alice swiftly turned her athame skyward.

"Go!" Alice cried. There was a loud crack as if thunder had broken right over us, and she disappeared. Within moments, there was a second loud pop, and Alice returned. She appeared completely unfazed. "Good one!" Alice congratulated me. "Your control is excellent."

"Where did you go when you disappeared?" I asked.

"Ah," she said. "That is another thing you must decide before you attempt this particular spell. Whenever you speak the word or phrase that you've chosen to use for disappearance, you must already have a destination in mind. Some place in which you feel safe and at home." Alice paused. "As I am a person who was not welcomed in my own home after I was found to be a witch, I chose another location. There is a little village called Fleetwood at the mouth of the River Wyre in Lancashire, where I was born. There is a legend about it that goes back to old Breton times about a lost city called Ys and the origins of witchcraft there. Whether it is true or not, I relate to it. I like that part of the Fylde Coast. It's changed greatly over the years, but at heart, it's still just a little fishing village. When I disappear, I imagine myself popping up in the queue for the Rose ferry boat that takes tourists back and forth across the mouth of the river to Knott's End."

"That's smart," Elliott said, nodding. "If for some reason you think that you might be followed, you can just step up on the ferry. Throw them off course a bit. Magick's more difficult to work over water."

"True," Alice said. "It also has fairly easy access to the Isle of Man, where many friends and members of the Craft have lived since before Roman times, if support is needed." Next, Alice asked if I would like to give disappearance a try.

Caught slightly off guard, I asked if I was allowed to change the destination point that I would disappear to. Alice laughed. "Of course! I've changed mine many times over the centuries. You can alter it every time you disappear if you like." I must have looked skeptical because she added, "Just make sure that it's a place you can visualize clearly. Otherwise, you might get stuck between points here and in the Otherworld. Then, I'd have to come fetch you. If you feel it happening, just will yourself back here and you'll be alright."

We repeated the same exercise as before, only with our roles reversed. After I deflected Alice's shove, I rolled to the side and thought as hard as I could about my dad's log cabin back in Oak Ridge. Everything went black for a moment. The next thing I knew, I was tumbling in the grass in our front yard. Sitting up next to a red, white, and blue real estate sign, I saw the cabin.

The lights were off. The front porch was empty of the usual tumble of tomato vines that crowded over the railings at the end of every summer. Containers of whatever tomato experiment Oliver had going on that year—yellow grapes or purple heirlooms—plus a few planters of ordinary Romas and Better Boys. Oliver grew those safeties, he said, in case the others died. Oliver's rocking chair was gone too. *Dad must have gone home and started packing up to leave for his new job with Albion right after he met with the realtor.* It made me sad to think about Dad there, taking care of it by himself and knowing that he was too late to save anything.

I heard a bird cawing and turned around to see Stella flying toward me. The rook alighted in the grass. I could see the note I'd written a few days ago was still attached to her leg. "I'm sorry, girl, I didn't know," I said, stroking the bird's shiny black head. She nipped at my hand nervously. I know it seems like I'm projecting human emotions on her, but I could swear Stella seemed anxious about not having completed her mission of delivering my note. Wrapping one arm around her wings and holding her close, I aimed my athame skyward and thought of the north lawn of Rookes College. All was black again for a few seconds. Then I found myself reeling in the grass. Stella hopped down and began cawing again, clearly happy to be back in more familiar surroundings.

"Well, I can see you do not need my instruction on how to reappear with company," Alice said. "Where did you find this girl?"

"My dad's," I said after a pause. It seemed weird to describe the place as Oliver's after what I'd seen. It felt like a lie. Alice studied me for a moment, her brows knit together as if she were trying to read my thoughts. From her reaction, I think she did.

"Oh, I see," Alice said. "Well, it will be alright. I have no doubt your father will land on his feet. He's a very resourceful man. He has a new job already, and everything. And as I said, you may change your disappearance safe destination at any time. A place you've enjoyed on holiday perhaps, or even here, if you're comfortable. Regardless, if he's closer you should receive responses from your father more quickly, as Mary discussed. Less than a day over to the site where the company team is staying, or so I've heard. It's quite handy."

I could tell the other girls and Elliott were listening intently to what Alice was saying. They wondered what I experienced during my disappearance. Yet, I hated the thought of talking about it. Telling them that my dad had already emptied our cabin during my time at Rookes because Oliver needed to rush away to his next job was too sad. Alice saved me from the inevitably embarrassing discussion by sorting everyone else into pairs so that they could practice disappearing and reappearing too. By the time they were through, it was clear that none of them experienced anything like what I had. Noticing that I was still processing it, Alice picked Elliott instead to help demonstrate her final spell.

"It's a common misconception that witches need brooms to fly," Alice said.

Tayen laughed. "You mean Harry Potter lied to us? Damn... I was looking forward to some Quidditch." The other girls and Elliott snickered. I did too, and Tayen winked. She could tell that something was bothering me too.

Alice closed her eyes and took a deep breath. "Tayen, has anyone ever told you that you shouldn't always be as funny as you can be?" Tayen shook her head *no*.

"Alright, well now they have," Alice replied to her question. "As I was saying, all that flight requires is your willpower to make it happen. Elliott, I know you have a bit of experience already. Would you like to give the girls an explanation and demonstration?

Elliott must have been glad to be given free rein to talk, or else he really enjoyed flying. He spoke for quite a long time, sailing around over our heads as he gave directions. About how best to summon the internal energy to levitate, then how to lean into the direction you wanted to go, and at last how to stop suddenly in midair without falling. The way he explained it, flying seemed quite similar to piloting a hoverboard. Only witches were actually in the air while they were doing it. "To sum up," Elliott finished, "The key is concentration. Just like musicians can miss notes in songs with which they're very familiar if they allow their minds to drift, so a witch can lose altitude and direction if they allow their thoughts to wander while flying."

Elliott looked at me strangely. "Whatever you do, stay aware of who you are and where you want to be. Don't lose focus."

"Well said," Alice replied, directing her comment to all of us. "I believe Elliott's advice could apply to many parts of life. Stay focused, and you can go anywhere." Then to Elliott, "Do you use any particular word or command?"

"Up," Elliott said simply.

"There you have it," Alice motioned for us to stand in a straight line in front of her in the grass. "Up you get, and give it a go. Try not to get higher than about the second-floor level there," Alice nodded in the direction of the main castle. "I'd hate to have to call Candy out so late to patch anyone up."

After a few tries, all the other girls were hovering at least a few feet above the ground. Not me, though. Elliott kept urging me to speak with more authority in my voice. Alice encouraged me to give it a little running start and jump to get going. However, no amount of yelling or jumping seemed to get me off the ground for more than a second or two. Even a good college basketball player with a strong vertical leap would have had more hang time in the air.

It went on embarrassingly long, my attempting and failing at everything that anyone could think of to suggest that might lift me skyward. Alice didn't even have an opportunity to tell her story, as was the usual pattern after the day's lessons. Alice claimed that it was fine and that her tale would fit in just as well during our next day's lesson with Mary on transmogrification. Still, I knew she was just trying to save my feelings.

"No worries," Alice said at last, clearly not as disappointed as I was when we walked back to the castle. "Not everyone flies on their first go. You are a Spirit witch, so it should come naturally after a bit more practice. The ability to fly isn't only about focus and concentration. Sometimes, one has to take a step backward first. Figure out what lingering thoughts are keeping them held down, tethered to the ground. Once we figure out what that bond is and cut it, you'll soar free as a bird."

"Which reminds me," Alice nodded at Stella. The rook had continued to await my command patiently for hours perched on a nearby shrub. The only lighthearted relief I'd had that evening was watching the rook nod off, begin to slip from her perch, and then regain her footing. Each time, Stella ruffled her feathers, pretending indignantly that it never happened. "After we've all rested, you should send Stella off again to your father in the morning. As close as he is, being out here on the coast now, you may get an answer by nightfall. That should help settle your mind some. Perhaps that's all it is."

Although I had my doubts, I wanted to believe Alice. I didn't want to think that I was the only witch in the world who couldn't fly.

Chapter Nineteen

B y the next morning, word must have spread to the other Mentors about my failure to fly. I was happy to have support from so many different directions, but I was still somewhat ashamed to have failed so miserably that everyone was concerned. It was like a whole army of witchy Red Cross workers stopped by during the night on an emergency mission. When I opened the door to my room, I couldn't even get across the threshold without carrying all the stuff in.

Candy sent a rose, lemon balm, and ginger elixir mixed into a little pot of honey, with a note that said to take two droppers full, morning and evening, to calm my nerves. Grace left a bundle of lavender incense to burn while I was in a cleansing bath with the special salts and more rose petals that Katerina had dropped by. Cora, Mary, and Alice piled up song and spellbooks in a stack waist-high, filled with notes and markers urging me to *Try this one! No, that one! Give them all a go!* My usual breakfast was replaced by a cornucopia of foods magically intended to make me calmer, more focused, and free of tension. It was a little overwhelming. I wasn't used to so many people hovering over me.

The worst part of all was that none of it seemed to do any good. If anything, it made me more anxious. By the time breakfast was over and Mary led us outside, I was relieved that everyone else was more concerned with the potential for an entirely different type of embarrassment during our transmogrification lesson.

Mary asked us to go back upstairs to collect our formal black dress robes that fastened completely shut from collarbone to ankle. "You can dress beneath them if you wish, but you'll only ruin whatever you wear. The robes will keep your modesty covered until you've changed into your familiar forms. After transmogrification, most find that the human desire to wear clothes fades away. Still, we will slip back into our robes before becoming human again. Going skyclad during rituals is not an easy thing to get used to. Many witches continue to use robes permanently."

"I think I'm always going to stay robed," Miranda said. She looked horrified at the possibility of being naked in public, to no one's surprise.

Tayen elbowed me and mouthed, *Unless the mermaids show up*, which made me giggle. Miranda wrinkled her nose at us, totally clueless.

Once we were in our robes, Mary led us out to the orchard near the Rookery. The wind blowing in from the ocean was cool and the day was gray. The thick, smooth satin lining of my robe brushed seductively against my skin with every step that I took barefoot in the soft grass. Mary instructed us to fold the hems of our robes beneath us to sit down, spread the sides and front out in a sort of fan, and tuck our arms close to our bodies inside the voluminous sleeves. Her reason was that it would allow us to slip smoothly out of our robes without tearing them as the changes occurred.

"My original intention was to train only Elliott in the art of transmo-grification," Mary began. "However, given the fact that our time may be shorter than what is usually spent in training new witches, I have decided to go ahead and work with all of you on how to change into your familiar forms. One way your Mentors and I were able to identify that each of you had a potential talent for the Craft was through your encounters with animals. Close your eyes, and if you can, try to recall a time in which a wild animal that was not part of your family showed a special affinity towards you."

Shutting my eyes as instructed, the first animal that popped into my mind was my corgi, Luna. Hopefully, she was with my dad by now. I hadn't seen her in my disappearance during my spellcraft lesson with Alice. I made a mental note to ask Dad in my next letter whenever Stella returned. At that moment, since we were supposed to be focusing on memories of wild animals, I tried to concentrate on that.

"Can it be a wild animal that was in a cage when we saw it?" Hana asked. Mary said *yes* and asked her to explain. "When I was a kid," Hana said. "My parents used to take me to the Franklin Park Zoo in Boston. I always loved all the big cats, tigers especially. Once we did this tiger encounter experience, where we got to go in and watch the trainers interact with them. I thought it was odd how the one female tiger kept watching me. When they would give her a treat, she wouldn't eat it. She kept trying to slap it out of the cage toward me. Being a kid, I thought it was funny and kind of gross, this tiger batting a piece of raw meat my way. The trainer said she'd never seen anything like it."

Mary smiled. "You have an excellent memory, Hana. I believe you may be onto something there, but I don't want to spoil the surprise. A witch's first transmogrification is truly one of the most exciting times in her life, I think. It is so freeing to let go of one's inhibitions and obey true instinct alone as the animals do. Anyone else? Tayen, I believe that you and Cora have already discussed your familiar form, but it will still be a joy when you experience it firsthand. Care to share with us any details that might help your fellow witches envision theirs?"

"Just don't force it," Tayen said, shrugging and almost opening her eyes until Mary reminded her to keep them closed. "The animal or its memory will come to you if you're patient. Try not to think too hard. Feel it."

"I agree," Mary echoed. "Excellent advice. Thank you, Tayen. Anyone else?"

The remaining group of us shook our heads.

"That is perfectly natural," Mary replied. "Just continue to meditate, and let your mind go blank. When you begin to notice sounds or smells that you normally wouldn't, that means that the transmogrification has begun and that your animalistic senses are awakening. Just remain patient and still. As Tayen advised, don't force it. The sooner you stop thinking and start sensing, the more quickly it will come."

Peeping a little, I saw Imani grimace. Her exasperation with having yet another lesson focused on feelings rather than concrete knowledge was clear. Even though I knew we weren't supposed to be looking, I couldn't help but notice the hood of Tayen's robe was beginning to sink. A fluffy gray tail popped out from beneath the hem. Last, the whole thing caved in, as a large, gray animal backed out of the pile of fabric where Tayen had been sitting. Even though Mary explained to all of us over breakfast what was going to happen, I still wasn't ready for it when I saw it. My friend Tayen had transmogrified into a coyote.

"Miss Todd," Mary called. "Eyes closed, please. Once we've all changed, we will reveal everything together. For now, please try to focus your meditation on finding your familiar form."

Easier said than done, I thought. From the rustling around me, I could tell the other witches were undergoing their transmogrifications. Yet, my mind continued to race from thought to thought, never alighting on anything. I began to fear that it was all just a repeat of the night before. *What would happen if I not only failed to fly but couldn't transmogrify into a familiar either? Did that mean I was a failure at being a witch?*

Suddenly, I felt a pair of sharp-clawed feet land on my shoulder. The prickle of pain made my eyes pop open. "Stella!" I exclaimed, louder than I meant to. A rolled piece of college-ruled notebook paper, taped closed, was tied to her foot.

"Miss Todd!" Mary said, exasperated. "Your mind simply isn't on the lesson this morning. Why don't you take Stella out to the Rookery and read that message? When you're finished, please return promptly and ready to work!"

Getting up from the ground, I could see that the grassy area beside the orchard was already full of animals that were my fellow students. A coyote and a tiger, formerly known as Tayen and Hana, along with a horse, an eagle, and a lion. It was fascinatingly easy to tell who was who. I hated to leave just as everyone's familiar identities were being revealed. Yet, I had a feeling that the message back from Oliver was crucial, and I didn't want to irritate Mary any further. I hurriedly followed Stella out to the Rookery.

Once inside, the warm, woody scent of hay calmed my nerves. Stella hopped into my lap and stuck her foot out for me to untie the scroll that Oliver sent. It read:

Dear Willow,

Thank you so much for sending word to me of where you are and what you are doing. I do not know how quickly or if this response will reach you, but I want to begin by saying please not to worry. Luna is with me and as rambunctious as ever. The sale of the house went smoothly. I've already arranged for most of the contents to be moved into storage in Wilmington. After I save up enough money for a down payment, I hope to purchase a new home there. Many other companies similar to Albion Oil are moving into the area soon. My services as a geologist might finally be in demand. Although I do miss our evenings among the trees and fireflies in the mountains, there is much to do to keep me well-occupied until your return. Most of the other staff here are scientists, so you needn't worry that I'm moping about or lonely.

As for the job itself, I appreciate your concern for the potential environmental risks, but so far nothing appears to be amiss. The operation is as well-run, from a safety standpoint, as any oil company might try to be.

Surveys have been completed, and drilling for the first wells is in progress. They should be operational by the end of the year. Mr. Capell has asked me to stay on indefinitely in an advisory capacity. Albert wants me to continuously monitor the state of the ocean floor around the wells, among other subaqueous conditions, as the enterprise continues to grow. If I see anything that might cause my opinion to change, I will most certainly let you know.

Last, I am not surprised by what you found in the forest and what has resulted from it. I always knew you were the most special little girl I'd ever met, but I could never figure out why. Now, everything makes sense.

Remind me to tell you about your grandmother Ursula in Scotland sometime. I believe that you will find her story very intriguing, all things considered.

All my love,

Dad

P.S. - Hopefully, the school will be okay. No, I don't think the part of your letter about the prophecy was hokey. We are in the height of hurricane season. I will keep my eyes peeled.

I rerolled the letter carefully and slid it into my back pocket. Relieved that Oliver and Luna had safely transitioned into his new life, I sighed. Placing Stella into her nesting box with a handful of acorns as a treat, I left the Rookery and returned to the orchard.

By the time I arrived, Tayen and Hana, the first two to transmogrify, had already reverted to their regular human shapes. They were sitting in their robes on the grass, patiently awaiting further instructions from Mary. A large lioness strode past me, took Imani's robe in her mouth, and dragged it over behind a cluster of pear trees to change. Overhead, a golden eagle circled in the sky, wheeling and diving in increasingly daring feats of acrobatics.

Getting closer and closer to the ground each time, Mary cautioned the eagle. "No, no, Miranda. Don't come in at full speed. That's why it seems frightening. Perhaps it would be easier for you to decelerate more gradually to a less threatening surface. Do you see that hedge over there?" The eagle keened shrilly as it made another swoop down. "Good! It's yew, so it should be fairly soft compared to other varieties. Just turn your wings so that they create a break, then glide down."

The eagle made one more circle, then brake-turned her wings. She landed softly on the yew hedge, just as Mary had instructed.

"Willow, would you be so kind as to go and drape Miranda's robe over her on the yew, please?" Mary asked. "I know she's a bit nervous. Perched on top, she should be able to transform back discreetly while covered as she sinks into the hedge."

I picked up Miranda's robe and carried it over to where the eagle sat waiting for me. The copper top feathers of her head and neck glistened like the human Miranda's own reddish-brown hair over the rest of her chocolate-plumed body. The gleam in her bright hazel eyes was uncanny. As I gathered the robe from hem to hood to slip over her, it was like I could still see Miranda's face, even though I knew I was looking at a bird.

As the eagle dipped its head through the hood opening, a fluff of feathers fell away. Just like Mary predicted, the weight of Miranda's returning human form caused her to drop down through the branches. "Ow!" she exclaimed, struggling to pull her robe to cover her bare legs where the twigs and leaves dug into them. Grabbing her forearms with both hands as they popped out of the robe's floppy sleeves, I pulled Miranda to her feet. She swayed against me, like a person trying to regain their land legs after being at sea too long.

"Flying during transmogrification always made me dizzy too at first," Mary reassured her. "It's not as natural a feeling as flying in one's true form. The change in physical dimensions tends to impair one's perspective temporarily. Have a seat and place the palms of your hands on the ground for a few moments. Contact with the Earth should rebalance you. And actually..." Mary paused, turning toward the shining, sable-colored horse with black legs that trotted up behind her. "Sometimes touching magick in another can help awaken the wild within oneself. Elliott, would you mind if Willow petted you for a moment since you're the last one still in familiar form? I believe it might help ease her transmogrification."

The horse snorted and shook his black-brown mane. Pawing at the ground with his right front hoof, Elliott seemed to say, *Go right ahead.*

Gently, I approached the horse. I ran my hand around his pointed ear, down the curve of his smooth jawline to his velvety nose. Even in his familiar form, he was beautiful. In his gray equine eyes, I could almost see a reflection of his human ones. Elliott blinked slowly once. A tingle of nerves coursed through my body from my fingertips down my legs to my feet. I began to feel myself shrinking. My hand fell away from Elliott's muzzle. In less than a second, I was lying on the ground in the collapsed tent of my black robe.

Inside this cozy burrow, I looked at where my hands had been and saw two slender, black paws and a coat ticked through with silver. Crossing my eyes, I looked down my long furry nose and pushed out from under the robe's hem. As I circled my fluffy black tail with a white tip on the end, the other girls cried out in joyful surprise. "A black fox!"

Excited, I raced about in the grass, darting in quick circles around Elliott's hooves. I know it must have looked silly, but I couldn't stop myself. For the first time in my life, I felt so light and carefree. "Yes, I thought that would do the trick," Mary said, laughing. "You two work well together, it seems. Your magicks must be compatible."

"Doesn't Todd mean *fox* in an older version of English?" Imani asked.

"You are correct as usual," Mary replied. "Middle English with Scottish origins. As I am sure you've begun to realize, our familiar forms during transmogrification usually display something about our heritage or true essence. Imani, you became a lioness, the queen of Africa. Hana was a tiger, long a symbol of Korea, although sadly reduced in numbers to near-mythical status today. Perhaps it is part of both your destinies to ensure a comeback for these big cats, as part of our duty to Mother Earth is to care for and preserve her creatures. In return, your powers of intellect and tenacity will grow through connection with their feline essences."

"I'm guessing that I transformed into a coyote because of the ones that I saw in the desert then?" Tayen asked. "Is that part of it? When you encounter a familiar, can they recognize you as a kindred spirit?"

"Precisely," Mary answered. "That was why I asked you to begin the lesson by meditating on a wild animal with whom you'd had a special connection. Animals are more in touch with their instinctual side than humans. Not only can they recognize their human brothers and sisters in spirit, but they often reach out to them in times of emotional distress to remind them to trust their instincts. Tayen, you became a coyote not just because of the animal's cultural ties to the Navajo, but because at your core, you think and feel like a coyote. I've noticed it since we began watching you. You're very playful and always sharp enough to recognize a way out of a tight spot. But a little bit mischievous. That's coyote magick."

Mary turned to Miranda, "Which is very different from eagle magic. Eagles are symbolic of internal fortitude and a willingness to see one's duties through, regardless of the cost. Given your sense of idealism, Miranda, and your heritage that is blended between Mexico and America—both nations that are connected symbolically to eagles—it is natural that the eagle is your familiar form. However," Mary glanced at the rest of us. "That isn't to say only those whose transmogrification changes them into animals that fly without magick must remain grounded always. As your powers grow, you may feel more comfortable combining flying spells with familiar transmogrification. One day, you may find that you've changed not only into the terrestrial species with whom you share a spiritual kinship but something even more magickal."

Elliott reared back on his hind legs and whinnied, pawing at the air. "Yes, Elliott. You are correct. Although your familiar form is a bit smaller than your father's, probably due to your mother Gwendolyn's influence, you are both Capells and horsemen. After you've come fully into your powers, you may become what Albert was, a flying horse. The Pegasus."

"Wait a minute!" Imani exclaimed, making the connection. "So my last name, Griffin, really means..."

"Exactly what you think it does," Mary completed her thought. "A winged lion. The gryphon. That's the funny thing about magick. Often, it hides in plain sight. Obvious only to those curious enough to look for it. This is why the final part of your identification and selection process for Rookes College included a test. Are you a seeker of knowledge who would pick up a key in the dust? Whether or not you are is the truest test for magickal ability."

We finished out the rest of the day practicing how to change back and forth between our human and familiar forms. The more times we tried it, the more we realized that we could do other things as animals too, including some spells. By dinnertime, almost all of us were very adept at slipping in and out of our robes to conceal the process. It was easy for canids, such as Tayen and myself, or even big cats, like Hana and Imani, to nose into our robes and curl up to transmogrify with some degree of modesty. After a few tries, Miranda became figured out how to use her beak to spread out her robe like a tent over some shrub so that she could duck under it too.

Only Elliott, much to his embarrassment, remained unable to transform in private without the help of at least one person holding his robe down over his withers. Even if he could succeed in nudging his front half through the hood, the bare rear end of his horse's familiar form always stuck out. This problem resulted in his pale butt left in the air, if only for a few seconds. Which I have to admit, I couldn't help peeking at just a little. Like the rest of him, it did not disappoint. Mary tried to reassure Elliott that some of the most notable witches in the history of the world always chose to perform magick skyclad. From the look on Elliott's face, though, I could tell he wasn't convinced that he didn't look ridiculous. In the end, he gave up and trotted over behind the grove of pear trees in the orchard every time he transformed.

Chapter Twenty

At dinner that evening, it was supposed to be Elliott's turn on the dais to speak with Mary. However, she insisted that since we'd missed the night that Alice and I were supposed to be in the center, we should join them. I sat opposite Elliott, and Alice was across from Mary.

"The need for more formal education in magick has ebbed and flowed through the centuries," Mary began. "Our discussion tonight will focus on the necessity of knowing one's audience before choosing to impart magickal knowledge or to come out of the broom closet." She enclosed the last phrase in air quotes. "For even in today's more liberal society, people still fear that which they do not understand. A witch is one of the most incomprehensible creatures the gods have ever created for those who are not among our number. Thus, I hope Alice's tale tonight will instill in you a sense of caution regarding those with whom you choose to share your gifts." Mary turned to Alice and asked her to begin.

"Like most tragedies of history," Alice said. "My story, the story of the Pendle Witches, started long before the trials. One might say that King James himself was the cause of it. A suspicious and superstitious ruler, King James came to the throne through a fog of many political enemies. So many that he became paranoid. When the ship that he was returning on from Denmark with his new bride was caught in a violent storm that almost sank them, King James was convinced that witches, hired by his enemies, were the cause. Then, in 1597, the same year that he supervised the rewriting of his version of the Christian Bible, King James wrote another book called *Daemonologie*. It was an instruction manual for finding and punishing witchcraft. Armed with the assurance their King condoned such actions, would-be witch hunters set out to find as many witches as they could, in hopes of winning his favor."

"Were there so many witches for them to find?" I asked.

"No," Alice replied. "In actuality, true knowledge of the Craft in Europe had dwindled almost to extinction by the Renaissance. However, two competing factions had a vested interest in pretending that witches were abundant. Early modern England was a very misogynistic place in which to live. Women had few rights to property or even their lives. Only widows could hold land or significant amounts of money in their names. As a result, many men considered wealthy widows a danger to society. Such women of independent means, unbound to a man for support or approval, might encourage other women to disobey or rebel against their fathers, husbands, the King, or the Church. The solution to divesting them of this place of power in society would be to find a way to take their lands and fortunes. That was the true purpose of witch hunting."

"Which makes sense, from a purely diabolical standpoint," Elliott shrugged. "Take away a woman's means of support, and you take away her power."

Mary agreed. "That explains why so many women accused of witchcraft in the early days were widows. It simply would not do to have middle-aged and senior matrons gallivanting around doing whatever they pleased and setting allegedly poor examples for younger generations of women. They had to be punished."

"True," Alice seconded. "However, on the opposite side of this battle of wills, women who were not true witches, or who possessed only marginal and often untrained abilities within the Craft, saw that there was power too in being thought of as a witch. These women, often quite poor economically and lacking in education, found places within society as minor herbalists or fortune tellers. Hoping that others' superstitious fear of witches would allow them to live free of harassment caused by their low social status, these women welcomed accusations of witchcraft. They viewed it as a shield."

"Some shield," Elliott scoffed. "Unless it was used in the old Roman way. To carry out the dead."

"Sadly, you are correct," Alice continued. "Which brings us back to my tale. By 1612, fifteen years after the publication of King James's *Daemonologie*, witch hunting had become an established method in England of getting rid of anyone. Especially women and girls who didn't conform to the ideals of society, for reasons of poverty, sexuality, or just irascible temperament. The county I was from, Lancashire, was especially given to such actions. My family, who were witches by both heredity and training, were mostly wise enough to keep mum. However, two families of women from the second category I have described were not. The Device family and the Chattox family, both very old and once respected, had fallen upon hard times. Most of the men had died, and the women attempted to make their living as folk healers and through basic efforts at prognostication. Having little real knowledge in these areas, though, their efforts were often unsuccessful. They began to make enemies due to their chicanery. Nevertheless, the Devices continued to live in the crumbling ruins of Malkin Tower, which had been their ancestral home. This drew the jealousy of the Chattox's, who were in even more dire straits. The two families began to squabble with one another. Accusations of theft and destructive magick started to swirl around their feud. Of course, all of it was brought out into the public eye in sordid detail when Alison Device was accused of murder."

"Did she kill one of the Chattox's?" I asked.

"Strangely, no," Alice replied. "Alison Device never killed anyone to my knowledge, unless it was through innocent ineptitude at concocting herbal remedies. No, the accusation of murder against Alison Device that started the Pendle Witch trials was simply absurd. Alison was on the way home one day when she came across a peddler named John Law. Alison asked John to open his pack to buy some metal pins, which were expensive and hard to come by in those days. Not wanting to bother with such a small sale, and probably because he thought Alison could not pay due to her shabby clothing, John Law refused. Angered at being dismissed because of her poverty, Alison screamed a curse at the man. John immediately stumbled, fell, and hit his head. The injury turned out to be more severe than anyone realized. John Law died the next day, after telling several people, including the Justice of the Peace, Roger Nowell, that a witch named Alison Device had struck him down with her curse."

"That was quite a stretch," I said. "Why did they believe him? Was Alison not articulate enough to defend herself?"

"You would think that might have been the case, but no," Alice shook her head, struggling with the irony. "'Twas the opposite. Thinking she could scare them into leaving her alone by claiming to be a witch, Alison stated she had made a pact with the Devil that gave her special powers. Also, she said she allowed a black dog, who was her familiar, to suckle on her, and the dog had helped her lame John Law. Last, Alison claimed her entire family, especially her grandmother, who was called Old Demdike, all possessed magickal powers, as did the family that they had feuded with for years, the Chattox's. Alison's confession was enough for the authorities to begin arresting everyone associated with the two families, whether young daughters, sisters, men, or merely friends who tried to help them. In the confusion, once they figured out that pretending to be witches would not help them gain freedom, they all turned on one another. Accusations of murder and consorting with the Devil flew so thick in the courtroom that it was impossible to follow who might be guilty of what. In the end, though, none of it mattered. They were all hanged, except me and Old Demdike. She died in jail, and I... well, I'm still ashamed to admit it after all this time. My father paid a hefty bribe to save me. Blood will out."

"Wait," I said, confused. "How did you get caught up in all their mess? Were you related to them?"

"By the stars, no!" Alice exclaimed, throwing up her hands. "Forgive me for sounding elitist, but I was never so ill-bred or ill-mannered as they. Being truthful and humble never cost anyone a shilling. I have known many fine people who maintained their dignity even in the face of extreme hardships. That was not the case with those women. They lied brazenly about their abilities within the Craft. Although no one deserves what happened to them, I cannot help but think the Rule of Three circled back upon them as punishment."

Alice sighed. "I became associated with the Device family because I tried to help them. After the first round of accusations landed Alison, Old Demdike, Mrs. Chattox, and her daughter in jail, the remainder of their families begged anyone in the community who might be sympathetic for assistance. A meeting was held in their home, Malkin Tower, to decide what might be done. Alice Nutter, who was part of a wealthy family in the area, took pity and offered money to help support them during their defense. However, they turned on her too. They thought that if one of the wealthy Nutter family were accused, then the court might be persuaded to see the absurdity of the situation. It didn't work, though. Mostly because the Nutters were too humiliated to go through with paying the bribe to save their daughter. Alice Nutter hanged alongside the rest of them. Being a real witch myself, I offered to visit the women in jail and teach them some simple spells that would help them escape. My family wasn't poor, but they weren't wealthy either. Just village merchants. Alison and the rest had often come in selling eggs or mushrooms. We had spoken about her wanting to learn more about herbalism to see if she could become adept enough at compounding potions and elixirs to charge for it. At the time, I saw no harm in teaching the poor woman a few remedies. However, when they were accusing everyone they could think of in hopes of saving their hides, my name came up. I was brought in to stand trial. Because my father, unlike the Nutters, went through with paying the bribe for my freedom, the court was willing to believe the tale I told. That I had no knowledge of witchcraft and merely knew the family through trade at my father's shops. Under oath, I claimed I had attended the meeting at Malkin Tower in hopes of persuading them all to confess to the crime," Alice rolled her eyes, "of witchcraft."

"That was good of your father, to save you," I said. "Did it cost him a lot of money?"

"My entire dowry," Alice replied sadly. "Perhaps it was just as well. No Lancashire man would have married me after the scandal. My parents and I decided it would be best if I went to live with my mother's family in Scotland. It was from her side that I inherited the Craft. There in Scotland, I learned how to wield it. Mother kept her practice secret for many years after her marriage. Yet, she and Father agreed that if I was going to have a reputation trailing after me as a witch for the rest of my life, at least I should be educated fully in what that meant and how best to protect myself."

"Which, as it turns out, with the benefit of three centuries of hindsight, was a very wise choice," Mary concluded. "Regardless, the lesson to be learned from Alice's trial is that sharing the knowledge of what you've learned here at Rookes College, or even the fact that you are a member of the Craft, can be extremely dangerous. Even in these far more enlightened times, the fact that outsiders, especially women, could have abilities exceeding anything that wealth could buy is threatening to those who have traditionally held that power."

Mary glanced around the room at all of us, then rested her gaze on Elliott. "However, that is not to say you must remain silent or believe yourself without allies. Never forget that although our secrets must be kept, you are never alone in keeping them."

Chapter Twenty-One

That night, not long after I fell asleep, I was awakened by a tapping at my window. Thinking that it must be Stella or one of the other rooks, I reluctantly rolled out of bed and drew back the curtain. The bird sitting on the windowsill was a stranger to me, with its brown wings and thick, white legs covered in speckles. A hawk, I thought, or something similar. When I opened the window, it hopped in and lifted its right leg toward me. I untied the note from its bright yellow foot, unrolled it, and read:

Meet me out by the boat slips. Bring Freyja back with you, but no one else.

The note was unsigned, but I recognized the untidy handwriting as Elliott's.

"What does he want?" I wondered aloud to the bird, who cocked her head sideways at me and shifted impatiently from one leg to the other. Wanting to seem as inconspicuous as possible, I did not put on a robe over my nightgown. Instead, I changed back into my old-fashioned outdoor outfit of riding pants, a button-down shirt, and boots. As I changed, Freyja followed me. She hopped around the room and occasionally fluttered up to just above shoulder height, circling, and then landing on the floor again. The bird seemed frustrated.

Then, I remembered how Elliott described his Nan's bird. Freyja wasn't a hawk; she was a falcon. I was supposed to carry her, but I wasn't sure how. The thought of her long-taloned feet on my shoulder made me wince. Looking back into the clothes cupboards, I found a brown tweed jacket with elbow patches, the kind English professors wore in old movies. Putting it on, I extended my arm. Freyja swooped up immediately to land on it. The bird was heavy, so I nudged her up to perch on my shoulder. She happily nibbled at the hair tucked behind my ear for a moment, as if to say,

Good job! You finally figured it out. Animals... we don't train them. They train us.

Slipping out the back door of the Spirit tower, I padded across the grass toward the pier. When I arrived, I saw Elliott sitting at the end of it, his feet dangling over the water. Freyja fluttered down from my shoulder to rest between us.

"What's with all the mystery?" I asked, sitting down on the pier next to him.

"Read this," Elliott said, passing me a rolled-up newspaper. "Nan sent it to me. We don't get them stateside."

The masthead said *The Augur,* and the headline read *Albion Oil's Grip on Southeastern American Coastline Tightens, Grand Council Concerned.* The article below included a map of the East Coast, dotted from Virginia to the tip of Florida with a series of tiny line drawings that looked like oil derricks. Each one had coordinates printed on the side of it and a line drawn out to a black-and-white sketch of a hurricane.

"Look at how many they plan to build before the end of the year," Elliott said. "The problem isn't just that some random hurricane might hit the area here at Rookes, it's that *any* hurricane would inevitably have to hit one of the new rigs somewhere. The Grand Council already knows it is an inevitability. They're trying to decide which pathway would be the least destructive to both people and the environment if it were subjected to an oil spill."

"That's terrifying," I said, continuing to scan the article. It ran for several pages, spelling out many different scenarios predicted by various well-known prognosticators, all of them disastrous. "The letter that I got from Dad yesterday said they were the most safely constructed oil rigs he'd seen. Why would the government allow them to be built if it were so sure to be a problem? Aren't there rules or laws or some kind of standards for that?"

"You would think there would be more regulations already in place before they even allowed construction to begin," Elliott replied. "But nope. Drilling on the East Coast is a new frontier. Albion's contracts with the Southern states were signed before there was any time to enact many restrictions. Are the rigs the safest that your dad has ever seen? Probably so, if he's only seen the ones off the coast of Texas, where hurricanes are less powerful and frequent. Will those same standards be enough to endure multiple direct hits, sometimes in a single season, as many parts of the East Coast get? The Grand Council doesn't think so. If you read to the very end, they're sending exploratory committees over from Britain to begin recruiting witches to get ready, since the news on this side of the pond isn't carrying the story."

"Ready for what? Relief efforts?" I asked, incredulous. "Wouldn't that be handled already by the National Guard or the Red Cross?"

Elliott lowered his chin and stared at me. "Witches believe in preventing disasters before they happen, rather than trying to clear them up afterwards. The Grand Council thinks that if they can gather as many witches together as possible to raise a large enough cone of power, then they can direct it at whatever hurricane might approach first. The thinking is that if they can allow it to come close enough to be a near miss, that might scare the American federal government into action due to public outcry."

"Maybe it's just because of how we did it earlier this week," I said. "But I thought witches had to be gathered closely together to raise a cone of power."

"They do," Elliott replied simply.

I should have known the answer to my next question before I even asked it. However, I've always been bad about ignoring the truth when it's right in front of my face. "Then, where would they all go to be together and still not conspicuous?"

Elliott motioned with his chin at the castle behind us. *Here.*

Of course, it made perfect sense. An almost empty castle that could house up to five hundred witches. Plus, Rookes was already veiled by centuries-old glamor, in one of the most common hurricane alleys on the East Coast. Even if they had to be moved to another location closer to the danger on short notice, hundreds of witches could already be assembled and standing by waiting for action when a storm approached. Still, my mind reeled with anxiety about what the influx of hundreds of witches might mean. *When would they arrive? Would we even be able to finish our training? What would happen to Rookes College?*

"Calm down," Elliott said. "One thing at a time. The Grand Council never does anything quickly. Since it's not likely the oil rigs will be completed and operational before the end of this year's hurricane season, the threat of a spill isn't imminent. They probably won't start gathering witches on campus until after we've dismissed for the summer at Beltane.

After that, who knows? Perhaps it would only take one season, and one close call, for the American government to intervene and put a stop to the drilling due to the hazards it poses. Or the Grand Council might still take a wait-and-see approach. That would cause the next year's class to be delayed or canceled. If they chose a more permanent solution," Elliott motioned at the copy of *The Augur* that I held in my hands, "then the Grand Council does have the right to commandeer any educational institution for witches as an essential outpost during times of crisis. If they decided that's what it would take to maintain safety from across the pond, it is well within their power to do so."

"That would kill Mary," I said. "Her whole life, her identity, is intertwined with this place. To have it overtaken by the Grand Council, whom she has argued against to maintain the vision of Rookes College as an institution dedicated to educating witches from all backgrounds, it would..." I trailed off.

"It would give the Grand Council a way to justify what they've always wanted to do," Elliott said. "To control magickal education and limit its access to only a few—the chosen elite of hereditary witches who were deemed worthy enough to pass on knowledge of the Craft. If the Rookes alumni or anyone else tried to protest," Elliott shrugged. "What argument could they legitimately make on behalf of keeping the college open and dedicated to its purpose? How could the education of an ever-dwindling population of hedge witches per year compare to the protection of an entire coastline for one of the world's most important countries?"

"It can't," I said, flipping through the paper and scanning the lengthy article once more. At the end of it was a political cartoon of an octopus. Each of its eight tentacles held either an oil rig blowing black gold out of its top or a bloated-looking politician clutching a fistful of dollars and wearing a top hat with the name of a state written on it: North Carolina, South Carolina, Georgia, and Florida. The beast itself was branded across its forehead with the name of Elliott's father's company, Albion Oil. Each of the politicians had a bubble coming out of his mouth saying something like, *Albert told us all was well*, or *If Capell agrees, it's good enough for me*.

"It must be hard," I said, setting the paper aside. "Being his kid."

Elliott snorted. "You have no idea. If Mary hadn't reached out to me, I'd have probably been the only magickal dude in England in decades who hadn't committed some wild crime and landed in juvenile detention to be denied an education. Do you know what happens to witches who never learn to control their magick?"

I shook my head *no*.

"Most of them end up in asylums. It drives them crazy, knowing that somehow they're different but they can't put their finger on why exactly. Learning what their powers are and how to use them properly saves them." Elliott looked down at the crumpled paper. "Most of them anyway. It didn't work for Pop, even though Mary tried. Sometimes, a bad egg is just a bad egg."

"I don't think you're like him though," I said. Elliott stared at the dock blankly but said nothing. "I mean it. Look, I don't know anything about your father or what he's like now, but at one time there must have been something inside Albert Capell special enough for Mary to have left him a key. And for Albert to have picked it up. Then, somehow his life took a turn, and he became whatever he is now. An opportunist at best, a pariah at worst, for what he's done. But the thing is, you don't have to take the same turn." I gestured out across the water in front of me. "From here, there are infinite possibilities."

As I dropped my arms, my left hand brushed against his. Surprisingly, he caught it for a moment and held it tight. His grip was warm and soft, but a little too firm. Trying to intwine my fingers more comfortably with his, I stepped closer to him and met his intense, searching gaze. Instantly, he dropped my hand and turned away.

"For you maybe, but for me?" Elliott shrugged. "Where do I go after I leave Rookes? Back to England, where anyone who cares to investigate will find I'm the dreaded Albert Capell's only boy? Stay here in America, where I'm soon to be the same? There's no path on this Earth I could choose that would lead me anywhere I'd want to be."

His frustration made me realize it. Why a gorgeous guy like Elliott would be interested in a girl like me. On the surface, we were opposites, but inside, we were very much the same. We both craved stability but were afraid of getting hurt if we tried to rely on it. His way of dealing with it was getting all self-doubting and philosophical. The stubborn horse who stood his ground. Mine was to run. Create a distraction. At that moment, I had no answers for him. I knew that running was only hope I could offer. When a person needs to get away from themselves, there's nothing better to be than a bolter. And there's no better bolter in the world than a fox.

"Then don't choose," I said. "Follow me instead." Instinctively, I pulled my feet back up under me, pushed away from the pier, and dove into the water with a splash.

The water was surprisingly deep just twenty feet from the shore. I kicked off my boots and swam down, further and further, until my feet touched the sandy bottom. Rebounding off it, I rocketed to the surface. Just in time to see Elliott disappearing beneath the water behind me. I ducked under again. Thinking of the black fox that I'd been earlier that day, I wriggled out of the rest of my clothes. I could feel the fur growing to cover my body. Paddling over to a sandbar, I pulled myself out and shook dry.

Elliott bobbed up from the water, still in human form. "What in the hell?" he sputtered. Then, he grinned and submerged beneath the surface once more. Moments later, the water churned as the sable stallion of his familiar form clambered up onto the shore. He sneezed. I hurried over and rubbed my muzzle along the side of his nose. The foxy equivalent of a hug.

Instantly, I could feel my paws rising off the sandy shore. I froze, catching my reflection in Elliott's big gray eyes. I could see that he was excited too, as he stomped on the ground.

I'm doing it! I'm really flying! I exclaimed. When Elliott perked up his ears, that's when I realized that not only was I flying, but I was speaking as a fox too. Yet, in my fox form, my voice was not my own. High pitched and strange, but in weirdly understandable English.

Still in my fox, I sailed across the inlet, over the boats, and back onto the pier. Looking over the water, I could still see Elliott standing on the sandbar. His horse's form paced along the water's edge, trying to decide how best to get back. Waving my tail, I bounced back and forth on the pier. Squealing and barking with excitement, I yipped, *Just jump! You can do it!*

Elliott pawed the ground, took off at a gallop, and jumped. He hit the water with a splash and went down. Then, rising from the water and into the air, he glided back across the inlet. He hit the deck of the pier with all four hooves at once, nearly knocking me back into the water. After we'd calmed down from the excitement of making it across, we realized we had a problem.

Our robes were back at the castle, and our clothes were somewhere on the bottom of the ocean. Elliott snickered, and I... well, I guess it is possible to say a fox can laugh. The sound I made was more like air escaping from a squeaking balloon. Without saying a word, the two of us trotted off to our rooms to change back into our human forms. Thank goodness I had left the door ajar as I crept out. Or perhaps someone was watching and propped it open for us? I've never really been sure. Sometimes, it's better not to know.

Book Two

The Wheel of the Year

Chapter Twenty-Two

The next weeks flew by in a blur of lessons that were thankfully free of further drama. Before I knew it, we were gathered around our tables for the Mabon feast. The center dais was decorated with five cornucopias were filled with tiny baby pumpkins of orange, white, and green, alongside an abundance of pomegranates. In the center, an enormous bouquet of sunflowers bowed their heads as a cloud of monarch butterflies fluttered, alighting here and there among them. Mary had charmed them into lingering to rest with us for a few days before continuing their migration.

It was tender-hearted Miranda's idea that our harvest meal should be vegetarian. She'd finally mustered up the courage to tell all of us that she'd never felt comfortable eating animals, even though her hunting-crazy Florida family made fun of her for it. We'd decided to pool our magickal cooking skills to focus on seasonal vegetables from the gardens around the college, with a variety of freshly made pasta and cheeses, and a rainbow of gelato flavors for dessert. Watching the other girls make food fly out from the kitchen and onto their plates was when it hit me. This was our life now. We could make any kind of small daily thing happen that we wanted. I suppose that was when it occurred to me too that, if we were lucky enough to have been gifted with the ability to enjoy the bounty of this extraordinary kind of existence, it only seemed fair that we should give something back.

After dinner, Alice and I went for a stroll out through the orchard. We'd become close friends after I'd finally confessed to her that I'd read her grimoire cover to cover, searching in vain for a spell that would make my hair perfectly bouncy and curly like hers, but found nothing. Alice almost fell down laughing before she explained it wasn't magick at all. She put pin curls in her hair every night. I asked her why she took the trouble when she could just make it happen so much more easily with a few words or a wave of her wand. Alice said she thought it was important sometimes to remind herself she could do some things without magick. Her comment was meant to be off the cuff, but I interpreted it as having a deeper meaning. I compared Alice's choice with similar habits I'd observed among the other mentors. For each of them, it seemed, magick alone wasn't always the answer to every situation.

As we walked, both Alice and I carried hand-woven wicker baskets to gather apples and pears. I could tell there was something on her mind and that she was trying to figure out the best way to say it. Finally, I just asked her. Subtlety has never been my strongest suit.

"The other Mentors have asked me if I would ask you whether you would feel comfortable speaking to your father again. To see if there was anything he could do to persuade Albert to wait until after the next hurricane season to open the wells," Alice asked.

"Why next season?" I said, answering her question with another. "I thought the goal was to get Albion Oil to stop operations completely as soon as possible?"

"It is," Alice replied. She pretended to examine the wormhole in one overripe apple before tossing it away. "According to everyone's predictions, Katerina's especially, it appears this upcoming hurricane season in particular is the one that we should worry about."

"So..." I stalled, not knowing specifically what Alice was asking of me.

"We'd like you to go out to the field station." Alice finished, looking like she was relieved to deliver the message at last. "Talk to Oliver in person. If we could get Albion to postpone opening the wells until at least the end of next year, that would give us time to begin work on trying to stop them from opening at all by persuading the proper governmental authorities. If you know what I mean," Alice leaned over her basket with this last statement, raising one dark, perfectly sculpted eyebrow.

I knew exactly what Alice meant. Although nothing had been stated explicitly, over the last eight weeks, I'd picked up on the fact that there were more than a few witches in strategic political positions. Women and men who were, in the parlance of the musical *Hamilton*, in the rooms where things happened. As I mentioned before, I had no problem with helping out the cause. I knew what the consequences of a hurricane strike might be.

However, I did have a few logistical questions. Even though Oliver and I had been corresponding through messages carried by Stella on a weekly basis, I still had no idea of his exact location. Most of his letters were vaguely upbeat, discussing my corgi Luna's latest exploits or describing some arcane details of his work. Yet, when I thought about it, Oliver said curiously little about his living situation. Even though I knew it must be a big adjustment, going from his cabin in the mountains where he'd nested for over a decade to a random temporary place on the coast. It made me feel a little guilty for not asking. Though, I suppose that's how things are with daughters and dads. We're often so wrapped up in our feelings that we don't stop to consider theirs. Dads are like trees in that aspect. Strong and sheltering, we don't notice they're vulnerable until they're uprooted or someone cuts them down.

"I'd be happy to help, but I'm ashamed to say I don't know where the field station is," I replied.

"Fortunately, I do," Alice said. "It's on Ocracoke Island. The only way to get there is to fly or to take the ferry. Since you're still a bit new to the air and unfamiliar with the territory, I'd recommend the ferry for your first trip. It doesn't stop here on our island, but the Cedar Island Ferry that passes just to the left, heading northeast, will take us there."

"You're coming with me?" I asked.

"Yes," Alice answered. "At least, along the way to meet the ferry and back. As I mentioned in our first lesson, the safe place that I always like to envision when I disappear is a ferry station in Lancashire. They are very handy places for magickal folk to meet. Our conversations cannot be eavesdropped upon while we're over the water. Since your father has moved on from your old home while you've been away here at Rookes, I thought the field station might be a convenient place for you to get to know. It's quite lovely and peaceful, especially in the wintertime when the tourists are few. Plus, I plan for us to take a rowboat out to meet the ferry. It will allow you to experience what it's like to go through the glamor surrounding our island physically over water, without disappearing. It's quite an experience. One that should be taken slowly to truly appreciate, I think."

"But won't we be kind of..." I searched for the right word. "Conspicuous? I mean, people don't just row up to a means of public transportation and climb over the side, do they? Aren't there, like, rules?"

Alice chuckled. "Perhaps. I'm not sure. If there are, then they don't apply to us. It's easier to show you why than to explain it. You'll see. Just meet me out by the pier tomorrow morning with your black formal cloak. It's the one we use for traveling. Wear your normal clothes otherwise, since you'll be among regular people most of the day."

The next morning was a Sunday when we usually practiced our lessons from the previous week one-on-one with our Mentors. After breakfast, I went upstairs as instructed to retrieve my formal cloak, which I stuffed into my sling bag. I changed back into the denim shorts and t-shirt that I'd had on when I first came to the island. Although I hadn't seen or thought about my old clothes in weeks, they were neatly laundered and folded in a stack on my dressing table. It didn't surprise me as it should have. By then, I'd become accustomed to things around Rookes falling into place just as I needed them.

What caught me off guard was Alice's appearance at the pier. Gone were her long black gown and perfectly curled hair. Instead, she was dressed casually, in dark jeans and a light gray cotton v-neck sweater. Her lustrous dark brown hair was not curled but instead caught up in a ponytail. Strapped across her chest was a slim, waxed canvas messenger bag, in which I assumed she carried her cloak. Although she was still very pretty, it was more of a normal kind of attractiveness. The kind that made one's glance linger an extra second or two at a train station or while waiting in line for coffee and wonder what life might be like to be born into a family wealthy enough that dressing flashy was considered passé. One in which sophistication was shown by polish rather than ostentation. Alice's uncomplicated beauty made me wonder how many times I'd passed other witches on the street and never guessed they were magick.

The rowboat was exceptionally ordinary too. Made of wood, the hull was painted green. It had two bench seats with a pair of oars tucked inside. After we pushed away from the pier, I reached for the oars, but Alice waved me off.

"We're not roughing it that hard," she said. "At least, not until we pass through the glamor, where anyone can see us." Reaching over the side, Alice wiggled her fingertips across the surface of the water, making little splashes. Suddenly, the boat lurched forward. I could see a small current rippling in our wake, carrying us along. The rest of the water further out continued to move smoothly in the opposite direction. For about fifteen minutes, we sped along, heading straight out into the Ocracoke Inlet. When I turned to look back, the main castle of Rookes College had receded in the distance so that it almost seemed like a very short lighthouse.

"Look ahead," Alice pointed. "Do you see it? We're going to go through the edge of the glamor in about ten more minutes."

I looked over the horizon to where Alice indicated. The morning sun, which always seemed as if it were behind at least a thin veil of clouds when we were at Rookes, was much brighter, though still far from the intensity one might expect when being on the ocean so soon after sunrise. Instead, it was as if I were seeing the sunlight diffused through a frosted glass pane or a sheet of waxed paper. I asked Alice what was causing the effect.

"That's the glamor," she replied. "If you think it's hard to see through on this side, just wait until you see it from the other." As we came closer, I could see the water too had an unusual sheen. The air became thickly humid.

"Better put on your cloak and pull your hood up to cover your face," Alice instructed when we were within about a hundred yards from the edge. "The glamor deflects the sunlight like a prism, which puts off heat. If it's too warm, you could get a steam burn from the moisture in the air. It's uncomfortable, but only for a moment, so you don't want to linger in it. Otherwise, you'll come out covered in sweat on the other side. Also, it's best if you close your eyes. It always makes me see spots for several minutes afterward if I don't."

Alice reached down into the bottom of the rowboat and took our cloaks from their bags. We both put them on, pulling them fully closed so that we were covered from head to toe. I didn't need to ask when we entered the glamor because I could feel the heat of it through my cloak. Even through the thick, heavy black wool and my closed eyelids, I could sense the intensity of its light. Then, after less than a minute, it was over. Tapping me on the shoulder, Alice told me it was safe to remove my cloak but to turn around and look forward, not backward, as we were still too close to the glamor's edge. Looking out over the bow, there was nothing but rippling waves as far as the eye could see. Behind me, I could hear Alice stirring around. She removed her cloak and picked up the oars to begin rowing away from the edge of the glamor.

"I wanted you to experience that and to have a bit of familiarity with the surroundings so you will know where to meet me on the way back," Alice explained. "I'm going to fly on with you to meet the ferry, but then I need to return to Rookes. I have another errand to run today. You can ask the ferryman the way to the field station from the harbor. It's not far to walk, and the path is obvious. I'll return at sunset to meet you right about here. There is an evening ferry that comes back along the same route. All you will need to do is fly in the exact opposite direction from how we are about to go. We're far enough away now that if you want to turn around and get your bearings, it's safe."

Rotating around on my bench seat, I could see the glamor from the opposite side. It was still insanely bright, but if I hadn't known it was there, it would have seemed like very hazy sunlight reflecting off the water. Weirdly, it was as if there were no end to it. I was completely disoriented. "So, that's what the sailors see," I said. "When they come up close to the island. No wonder they can't tell it's there!"

"Yes, a great many ships were wrecked in these waters, from here up to Cape Hatteras. That's why the Outer Banks are called the Graveyard of the Atlantic. Hundreds were lost to storms and sandbars, and long ago, to pirates or local wreckers. One of my dearest friends was aboard one of those unlucky vessels that caught hell from all of them. Thank God Mary saw it in time. You may have heard of her. Theodosia Burr, daughter of Aaron Burr?"

"The Vice President who killed Alexander Hamilton?" I asked, incredulous. "Um... how could I not know? I've only seen the musical twice in person and dozens of times on streaming. And the soundtrack was number one on my phone's most-played list last year." Alice gave me a puzzled look, as I realized she had no idea what I was talking about. "Forget it. How do you know Theodosia Burr?"

"That's a long story for another time," Alice replied. Pulling on her cloak again, she motioned for me to do the same. As she covered herself, Alice disappeared from view. "We will fly the rest of the way to the ferry from here. The cloaks will keep us concealed. I've already purchased a ticket for you, but I'm going to turn around once it's in sight." Alice reached out a hand from beneath her cloak to give me the ticket. It looked strange, kind of like Thing from the Addams Family, just floating out there in the air. I took the ticket and stuck it into the back pocket of my jeans.

Alice continued. "The way I've always done it is to keep my cloak on until I find a washroom. Then, I go inside one of the stalls, take it off, and put it in my bag. Then, whenever I'm ready to fly off again, I just reverse the process. Go into a stall, put it on, and slip away. Works like a charm unless the washroom's crowded. You'd be surprised how little people notice one another in public spaces."

She must have felt me staring at her, because Alice added, "What? You're surprised the cloaks have a practical function, beyond being the height of gothic fashion? I assure you we don't use them to spy on one another at school. Their invisibility only works when we're outside the glamor. Even then, only the black ones are treated with the spell that creates the effect. The brightly colored robes are just ceremonial. Formal travel cloaks are always dyed black because the ingredients stain the fabric dark anyway. It's more sensible. Hides dirt too."

"New magic isn't that shocking to me anymore," I answered. "I've learned to expect the unexpected in that department. What I'm wondering is why you bothered to buy a ticket for the ferry. Couldn't I just keep my cloak on the entire time and ride for free?"

"Free riding!" Alice scoffed. "Certainly not! Have some dignity. An upstanding woman always pays her way. We're witches, not criminals!"

Chapter Twenty-Three

Following Alice's directions along the walk from the ferry harbor to the field station, I found the building Oliver described in his letters easily enough. It was much larger than I imagined. A quick search on my once-again operational cell phone informed me that the large white structure with the red roof had been a Coast Guard station but had transitioned into a research center. Appropriate for what Oliver was working on since it was likely to have plenty of room to house all the laboratory equipment that he would need.

Walking around the perimeter of the building to the pier, I spotted Dad. He was wearing his usual early fall uniform of jeans with a plaid shirt rolled up to the elbows. Walking Luna while chatting on his phone as I approached, Oliver didn't notice me right away. Luna did, however, and she immediately began yipping and struggling against her leash to run to me. Ending the call, Dad unfastened Luna's leash. Like a streak of furry, tri-colored lightning, Luna darted through the marsh grass, nearly knocking me down as she leaped into my arms.

"Somebody missed her big sister." Dad smiled as I struggled to breathe through a cloud of free-floating corgi fur. "I have too. Come here!" We hugged and then walked back up the path to the station, both careful not to acknowledge the oddity of my unexpected presence.

Inside, Dad showed me around his apartment in the upstairs rooms, which were maintained like a private officer's suite from the main building's Coast Guard days. It was a little bland but comfortable, with an iron bed and coastal-style, whitewashed wooden furniture throughout. In his usual way, Dad had done his best to bring the outdoors in. He'd filled the shelves not only with books but also shells, sea glass, and pieces of driftwood doubtlessly picked up on the surrounding beaches. I noticed too that all of my geodes and crystals had been carefully arranged among them. Seeing them made me remember all the hours Dad spent over the years telling me stories of his travels. It made my heart hurt to think of him alone here, with only Luna for company.

Following him downstairs, Dad showed me around his lab. Oliver had all sorts of experiments working, from seawater composition analysis to geologic mineral testing with samples taken from the ocean floor around the rig building sites. As we weaved our way among them, I tried to keep up with the swift pace of his explanations on the significance of each one. Soon, I was lost. Mostly because I was distracted thinking about my reason for visiting and also by seeing how settled he was in the place. It dawned on me that he'd set up an entirely new life during my absence, a feeling that gnawed at the pit of my stomach. I realized why some witches chose to leave the magickal world behind periodically, in which time stood virtually still, even though it caused them to age in real-time. Stepping back into reality without enough mental preparation could be jarring. The longer one was away, the worse it would be.

Oliver could tell something else was on my mind near the end of the tour. "Well, I think that's about enough pebbles and ponds for the day. Don't want to bore you stiff. Why don't we take the boat out for a spin?" Dad suggested.

In several of our letters, I'd mentioned Alice's recommendation regarding the usefulness of speaking over water to shield private conversations. I've always been grateful for my dad's very British sense of subtlety, his uncanny sense of knowing just when a change in conversation was needed, and his ability to understate the obvious. Parental intuition is perhaps the most underappreciated type of magic. Nodding, I agreed and followed him once more out to the pier. Luna trotted along behind us.

Once we were aboard a smallish red and white cruiser, Dad steered the boat along the coastline of Silver Lake to a likely-looking fishing spot, then cut the motor. Tossing Luna a rawhide chew and handing me a fishing rod, we baited our hooks with shrimp for flounder as he waited on me to get around to what I'd come there to say.

"Do you remember Alice from my letters?" I asked.

Oliver nodded as he cast his line along an abandoned boat dock that drifted loosely behind us. He twirled the reel slowly, allowing the bait to sink to the bottom.

"Well, Alice wanted me to come here and speak with you about finding some sort of legitimate reason for delaying the opening of the new offshore rigs until after next year's hurricane season has passed," I continued.

Oliver's eyes remained fixed on the calm ripples of the water as he reeled and cast again. "You know that's not going to happen. And it's not just because Albion's got investors breathing down their necks. A lot goes into an operation like this, and there are many moving parts. Four state governments have plenty riding on an on-time opening too. It's already figured into their next year's budgets. That's why they've put me up here." Oliver motioned over his shoulder back toward the station. "It's state property. After this initial construction phase is completed, they've been talking about keeping me and the rest of the team on permanently as government employees to make sure that all regulations continue to be followed. It would be a secure job that would allow us to buy another house. Also, it gives me peace of mind that, even if I did have to sell out to *The Man*." Dad placed his fishing rod in the holder attached to the side of his seat and made air quotes with his fingers. "Then, at least, it would be on the up and up."

"But what if something went wrong?" I asked. "Something unexpected."

The end of Oliver's line jerked a bit in the water, and he picked up his rod. "Willow, you and I both know there are risks associated with any petroleum extraction operation. But believe me, after dodging this kind of work for so long on ethical grounds, even though it paid three times as much, I wouldn't be involved with this one if it weren't the safest I'd seen. The seafloor conditions truly are ideal. Resources are close to the surface and easy to extract with minimal disturbance. Albion's got a huge team—not just me—monitoring it ceaselessly. They've staked their entire future on this being a success. And even though Big Oil is usually the last place anyone would look to protect the environment, this time, they're trying to do it right. Mostly from monetary motivations, I'm sure, but that's beside the point. Barring some unforeseen catastrophe, nothing is going to stop Albion Oil from opening those wells before the end of May next year."

"What if a catastrophe were foreseen, though?" I insisted. "Like a hurricane."

I could almost see the wheels turning in Dad's brain as he cautiously rotated the reel until it clicked, carefully setting the hook to pull. "I think I know what you're getting at. Even if that lot you've been studying with had the most accurate crystal ball in the world and were able to tell the exact day that a hurricane was going to land right on top of us, it wouldn't matter."

Oliver jerked the line, and the empty hook popped out of the water. Sighing, he finished reeling it in, threaded the shiny hook with another shrimp, and cast again. "Don't you think every possible weather condition has already been taken into account in building these rigs? The upper brass at Albion hired the best concrete and steel engineers to build the platforms, the best mechanical engineers to design the safety cut-off valves, and the best meteorologists to tell them when to use them. Witches don't have the market cornered on predicting the weather, you know. Scientists have their kind of magic for that too."

"But what about..." I began.

"What about if you worry too much?" Dad finished, setting the rod back into its pocket beside his seat. "Willow, look. I'm not doubting that a hurricane will hit this area at some point. And I'm not doubting that Alice and Mary and all the rest of the ladies at Rookes whom you've written about can accurately predict when Nature will act. What I do doubt, though, is whether they've taken into account how far science has advanced to protect men and their investments on this Earth when it does. You know I'm as big of a tree-hugging old hippie as there can be in this world. Sometimes we've just got to change with the times and put faith in ourselves. We've got to believe that science can help us protect our efforts in utilizing the resources that the Earth has to offer. Otherwise, how can we continue to move forward? How are we going to survive?"

Dad's earnest blue eyes locked with mine. I could see he believed in what he was saying, but I could also tell that it was because he desperately *wanted* to believe it. My dad needed this job badly. Not just for his day-to-day livelihood—he could go pick up a gig teaching science at any community college in America and make ends meet—but for reassurance. To prove to himself that by standing his ground and sticking to his career in fieldwork rather than switching to academia and moving to a bigger city, he hadn't just thrown his marriage and our family away with both hands for no legitimate reason.

Oliver wanted this gig with Albion to be both a path to financial security for us and also something more. An innovation. A new way of life. A solid piece of concrete evidence that he had made the right choice to let Mom walk away, and for me to stay with him. The need to have that kind of hope made his otherwise rational and highly skeptical brain incapable of entertaining any other possibilities besides success. Perhaps I knew that because I'd spent the last few weeks learning how to look into people's eyes and read what was written on their souls. More likely, it was because I was seeing something that I'd never seen before from my father. I was seeing him open up to me, as much as he was able, about being afraid.

I didn't press Dad any further. We spent the rest of the afternoon catching up and catching a few flounder. We brought the fish back to the field station. There, we filleted and roasted them with Cajun seasoning over the fire pit with some skewers of yellow squash and zucchini. We ate the flounder accompanied by white rice spiced with peppers, followed by s'mores for dessert. Oliver was mostly quiet, absorbing every detail of what I told him about my new life and what I was learning at Rookes while we were still out on the water. He waited until we were back onshore and had finished eating to ask questions.

"Show me," Dad said after dinner, rolling up the bag of marshmallows. Luna whined with dismay. He tossed her a graham cracker. She fell upon it, crunching. Then, Oliver pointed at the fire pit. "Make the fire go out. I want to see you do it."

Swallowing my last mouthful of chocolate, I put down my toasting fork, raised my right hand, then paused. Other than using my cloak to conceal my entrance onto the ferry, I'd never used magick outside of the Rookes College grounds. I had no idea if it would work.

Not wanting to give myself time to get psyched out, I moved quickly. Reaching as high as I could with my right hand over the fire, I swiped downward as if I were slamming a lid shut. A swift gust of air extinguished the fire, blowing a cloud of gray ashes over us. Dropping the remains of her graham cracker, Luna jumped up and growled at the now-inanimate fire pit as if it were alive. Through a fit of coughing, Oliver began to spout alternative explanations about why the fire had gone out. I was standing so close that my arm acted like a fan, he said. Pop-up storms caused all kinds of depressurizations in the air along the coast too. It must have been a coincidence.

"Wanna see me light it again?" I asked, smiling at his skepticism. This was the Dad I knew. Not the one who was scared to look too closely and see that he'd failed. The one who never believed anything anyone told him until he'd seen it with his own eyes at least twice.

Before he let me try, Dad set up a sort of magickal obstacle course. First, he made me turn out my pockets for anything flammable and stand on the far side of the patio. Next, he placed an easel with a giant-sized sheet of sticky pad note paper clipped on it between where I was and the fire pit. Then, he sifted through the ashes of the old fire with his bare hands, making sure there were no latent smoldering embers, restacked more kindling on top, and gauged the wind speed with a digital anemometer. Finally, he brought out his digital tablet, mounted it on a tripod at an angle to catch me, the paper, and the firepit, and pulled up a video recording app.

"Now," Dad said, pressing record. "Make it burn."

"I don't want to ruin your easel," I warned.

"I would love nothing better than for you to melt it down like a ball of foil," Oliver replied, peering into the tablet screen. "Go for it!"

All our Mentors at Rookes warned us against being overly theatrical when using our magick, but that time, I just couldn't help myself. Sure, I wanted to impress my dad. Also, I wanted to scare some healthy skepticism back into him by showing him something impossible to explain using science alone. Reaching into my sling bag, I pulled out my wand and thrust it skyward. Immediately, I could feel the energy begin to crackle in the air, through the wood of my wand, and warming my palm. From one tiny cloud high in the sky, a small roll of thunder echoed. The hair along Luna's spine stood up as she spun around barking.

"Dad," I said, as calmly as I could, echoing Cora's words from our first day at Rookes. "From today forward, you will know what it's like to have a daughter who can hold lightning in her hand." Whirling my wand in a circle, I felt the wind churning as I caught the thin, single streak of lightning that raced down from the sky. Throwing my wand arm forward, I cast it toward the firepit. The new kindling burst into flames with a loud crack that sent pieces of smoking wood flying in all directions. Luna dove for safety under a bench and began to howl. Dad staggered backward with the tablet tripod still clutched in his hands, tripped over the stone perimeter wall, and tumbled into the grass. I dashed over, hoping he wasn't hurt.

"I'm alright," Dad called gruffly. Waving me off as he stood up, he patted at a singed spot on the shoulder of his shirt. "Think I bodged the video though," he said, frowning as he peered into the replay on the tablet and holding it up for me to see the screen. "That pink blob's my finger over the lens. Must have grabbed onto it when I fell."

"That's okay," I replied. "It's probably best not to make a record of it anyway. Now that I think about it, I'm not sure what I'm allowed to do regarding magick outside of school."

After comforting Luna and tempting her from beneath the bench with a few otherwise forbidden marshmallows, we examined the remains of the easel. The paper was completely incinerated. All that was left of the top and legs were four globs of aluminum that had melted onto the stones of the patio.

"Blimey," Dad whispered several times. He held his hand over them, aware that the metal was still much too hot to touch. My whole life, I'd never known Oliver to lapse into the British slang of his youth unless he was, to use his parlance, *gobsmacked*, so I knew he was impressed. He glanced at the charred remains of kindling scattered around the patio, then squinted at the tiny cloud, gray and uncertain, from whence I had drawn down the lightning.

"And you can do that anytime now?" Dad asked finally after he rediscovered his vocabulary.

"I can do a lot of things," I replied, knowing he'd appreciate the understatement.

"I bet," he nodded, clearing his throat in the way that all dads do when they'd rather not call attention to being impressed by something. "I have another meeting with the structural engineers on Tuesday. I'll bring up what we discussed on the boat and send word of what I find out. The usual way. There may be some things we've overlooked on safety protocols after all."

We tidied up the patio area together, sweeping the burnt bits of wood into the fire pit, prying the cooled nuggets of aluminum off the flagstones, and tossing them in the recycling. Dad walked me back to the ferry stop with Luna in tow. I bought my ticket, and we stood waiting in that awkward kind of limbo that makes people feel as if they need to say something great.

"Yanno, some days, like today, I feel like a really lucky chap," Oliver said. "To be your dad, I mean. Other days mystified and confused. But today, really lucky."

"I feel lucky to be your daughter every day," I smiled, as I hugged him goodbye.

I timed everything just right on the way back to the college. Moments after the harbor on the south end of Ocracoke Island faded from view, I began to see the shimmer on the horizon indicating that the boat was nearing the edge of the glamor surrounding Rookes. Stepping into the tiny bathroom on board, I donned my black formal cloak. Slipping out again over the railing, I was unseen by the handful of passengers day-drinking their way back to the mainland. Guided by the setting sun to my right, I glided southward until I saw the rowboat Alice and I had taken that morning. Although it looked empty from a distance, I knew that was only because Alice was concealing herself with her cloak as she waited for me.

Sure enough, as soon as I landed and pulled back my hood, Alice did the same. We both laughed at how funny we looked. Two disembodied heads just floating there over a rowboat in the middle of the Atlantic Ocean. We rowed up to the edge of the glamor, chatting about my day. Once we'd passed through, Alice showed me how to work the spell with the water that propelled the boat on its own.

Alice was happy about my day with Oliver, but when I asked how her other errand had gone, she became serious. "The reason that I rushed off this morning is that I needed to help Elliott go through the glamor a different way," Alice explained. "Mary and the rest of us agreed that Elliott would go back and try to reason with Albert, just as you went today to speak with Oliver. About the visions we've all seen and the reason to wait until after the end of next season before opening the wells. Elliott flew to America on an airplane like a regular person when he first came to Rookes, but today we disappeared to Ireland. He'd never disappeared across the ocean before, so we thought it was best if he had some guidance. Sometimes, it can be difficult to keep oneself together when you've got so far to go. And I know you've felt firsthand how any kind of magick can become complicated to work after one's had an emotionally disturbing episode."

"What happened?" I asked, concerned. "Is Elliott okay?"

"Elliott's back at the college now," Alice answered. "In his room, when I left him. He's fine, I suppose. A little sad, because his father wouldn't see him, but he'll be alright. Albert's put a glamor of protection around Desmond Manor so that it looks like the ruins of an old castle to non-magickal folk passing by. He doesn't let anyone in or out when he is at home."

"Wait," I said. "I knew that Elliott and his dad hadn't spoken in a long time, but I thought Albert was banned from Britain?"

"They haven't spoken," Alice answered. "Not since Albert's expulsion by the Grand Council from the Circle of British Witchcraft, after the trial following Gwendolyn's death. However, only Northern Ireland is part of Great Britain. The Republic of Ireland is an independent nation, with its own Council and system of justice. In the Republic of Ireland, there is a verdict between guilty and innocent, called *not proven*. That is how Albert Capell is regarded in Ireland. As a man who is *not proven* to have killed his wife. Thus, Albert is still allowed into the Circle of Irish Witchcraft. The place that Elliott and I attempted to visit him today was at the castle Albert owns near Shanagolden, in the Republic of Ireland. We were hoping that perhaps Albert might have changed his mind somewhat about seeing Elliott now that his son is attending his alma mater. Also, the matter regarding which we sought his audience is his preeminent business concern with Albion Oil. Alas, Albert's answer was no."

"Poor Elliott," I said, shaking my head. As we arrived at the pier and tied up the boat, I thought about the night that I barged up to the door of Elliott's room and asked where his father lived. When Elliott told me, I was too lost in my self-pity about being the poorest girl at Rookes to even consider his plight. What would it be like to be a student there with the richest father but who lived in a castle where his son was not welcome?

Upstairs, I waited until almost midnight to walk across the hallway and knock on Elliott's door. I wanted to give him the chance to talk about what had happened. Waiting expectantly as I listened to his footsteps approaching, I heard him lock the door from the inside. Anticipating this response, I'd already written him a note. A simple message asking him to meet me in the orchard, saying nothing about what Alice told me or about my day with Oliver. Slipping the note beneath the door, I waited in the dim glow of the candle-lit hallway. It was so quiet, I could hear Elliott sniff loudly on the other side as he crumpled the paper and then unwadded it.

When it returned to me from beneath the door, the opposite side had two words on it in his usual sloppy penciled scrawl.

Not now.

I wanted to tell Elliott that those two words alone meant that he would never be the kind of man his father was. The kind of man I knew he lived in fear of becoming. The fact that he'd chosen to answer at all proved it. However, I also knew Elliott didn't want to hear that.

Not now.

I pulled out my pencil and wrote two more words, which I slipped back to him.

Not ever?

Elliott swore under his breath from the other side and quickly scribbled his response.

No, just... Then a circle was drawn around his first answer. *Not now.*

Then beneath it, printed in crooked all caps. *GO AWAY.*

And at the very bottom, in the lower case, an afterthought—*please.*

Tucking the paper in my pocket, I crossed back to my room and shut the door. Loudly enough to be noticed across the hallway, but I left it unlocked.

Chapter Twenty-Four

"Isn't it beautiful?" Miranda mouthed silently to me, her hazel eyes sparkling with golden flecks as we sat in a circle around the crackling bonfire on the beach next to the pier. The clear night air twinkled with stars as the full moon shone down upon us in our black formal cloaks. Beneath the hoods, our partially concealed faces looked like phases of the moon. At my back, I could hear the rush of the ocean and smell the salt of the tide coming in, mingling with the warm odor of wood smoke.

Sitting between each of us and the fire were jack-o-lanterns we'd carved early that morning. Using only our magick to guide the knives, the idea was to recreate interpretations of our familiar forms. I was particularly proud of mine, an elaborate multi-dimensional fox face with long whiskers, paws, and a fluffy tail. The fox's mouth was open to display a grin full of sharp teeth that made it look simultaneously merry and menacing. Tayen's was awful because she'd gotten impatient. She'd slashed away until hers had the sadly unimaginative triangular visage of something a not-particularly talented elementary schooler might think resembled a coyote. Everyone else's pumpkin carving was somewhere in between, aesthetically speaking.

We'd each brought a picnic basket filled with foods we'd magickally prepared to honor our ancestors with a dumb supper on Samhain night. Mine contained fish and chips for Oliver's British side of the family and a pecan pie for my mom, Darla's Southern roots. To my knowledge, Oliver's parents were long since deceased. They were buried in some massive cemetery near Edinburgh, where his grandparents were from. I presumed both of Darla's parents were alive and kicking, still selling used cars in Columbia, Tennessee. That's what they'd been up to when I'd last seen them anyway, about fifteen years ago, when my folks split. Like everything else about my mother, her parents had faded into the background of my life after she left and married the plastic surgeon in Brentwood.

As the other girls put away the remains of their suppers, Mary cautioned us again, as she had when we were unpacking the food earlier. No one was to speak from the time the meal began until the last bite was swallowed. Instead, we were supposed to eat in silence, contemplating our ancestors as we gazed into the flames. If they had any messages for us, Mary claimed, they would do it through our fire scrying. After one final glance around the bonfire to see that everyone was finished, Mary and the other Mentors cast several additional layers of protection around our perimeter circle using more elaborate incantations than usual.

"The veil between the world of the living and the Shadowlands is at its thinnest on Samhain," Mary explained. "Which can be both good and bad. For those seeking to communicate with loved ones who may have passed on, it provides an excellent opportunity. However, one must always carefully question spirits who appear to us during Samhain visions. Evil entities can prey upon our eagerness to interact. They might tell us falsehoods as they attempt to overpower our will. Some even try to enter human bodies to consume them from within."

"You're talking about possession," Miranda shivered. "When a demon steals its way into a person's soul."

"Precisely," Mary acknowledged. "Although an entity needn't necessarily be a demon to take up residence within the space normally reserved for a living soul. Numerous kinds of spiritual beings may try to latch onto the living, leaching them of their life force. Some may even have been human once themselves. Others might be from other worlds. Regardless, these entities can hear our innermost thoughts and deepest insecurities. The evil ones seek to instill doubt and fear wherever they can. To protect ourselves, anytime we encounter a being who comes in the shape of a loved one, we must question it thoroughly. Ask its name, why it has come to us, and something that only the spirit they appear to be would know. If they cannot answer, often they will become outraged and give their true selves away, allowing us to flee or banish them from our presence before they can harm us."

"Like that scene at the end of the first act of *Hamlet*," I said. "When Hamlet questions the ghost he believes to be his father, and it tells him to avenge his murder."

"Yes," Mary nodded. "William Shakespeare was very aware of the Old Ways, which were experiencing a Renaissance during his lifetime. Ironically, due to King James's efforts to control them for his ends, and if he could not, then to suppress them. Hamlet is perhaps the best example that we have in literature from that era of a character trying to question a spirit but ultimately failing. His reluctance to act on evidence that he knew in his heart to be true points to the suppression of his free will by the Spirit that presented itself in the form of his father."

"So you're saying *Hamlet* was a possession story?" Imani asked, incredulous. She, Miranda, and I—the big readers of the group—were hanging on Mary's every word of this literary digression. However, Tayen yawned openly, while Hana and Elliott also looked bored.

Sensing their disinterest, Mary redirected the conversation. "In short, yes, Imani. But we can discuss that in more detail tomorrow if you wish. Tonight, our focus is on celebrating the world of the spirits who live in the Shadowlands and learning how to discern their helpful and benign communications from the dangerous. Candy and Grace have prepared some sachets of herbs to assist us in setting the intentions for our scrying session tonight. Sisters, if you would?"

Mary motioned to the two Mentors sitting to her left. With a few flicks of her wand, Grace opened the enormous crossbody bag she always carried and guided small natural linen pouches of dried herbs tied with jute thread around to float in the air before each of us.

"A mixture of bay leaf, rosemary, dandelion, lavender, nutmeg, and pennyroyal," Candy explained. Taking hold of my sachet, I gave it a sniff. I couldn't identify the scent, but Tayen's assessment was pretty accurate. "Smells like the Thanksgiving episode of the Golden Girls, after Rose takes the cookies out of the oven, and then Blanche walks in." I laughed. Mary frowned.

"A little less levity, Miss Kennerly," Mary said, speaking across the fire. "Hana, why don't you begin the scrying ritual for us, since you are the most visually gifted? Shake out a handful of herbs and toss them onto the fire. Then relax and breathe deeply. Allow your gaze to come to rest in the heart of the flame. Beyond the realm of focused consciousness, the mysterious history of the Shadowlands always waits for us."

Hana did as instructed. The herb mixture whirled and burst like a small handful of firecrackers, giving off a more intense concentration of scent. As the tension of Hana's shoulders fell and her dark eyes focused, I could see a tiny reflection of the bonfire dancing in them. We sat in silence for several minutes. Beneath the tent of sticks piled into a cone that formed the center of the fire, a hazy shape began to emerge, then split in two. Slowly, the pair rose and became part of the smoke at the top, taking the form of two humans. It was like watching a black-and-white movie on an old analog television set that was going bad and kept fading in and out of a snowy background.

Gradually, I could tell the people were a man and a woman. The woman was dressed smartly in a trim skirt suit. Her ghostly profile was as perfect as a doll's. The man's face was heavier and his expression hard. He appeared to be wearing a military uniform of some kind. They embraced, seemed to argue, and afterward, the woman disappeared in a whooshing updraft. Then, the smoke coalesced, and the uniformed man appeared again. This time, he carried a bundle wrapped in his arms. Looking nervously back and forth, he walked down an alleyway next to a church. Stopping, he pulled on a handle that opened a chute of some kind and placed the bundle into it. Closing the door, he took two halting steps backward, covered his anguished face in his hands, turned, and ran.

The innermost logs of the bonfire broke and collapsed, causing everyone around the circle to jump. We'd all been so captivated by Hana's vision that it was as if we were coming out of hypnosis. The relatively mundane sound of wood breaking resonated like a gunshot.

Finally, Katerina spoke. "Hana, I believe that I understand the nature of your vision. However, would you like to explain it to the rest of us?"

"Those were my parents," Hana said quietly, still in shock. "My birth parents, not the Atwaters. They lived in Seoul, and their names were Bitna and Kyong." Hana seemed bewildered as she blinked several times, like someone who'd stared too long into the sun. Then, she took a deep breath as the rest of the story burst out of her. "Bitna's family wasn't wealthy, but they were trying to appear so. They sent her to university, and she got all perfect marks. Her family wanted her to go to medical school, but she didn't get in. I don't know why she didn't, but she didn't, and they were angry with her. Her parents thought Bitna hadn't tried hard enough. They kicked her out of the house. She got a job as the office manager at a hospital, and she was going to try to take the entrance exam for medical school again, but she met Kyong. He was poor. A soldier. Bitna became pregnant. They argued. Kyong wasn't ready to be a father. He didn't want to get married. Kyong was going to leave her, but then Bitna... she..."

Hana gasped for air. "Bitna died. The hospital called Kyong because he was the father she'd put on the birth certificate. When he came, Kyong still didn't know what to do. He was angry at himself. He was angry at Bitna for dying before he could apologize and figure out a way for them to get back together. And Kyong was angry at the baby. Every time he looked at her, all he could see was Bitna. Bitna constantly watching him, needing him, accusing him of abandoning her. The baby was like a ghost, so he left her. He left her in a box at a church where they take in babies people don't want. He left her... he left..." Hana's voice choked into a whisper, "Me."

Her eyes filled with tears. As she turned to Katerina, Hana's whole body began shaking. "I've always known they were dead, but every other time I've tried to see them, I couldn't. I tried everything! Why did I see them now? Why? What good could it do when I don't even know their last names? All I know is that they didn't want me. Just like my other parents don't want me, but at least they picked me out. Kyong—my real father—he left me in a box! What's wrong with me?"

Katerina leaned closer to Hana in a much gentler voice than usual. "Nothing, dear heart. What spirits show us in the fire is often a reflection of their deepest regrets, which they share to help us interpret what we might not be able or willing to see otherwise. Did you see the expression on Kyong's face as he turned? Your father was in pain, Hana. He didn't want to leave you, but he felt inadequate to raise you on his own and deeply sorrowful that he quarreled with your mother. So he left you in a place where he thought others would take better care of you than he could."

"Those baby boxes," Miranda added. "My father's ministry works with charitable groups all over the world to help staff and support those boxes twenty-four hours a day. They're pretty well known. The children get good placements in homes with families who want babies. At the one closest to us in Florida, someone leaves a baby almost every other day. If your dad were in the Army and about to be deployed to somewhere that he wasn't sure he'd come back from, he might have thought that choosing to leave you in the hands of the ministry, where he knew you'd be safe permanently, was better than just parking you with some random acquaintance and not knowing where you'd end up if he died."

"That's a very thoughtful interpretation, Miranda," Katerina continued. "Also, I believe that by sharing with you the unfairness of how she was ostracized by her parents for not fitting into the plans they'd set out for her, your birth mother, Bitna, was trying to tell you, Hana, to reconsider what is important about your adoptive parents' expectations for you. Is it really that they want you to be a doctor, or would they accept some other destiny that is more aligned with your talents?"

"They want me to be the best," Hana sniffled. "Because that's what the Atwaters are, they always tell me. They're all geniuses. They're the best at everything. But it's so hard. I feel like I'll never be good enough to be one of them. Like their choosing me was some kind of mistake."

"That's BS," I interjected, then clarified. "Not how you feel about it, but the fact they make you feel that way. My boyfriend Stephen's parents put out the same crap, and I'm sure you're trying just as hard and are just as smart as he is, if not more so. Heck, you got into Harvard! *The Harvard!* Stephen's parents would pass out if he'd gotten accepted there."

"All of the Atwaters go to Harvard," Hana shrugged. "Or MIT. It's nothing special. It's what's expected."

"Then show them something special. Something more than what they expect, that is beyond their understanding," I replied. "Hana, I've never met your parents, but from what you've said, I think I know a few things about them. They don't know how to appreciate what they have. Or even if they do, they don't know how to express it in a way that makes people feel good about themselves. Perhaps that's why if they're supposed to be so successful, I've never heard of them. Nobody likes listening to anyone who deliberately talks over their heads. It's unrelatable. Hana, you say smart stuff in ways that are engaging so that people want to listen."

"What Willow is getting at," Mary concluded, "is that communication is your gift, Hana. Your life experience of being displaced from the world of your birth and raised in a completely alien environment has made you an empath. As a witch whose natural affinity is with water, you can understand the emotions that ebb and flow between people. Learn to utilize that strength, and you will be the best at whatever you set your mind to. Meanwhile, the Atwaters will be left puzzled at the mystery of your success."

After Mary replenished the fire, stacking up the kindling in a small pyramid with a few waves of her wand, she asked Grace to smudge the circle with sage to cleanse it. When Grace finished, Mary asked if anyone else was ready to try fire scrying. Imani volunteered. Pouring out a handful of the dried herbs from her linen sachet, Imani tossed them into the newly rebuilt pyre. It leaped and crackled as we settled in once more to await the spirits that she summoned.

This time, the smoke gathered into the silhouette of only one figure: a tall, muscular young man. Facing Imani, his empty eye sockets seemed to be staring at a figure right above where Imani was sitting. From his facial expressions and hand gestures, I could tell the young man was pleading with someone but seemed to be having difficulty getting them to listen to reason. As she sat with her gaze fixed on this smoky figure, Imani's expressions twitched through a series of emotions, from shock to bewilderment and finally anger.

Clearly disturbed but working hard to maintain her composure, Imani began asking the shape questions. *Who are you? Why are you here? What is my name? The name you called me?*

Gradually, as I strained to hear what Imani was listening to, I began to hear a low rumble. It sounded like a single voice talking to itself through a thin wall in another room. Several minutes passed, and the noise grew louder. I could hear not just one voice but many, clamoring and gibbering. The gray shape of the young man hovering over the fire started to flicker. Then, his head snapped abruptly to the side, and the sound crescendoed into a deafening crash. Imani fell forward onto the ground, covered her ears, and screamed as the shimmering edge of the circle of protection behind her bowed inward.

Instantly, Candy was on her feet, her wand slashing the air above where Imani lay. "Be gone, demon! I banish thee!"

The atmosphere within the circle of protection pulsed. I felt the pressure in my eardrums grow painfully tight as if I were on an airplane that dropped altitude too fast. An otherworldly shriek cut through the air as the bonfire surged up into a column of flame. The shadow figure disappeared, and then all was silent.

"What the bloody hell was that?" Elliott exclaimed. He'd been so quiet the whole time, I'd forgotten he was even there.

"My brother Isaac," Imani replied, sitting up. Her jaw was trembling. "In the smoke. And my mother, outside the circle." She turned to Candy, her eyebrows knit close in thought. "Only, that couldn't have been just them, could it? My mother is still alive. She wouldn't be able to speak to me as a spirit. And my brother..." Imani rubbed her ears, probably trying to clear the ringing in her head that I heard too. "Isaac called me Imma for as long as I could remember. Because when I was a kid, I used to run after him, going, *Imma gonna do this,* and *Imma gonna do that,* after everything I saw him doing. There's no way he wouldn't be able to remember!"

"No," Candy answered, her face serious. "Although your brother Isaac came through the veil first, another entity, perhaps more than one, followed him. That happens occasionally. I knew something was happening, but I chose not to interact at first because you were managing the situation correctly. Having the confidence to question unwanted spirits can sometimes be enough to frighten them away. It's an important skill to build and requires much self-control."

"Ghosts can be scared of us?" Tayen asked. "That's pretty wicked."

"Of course they can," Candy answered. "Think about it. All ghosts—real ghosts, not other entities masquerading as ghosts—are humans who used to be alive. Newly released ghosts are the most afraid because many of them have no idea where they are or how to negotiate the divide between this life and the Shadowlands. Confused and lonely, they want nothing more than the reassurance of speaking with another live human, but they don't know how. Some try every way that they can think of, making sounds and moving objects, but nothing works because no one is paying attention. Thus, when one of us makes an effort to contact them, and it works—when we're able to get through the fog of the veil—it startles them. Unless they're very old or experienced in such interactions, quite often it scares them into silence."

"But Isaac," Imani thought for a moment, massaging her temples. "Isaac wasn't trying to speak to me. I was concentrating very hard and trying to ask him questions, but he wasn't answering. It's like he didn't even know I was there, and I was watching him argue with my mother."

"What were they arguing about?" Elliott wondered aloud.

Imani stared at Elliott for a moment, chewing her bottom lip. To me, it was clear she was trying to decide whether or not to answer his question, and if so, to what extent. She closed her eyes and said softly. "They were arguing over whether Isaac should come out to my father. His football career was already over because of his injuries, and he didn't see any point in keeping it a secret anymore. There was no image," Imani made air quotes with her fingers, "of this big macho guy to protect. Most of his friends and the rest of his family, including me, knew. Plus, Isaac had been seeing a man who was a sportscaster for a while. He was out, and nobody made a big deal about it. Honestly, I hadn't thought very much about him being ashamed to tell Dad or that keeping it a secret might have been part of the reason Isaac committed suicide. Dad keeps his feelings pretty close about everything. I just assumed he knew, but it was one of those things he chose not to talk about. Isaac was in so much pain with all the nerve damage and neuropathy after his last spinal surgery that he stayed constantly depressed. When his autopsy revealed that he'd had CTE too, well... I think we all thought that explained it."

"Was that what the demon argued with him about?" Miranda wanted to know. I could sense a bit of personal interest in her voice. Tayen must have too, because she shot me a look across the circle.

"Yes and no," Imani answered. "It was weird. When the vision started, it was like I was a ghost. I'd accidentally walked into Mom and Isaac arguing, and they couldn't tell I was there. I couldn't see Mom, but I could hear her voice. Mom was screaming at Isaac for being selfish. How he shouldn't say anything to Dad because it would kill him. Also, how it would stir up too much controversy and ruin our little brother Ivan's chances of getting picked up by a big-name college team if it got out to the press. However, as I began asking the spirit that was Isaac questions he should know, he kept ignoring me. That was when the voice that started out sounding like Mom changed. Isaac was pleading with her to calm down, but she kept getting angrier. Again, weird, because Mom's never like that. She's always been the rock of the family—Dr. Zuri Griffin—the voice of reason. I mean, she was a professor for crying out loud. That is, until after her stroke and the dementia that followed. Now she can barely even speak." Imani took a deep breath and closed her eyes again. "I just don't understand any of it."

"Imani, I know that you are a very rational person, but interactions with the spirit world often defy logic," Candy said calmly. "Possibly, what we were watching was a moment in which your mother was not communicating as herself at all. Perhaps the repression of her had already begun. How long was it after your brother passed before Zuri had her first stroke?"

"Not long," Imani answered. "A few months. Her doctors said the stress of it was a contributing factor."

"No doubt it was," Candy agreed. "If your mother was possessed by an evil entity that caused her to lash out at her son when he sought to confide in her, and then he committed suicide, then the guilt from that confrontation must have caused her a great deal of anguish. It may have been too much for her body to bear, and then, something snapped inside. Having broken both her spirit and your brother's, the demon could have left them in search of other life forces to destroy."

"Which could explain the entity all of us witnessed pressing against the circle of protection," Mary concluded. "For whatever reason, Imani, there is an entity that appears to have taken an interest in harming your family. Fortunately, your powers are grounded in the Earth. You are focused enough to keep your wits about you when you encounter it, as you have demonstrated tonight. However, I believe that Isaac's spirit appeared to you as a warning and that you must be vigilant in protecting members of your family who might not be so aware. Your younger brother, Ivan, and even your father, Richard."

"Ivan, I can see," Imani replied. "He's always taking risks and is spoiled rotten, being the baby. Especially now that Isaac's gone. But Dad?" Imani smirked. "I mean, I love him, but I don't think Coach Wreck-em Rick Griffin is in danger of anything, other than his ego overinflating."

"On the contrary," Mary disagreed. "That's exactly why your father might be more susceptible. Nothing attracts a demon more than pride. You should keep an eye on him. The spirits never speak without reason. We just have to interpret what that reason might be."

"We should also be mindful of the time," Alice added, glancing up at the moon. "It's almost midnight. Cora should be back to lead us in the Wild Hunt any minute."

"You are quite right," Mary replied. "Although I am aware that communication with the spirit world is rarely what we would expect. Hopefully, tonight's messages from the Shadowlands have been insightful, if not comforting, for both of you." Mary nodded to indicate Hana and Imani. "But we should move on to the finale of our Samhain celebration. Is there anyone else who would like to attempt communication before we open the circle?"

This time, Mary looked directly at Elliott, who shook his head quickly. "I tried fire scrying once," Elliott murmured. "It wasn't for me." Mary studied him with a knowing look.

"Alright then," Mary said, turning back to the group. "Sisters, let us remove our layers of protection about the circle so that we can draw down the moon. Artemis's winged chariot draws near. The time of the Wild Hunt is almost upon us."

Chapter Twenty-Five

While Mary and the other Mentors unwound the protective charms they'd cast around the bonfire circle, the rest of us returned to the castle to retrieve our besoms, the little natural twig brooms that we'd made in anticipation of Samhain. As we made our way back, the wind began to pick up, swirling the dead leaves from the orchard in tiny tornadoes across the back lawn. The air smelled crisp and nutty, so much that even Elliott's usual dour mood picked up. Tossing his besom playfully into the air, he showed off by making it spin an impossible amount of times, then cartwheeling over to let it drop to where he could catch it behind his back. It was a cool trick, but I didn't dare attempt it. The last thing I wanted was to look like a fool by knocking myself out cold in front of Elliott with the handle of my broom. Instead, I asked him what Mary meant about Artemis and the Wild Hunt.

"The Wild Hunt is a sort of spiritual procession that flies across the sky on important nights of the year. Samhain, Yule, Imbolc..." Elliott explained. "Sabbats when the weather is cold. Other nights during winter when the moon is full and the veil is thin. In different parts of the world, it's led by different deities. According to what I know about Rookes College, it's always been closely associated with the Greek goddess Artemis. It makes sense that Mary would choose her as the deity to lead our Hunt tonight."

"Who else is hunting?" I asked. "And what are they hunting for?"

"That depends again," Elliott continued. "On locality and several other factors. Considering that we're invoking Artemis, it will probably begin with the goddess and her traditional symbols. A white stag, pursued by Artemis in her chariot with her hounds, and perhaps a small army of fae, with bows and arrows. They go very fast and can turn quick as a wink." Elliott rolled his broom over the back of his hand and flicked it up in the air with his elbow, rotating to catch it again behind his back before holding it out toward me.

"That's why Mary wanted us to bring our besom's. It's much easier to turn and change direction abruptly in the air when a witch is riding one. Flying unassisted is fine under normal conditions, but nothing beats a well-made besom for cutting corners quickly."

"So, it's like a game then," I said. "Sort of like when upper-class English people go out on fox hunts. Only this game is played by a kind of Ghost Riders in the Sky following the charge of a goddess."

"Technically, they're not ghosts," Elliott corrected. "They're fae. Huge difference, and I'd probably not let any of them hear you mistake them as such. Fae can get testy, especially around humans. Most of them think we're not all that bright. But otherwise, yeah. That's the general idea of how it starts anyway. The Goddess Artemis leads, then the fae next, and since we're usually a good bit slower, witches follow after, all going round and round. Once Artemis shoots the stag, though, that's when the more traditional ceremony ends, and it gets fun. All bets are off, and the Hunt changes to become even wilder. It's kind of a free-for-all. Witches drop their besoms and change into familiar forms, with everyone chasing each other. It's pandemonium, sometimes for hours, but in a good way. Like a race with no rules or finish lines. No inhibitions either, just the exhilaration of the chase." Elliott's eyes sparkled with mischievous energy.

"So, I take it you've done a Wild Hunt before?" I asked.

"Eh, only once, a couple of years ago," Elliot said. "And not for long. Nan and Pop are getting older now, and their reflexes aren't what they used to be. Since I was like thirteen or fourteen, they've only partic-ipated in the first round, which moves slower and is more ritualistic than anything. They're at that age witches get to, you know, when they can still heal themselves magickally, but it takes longer. So they try to be careful." Elliott shrugged as if I should know exactly what he was talking about, forgetting I didn't have the same contextual background.

"Anyway, the year I turned seventeen, I stayed up late to watch them on Samhain as usual. When Nan and Pop toddled off to bed around three in the morning, I snagged one of their besoms and gave it a go. I'd sneaked in a little flying practice here and there, which I think Nan knew about but didn't say anything. But this, whew!" He whistled. "It was like riding the wind itself. I'd have never gotten caught either, except for that stupid seagull. See that?"

Elliott pointed to a thin, white scar just barely visible in the hairline above his right ear. "That's where its beak snagged me. Gull lived, though it got knocked silly for a bit. I fell off the besom, and splat!" He slapped his hands together and staggered comically. "Flat on my back. Knocked me out cold. Nan and Pop lost it once they figured out I wasn't going to die and all my brains were still packed in my head." He chuckled to himself. "That was the end of my sneaking out flying. They kept both besoms under spell-locks until I left for Rookes."

"Wow," I said. "You're really lucky that..."

"That we're about to start the Hunt so we don't have to keep listening to the wild tales of Crash Welles over here?" Tayen snarked. "Pro tip, Holmes. Chicks only think it's impressive when you *don't* fall off the broom." Elliott glared at her. Tayen blew him a kiss.

"Would you look at that!" Miranda exclaimed, pointing back over to the shoreline where the last embers of the bonfire smoldered. Hovering about twenty feet in the air above the circle where we'd sat before during the fire scrying were our jack-o-lanterns. Beside each of them was an open, leatherbound book. The wind continued to pick up, but the pages of the books didn't even flutter. Already astride their brooms, all the Mentors besides Cora swooped and darted around the circle, trying to hold their places in the stiff gale. Their black formal cloaks flapped around them.

"Mount your besoms and move into place, please!" Mary called. "The scripts for our incantation are already open for you on the correct pages. Tonight, we will be reading from the Dutch poet Johannes Carsten's verse in tribute to the Wild Hunt as our invocation to the goddess. Tayen, since Cora is your Mentor and she will be guiding Artemis to us for the opening ceremony, you shall recite the first verse. Continue as you hear Cora respond. As Cora starts into verse two, Miranda, you begin, and Grace will follow. Then so on around the circle, clockwise and back widdershins, until we end with me. Although," Mary shielded her eyes from the leaves and debris flying through the air as she scanned the moonlit horizon, "I don't think we'll be reciting the poem's entirety. They're already very close."

"How will we know when they're here?" I asked Elliott, putting a leg over my broom and floating off the ground.

He laughed. "Trust me, you won't miss it."

With everyone at their stations, Tayen began to read, in a loud, clear voice, the opening stanza of the poem.

When they thought that Denmark's king
Soundly in the graveyard slumbered,
Words incredible, unnumbered,
Through the land crept whispering.

Mary wasn't kidding. That's really about Hamlet, I thought silently. As Tayen proceeded to the next verse, I heard the hushed tones of Cora's voice echoing from the west. Turning to look over my shoulder, I could just barely make out the faintest glimmer of intense white light, like the speck of a star hovering past the edge of the island.

Although none of us acknowledged it, because we were quickly absorbed in the incantations of the poem, by the time Miranda started her recitation, our students' inner circle and the Mentors' outer circle began to rotate gently in opposite directions. As each witch began her round of speaking the verses, our speed within the circles increased. The glowing white star became larger and brighter as it neared. By the time it was my turn to read, it felt as if we were inside a centrifuge, moving so swiftly around that I could feel heavy pressure on the skin of my face. I struggled to hold my place steady in the air on my broom. Just as it had earlier that evening, when the bad spirit was trying to break through our circle of protection, the space inside my ears felt tight. The air surrounding me was as dense as just before a thunderstorm. Yet, strangely, I wasn't afraid. The snugness of the air was almost comforting, like when I was a baby and Oliver would have to put me in the car and drive fast on the interstate to get me to sleep.

This must be what Shakespeare meant when he described Hecate's charm as being wound up, I thought. *It's like we're winding tight the springs of time with our words.*

From the corner of my eye, I caught glimpses of our Mentors rocketing around the circle on their besoms. Each chanted the verses in endless repetition, with her black cloak whipping behind her. About the time I got to the ninth verse, I could see her clearly. Artemis, leading the hunt in pursuit of an enormous, glowing white stag. Her great hounds leaped through the air at her sides, just as the poet Carsten's verse described:

Her long hair flickered in the midnight blast,

She sighed with sighs inhuman;
On a snow-white horse, she galloped fast,
The fairest of all women.

Mesmerized, I stopped reading, stopped breathing, unable to do anything other than stare at her. From the perfect shape of her face to the clearly defined muscles of her arms as she held her bow pulled back tight with its arrow, the goddess Artemis truly looked as if she'd been cut from marble.

Somewhere in the distance, I heard Cora yell, "Hold fast to your lights!"

I had just enough time to register that someone had spoken, although not to decipher what was said when my jack-o-lantern smacked me hard in the chest. Instinctively, my right arm clasped around it. I clutched onto my broomstick with my left. The books that were magickally held in place during our incantations dropped like stones. I felt myself tumbling sideways through the air to the ground.

The tension in the sky burst like a cloud, with a downward whoosh of icy air as Artemis and the Wild Hunt passed over us. Dozens of fae followed behind her, fanning out in a white-hot V like a moving constellation of comets. *Fauns*, I thought, *and satyrs*, as I watched their hairy legs and glowing naked torsos passing above, each one carrying a long spear. Their hooves seemed to be running on the fabric of the clouds themselves. Elves raced alongside them, sharply angular in every part of their body structure, from their chiseled chins to their spider-crooked legs. They whistled to one another, swooping in and out among the larger fae in search of clear shots from which to launch their arrows. It was like a scene out of some CGI remake of *A Midsummer Night's Dream*, in which the director had gone completely mad.

Wheezing as I tried to regain my breath, I lay in the grass with the pumpkin, still lit by some feat of magick, balanced on my stomach. Above me I watched hundreds of birds, everything from owls to hawks to our rooks, whirling in a confusing, cacophonous swarm. The edges of my vision swam, and I must have blacked out for a second. The next thing I knew, Cora's luminous face and long veil of white-blonde hair hovered over me. Placing her deathly pale, long-fingered hand lightly on my brow and then sweeping beneath to support my head, Cora closed her ice-blue eyes in thought as she searched for injury.

"No harm done," Cora said. Catching me in her startling gaze, she pulled me to my feet. "Just took a tumble off your besom. Happens to the best of us. You'll catch a second wind. Hold fast to your light and follow me!"

Mounting my broom again, I tucked my pumpkin underneath my arm and wavered unsteadily through the air in the wake of the massive flock of birds. However, something in the energy of the night must have recharged me. Within minutes I began to catch up to the rest of the witches again. The gleaming white stag darted sharply through the air as if avoiding trees in an invisible forest. One by one, as he came within range, each witch hurled her jack-o-lantern at him, as if we were a whole squadron of headless horsemen. Mine passed right between his two massive antlers, but I didn't care. By the time Artemis's arrow finally found its mark in the stag's neck, none of us did. We were simply enjoying the pursuit.

Just as Elliott described, after the stag disappeared, the Hunt changed. Witches dropped their brooms and changed into familiar animal forms. That seemed to shift our chase into a faster gear that allowed us to keep pace with the fae, rather than trailing behind. Freed by my more agile fox shape, I wove among the churning hooves of the fae to the front of the group. Around and around we went for hours, sailing over land and sea in an exhilarating surge, until I realized the edge of dawn was just beginning to color the horizon. Artemis turned to follow the fading darkness in the west. The fae started to disappear like winking stars. As the chase wound down, each witch changed back into human form. We landed naked and then rewrapped quickly into our cloaks.

Gathering around the now-extinguished bonfire, we chattered excitedly. At last, someone noticed Miranda was missing. With the sky empty, the Mentors began to worry, but not for long. Out over the ocean, illuminated by the sunrise, we heard first one, then a chorus of conch shells being blown.

"That is the call of the Merfolk," Mary said, picking up her broom once more. "They must have found her. Candy, bring your bag and fly with me. Miranda may be hurt, and if so, we will need you." Exhausted but hopeful Miranda was not harmed, the rest of us followed.

Touching down on a sandbar exposed by the low tide, I saw a group of Merfolk surrounding Miranda. She lay propped with her back against a saltwater-worn boulder and covered head to toe in what appeared to be a kind of cocoon made from seaweed plaster. Her face was ghostly pale, and her eyelids drooped like someone awakening from sedation. Mary approached the most ancient-looking merman, whose skin was tanned to the shade of worn leather. She curtsied deeply, asking what happened. The old merman stroked his long white beard, the tiny braids of which were interwoven with spiral shells, as he explained.

"Near the end of the Hunt, when the rest of you were returning to human form, this one," he tipped the end of his trident toward Miranda, "seemed to be having a bit of a struggle. She kept swooping down near the water, half-transforming, and then changing her mind. After five or six attempts, she simply fell out of the sky. We knew she was one of yours, Mary. We've seen her often enough out by the pier, listening to our singing in the evenings. Immediately, I dispatched a group to rescue her. She took in a bit too much seawater, I'm afraid, for human lungs to bear in good health, but she's lucky. If she hadn't still been in the shape of an eagle when she hit the surface of the water, she would not have been as buoyant and might not have survived."

Grace, Miranda's Mentor, knelt beside her. "Were you having difficulty transforming out of your eagle, dearest one?" Grace asked. "It can be easy to get caught up in the excitement."

Miranda swallowed with difficulty. Her voice sounded hoarse and raw from the salt water. "No, it wasn't that. I was, well... I felt like I was stuck. I didn't know where my robe was, and I didn't want to land on the lawn, where everyone could see me without it. I was trying to land in the water, but I was scared because I knew I couldn't swim. Still, I was willing to risk it because I thought if I landed close enough to the pier, I could perhaps catch onto it before I went under. Then I might hang on, covered by the water, until I could call out for help. I kept chickening out, though, and each time I half-transformed and then had to switch back, it seemed like I got weaker and weaker. That was when I must have fallen..." Miranda trailed off, blinking with effort. Her eyes were red and irritated, probably from being open in the gritty ocean water.

"So, what you're saying," Tayen said. "Is that modesty almost killed you?"

"This is no joking matter," Mary replied sharply. "Miranda, I am surprised at your reluctance to let go of prudish notions that were doubtlessly instilled by your upbringing. There is nothing shameful about being skyclad for a few moments before or after transmogrification. I understand everyone has different levels of comfort with their bodies, but it is simply a practical necessity of the process, no more than consulting a physician. No one here is going to be looking at you with improper intent. And we simply must see to it right away that you learn to swim. It is too dangerous to live the entire year of your education on an isolated island without knowing."

"Arnaud," Mary addressed the eldest merman. "Is there anyone among your people who would mind taking it upon themselves to assist Grace in teaching Miranda to swim? Hopefully, before the water becomes too cold for the season. I'd rather not warm it artificially with magick, because it disturbs the fish."

"I would be glad to," replied one of the young mermaids. Her golden hair fell in effortless, natural ringlets across her shoulders and cascaded down to cover her bare breasts. Like all the Merfolk, she wore no clothing. She was covered in scales from just below the navel to the end of her tail fin. "My name is Celine. I was among those who rescued her. I think she might be less afraid to learn with someone who appears to be closer to her age."

"You have my utmost gratitude, Celine," Mary said, curtseying to the young mermaid. "I believe your influence overall will be most beneficial. For now, Alice, could you assist me in transporting Miranda back to the college so that Candy may begin work with some restorative practices? I believe it would be easiest if we used her robe to carry her. Grace, do you have it?"

Grace pulled Miranda's black formal robe from her bag. With a few whisks of her wand, Alice lifted Miranda from her resting place against the boulder and swaddled the robe around her encasement of seaweed plaster. Then, as we said goodbye and got on our brooms, Alice held her wand arm out behind. She pulled the tightly wrapped Miranda along as if with a magickal tether.

By the time I went to bed, I was so exhausted I could hardly undress. Every muscle in my body ached like I'd been working out for hours. However, it was a satisfying kind of soreness. Also, I was famished. We'd eaten dinner in the Great Hall as usual before the Samhain ritual, but I was still as hungry as if I hadn't eaten anything all day. Summoning a tray of hummus, pita bread, olives, and dipping vegetables, along with a big tumbler of pineapple smoothie from the kitchen downstairs, I dove on the food the moment it floated to rest on my desk.

Elliott must have had the same idea. A few minutes later, he knocked on the door of my room. When I opened it, he had the most enormous charcuterie board I'd ever seen floating beside him, with at least a dozen different kinds of meat and cheese and a glass of ale that must have been a foot tall.

"Thirsty?" I asked, watching him drain the beer completely.

"As a man who's been stranded in the desert for a week," he answered, wiping his mouth and waving his wand to summon another drink. "The Hunt does that. Awakens the appetite."

"Yeah," I mumbled through a mouthful of hummus. "I can feel it." The straw in my smoothie hit bottom, making an empty gurgling sound.

"I'll make that two," Elliott said, swirling his wand in an *X*, then tapping twice in the air.

"What a gentleman," I joked, popping the last baby carrot into my mouth and crunching. "Changing the subject, but what was that stuff the Merfolk had wrapped around Miranda? I know I could look it up, but I'm so tired I don't know that I could pull a book off the shelf."

"Mmm..." Elliott chewed a roll of prosciutto-wrapped cheese as he thought. "It's hard to explain. Candy would know more. You should ask her. Kind of like a poultice, I guess. Supposed to draw out toxins. Merfolk are big on remedies that involve wrapping themselves in things, according to Nan. It makes sense. Maintaining hydration is super important for them. They can't live for more than a day or so out of the water."

"Hydration is important for everyone," I replied. Then, seeing the drinks that floated into the room, I added, "What are those?"

"Piña coladas," Elliott grinned, pulling one out of the air and handing it to me. Seeing my expression, he added. "What? I thought you liked pineapple?"

"I do," I said, taking the enormous pineapple carefully in both hands. It had several maraschino cherries, a pink umbrella, two hibiscus blossoms, and a striped bendy straw sticking out of it. "But this feels like we're day-drinking at brunch on a cruise in the Bahamas."

"Live a little," Elliott said, gulping piña colada as he put his feet up on the ottoman and relaxed back into one of the armchairs by the bookcase wall. He swirled the straw around in his pineapple, mixing the contents. "We've only got one, yanno. Life."

"Yeah," I said, taking a sip out of my pineapple. It was delicious. "I know. That was my takeaway from the fire scrying tonight. I've never lost someone close, but it made me think about how lucky that is. To have a dad like Oliver and Mom, well..."

"You're lucky to still have time to patch things up with her," Elliott finished. "You should do it, too. After we're finished with school. Learning the Craft gives you a different perspective on things. It has for me a bit already."

"Like what?" I asked, taking another sip.

"Oh, I dunno..." Elliott replied, staring down into his pineapple. "About how having power changes people. Mum and Dad argued a lot, sure, my whole life. But it got worse the more successful Albert became. Gwen, my mum, she was used to being the center of Dad's world. As Albion expanded operations, it took more of his time. That's why I think Gwendolyn got into more dangerous magick. The longer I'm here, and the more I understand how magick works, the more certain I am of it. The darker arts are all about control. Of money, people, you name it. They're about bending someone else's will or the natural order of things to the way you want them to go. That's why they're so appealing to people who feel as if the world disregards them. Everyone's eyes are always on a villain. To them, it doesn't matter if it's negative attention. Because that's what practitioners of destructive magick live on. That's their food and drink. Attention and power."

His voice was firm, and a little angry, yet whisper-soft. I could tell that he was choosing his words carefully, like someone who'd practiced giving an interview after being caught off guard too many times and forced to speak about something painful.

"That's why you don't like to talk about your parents," I said, sensing I needed to be respectful and not suggest too much. "Because they were into evil magick."

"Not they," Elliott corrected, taking another lengthy sip. "She. My mother, Gwendolyn. That's what everyone always gets wrong about my folks. Dad wasn't always the bad one. At least, not at first. Albert was born to a darker magick family. They'd been that way for hundreds of years, maybe longer. It was how they made their money, initially. When

Albert was young, I think he was looking for a way out of it. That's why I believe Mary left him a key. She felt that by bringing him here, to a gentler environment, she might help him to change his path."

Elliott shrugged. "And it might have worked, who knows? But fate has a weird way of catching up with folks in the most twisted ways. Gwen was a good girl here, from a good family. Nan and Pop weren't rich, but they were well-respected. Their daughter, my mum, was beautiful and a talented witch. Gwen was like a prize to Albert, and she knew it. She loved being the center of attention. However, Albert was working so hard to turn his life in a different direction, to find a way to make legitimate money without having to manipulate people, that he forgot you have to polish a brass cup, or it tarnishes. Mum felt bored and neglected, and I'm pretty sure that's why she took up a more sinister style of magick. The resources were all around her there at Albert's home in Shanagolden. All of Lady Desmond's forbidden books, and Gwendolyn had nothing but time to read them. To practice their darker magick as she tried to recapture that feeling of natural power over people that she had when she was younger. Albert's family encouraged her too, of course. I'm sure they persuaded her that was the way to win back his attention. By showing him how much further he could expand his empire if only he would embrace his legacy. What he could accomplish by using more manipulative magick."

"Was that what you saw in the fire when you were younger?" I asked.

Elliott set his pineapple down on the coffee table. "I saw the end of it. Of her, and what she became. Everyone here remembers Gwendolyn Welles, the bright young woman whom everyone loved. What they didn't know was that her time at Rookes College was the most promising year of her life. They miss the Golden Girl. I mourn the mother who became the new Black Hag of Shanagolden. Mum was lost to me years before she died. What I saw, when I tried to scry for her spirit several years ago, was exactly where she was and what she'd turned herself into. It terrified me that someone could become so unrecognizable. So completely changed."

"Everyone changes, and not always for the better," I said, thinking about my mother, Darla. Feeling it might finally be the right time to mention it again, I added, as gently as I could, "Maybe that's why you had a hard time seeing your dad. He's scared that by being a part of your life, he'll be cursing you. Drawing you into the same circle that he feels ruined Gwendolyn."

Elliott sighed. "If that's how he feels, then he's just as confused as she was. Neglecting Mum after he worked so hard to win her over is what drove her to take up exactly the life that Dad was running away from. In a weird way, she was trying to use it to win him back. All Albert's doing now is hiding in his work, wallowing in self-pity, and repeating the same mistakes."

"But with a different person," I insisted. "I know you don't want to be like your father, and you're not, but you're not like your mother either. You're more straightforward. I know because when you want to say something, you say it. You don't suppress your thoughts very well. It might take a while, yes, but you get around to saying what you mean eventually."

"That's what you think about me?" Elliott smirked. "Well..." I could tell he was about to say more, but he stopped himself. Picking up his pineapple as he stood to leave, he swayed a little, tipsily studying it. "Pineapple. Interesting. In a place where you're thirsty and you can have anything your heart desires, you choose pineapple. They say it symbolizes a happy home."

"You chose it too," I replied. "And you even added little flowers and paper umbrellas. I'm keeping mine, by the way," I said, pulling the toothpick umbrella out of the pineapple and tucking it into my hair over my ear.

"I'm glad I could give you something worth keeping," Elliott remarked. Rising to leave, he lingered in the doorway, watching me for a moment. "I would kiss you, but I have a personal policy about never kissing girls with umbrellas in their hair," he murmured, and slipped away.

Chapter Twenty-Six

Early in December, Mary announced that we were going to have visitors. According to custom, she explained, all witches' colleges took turns hosting a Yule Ball each year on the Winter Solstice. For the last few decades, Rookes had alternated hosting with another small institution, Devereaux College, in New Orleans. This year was Rookes' turn. In the weeks following Mary's announcement, we spent several hours every day weaving the spells that transformed Rookes College into a magickal winter wonderland. Although by that point, I had become accustomed to using magick every day and seeing all the amazing feats that could be achieved by those who knew how to wield it, I was still in awe of how beautiful the college became at Yule.

The morning after Mary's announcement, I awakened to find a foot of snow blanketing the entire island. Not the slushy-mushy stuff that falls on most of the South during the winter months, but real, fluffy, perfect drifts of snow almost knee-high. The kind I'd only seen a couple of times on trips to the Rockies with Dad. After breakfast, Katerina, who'd summoned the snow, led us outside and demonstrated how to make snow-piaries using magick. I say snow-piaries, not snowmen or snow people, because using a wand one can shape any kind of creature, human or animal, much in the same way a gardener shapes a topiary.

Beginning with one large ball of snow, which Katerina also showed us how to pack into a tight roll using only magick, we simply whittled away until we achieved the shape of the creature we wanted. My natural inclination was to carve a snow fox, and I have to say it turned out pretty lifelike. Each of the others chose a different animal. I noticed that even Tayen took more care than usual. Her coyote truly resembled a canid. Once everyone was finished, we moved the figures around again by magick, so that they lined the path to the main college door in a frosty menagerie. If

I'd been able to snap a picture with my phone, I would have proudly posted it to all my socials. Alas, glamor-shielded islands have no cell service.

From that point onward, it seemed as if every day brought a new crafty thing for us to learn to create by magick. As they had during our first week at Rookes, the Mentors took turns leading these lessons. Grace taught us how to expedite the fermentation process for red wine and afterward how to warm it, adding oranges, cinnamon, and other herbs to make wassail. Cora explained the tradition of the Yule Log, along with some fire spells to rid oneself of negative energy as the Wheel of the Year made its rounds. Ever practical, Candy taught us spells to ward off colds and other respiratory ailments common with the winter season, filling the whole castle with the scents of peppermint and eucalyptus mixed with more healing herbs. Then, about a week before the visiting group from Devereaux College arrived, Mary and Alice showed us how to weave wreaths and garlands from branches of pine and fir. We spent several days festooning every banister and room with carefully wrought boughs that were tied in sparkling gold and silver ribbons and lit with never-ending natural beeswax candles. Mistletoe danced above every doorway. Their combined woody perfume intermingled into an intoxicating blend with all the other holiday food smells that wafted through the castle in a delectable fog: spiced apple cider, toasted hazelnuts, and gingerbread cookies.

Finally, on the night before the students of Devereaux were scheduled to arrive, Alice brought in a tree to decorate. It seems like a simple thing unless you've seen it. First of all, unlike any regular Christmas tree I'd ever seen in my life, this one wasn't cut at the bottom to fit into a base, nor were its roots bound into a little burlap ball for replanting. Instead, the entire tree, from the twenty-plus feet of it normally visible above ground to the ends of its root system, was brought inside the Great Hall. There, Alice set the tree upright beneath the central dome and cast a magick circle around the root ball of this enormous, cone-shaped fir. Then, she raised a clear glass wall surrounding the circle's circumference, which she filled with dirt. Last, after she'd decorated every branch with twinkling lights and intricate crystal ornaments that replicated the fir's natural cones with dancing prisms, she walked around the magickally encased roots of the tree, tapping at the glass.

I didn't know what she was doing until I noticed that every place she tapped became hollow. Then, when Alice whisked the main front doors of the college open, a scurry of ground squirrels and chipmunks ran inside. The chipmunks dashed up the tree trunk, squeaking and chattering among the branches, while the ground squirrels dove into what I realized were a series of tunnels, visible among the tree's roots. Through the thick wall of glass, the ground squirrels seemed to be playing peek-a-boo with us. Running to where each tunnel ended in a circular window and chittering, then reversing course and sprinting back up to what would have been ground level if the tree were naturally planted.

"As above, so below," Mary said approvingly as she walked around the glass-encased base of the tree. "What a lovely reminder, Alice, of how life continues underground, even during the winter months! While the goddess Persephone slumbers, we take comfort in awaiting her return with the warmth of the sun."

On the day of the Yule Ball, I awakened to the smells of baking wafting through the castle. We'd been given time off through Twelfth Night as a holiday, and I realized I must have slept through breakfast. A tray of cinnamon rolls, fresh fruit with sweet cream for dipping, and coffee sat on my dressing table. Hanging on the back of the plush green velvet chair beside it was a black dress bag with a note pinned to it. Taking a sip of coffee, I unpinned the note. It read:

The theme tonight is Old Hollywood glamor. I chose this for you.
Thought you might enjoy something a little more festive to wear,
Perhaps for you-know-who?
Alice

Setting down my coffee mug, I unzipped the bag. Inside was a dress like I'd only seen in the movies. Pulling it out, I held it up against myself in the mirror. Ending about halfway up my thighs, every inch of it was covered in silver beads that shimmied with the slightest movement, making a seductive rattle. The dress was extremely heavy. When I examined the beads more closely, I could see that they weren't ordinary beads but real silver. Tucked in the bottom of the bag were a pair of strappy silver sandals to match, wrapped in tissue paper. Feeling like I'd stepped into someone else's dream, I slipped the dress on and buckled the shoes. The whole ensemble made me stand straighter and at least three inches taller. Admiring my reflection, I removed the overnight pin curls from my hair. As I was smoothing the tight curls out into softer waves, Elliott knocked on my door.

"Hey, I think I'm going to need your help again tonight. Mary's left me a bowtie." Elliott mumbled, wandering in wearing half of two different outfits as usual, and generally not paying attention. Then, he noticed the dress. "Gods help us! What's happened to you?"

"You don't like it?" I asked, spinning around quickly to make the beads flare out.

Elliott swallowed hard, stammering, "No... I mean, yes. Oh, blast it! You know that you look marvelous; why are you asking me?"

Feeling flirtatious, I leaned in to whisper in his ear. "Because I wanted your opinion."

"Well, you have it. I think you're gorgeous, but that's nothing new. There! Are you satisfied?" he asked gruffly.

"For now," I replied, giving a little celebratory wiggle. The beaded layers of the dress tinkled like tiny bells.

"Good. Now help me with this tie. Mary wants us downstairs and dressed as soon as possible. The Cajun Invasion is imminent, or so I've heard. I wish it were over already."

"Why?" I asked, swinging my arms left and right as I made little back-and-forth Charleston steps toward him. After a decade of ballet and then four years on the Oak Ridge High Dance Team, dancing was one talent I felt pretty confident about. "Don't you like dancing?"

"Cut that out!" Elliott said sharply. "It's like you're mocking me."

I stopped abruptly. "You can't dance, can you?"

"So what if I can't?" he stated indignantly. "The West End of London is full of dancers. They're worth a penny a pound. If I were so mad about dancing, I could learn, easy enough."

"Good," I said, patting his freshly tied bow. I ushered him out before he could protest so that I could put my makeup on in peace. "Then you can be my partner tonight."

I'd just finished clipping my pin-curled hair up over one ear with a silver barrette into what I hoped resembled an Old Hollywood style when Stella came sailing in through the window with a note from Alice tied to her leg and cawing up a storm. It said the entourage from Devereaux College was arriving. We were to assemble on the front lawn as soon as possible, accompanied by our rooks. Giving my lips one last swipe of red lipstick, I stroked Stella's smooth black feathers where they joined her beak and then ran my fingers down lightly to the tip of her tail, just as I knew she liked.

Stella clucked approvingly, and I offered her my arm. When she hopped on, I turned to admire how we looked once more in the mirror, wishing that I had a way of taking a picture. I'd never looked or felt more like a witch.

I don't know what I was expecting, but it was not a dozen devastatingly hot men on gigantic flying bears. Coming from the southwest, the bears soared gracefully despite their huge size, just like the satyrs weeks before during the Wild Hunt. The bears wore no bridles. The men who sat astride them merely clasped handfuls of their thick, heavy fur. As they came closer, I could see that all of them were wearing the long black formal traveling cloaks to which we'd become accustomed. The men sat up close to the bears' shoulder blades because behind them each animal carried two large leather cases balanced like saddlebags on either side.

"Seriously?" Tayen hissed next to me as the enormous animals touched down gracefully on our front lawn. Tayen was dressed in a gold sequined sheath as short as mine. Her long, straight black hair was swept up into a high ponytail. She looked, not surprisingly, like the model she was. "That's a bit much."

"Not really," Imani quipped, also radiant in shimmering gold. Only hers was a long gown with a daringly high slit that exposed her toned thigh. "The mascot of Devereaux College is the black bear. It's the state animal of Louisiana." Imani preened, patting her silky hair. Over one ear, she had tucked a white gardenia like Billie Holiday.

"Forgive me for not paying attention in geography class," Tayen returned.

Imani ignored her. Her eyes were fixed on the tallest guy, who had a smile like Taye Diggs. He was laughing with his friends as he unfastened one of the leather cases strapped to the side of his bear and pulled out a silver trumpet.

From the back of the group, another man approached. He looked about the same age as Mary. His straight black hair was shoulder-length, and he had a close-cropped beard. He was wearing a solid white tuxedo with a long vest and looked perhaps like the DJ Steve Aoki would have if he'd popped into Rick's Bar in the old black-and-white movie *Casablanca*.

"How delightful it is to see you again, Kano!" Mary said, extending both of her hands. Turning to face us, she announced, "Sisters, this is Kano

Crane. He leads the jazz orchestra for Devereaux College and serves as one of their Mentors."

"The pleasure is mine," Kano replied, taking Mary's right hand and kissing the back of it as he bowed. "However, I'm afraid I will not be conducting the orchestra for much longer. As soon as we return to Devereaux, I'm to be installed as the new Head of College. As I wrote to you, Master Devereaux is not well, which is why he will not be in attendance this evening. He plans to step down from all official duties with the College as the wheel of this year comes full circle. Moses Tembo," Kano gestured to the fellow with the million-dollar smile, "one of my mentees this year, has been selected to succeed me in my current position as orchestra leader."

"Are you taking notes?" Tayen whispered to Imani. "Grab him while you can. He's on his way up in the world. Ow!"

Imani elbowed her sternly in the ribs. "Be quiet for once!" She hissed back through clenched teeth. "Have you no manners?"

Mary pretended not to hear them. "Yes, I recall. I believe they've made an excellent choice in naming you as successor, Kano." Mary motioned for Moses to step forward. "And you must certainly be a very talented young man, Moses. Devereaux College's jazz orchestra is considered the best in not just America, but dare I say it, the magickal world?"

"You're too kind, Mrs. Rookes," Moses replied modestly, flashing his breathtaking smile again as he kissed Mary's hand. Literally breathtaking, as I heard Imani inhale deeply beside me.

"What's up with you?" I asked her. "You're acting all weird."

"It's him," Imani whispered back. "Moses is the man from my vision."

Chapter Twenty-Seven

"What vision?" I asked Imani.

"Remember that first week, when Katerina asked us all to scry using crystal balls? Well, when I asked mine who my true love was going to be, it showed *him*." Imani nodded in Moses's direction as he continued to speak with Mary about where they should set up the orchestra.

"Well," I replied, digesting the information, "that should make it easy then. Just go over there and introduce yourself. Maybe say something like," I tossed my hair lightly over one shoulder. "Hello. You don't know me, but my name is Imani. I'm the woman of your dreams."

"Be serious!" Imani snipped. "You're as bad as Tayen!"

"I know what would catch his attention, Imani," Hana interjected. "Why don't I go over and strike up a conversation with him about what a wonderful voice you have?"

"You sing?" Tayen asked, skeptical. "What, like opera?"

"No..." Imani drew out the word. "For your information, I sing jazz, hip hop, R&B, some rock, and a lot of show tunes. I was big into musical theater in high school. Considered trying out for a few conservatories but decided to go the pre-med route instead. More study time."

"Her vocal range is amazing," Hana seconded. "You should hear her version of Defying Gravity. It gives me chills."

"So that's what you girls do over there in the other hallways at night," Elliott joked. "Showtunes from *Wicked*. Brilliant, considering..." He trailed off, gesturing to the castle.

Hana interrupted him, motioning for all of us to follow her as she stepped back out of hearing range from the Mentors and the musicians from Devereaux. "Let me speak to him, Imani. It's a lot easier to make the first move after someone else has already put in a good word." Hana's dark eyes sparkled mischievously. "Besides, I live for this kind of thing. It'll be fun!"

"Fun for you maybe," Miranda said. "I'm no good at meeting people at parties."

"It's easy!" Hana insisted. "Haven't any of you ever practiced conversation rotation?"

We all shook our heads.

"Seriously?" Hana asked in disbelief. "I swear, people give sororities a bad rap, but we learn a lot of useful things. Conversation rotation is something you can use to work a room when you want to make sure you speak to as many people as possible. It keeps you from getting trapped on an awkward tangent with someone who is long-winded. You simply agree on a series of hand signals that indicate whether you're happy with the conversation you're engaged in or if you need one of your sisters to swoop in and rescue you. The way we do it in my sorority back home is by holding our hands behind our backs as our other sisters walk by."

Hana dropped her hands casually at her sides, then brought them together lightly behind her back to demonstrate. "As long as we're moving our arms normally, we're engaged in the conversation. Feel free to join if you like, but there's no rush. When we clasp one arm like this," she circled her wrist with her thumb and middle finger. "It means things are getting boring or awkward. We're ready to move on. But if you see this," she crossed the fingers of her hand beneath the clasped wrist. "It means someone should come to rescue me immediately; I'm floundering. You don't have to do anything else. Just signal me. I'll be watching."

Imani massaged her temple. "Is this how sorority parties go? I feel like I'm in the dugout of a Reds game."

"Not all of them," Hana shrugged. "Just a formal rush event or some of the more important mixers. You know, the kind where everyone's checking out your every move?"

At that moment I realized witches were perhaps not the most socially savvy people in any given room. However, I knew someone who would comprehend what Hana was saying immediately. "My boyfriend Stephen from back home would get it. He just finished rushing his fraternity for the fall. All he could talk about for weeks was stuff like this, even though he wasn't supposed to. So many secret signs and handshakes, and ways to figure out who was whom without asking directly. It's like some kind of code."

"Exactly," Hana replied. "Willow, you're pretty good at striking up random conversations too, so you can help me watch for signs. Everybody else just acts normally. If you don't recall anything else, just remember to hold your hands behind your back if you feel uncomfortable. Willow or I will come running."

"Sisters," Mary called, her tone bright but inquisitive, as I could tell she was wondering what we were up to, whispering together several yards away. "Let's be proper hostesses, shall we? All the rooks will be roosting in the College for the evening. Willow and Elliott, could you please show a few of these gentlemen where they might shelter their bears for the night in the Rookery? Kano and the rest of us will finish making arrangements to set up the bandstand before everyone else arrives."

"Everyone else?" I asked Elliott as we began walking across the lawn toward the Rookery. "How many more are there?"

"This year?" he shrugged. "Eh, enrollment is down everywhere. It's getting harder for colleges to recruit new witches when so much new technology seems like witchcraft. But these guys," he motioned at the Devereaux students leading their bears on short silver leashes behind us. "I figure a couple hundred at least. Devereaux's a pretty big-name school. New Orleans has many lines of hereditary witches to pull from."

"Then, no offense, because I love everyone here and everything we've been learning," I qualified. "But why would a school with so much larger of a population choose Rookes as the college to exchange Yuletide visits with?"

Elliott looked at me for a moment, puzzled, before he answered. "I keep forgetting you have zero frame of reference for the magickal world. Devereaux maintains its relationship of exchange with Rookes because everyone knows Rookes students are the most talented outside of Europe. Maybe even in the entire world. No other college uses Mary's method of observing potential witches from birth to the age of training for the Craft combined with the key component of intellectual curiosity. At Devereaux, everyone is a legacy. A hereditary witch. Some of them have the aptitude for magick carried through in their bloodlines, yes. However, others do not. In contrast, Mary's method of selection ensures that every student who comes to Rookes has a strong natural affinity for magick. We are all gifted, and that's why schools like Devereaux see value in socializing with students from a college like Rookes. No matter whom one of their students develops a friendship or something more with, they're assured that the thread of magick they carry is very, very strong to have manifested, even in children from non-magickal families."

"So we're like unicorns to them?"

"Yes," Elliott answered, looking a bit uneasy, as he glanced behind me. "Or maybe rhinoceroses, which have been mistaken for the same things. By the gods, I wish that guy hadn't come."

"Which guy?" I asked, looking over my shoulder at the three young men who followed behind us. They led two bears each on either side by long leashes.

"Don't turn around," Elliott replied. "Just keep walking. Hopefully, he won't notice me."

"Hey, Capell!" A haughty voice called. Elliott winced and mouthed the words *too late* as he turned around, stopping in the middle of the pathway to the Rookery. Leading the group behind us was a tall, muscular blonde guy who looked like he'd stepped out of an advertisement for a sailing team. He had the kind of golden tan that only people whose families used the word *summer* as a verb could cultivate.

"Yeah?" Elliott replied. He kept his hands clutched in his pockets.

"I thought that was you," the blonde guy said. His upper lip curled into a grin only on one side of his mouth. From his accent, he sounded like he was from Texas. "Glad you finally found a place. Didn't know you went to Rookes. I thought it was only a girls' school."

"No, Brock," Elliott replied, crossing his arms over his chest. "They accept men too."

"Well, from the looks of it," Brock glanced back over his shoulder where Mary and the rest were whisking their wands to transport the packs of gear that had been carried by the bears through the double doors and into the Great Hall. "They can't be too choosy these days in who they accept, can they?"

"What's that supposed to mean?" I asked defensively.

Brock turned his smug grin on me. Elliott shot me a fierce look that said, *Be quiet!*

"I mean that there aren't as many legacies to go around these days who are choosing to take up magick. Some colleges that haven't done as well in keeping up with the times have to settle for whoever they can get," Brock replied in a saccharine, condescending tone.

"Knock it off, Brock," Elliott said, stepping between us defensively. "If you've got a problem with me, then come out and say it. But I'll not stand here and allow you to insult my friends or our college."

"Whoa, ho, ho!" Brock laughed derisively, taking a step backward and putting his hands up with palms facing us. "Don't get so touchy, Capell. I was just stating the facts. Frankly, I'm glad you're here. Even lost causes deserve a chance. And speaking of lost causes, how's your old man's new operation panning out? Word is that the whole enterprise isn't very popular with the Grand Council."

"Albert's fine," Elliott answered, his jaw muscles tightening. From the shape of his trouser pockets, I could see him clenching his fists. "Everything's running right on schedule. Albion should have the new rigs open this summer."

"Unless," Brock smirked, "some unforeseen circumstances were to prevent that from happening, right? Some kind of accident, maybe, that demonstrated how unsafe they were?"

"Dad's engineers are building the foundations stronger this time," Elliott answered curtly. "Short of someone deliberately setting off explosives underneath them, everything should be fine." A challenge flashed between the two of them. Although I couldn't detect what it was, I could feel the hostility pulsating off both men in waves. The bears must have sensed it too, as they began to growl. A low, guttural rumbling sound that was a universal phrase in the animal world for *Check yourself*.

"Give him a break, Brock," one of his companions said. He had shaggy brown hair and a fairly thick Southern accent too, but more of a laid-back Gulf Coast drawl than Brock's Texas twang. "It's a Yule party. We're supposed to be here having fun. Don't go around starting your crap." He extended a hand for me to shake.

"Let's begin again, shall we? My name's Fred Jeffries. Capricorn, standard Earth magick witch, if we're going to do the whole sign thing. When I'm finished at Devereaux, I'm going to vet school. I'd love to be in residence at one of the bigger zoos that has an open-range conservation program. Really into the larger and more exotic animals, lions, tigers, and..." he pointed at the four bears he was leading. "These guys. How about you?"

"Lions, tigers, and bears, oh my!" I said, finishing the corny joke and forcing a chuckle to break the obvious tension. I shook Fred's hand, which was warm even in the frosty air. "Willow Todd. Also a Capricorn. Spirit witch, though. And... still trying to decide on life post-Rookes. I'm really into history and cultural studies, but my dad's a geologist. That's interesting too, so we'll see." We walked the bears into the Rookery and unbuckled their leads. "I don't think I've met a Fred under forty. Is it a family name?" I asked him.

"Yeah, I'm Fred the Fourth, which kind of sucks because there aren't any good nicknames for being a fourth. What are people going to call me, Quad? IV? One sounds like an all-terrain vehicle, and the other one like I'm running around perpetually dehydrated. Maybe the coolest part of being a fourth Fred is that Fred Rogers was my great-grandpa."

"Really!" I exclaimed. "That's awesome. Who doesn't love Mr. Rogers?"

Fred covered his mouth and wheezed, "No, not really. I'm bullshitting you. I'm just plain Fred... again." He rolled his eyes and sighed playfully.

I laughed, for real this time. Fred was pretty funny and also pretty cute. Elliott tapped me on the shoulder. "We should be getting back. Mary's probably wondering what's taking us so long. We can send the new arrivals down here to Mr. Rogers and friends if that's okay." Elliott glanced over at Fred, who returned a *whatever* shrug as we left, heading back toward the castle.

Halfway down the path, when we were out of earshot of the Rookery, Elliott said, "I feel like I should explain what just happened with Brock. So that you don't think I'm some kind of insecure ass who goes around with a massive chip on his shoulder all the time." I said nothing and just waited for him to continue.

"Brock's father owns Owens Petroleum. It's one of the oldest independent operations on the Gulf Coast. My dad tried to start Albion's North American expansion by buying up a few older offshore rigs from one of their smaller competitors. For some reason, the former owner was ready to retire and wanted to sell out to anybody *but* Owens. Not long after the buyout, one of the rigs exploded. An investigation found that everything was mechanically sound, so it was more likely to have been sabotage than an accident. Afraid of the bad press on their first venture here, Albert sold those rigs again, that time to Owens. I think he barely broke even after the insurance payout. That's why he decided to refocus Albion's efforts on trying to persuade the state governments here to open offshore drilling in the Outer Banks."

"So, what you're saying is Albert thought Owens deliberately sabotaged his operation to make him sell after the original owner refused," I replied. "Wow. If that's true, then Brock's a total jerk. I mean, to show up here and immediately start ragging on you about it. Do the two of you even know each other personally at all, or just through your dads?"

"Not really," Elliott answered, as he slowed down a bit. I could see the reluctance in his face as we approached the rest of the crowd from Devereaux. They were waiting in line to be formally greeted by Mary as they filed into the Great Hall. "We kind of don't have to. I'm the sort of guy whose name precedes me in the magickal world. And not in a good way. The year my mum died, every witch in the world must have seen my school photo. It was plastered across the front page of *The Auger* for months. Usually accompanying some tear-jerking story about what would become of the poor child produced by such a nightmare family."

"What an awful thing to go through. I'm so sorry." I murmured, sensing that Elliott didn't want to be overheard discussing the whole situation.

"Don't be," Elliott whispered back. "I've lived with it so long, the last thing I need is pity. Especially from you. I just wanted to clarify the motivations for my behavior so that you can judge accordingly."

"Judge what?" I asked.

"Judge if you'd rather throw over your old non-magickal boyfriend back home for a nice guy like Fred or someone like me." I gave him a look. "Stop it," Elliott replied. "I saw you flirting with him. And it's alright. I know I've been super lucky to have the market cornered on your attention by being the only dude here for a few months, but this won't last forever. The real world is still out there waiting for us, you know. Someday soon, we'll have to face it."

"Thankfully, not tonight," I concluded, as Hana bounced up to me.

"I'm so glad you're back. You've got to help," Hana pleaded, grabbing me by the hand and pulling me inside the castle doors. "Tayen keeps teasing Imani while she's trying to talk to Moses. From the look on Imani's face, she seems about ready to slap her. And Miranda just keeps standing there, blushing and not talking to anyone at all. Except me, through sign language. She's had her hands behind her back the entire time, calling for a rescue, but I haven't made it over there."

"Relax," I said, glad to have an easier problem to solve than trying to bolster Elliott's self-esteem. "I'll handle Miranda. She just needs someone to help get the ball rolling. Send Tayen over to us so that she'll give Imani some room to work her charms on Moses."

Squeezing my hand in thanks, Hana dashed off toward the other side of the room. Although she was momentarily flustered by the fact her friends weren't having a very good time, as soon as that drama was over, I could tell Hana was really in her element. Buzzing around the party, Hana knew every Deveraux student's name and half of their life stories before we even sat down at the banquet tables.

"Does everyone just randomly pour out their hearts to you all the time?" Tayen yawned, when Hana finally landed at our table an hour later, spilling over with tea about everyone in attendance. "That must be exhausting."

"Oh, I think it's fun!" Hana replied, bursting with energy. "I miss being in a roomful of people. I mean, you guys are great and all, but..."

"But we're not exactly a night at the sorority house?" Miranda joked, feeling more at ease now that she was sitting with us and not lingering awkwardly in the middle of the room.

"Hana! There you are!" A male voice called over the announcement that the band was about to start playing. "Come dance with us!"

"You know I love you," Hana gushed, popping up from the table and kissing Miranda on the top of her head, then darting off once more.

"There she goes, Miss America," Tayen said in a sing-song voice. She swirled the cinnamon stick around in her hot mulled wine and downed the remainder of her glass in one swallow. "We should probably go be congenial." Setting the glass down, Tayen strode out toward the dance floor.

"Look!" Miranda pointed at the stage. It was set up in front of the entrance to the Spirit hallway. "Imani's up there! She's going to sing!"

Posing in a perfectly placed beam of magickal light, Imani seemed to glow as Moses announced the first tune of the evening would be "As Time Goes By," from *Casablanca*.

"May I have this dance?" a female voice asked. Elliott turned to see a slender woman with a wavy blonde bob hovering behind us in a short, black beaded dress very similar to mine. Her eyes were winged with cat's eye liner, and her lipstick was a deep shade of plum. A look of surprise passed over Elliott's face as he glanced up at her, then at me. For a moment, I was relieved.

"No, not you," the young woman smiled, extending her hand to Miranda. "Her." Initially looking bewildered, Miranda accepted her hand. After understanding her intention, Miranda beamed.

"Well, what do you know?" I said, shaking the ice in the bottom of my glass as we watched Miranda being led away onto the dance floor by the woman with the plum lipstick. "Tayen called it. She's going to die because she missed seeing Miranda's moment of awakening, finally."

"I don't think she missed it," Elliott replied. Tayen waved at us to come join her from across the room as the band began to play. He rose, carrying his drink with him. I cleared my throat loudly. "What?" he said in an irritated voice, then realized what I meant a moment too late.

"Hey, could I have the first dance?" Fred asked, appearing from the crowd beside our table. Hesitating, I watched Elliott's expression drop when I replied, *Sure*. Trapped by indecision and unable to speak, Elliott sank back down as we passed by him on our way to the dance floor.

Fred was an excellent dancer. He even knew the right patterns of steps for a waltz, unlike most guys, who tended to just sway back and forth during slow tunes. Putting my head on his shoulder as we twirled around, I inhaled his scent. He smelled like a mixture of warm sandalwood and vanilla. Blended with the sound of Imani's lush, smoky voice over the shimmering piano solo, it felt as if I were being carried into a dream on a pillowy cloud of jazz.

"Duty calls," Fred smiled as the song ended. "I couldn't resist just one dance before we got into the full swing of things. You look stunning." Twirling me away from him dramatically, Fred returned to join his bandmates. Picking up his saxophone, he gave me a wink as the band launched into the more upbeat tune, "Jump, Jive, and Wail."

"You could not have played that better," Tayen almost shouted in my ear as we scurried back from the stage so that we could hear one another talk. "I'm so proud of you!"

"Why?" I asked. "Where's Elliott?"

Tayen smirked. "Probably sulking somewhere. Which is good. Hopefully, it will be a learning experience. Did you see the look on his face while you were out there?"

"No... yes, I mean," I scanned the crowd but didn't see Elliott anywhere. Our table was empty. "I should go find him."

"Nope," Tayen put her hands on my shoulders. "You should stay here and have a good time. Stop babysitting him. It's clear to anyone with eyes that he adores you. Make him say it."

Reluctantly, I agreed. Over the next several hours, we had a blast. Tayen was a master in the art of ignoring people just enough to be intriguing. Combined with Hana's over-the-top energy and my ability to improvise choreography, the three of us owned the dance floor. Miranda and her partner joined in for a while. However, toward the end of the evening, they settled into chatting and giggling at a table by themselves. In contrast, Imani reveled in her night in the spotlight. Her sultry voice circled through dozens of tunes, with Moses's trumpet solos weaving among her words in perfect accompaniment. By the end, it was clear to everyone present that they were head over heels for one another.

The party broke up in what must have been the wee hours, judging from the position of the moon in the winter-bright sky. Mary handed each of the Rookes Mentors and witches a ring of keys for our respective hallways, along with a list of corresponding rooms for our guests from Devereaux. It was a fact universally acknowledged, even if unspoken, that whatever romances might have been sparked that night would have to continue at another time. Given the number of us present, along with the possibility that our Mentor witches could overhear every word, the only thing we lacked that would have made the end of the night perfect was some privacy.

Nevertheless, after everyone was settled in and the candles dimmed, I heard a tapping on my window. Setting my hairbrush down on the dressing table, I went over to the window and opened it. There was Stella, with a note and a sprig of mistletoe tied to her leg. The note read:

Tonight was wretched. I felt awful. Went to bed early.
If you forgive me, bring this to the orchard tomorrow after everyone leaves.
It didn't need a signature.

I almost stomped across the hallway to pound on his door and ask for an explanation. Almost. Though remembering what Tayen said earlier, I thought better of it. Instead, I attached another note to Stella's leg with the spring of mistletoe. That note replied:

Nope. Downstairs. Great Hall. Now or never.

Her eyes glittering with the excitement of two messages in one night, Stella was off in a flash. I took my time and finished brushing the curl out of my hair into soft waves that tumbled down over my shoulders. Slipping back into my dress, I left my silver shoes behind so that no one would hear me clopping down the hallway.

As I descended the stairs, I saw Elliott sitting at the same table where we'd begun the evening. Still in his suit, although he was also barefoot and his tie was undone. He looked like he'd been crying. The sprig of mistletoe lay on the table, illuminated by a single candle. When I sat down beside him, he kissed me immediately, lingering for a long time.

"Was that so hard?" I asked.

"Yes, dreadfully," he replied and kissed me again.

Chapter Twenty-Eight

Six weeks after our snogfest at the Yule Ball, Elliott still wouldn't discuss it. Every time I tried to bring it up, he'd change the subject or get all weird and pretend that he had something urgent to do elsewhere. However, I knew he had to be thinking about it as much as I was. I kept catching him staring at me when he thought I wasn't looking. Which was exactly what he was doing while Cora was teaching us how to use a heating spell to dry out corn husks quickly so that we could use them in our Imbolc ritual. That morning, we each sat in front of one of the ten stone fireplaces that flanked the first-floor entry to the five hallways.

"Hold your left palm up close to the fire," Cora instructed. She paced around the circle of the Great Hall behind us. "As if you're warming it. Focus your eyes on the flame and try to relax. Then, place your other hand just above the corn husks. Draw the heat and channel its energy. You may feel a slight itching or tingling sensation as it moves, but that is expected. Fire spells occasionally make the skin dry and the muscles numb. Also, if you are sweating, then that means you have established the energy channel correctly. Just be patient and wait. Don't take your eyes from the hearth. You will smell it when the heat begins to wilt the leaves."

Sweat dripped from my temples and ran down my chin as I tried to concentrate. Feeling his gaze burning even more intensely than the real fire in front of me, I snuck a glance to my left at Elliot. He was sitting before the hearth on the opposite side of the Spirit corridor. Sensing me staring at him, Elliott averted his eyes immediately.

"Focus, Willow!" Cora intoned, tapping me on the shoulder with her wand as she paused behind where I sat on a wooden stool before the hearth. "As the saying goes, a wandering mind kindles no flames." To Elliott, Cora said nothing.

Gazing into the dancing embers once more, I sighed and tried to let the tension go from my shoulders. As I did, I felt a prickly warmth spread up my right arm, across my chest, and down my left arm. Moments later, I could smell the unmistakable odor of roasting corn.

"Excellent," Cora said. "With proper focus, it only takes a moment. See for yourself."

I looked down at what had been a stoneware platter piled high with freshly shucked green corn leaves sitting on a small, low table beside me. Those same leaves had withered to a dry, crispy brown. When I touched the platter, it was warm. Turning to take them over to the larger table, I saw the other students finishing up as well. Everyone, that is, except Elliott, whose shucks were still as green as if they'd just been harvested from the field.

After I placed my platter on the table, I started to return to the fireside in hopes of assisting Elliott. However, Cora discouraged me, wanting him to finish the spell on his own. That was part of his recent weirdness. Since the Yule Ball, Elliott's magick had become more difficult to control. At times, he had trouble summoning it at all.

Sitting at the table instead, I pulled Alice's grimoire closer to examine the diagram of the corn dolly that I was supposed to assemble. It was easy enough. Bending, twisting, and splitting the crackling leaves into the shape of a woman in a full skirt. More complicated was figuring out what messages to write on the small slips of parchment that were stuffed into her head and chest along with the cornsilk. The instructions said I was supposed to write down some current trouble that worried me and something that had weighed heavily on my heart for a long time. After thinking about it, I wrote, *Where will I go after I leave Rookes College?* for one, and *my mother Darla's indifference* for the other. Putting them inside the dolly, I tied her waist and neck securely with thinner strips. Then, I added more dried cornsilk to her hair, capping it off with a little leafy peaked bonnet. It didn't look exactly like the drawing in Alice's grimoire, but it was very close.

For once, it seemed that I was the first to complete her preparations for the spell. Tayen, a natural Fire witch, had roasted her shucks almost immediately. Yet, she was struggling with how to assemble the doll. Mostly because she wasn't looking at the instructions. Cora's grimoire lay on the table beside Tayen, unopened. Gliding around the room, Cora noticed this too. With a few flicks of her wand, she flipped the book open to the correct page and whisked it onto the stand right in front of Tayen's face. Watching the quiet battle of wills between those two always made me chuckle. Although both were impulsive by nature, Cora's ability to keep her temper under control when dealing with the nearly impossible-to-teach Tayen was a marvel.

"When you've finished, ahem..." Cora stated, clearing her throat for Tayen's benefit. "You may proceed to the final step of the Banishment Spell, in which you return to your place by the fireside. Meditate for a few moments until you have a thorough understanding of the messages that you've inserted into your dolls. When you can see the sources of your consternation clearly in your mind's eye, toss your dolls into the fire. Keep your eyes closed. A vision either of their release or what you must do to release them will come to you. Last, please remember that we will not share our visions with anyone until later tonight at the sabbat."

As instructed, I picked up my corn dolly and sat down once more before the hearth. Beside me, Elliott continued to struggle with the warming and drying part of the spell. Wanting to help him but not desiring to disappoint Cora with my disobedience either, I turned to face the fire directly so that I wouldn't be distracted by his efforts. Closing my eyes, I whispered the problems that I'd tied into the doll over and over. It seemed as if they ran around in my brain like an endless ticker at the bottom of a television screen. At last, I took a deep breath, and with my eyes closed tightly, threw the doll into the flames.

While I listened to the fire hiss and crackle, the first image I saw was my mother, Darla. She lounged in a long, form-fitting light gray jersey dress on a dark slate gray velvet sofa. Although I couldn't tell if it was just the way I was receiving the vision or if the colors were true, it seemed as if everything else in the room was some other shade of gray too. Gray floor, gray walls, gray coffee table, gray everything, as if she were in a cave. In one hand, Darla held a massive balloon glass of pale white wine, and in the other, a digital tablet. As she scrolled through it listlessly, something that I couldn't see in the scope of the vision made her jump. Darla flipped the tablet shut and downed a big gulp of wine. She sat there looking guilty as a man walked into the room. As he turned toward her, the vision began to fade. Before it went completely black, I saw the man was Plastic Kurt, her surgeon husband.

The second vision felt like it took an eternity to materialize, but I remained patient. When it did, I was no longer sitting still, observing the scene from a fixed perspective. Instead, I hovered over it, looking down from above. Realizing that I was flying, I began to maneuver around. In contrast to my initial vision, this one was in full color. The green rolling hills were so bright and lush that they hardly seemed real. More like a supersaturated photo on a tourism website. I sailed above a narrow river with an old rock bridge spanning over it in several arches. On the other side, I passed the moss-covered ruins of an ancient castle. The side walls were mostly caved in, but the front wall maintained its original, tall Gothic window, now empty of glass. Continuing onward, I flew over several fields and a second set of Gothic ruins, more decomposed than the first ones.

It was then I began to have the sensation that someone was watching me. Wondering if it was Elliott staring at me so hard back in the material world that I could feel it through my trance, I wanted to say something. However, I didn't want to spoil the vision. Instead, I flew on, touching down at last on the meticulously sculpted lawn of a massive Gothic manor house. A river ran beside it, and there was a hedge maze cut into intricate spirals out front. Around the back, a mirrored glass atrium several stories tall sheltered an indoor pool. Back on solid ground, I walked up to the wall of glass and tried to peer inside.

Once more, I sensed the uncanny pressure of staring eyes. The air around me suddenly became thin. I felt my heart rate increase as I inhaled more deeply to get enough oxygen. A wave of tingling chills pulsated through my spine. I heard a voice from somewhere telling me not to turn around. Then, my shoulders began to shake involuntarily back and forth. Just as I came to, I saw a quick flash of an image. The kind of thing that you might see if you flip the lights on and off in a room in front of a mirror. A dark shape of a pale-faced woman dressed all in black. Her large, red-lipped mouth filled with sharp teeth opened wider than humanly possible.

She shrieked an otherworldly sound that reverberated around the interior of my skull like the echo of a gunshot in a deserted valley. The scream broke my meditation and jerked me out of my vision so forcefully that I fell off the stool and onto the floor.

When I opened my eyes, Elliott's terrified face was inches from mine. "Willow? Are you alright? What did you see? Say something!"

"Something?" I replied, groggily realizing that he must have been the one shaking me by the shoulders.

"I'm sure that she's perfectly fine, Elliott. Calm down. Please step aside and let me see." Cora said firmly. She knelt beside me, putting a hand on my forehead.

"No!" Elliott shouted. "It's like she was having a seizure. She saw something that wasn't right. I need to know what it was!"

"What is all this yelling about?" Mary said, descending the staircase with Gregor on her shoulder. Cora stood up and whispered into Mary's ear. Mary nodded and told Gregor to fetch Alice. The bird swooped off in search of her. Last, to Elliott, she said, "We need to have a word. Come with me. Cora and Alice will attend to Willow."

Reluctantly, Elliott followed Mary up the stairs, stealing a few glances back in my direction as Cora helped me to stand. By the time I was steady enough to walk, Alice had arrived. She asked me to follow her out into her office in the Spirit tower rotunda, where we could speak privately while Cora finished up the lesson with everyone else.

"So," Alice began. "Care to tell me what all the commotion is about? I know it's tradition to wait and share the visions from Banishment Spells until the official Imbolc ceremony, but I promise that I will act surprised regardless."

"To be perfectly honest," I replied. "I'm not quite sure I understand what I saw."

"Well, let's start with what message you put inside the doll. It's about the head and the heart, right? What worries you in the present, and what emotions are holding you back from your past? Something along those lines? What did you write, and then what did you see?" Alice asked.

"For the current worry," I answered, "I asked where I would go after Rookes was over. For the longer-standing negative emotions, I wrote asking about why my mother was so indifferent towards me. I think the vision responded to the second question first. I saw my mother, Darla, in this strange, all-gray house, wearing a gray dress. She was sneaking to read something she'd found on the internet. It made me want to reach out to her because she seemed very sad."

"Perhaps you should," Alice said. "The grayness of her world could be interpreted as either boredom or loneliness. In either case, she might welcome a visit from her only daughter. Alternatively, it could point to feeling trapped in a morally ambiguous situation, in which she knows that she must act in a devious manner to save herself. Regardless, I do think that part concerns reconciling with your past, particularly your mother. How about the other one?"

I explained to Alice what I'd seen in the second part of the vision. Also how startled Elliott had been when he woke me up. She listened carefully, asking me to repeat the description of the house and grounds. "Well," Alice said at last. "Although it's going to spoil the surprise for at least two more people during the ceremony tonight, I think we should tell Mary and Elliott about what you've seen as well. Once Mary knows, I believe she'll have a better understanding of why Elliott was so upset. It explains why he's been watching you like a hawk. Also, I think it will give Elliott some peace of mind to know that his magick has been off for a definite reason."

"So you've noticed that too?" I asked. Alice nodded. "What do you think is going on? How could all of it be connected to what I've seen?"

"I believe that the place you envisioned was Elliott's father's estate in Ireland," said Alice. "The face that you saw reflected in the mirror was the spirit of an evil witch who drove Elliott's mother insane. Just to be sure, I would like a second opinion, though. Follow me."

Once upstairs, the four of us sat in Mary's office. Elliott's expression was somewhere between desperation and total panic. "So, you've seen her?" Elliott asked.

Mary didn't allow me to answer. "Elliott, I believe it's clear the Black Hag was part of Willow's vision. However, we must be mindful of the fact that sometimes what we see in visions are only glimpses of what could be, not what must be."

"But Willow's question," Elliott's eyes caught mine for reassurance, "was to ask where she would go after Rookes. How could that not be a sign that the Hag is watching her? Waiting for just the right opportunity, just like she did with my mum, to tempt her to unthinkable things?"

"We can't," Mary replied patiently. "However, I believe it's a bit rash, based on a singular vision, to believe that Willow is fated to be pursued and then persuaded into the practice of dark magick by the same nefarious being who plagued your mother. Instead, we must look at the practicalities of the situation. Is it likely at some point, given the bond that Willow and you have forged during your time here, that she will visit your father's home in the future? Yes. Is the Black Hag a resonant spiritual entity on that property who frequently attempted to influence the behavior of living witches? Also, yes. Yet, the difference in this situation is between the two women. Would Willow react in the same manner as your mother, Gwendolyn? No one can say for sure. However, it is folly to judge any one human being by the actions of another. Every life is singular in that aspect. It doesn't account for free will, individual choice, or other differing factors. Simply put, the likelihood that Willow would repeat precisely the same mistakes as Gwendolyn is minuscule. They are simply too different in every aspect of their temperament and motivation."

Elliott seemed as if he were about to object again but held it back.

"I'm sure the two of you will have much to discuss going forward," Mary continued. Eyeing my reaction as well, she attempted to redirect the conversation. "However, this is not the moment. Nor do I believe that one vision alone is a sufficient cause for concern regarding Willow's well-being. If later events prove otherwise, we shall revisit the issue. At present, we should go down and rejoin the other witches while they finish preparations for this evening."

Mary stood and crossed the room to open the door for the rest of us, effectively declaring the conversation closed. Elliott did not look at me as we followed Alice downstairs, where our fellow students and Mentors were waiting, having completed their spells and prognostications. Although no one asked directly, I could tell they were all dying to know what had happened.

Not wanting to allow time for speculation to fester and grow, Mary immediately began her speech about the holiday. "Imbolc is the smallest and quietest of the eight sabbats that make up the wheel of our year," Mary began. "Yet like the tulip bulb that bursts into full flower at the first sign of spring, so are we to interpret the visions and inspirations that we receive at Imbolc. As the proverb goes, from a seed, a meadow grows. Thus, let us take this winter interlude of deepest darkness to reflect upon how we might choose to begin again if all doors of possibility were open to us. The first step toward any journey isn't just the walking itself. Rather, it's in the giving of permission to oneself to move forward. To proceed in harmonious acceptance and agreement with the divine movements of fate."

Plucking one of the numerous corn dollies from the table arrangements of winter wheat around her, Mary examined it. "Imbolc is a sabbat of quiet reflection. A time of personal rededication to the Craft. A subtle, often unspoken, agreement between a witch and the universe to use magick only for good and to hold oneself accountable for its results is made while the rest of the world slumbers. Such modest magick is essential in this day and age when so many utilize glamor to conceal their bodies and motivations from others. Thus, we call upon the spirit of Brigid, the warrior mother, goddess of the heart and hearth, to give us the strength to endure hardships. We ask her to guide us, like a flower bulb searching for the sun in springtime. Through the darkest nights of our winters and into the warm light of revelation gained by self-exploration."

With a few waves of her wand, Mary summoned a series of baskets from the kitchen. As they floated down into place before each of us at the tables, she continued to explain. "Tonight, as we begin the Imbolc period of quiet reflection, we honor Mother Brigid. Goddess to the pre-Christian Irish, and also the only female patron saint of Ireland, on her feast day. In one of your baskets, you will find potato bread and cheese, along with blackberry jam, wild honey, and butter. Foods all native to Ireland for us to enjoy during this evening's meditations. In the other basket are bundles of rushes that we will shape into a symbol of the goddess."

Mary paused to point to a large square cross made of straw that hung over each archway leading into the five corridors. "Brigid's cross has been a symbol of protection for over a thousand years. It represents the fact that no matter how dark life may seem, the great wheel in the sky will continue to turn. As such, it may be carried in one's pocket or hung over a doorway as reassurance of brighter days ahead."

Picking up a smaller version of the woven cross from the basket of reeds by Elliott, she handed it to him. "Your Mentors have woven a cross for each of you to observe as you shape your own and also to carry in the spirit of motherly protection. Later this evening, when we have finished our weaving, I will inquire which of you would like to visit briefly with your mothers. If you so desire, you may tell them what you've experienced so far, here at the midpoint of your education at Rookes. When you return, we will share those experiences over our Imbolc feast. That will also include strawberry shortcake and ice cream, the favorite of a certain witch here, in honor of her birthday." Mary glanced over at Hana, who smiled back, as she concluded.

"You may be surprised to find that your interaction tonight helps to create a bridge between the two of you that strengthens your bond. Communication with our mothers can be difficult and our relationships sometimes fraught with growing pains over the years. However, we must always remember that every mother was once a girl herself."

Chapter Twenty-Nine

After we'd finished weaving our Brigid's crosses and exchanged them with our Mentors, we received their blessings and gave ours in return. Mary asked again if any of us would like to conclude our observance of Imbolc by visiting our mothers to tell them about our lives at Rookes. Imani said no, for the logical reason that in her mother Zuri's advanced state of dementia, expecting her to comprehend anything new would be very difficult. Elliott also declined because visiting Gwendolyn was impossible. Although Hana pondered it, ultimately she decided against attempting to contact her adopted mother, because Camilla would simply refuse to believe that something as unscientific as magick could exist. Last, Miranda claimed that her mother, Viola, would wrongfully interpret any mention of magick as the Devil's work.

Ultimately, it came down to Tayen and me to complete the ritual by visiting our mothers. Both my mom, Darla, and Tayen's mother, Bly, were big into astrology, tarot, and the whole New Age nine. It should have made them the most receptive to hearing that their daughters were real-life witches. That would have been the sensible reaction. However, my mom has rarely done anything in her life that made sense. After that night, I found out that Tayen's mom was pretty irrational too.

Using our newly developed skills of disappearance, Tayen and I each transported ourselves magickally to our mothers' respective homes after dinner. Tayen went to Bly's compound in Calabasas, and I went to Brentwood.

Darla and her second husband, Plastic Kurt, had lived in one of those monstrous fortresses of brick, marble, and glass out on Concord Road since they got hitched when I was still in grade school. Even though I was told that Plastic Kurt had built it as a same-size replica of some Newport Gilded Age cottage, I recalled being unimpressed with the mansion upon my first visit as a child. Chiefly because it had eight bathrooms but no swimming pool. I also remembered being terrified by the uncannily realistic humanoid statue in my mother's dressing room closet that was made out of tiny pieces of mirrored glass. Even after Darla explained to me that it was just a piece of expensive sculpture, I remained unconvinced that it wasn't some cleverly disguised cyborg or replicant waiting for the right moment to strangle me the moment my back was turned. I'd seen the original *Blade Runner* on Blu-ray with my dad and enough of the *Terminator* films to believe anything that looked like a humanoid robot was not to be trusted.

The statue scared me so much that after two or three more visitation weekends, Mom gave up and started driving out to Oak Ridge to see me twice a month. However, it wasn't long before her twice-a-month trips dwindled to once a month, then once every six months. By the time I was in junior high, Darla visited only on the major holidays. Weirdly, for reasons unbeknownst to me, Darla never sent presents. We never visited on the actual day of the holiday either, but a day or two before or after. She and Plastic Kurt usually threw some kind of swanky soiree in their tennis court-sized ballroom on the actual days, to which I was never invited until I was much older. By then, I didn't want to go.

Darla rarely attended any of my dance performances that I could recall. Oliver was almost always the only dad out there in a sea of moms. He seemed super awkward in his scruffy beard and plaid flannel as he held my glittery tie-dyed unicorn backpack full of costumes. Looking back on it, Oliver was probably a big hit with the mom squad, though. Most moms dig it when a dad tries to be an involved parent. He's got a cool accent and is a decent-looking dude, I suppose. Better than Plastic Kurt, if only because Oliver can still move all of his facial muscles. And, unlike Plastic Kurt, Dad's not over seventy years old. I know Mom's choice of Kurt over Dad was primarily about money. Still, I've never been able to understand Darla's taste in anything. I mean, she spent a wad of cash on a terrifying cyborg mirror statue in her closet and called it *Art*. That's all anyone needs to know about my mom's sense of aesthetics.

Regardless, when I appeared on the lawn of Mom's house in Brentwood that evening, it had been about nine months since Darla last graced me with her presence at my high school graduation. She'd stayed long enough to hear me give the valedictorian speech, cross the stage, collect my diploma, and snap a couple of pics. Mom made a beeline for the door when she saw Dad weaving his way through the crowd. During the years since they separated, I don't think I'd ever heard Darla speak more than a few words at a time to Oliver. Even then, it sounded painful.

From the outside, Darla's house looked about the same as always. Fifteen thousand square feet of two-story brick consisting of a main hall and two wings of what Darla referred to as "occasional rooms." Plastic Kurt's wing was full of more subtly creepy modern art. All of it had some highly esoteric symbolic meanings that only he claimed to understand. He considered them "investment pieces." Kurt's wing also had three guest bedrooms for when the three grown children from his first marriage came to visit. According to Darla, that was only about once a year. They're all just a few years younger than Darla. I've never met any of them. The daughter was some kind of surgeon who was always off on a medical mission trip in some far-flung part of the world, and the sons were both in financial consulting. When I'd asked Darla to explain what financial consulting was, she said it was a polite term for wasting other rich people's money.

Mom's wing looked like a small music museum. Since marrying Plastic Kurt, she'd expanded her guitar collection from the three she used to play to literally dozens. All were signed by famous artists. They hung in climate-controlled plexiglass boxes on the walls. A man came by once a month to tune them so that their necks didn't become strained, or so I was told. Darla also had a couple dozen of those old-school rhinestone cowboy-type suits that a bunch of dead country music singers I'd never heard of had worn in the sixties and seventies. To me, the whole thing looked like something out of a Wes Anderson movie. Like I said, I've never understood my mother's sense of taste.

By the time I was born, Darla didn't play much music anymore. Back in the nineties, when country music was popular, she'd had a band that did a lot of touring and even had a record deal for a little while. Nothing much ever became of it. Her debut album did okay, but she froze up during the production of the second. She was still playing around with little club gigs but couldn't seem to write anything new. Then, she tried college at the University of Tennessee for a couple of semesters but didn't graduate. That was where Darla met Oliver. Dad had just finished his PhD at the University of Edinburgh and was doing a post-doc fellowship in Geology at Oak Ridge through UT. Things trucked along okay with them for a year or two. They got married, and then she found out she was pregnant with me. She was still working with her band some. While she was pregnant, it was like some kind of light went on, and she could write again. However, it was hard for her to lose the baby weight, and her label was getting tired of how she kept dragging things out. Plus, she became difficult to work with, or so I heard. Drinking too much, showing up late for rehearsals, and yelling at her bandmates when she finally arrived. Despite all this, Darla chose to place all the blame for her lagging music career on the fact that she'd gained weight and looked older. By then, most of her old Nashville friends had hit the age where they started having what they called "work done." On their faces, hips, and whatever other parts of their bodies they were tired of looking at. That was how Darla met Plastic Kurt and ended up living in the country music mausoleum. Mom allowed Kurt to mold her whole body to suit him and then he installed her in the live-action display case of their Brentwood mansion just like a collectible classic guitar.

Anyway, the middle part of their compound was decorated in the front half like any other rich person's house who was trying to show off a bunch of new money. High ceilings dripping with crystal chandeliers. Coffered walls stuffed with gigantic, gilded mirrors. Dozens of antique whitewashed chairs and settees no one was allowed to sit on. White marble floors in a ballroom that stayed empty except for a white grand piano that no one played except when they hired a pianist to come out for parties. Passing beneath the sweeping white marble staircase into the back of the center portion was the smaller part of the house that Mom and Plastic Kurt lived in. It contained their bedroom suite upstairs, with his and hers closets and baths. The main kitchen, a home theater room with a real movie screen and those automated reclining leather seats, and a living room with a bunch of custom sofas downstairs. The last time I'd seen her at graduation, Darla said they were remodeling it, but until that evening, I hadn't laid eyes upon the results.

Although I tried to walk around to the back to knock on the door where I could be heard, there was a new security fence that prevented my entry. I returned to the main front door and rang the bell. I waited patiently by the winter-dry, white marble fountain shaped like a trio of swans as the chimes echoed through the empty ballroom. Eventually, a maid whom I'd also never seen before answered. She asked my name and the reason for my visit. When I told her who I was, she asked to see my identification, which of course I didn't have with me. Instead, I just told her to say that Oliver's daughter was there to see her, and Darla would know what I meant. The maid toddled off again. After what seemed like an eternity, the maid returned and allowed me into the house.

I shouldn't have been surprised at what I saw when the maid opened the door to the back living room. After all, I'd seen it only a few hours before in my vision. Still, it was jarring. There was my mother, in a long gray dress, sipping from a comically large balloon glass of chardonnay while lounging on a plush gray velvet sofa. It was placed in the middle of a slate floor so highly polished that it shone like the surface of the ocean at midnight. The slight sheen on both the sofa and her curve-hugging dress gave her the overall appearance of a very sleek and luxurious seal. When she turned to face me, Darla's cheekbones looked more prominent than I remembered. I realized that she must have had more work done. This time, it was likely a buccal fat removal courtesy of Plastic Kurt. That was his new specialty. Her whole face seemed blurry to me, but I chalked that up to the surgeries. Every time I'd visited with Darla during the past few years, it was as if a different part of her had been erased and redrawn. The result was a slightly skewed, modernized portrait of the mother I used to know.

"Willow!" Mom cried, her eyes bright with welcome but the rest of her face frozen by Botox. Opening her arms wide in a grandiose sweeping gesture but not standing up, Darla motioned for me to sit down on the sofa close to her. She offered me chardonnay that she poured into a second empty balloon glass. "That was supposed to be Kurt's, the old buzzard," she whispered conspiratorially, as I took a cautious sip. It was good. Buttery, as the wine critics say.

"But he's late, so too bad! I'm glad you're here instead. He's a bore." Draining the last of her chardonnay, Darla set her glass on the coffee table and turned down the volume of the flat screen television the size of a pool table mounted on the gray wall inside an art deco, geometric brushed pewter frame. On the screen, the Kardashians reclined on an almost identical sofa. Only theirs was white instead of gray. To the side of the television was that damned cyborg-looking mirror woman statue. Why Mom saw fit to drag it out of her closet and give it a starring role in her new living room, considering its troublesome history with me, I'll never know.

"That's a beautiful dress. Where'd you get it?" Darla said, genuinely admiring what I had on. She twirled a section of her long, bleached-blond, perfectly beach-waved hair around one finger. Until that moment, I'd forgotten what I was wearing. The official gown for our Imbolc ceremony. A forest green velvet dress with a ballerina neckline and long sleeves that tapered down to delicate points at my wrists. The bodice was fitted, but the long skirt had a slight flare to it so that it rippled when I walked. As for where I'd gotten it, the dress came out of the same wall of wardrobes in my suite at Rookes from whence I'd been pulling perfect-fitting, old-fashioned clothing for about six months.

Deciding that was as good a segue as I was going to get into telling Darla about the college, I replied, "It's a formal dress for this new school I'm attending."

"What?" Darla's blue eyes widened as she slapped me playfully on my arm. Over the years, I'd become accustomed to Mom's every gesture being like some version of play-acting. Slightly exaggerated, as if she considered herself the star of her reality show before invisible cameras and was trying to increase the level of drama. Affected, yes, but she'd done it so long I think that she'd forgotten how to have a genuine reaction. It was just a part of her. "Get out! You've started college already? I thought you were taking a gap year," Darla asked.

"I am taking a gap year from a traditional college," I answered. "This is a different kind of school. For girls who have certain..." I searched for the right words. "Natural talents and skills that are not the kinds of things taught in a normal university."

"Ooooohhh..." Darla breathed as if I'd just let her in on some kind of top-secret conspiracy. "And you can't tell me what it is? Judging from that dress, it's not the government. Is it a conservatory? Are you studying dance or acting?" At this point, I felt that Darla was genuinely interested. Darla had always dissuaded me from pursuing music. I could tell that she considered music her artistic turf alone. Yet, on the rare occasions when she'd taken an interest in my education, it was to encourage me to pursue something else creative.

"Mmm..." I hemmed. "It's closer to acting really, but it's definitely a creative art form." Even though I'd practiced what I was going to say half a dozen times in my head as I was waiting at the front door for the maid to return, I lost my nerve when sitting in front of Darla. Then, I had an idea. "Perhaps, it would be better if I showed you. Do you remember when I was in high school drama, and we did that awful version of *The Little Foxes*?"

"Oh yes," Darla shuddered, taking another long sip of chardonnay and reclining into the sofa, with her head propped on one long-fingered, slender hand, exposing the delicate outline tattoo of a desert chameleon with its tail encircling her wrist. A reminder of her misspent youth, she'd always claimed. "It was ghastly. Why in the world would a director put on a production filled with teenagers in such adult roles? Especially with you as the Bette Davis character in the lead?" Darla snickered her little wheezing laugh that she normally reserved for company. It sounded as if she were trying to stop herself. I don't think I've ever heard my mother laugh fully out loud, like a normal person. "I mean, it's not like anyone with sense would cast you in a leading role. You simply don't draw the eye. I've always envisioned you more in character-type roles. Kind of like..."

I didn't wait for Darla to finish. Over the years, I'd heard enough of Mom's backhanded recommendations. Once she got wound up, she could go on for hours offering unsolicited advice. Although I knew it was petty, at that moment, I wanted to go for shock value. Something to finally shut her up for once. Clamping my eyes shut, I inhaled deeply, willing my body to change into my fox familiar form with every fiber of my being.

Instantly, I fell down into the folds of my dress. Darla shrieked and dropped her wine glass, which shattered on the floor. Wiggling free, I hopped up on the coffee table, accidentally knocking the other glass and empty chardonnay bottle over. Darla skittered across the room and dove behind a loveseat, peeping over the top of it like a little girl who'd seen a ghost. Behind her, the Kardashians continued chatting and preening their hair like cats with their long nails.

"Mom, don't be scared," I said, realizing how bizarre my squeaky fox voice must sound. "It's still me. Willow. This is what I've come to tell you. I've been going to a school where I'm learning to practice magick."

Darla's whole face appeared over the back of the gray velvet loveseat as she rose cautiously. "Wha..." her voice trembled. If she'd been able to raise her eyebrows, they would have been near her hairline in surprise. "What kind of magick?"

"There's only one kind," I yelped, springing over to the sofa and bouncing on the cushions. Darla never allowed me to sit on the old leather sofa that used to be in her living room before the remodel, let alone jump on it. Given how high I could jump in my fox form, bounding around on this new velvet one was especially fun. Darla's mouth gaped open and shut like a fish as I bounced from cushion to cushion. I could tell she wanted to tell me to stop, that I was getting my dirty paws all over her brand-new velvet. But how could she scold the miracle that was her daughter, who had turned into a fox right before her eyes?

"I can do other things too. Watch!"

Deciding to show off a bit, I got a running start and took off, flying in a circle up to the balcony overlooking the room. Scampering along the length of the rail, I slid down the banister back to the main floor, another *no-no* when I was a child. I stood panting in front of her, swishing my fluffy black plumed tail.

Stunned, Darla grabbed the back of the sofa with one hand and put the other to her forehead. Tiptoeing around the broken pieces of glass and puddles of spilled wine on the floor, she settled uneasily onto the sofa, still shaking. Unable to take her eyes off me, Mom started whispering to herself. "This must be a dream. I fell asleep drinking on the sofa, and this is all a dream." Darla reached for the spot on the coffee table where the wine bottle had been. Her hand grasped nothing but air. It was like she forgot her hand was attached to her body.

Worried that I might have overdone it and pushed Mom over the edge, I climbed back onto the sofa and lay down beside her, putting my paws on her lap. "No, Mom. This is real. I'm real. Touch me." Absent-mindedly, Darla stroked my head, like a child being told to pet a dog. The motion seemed to ground her. As she ran her hand over the thick, dark fur, her fingers found the thin length of cord around my neck with my silver key on it.

"What is this?" Darla asked.

"It's a key," I replied. "The key to Rookes College. That's where I have been these past few months. Where I've learned to work with magick."

Leaning in, Darla pulled the key closer to her face, studying it in her open palm. "Where did you find it?"

"Out on one of the wilderness trails where Stephen and I were hiking," I said. Glancing up, I could see the emotions churning behind Darla's eyes, even though she couldn't express them with her frozen face. "I picked it up. It just pulled me to where it wanted me to go. That's how Mary and the others choose the new witches. They leave keys in the dust out for them to find. If they're curious enough to pick the key up and follow it, then it leads them to the college where they can learn magick and never grow old."

Darla's fingers closed around the key. "Where they can learn magick, and never grow old," she repeated, closing her eyes. With my fox's heightened senses, I could hear her heart beating faster and harder as she began to cry. "Once, I found a key like this. When I was out in the woods, just like you said. I was nineteen and on a date with..." She paused to wipe her eyes. "Oh, it doesn't matter. But when you say it pulled you away—yes! That's exactly what it did. It almost slipped right out of my hand."

"What did you do next?" I asked, kneading Mom's lap with my paws, trying to comfort her. "Did you follow it?"

"No," Darla shook her head. "No, I just left it there. The guy I was with called my name, so I dropped it and ran back to him. I didn't give it another thought until later that night when I woke up and realized I'd been dreaming about it. The key. We were staying in a cabin in the woods. I ran out into the night, without any shoes on, as fast as I could go. It felt like I had lost something very precious, and I had to find it. I ran all night through the forest again. Up and down every trail, falling in the dirt every time I caught the slightest glimpse of something shiny until I must have passed out from exhaustion. By then, the guy I was with called the wilderness patrol who found me. They thought I must have been on a bad trip mixed with too much booze, but I knew..."

Darla's speech trailed off as her gaze fixed on the key once more. "I knew that I had missed something."

"Did you ever find it?" I asked. The end of my tail began to twitch involuntarily as the hairs on the back of my neck stood up. Darla's free hand, the one that she'd been petting me with, stopped moving. Cautiously, I drew my paws back beneath myself.

"Not that one, no," Darla answered. "But this one," she said as she began to pull on the cord that held the key around my neck. The muscles of my legs and shoulders tensed as I readied myself to spring. "This one is almost identical to it. Only they must have made some mistake. It's supposed to have a letter D on top, instead of a W. Give it to me!"

Darla yanked the cord. It broke free from my neck. Instinctively, I nipped her hand with my short fangs and leaped away. She yelped in pain and dropped the key. She staggered backward, bumping into that awful, mirrored statue. Then, as Darla and I watched, her with horror and me with glee, the statue toppled over. It broke at the neck and waist. The head popped off and rolled across the floor, shedding broken pieces of mirrored glass as it went.

Scooping up the key and cord in my mouth, I dashed toward the door. Realizing that I'd need my dress too, I circled back, pouncing on top of it. I pressed the folds of the skirt between my paws, hoping that would be enough contact to make it disappear with me. Darla began to howl in pain as tiny red dots of blood emerged from the wedge-shaped bite mark on her hand. Behind me, I heard a rush of heavy footsteps echoing across the ballroom. I felt the vibrations coming up through the sofa from the floor.

"What in God's name is going on here?" Plastic Kurt yelled as he flung open the door leading in from the front of the house. The bright lights of the crystal chandelier glinted off his highly polished bald head, which was as smooth as his eerily seamless face. He looked more like a robot with a silicone skin stretched over the machinery of his workings than a seventy-year-old man. I crouched down as flat as I could, hoping to hide myself from view behind the sofa cushions. Closing my eyes, I concentrated on the mental image of the Great Hall at Rookes. The calm circle of crackling fireplaces and the faces of my friends.

The last thing I heard before I disappeared was my mother crying out to Plastic Kurt, "That little bitch bit me!" When he asked who, Darla screamed my name. *Willow!*

Opening my eyes, I saw that I was once again just where I'd willed myself to be, back in the center circle of the Great Hall. Tayen's look of shock said it all. I knew no one expected me to return as my familiar fox. Sensing that something had gone wrong but choosing to wait for my explanation, Alice carried my dress upstairs and waited patiently outside the door to my room. I changed back into my green velvet gown and tried to regain some sense of composure along with my human form. Downstairs once more, I told everyone what happened.

Tayen shook her head sympathetically. "Things didn't go so hot in Calabasas either. I'd just gotten through regaling everyone with that disaster when you showed up." She then proceeded to recap what happened during her visit with Bly for my benefit.

When Tayen arrived on the pool deck at her mother's home in the Valley, Bly was entertaining a dozen or so of her female friends. Tayen dismissed them as a bunch of "Real Housewives candidates." After pulling her mother away from the party to tell her about her new life at Rookes,

Tayen said Bly didn't believe her at all. Instead, Bly accused Tayen of being high on drugs. Bly escorted her into the pool house. After the door was shut and they were out of earshot from her friends, Bly let Tayen have it. Tayen's mother told her that if she didn't stop drinking and doing drugs, she would lose her looks completely and her modeling career would be over.

Before returning to her friends, Bly also made Tayen promise not to tell another living soul about all the witchy stuff. According to Bly, "Nobody wants to hear a model spouting New Age philosophy. Her job is to stand still and look pretty." When Tayen protested, Bly picked up her cell to call her therapist. She'd set an appointment for Tayen later the following week. If Tayen didn't cooperate, Bly claimed that she would call the police and put her on a psychiatric hold, forcing Tayen to submit to rehab. Rather than sticking around for any of that, Tayen simply chose to disappear. Right there from the pool house, with her mother watching.

"At least she can't deny there was something very unusual about the way you left," I offered, trying to sound comforting. Tayen shrugged, unconvinced.

"I would not give Bly's reaction a second thought," Mary added. "Tayen, your mother showed promise when she was young. Who knows how different her life might have been had she answered the Craft's call? However, she has become a very solipsistic woman. Although I cannot read her mind from this distance, I have met many who are similar. Her selfishness is reinforced by the company she keeps. It has been my experience that women who are unwilling to believe that there is anything special about their daughters are usually dissatisfied with their own life choices. Lost in their insipid narcissism, they are unable to find beauty in others. Even in the lives of those they have physically created, and who should naturally benefit from the wisdom and experience of their nurturing."

Turning to me, Mary continued. "The same for you, Willow. However, whereas Bly's dismissal of her daughter's revelation stems from different discontents, I believe that I am at least partly to blame for Darla's reaction."

"You are?" I asked Mary. "Why?"

"Because I was the one who left her the key when I should have known that she was not prepared to accept it. Yes, Darla was exhibiting most of the elemental signs of an Air witch. Hawks, lizards, and other desert animals would follow her from a watchful distance. Dangerous storms would go completely around her, leaving her unharmed. I am sure Darla told you about the tornado she survived when she was a child."

"Yes, I remember. She said her parents lost the entire house. Her family only survived because they were locked in the central bathroom," I said.

Mary smiled sadly, "On that one point, Darla underestimates herself. The Dentons survived because she was there to move the eye of the storm, with her fear alone. Your mother would have made a fine witch, Willow. If only she'd had the open-mindedness to listen to the signs that the universe was trying to send her. Nevertheless, she did not. So she is where she is, and you are where you are. Whether Darla is satisfied with where her decisions have led her is inconsequential. The three sisters, Clotho, Lachesis, and Atropos, see all and know all. They have bestowed upon Darla the fate that she earned."

The fires in the ten hearths surrounding us crackled quietly as I contemplated this. My entire life, I'd thought that Darla left Oliver and me because we weren't up to her expectations. Somehow, Oliver, through his inability to afford the lifestyle that his wife wanted, had fundamentally let her down. Also, try as I might to be the ideal daughter, I could never make up for that disappointment. I'd never considered the other possibility. That I possessed something Darla wanted. Something that she'd given up long ago before she even knew what it was, or that it was valuable. Her free and independent self.

Glancing toward Tayen, I could see that she too was lost in thoughts probably similar to mine. When I first met her, Tayen's statuesque beauty and aloof personality made her seem untouchable. However, even though she'd grown up in a world very different from mine, at that moment, I realized we were much more alike than I'd known.

My contemplation was interrupted as a series of silver trays drifted down onto each of our tables. As one glided down at my place, the wicks of a round, white pillar candle ignited. In its glow, I saw a dish of vanilla ice cream and strawberry shortcake. Beside it was a huge chunk of raw white quartz crystal about a foot in diameter and something in a gauzy white pouch.

"Although tonight's revelations might not have given us the results we desired," Mary intoned. "They have brought us something more important. Wisdom. Now that the wheel of the year has made exactly half of its turn, all but one of you has celebrated a birthday. Thus, before we enjoy

Hana's selection of our dessert tonight, your Mentors and I would like to give each of you a present. In honor of the goddess Brigid, the nurturing mother to all. She reminds us that patient acceptance and true knowledge of oneself is the greatest gift." Mary motioned for us to open the small gauze parcels.

Loosening the drawstring, I tipped the pouch out into my hand. Inside was an intricately wrought silver bracelet in the shape of a snake. Each of the other witches had a similar one too. Slipping it over my hand and onto my arm, I felt a warmth radiating from its tiny head at my wrist, up my arm, and into my shoulder. Following Mary's suggestion, I took the large piece of quartz from the tray and placed it on the table. Putting my hand on top of it as she spoke, the same energy rippled through my entire body, making my scalp tingle. It was the same sensation that I had on the day that we'd raised the Cone of Power. The quartz began to glow brightly.

"Although our time together here at Rookes is half-completed, we offer these remembrances to you in this time of hibernation," Mary concluded. "That along whatever path your life might lead, your sisters await your call. You need only to make contact with the Earth, sky, wind, and air to summon them. For in the triple aspect, and at every age, from maiden to mother to crone, witches serve as Mentors to themselves and one another. Without judgment, forevermore. Let the circle be unbroken. In perfect love and perfect trust."

"In perfect love and perfect trust," the rest of us repeated, closing the invocation. Instantly, every flame of every candle and every hearth in the castle blew out in a puff of ash. Lit from within, the blocks of clear quartz on each table continued to radiate with a luminous phosphorescence.

Chapter Thirty

About two weeks later, we spent a Saturday afternoon picnicking on the pier. It was one of those random, unseasonably warm days that sometimes happen in late winter. Miranda announced to everyone just before lunch that she wanted to show us something, then mysteriously dashed upstairs to change. When she returned, she was wearing a wetsuit and beaming. She wanted to demonstrate her newly acquired swimming abilities. Grace, Miranda's Mentor, seemed to have been tipped off beforehand because she already had everyone's food packed into baskets to carry along.

"I think the cold weather has helped her," Grace whispered to us as we filed out the back door of the Great Hall. Even though she didn't state so specifically, I knew what Grace meant. Covered in a thick layer of black neoprene, Miranda lost the painful self-consciousness and fear of revealing too much skin in a normal swimsuit that had kept her out of the water for most of her life. For Miranda, the wetsuit was like body armor protecting her from her negative thoughts.

Nibbling at bread bowls full of homemade soup, we applauded as Miranda dove off the pier. Then, she maneuvered through several different styles of strokes. What impressed me the most was that Miranda could even do that flip-turn thing like a professional swimmer, a move that has eluded me forever. When she'd finished, Mary congratulated both Miranda and Celine, the mermaid who'd been teaching her. She noted that Celine must have spent a lot of time and effort for Miranda to have picked the skills up so quickly. Both of them blushed and giggled at one another, which caused Tayen to elbow me in the ribs. I nodded, catching her drift. By then, Miranda's interest in her mermaid swim coach was a fact acknowledged by everyone, even if never discussed.

As we were all walking back, Alice announced we were to have a special lesson that evening. In honor of Lupercalia, Alice said she was going to teach us how to cast glamors. Although we were all tired and looking forward to a day off, everyone perked up at this news. Glamor casting is high magick, a transformative power normally reserved only for witches who'd nearly completed their training. Although no Mentor was specifically limited to teach only one type of magick, it made sense to me that Alice was chosen to teach us about glamor. Her familiar form was a hare. An animal often considered in the magickal world to be an intermediary between this world and others because hares live both above and below the Earth's surface.

"In essence," Alice explained, "being able to cast glamors allows witches to live multiple lives. Their own, and others under any disguise they choose. Many people would like to change their appearance, especially in this day and age when image is everything. With so many tricks at their disposal, from contouring makeup to plastic surgery and filtering photos, even non-magickal people can use a type of glamor to seem more attractive than they are. What those people, and also many witches who use actual glamor casting techniques, don't realize is that all glamors, even magickal ones, fade. This is why I would strongly discourage you from using what you learned today about working with glamor spells in combination with love spells. Although glamor spells can assist in forming initial attractions by allowing a person to show only the best version of themselves that they can imagine, the temptation to push too far is real. Many witches have found themselves in uncomfortable and even dangerous situations when they attempted to appear as someone else entirely for too long. Sooner or later, their true identities are always revealed."

By this time, we'd made it to the patio behind the central Spirit hallway door of the college. The other Mentors went inside. Alice motioned for the rest of us to sit. Conducting a series of small spells with her wand, Alice made six silver bowls of water appear on trays. They were accompanied by small wicker baskets of red and pink rose petals. Looking over into the bowl that glided to rest on the stone table in front of me, I could see that in the bottom was a highly polished, thin disc of solid rose quartz, about six inches in diameter.

Alice squinted at the brightly contrasting colors of the sunset as they shone in a spectrum of pinks and golden oranges against an impending curtain of dark blue. "We'll wait about another half-hour until the moon is visible, and perhaps a bit afterward, before we begin. Moonlight is necessary to charge the energy of the crystal and purify the water, allowing for maximum clarity. Then, I'll ask you to take a handful of rose petals and sprinkle them over the water. Allow them to float freely as you close your eyes and visualize how your natural reflection looks. Examine your face carefully in your mind's eye. See if there is anything you'd like to change about it. Perhaps you have an old scar, or freckles that you're not fond of, or whatever it may be. Then, imagine what your face would look like if that perceived imperfection were removed, and you appeared instead as an idealized version of yourself. When you have that new visage impressed upon your consciousness, open your eyes. Allow them to focus softly on the circle of rose quartz at the bottom of the bowl. Using a similar technique of energy control as in some of the other spells we've practiced, concentrate on pushing the image you've just imagined of the most perfect version of yourself out of your mind and onto the stone. If you've done it correctly, after the spell is over and we pour out the water, you may find that your self-impression was so strong that it etched itself into the crystal."

Imani raised her hand. "Isn't quartz one of the hardest gemstones? That would take a pretty extreme amount of pressure."

Tayen elbowed her. "Listen to Miss Gemologist over here!" Imani half-scowled, eyeing Tayen with suspicion. Even though they'd become friendlier over the past few months, it was clear that Imani was never quite sure whether Tayen was laughing with her or at her.

"You're correct as usual, Imani," Alice answered. "The impressions that we have of ourselves are so deeply ingrained by our lives and external circumstances that when we push that energy outward, it can carve quartz. This is why we use rose quartz combined with water scrying in the facial glamor spell. Rose quartz is the stone of self-love and acceptance. Seeing our images in it through water allows us to pull our internal beauty outward so that everyone can see it reflected on our faces. Brace yourselves. You may find seeing the amount of beauty that you harbor inside exceeds your greatest expectations. Or it may manifest itself in a way that you'd never expect."

By this time, all the bright winter sunset colors had faded, leaving only a band of deep cobalt blue stretching beyond the horizon. Turning my attention to the silver bowl in front of me, I closed my eyes as I tipped a handful of rose petals into it. Concentrating on the facial features that I would like to change, my first thoughts were of my nose and my eyes. When I was in kindergarten, a mean little girl named Bentley smacked me in the face with a tee-ball bat. It gave me two black eyes for weeks afterward. According to the doctors that Oliver took me to, if the cartilage in my nose had been fully formed at the time, Bentley would have broken my nose. However, because I was so young, the damage was minimal. Still, it seems to have changed the angle of my nose. Looking back at childhood pictures of myself, it was clear that my nose was straight beforehand but turned up afterward. Also, I've always wondered whether some of my sinus trouble was caused by the incident. Focusing on that imperfection first, I watched my nose straighten in the water's reflection.

Encouraged, I decided to try to improve the area around my eyes as well. I've never liked the fact that I have hooded eyes. If I'm not careful doing my makeup, my eyeliner always gets stuck to my brow bone, leaving this weird line. I focused on my eyelids next, mentally pushing them higher until they looked more round and open. Satisfied with the result, I opened my eyes and focused on the disc of rose quartz at the bottom of the bowl. I tried with all my might to impress upon the stone this improved version of myself.

When I stared at my reflection in the stone beneath the water, I was equally amazed and horrified by the image that looked back at me. With my straightened nose and unhooded eyes, I was the spitting image of my mother, Darla, before all the years of plastic surgery altered her face beyond recognition. Although Mom's eyes were bright blue and mine were green, her hair was bleached blonde and mine was dark brown; every other feature was of the same face. The resemblance was uncanny.

"It seems as if each of you have decided how you would like to be seen and have made the necessary changes," I heard Alice say, in some faraway echo. I sat transfixed before my disturbing reflection in the water. "Now, I would like for you to look up from your bowls and make eye contact with the person nearest by. Take some time to share your thoughts on how your appearance has changed. However, remember to be kind, for each person's idealized version of themselves is highly individualistic. We must respect their choices."

Following Alice's instruction, I forced myself to look up from my silver bowl. Wouldn't you know it, the first face that I saw was Elliott's. He sat at the table next to mine. Until I saw it, I would have had no idea that his beautiful face could have been improved upon, but somehow he had. His jawline was even more defined, and his eyebrows were raised slightly from his usual melancholy expression. Elliott, or this recently improved version of him, looked almost like the poster of Timothée Chalamet that I'd kept in my high school locker. His lips, though... Elliott's perfectly bow-shaped lips drew me closer.

Alice laughed and interceded, stepping between us. I had no idea that I'd been leaning toward Elliott, or him toward me. We blinked simultaneously, aware of the mutual attraction. "Yes, Willow, I agree," Alice said. "Elliott's glamorized version of himself is quite charming. However, we must remember that these are only the effects of a well-articulated glamor of whatever version of ourselves we choose to project."

Regaining awareness of myself within the disorienting glamor, I refocused my gaze upon Elliott. He was staring intently at me too. I found being the recipient of his attention equal parts unsettling and a relief. Examining closely every part of his face, from the widow's peak of his untamable dark curly hair to the beguiling wildness of his gray eyes and the wry, upturned corners of his perfect lips, I found his every feature flawless. Knowing his true nature, I longed to hold him, to walk beside him along every adventure of life, and when it was done, to lie still next to him, content in the adventures that we'd shared. This voluptuously tender man who had captured my heart. As my mind drifted through this fantasy, I began to lean toward him again.

"Willow!" Alice exclaimed, snapping her fingers. Emerging from the romantic trance of my glamor, I snapped back into reality. "Focus, please!" Around me, I was vaguely conscious of the other girls whispering and of Elliott's silence. "As I was saying, now that we've had some time to experience the effect of facial glamors, perhaps it is now time to move onto more extensive spells that include whole body involvement."

Having regained our attention, Alice continued. "For the next part of our glamor lesson, I would like for each of you to return to your rooms and prepare for a ritual bath. We'll be working with the goddess Aphrodite to assist in casting our glamors, so it helps to use some of her symbolic correspondences. Stop through the kitchen for some cinnamon tea, fresh berries, and cream. Take your baskets of rose petals for the bath as well. There should be a bottle of rose oil in the cabinets for each of your bathrooms. Put a few drops into the water as you are filling the bath. Also, light some lavender vanilla incense and at least a half dozen or so corresponding red and pink candles from your candle boxes. Place them around the tub. Last, take the silver hand mirrors from your vanities and speak aloud the changes that you would wish to see in your bodies. Ask to become your most perfect form. Repeat these intentions several times, alternating with an invocation to the goddess, until you can begin to see the changes. Don't become frustrated if nothing happens right away. Remember that Aphrodite is the weaver of wiles. The fabric of glamor may take time to weave, so be patient. By the time the water is cold, your spells should be complete. When you've finished, please redress, and we'll meet downstairs in the Great Hall to discuss the effects. Don't drain the water; save it for when you return. You can heat it again with your wands to dissolve the natural sea salt solution that we use to reverse the glamor. There should be some little pots of salt in your bathroom cupboards for that purpose."

"Um," Elliott began hesitantly, "I don't mean to question your directions, Alice, but should I be attempting to invoke Aphrodite too? Because obviously..." he gestured toward himself.

"Oh, yes. I almost forgot," Alice added hastily. "Although Aphrodite is the deity primarily associated with feminine beauty, men can work with her as well. This practice is most commonly done through the simultaneous invocation of Adonis, her lover. He is considered her equivalent of male attractiveness. If you look closely in your basket of petals, Elliott, you'll see that I've intermixed some anemone blossoms with your roses. Anemone is the flower correspondence for Adonis. By combining the two, your glamor should work just as well."

After gathering our tea and other offerings, we parted ways to set up everything needed for our ritual baths. As I waited for the water to fill, I pondered what changes I would make to myself. I'd always wanted to be taller and to have naturally curly hair, so I decided to concentrate on those first. Examining my hands, I thought it would be nice to have longer, more delicate-looking fingers too. I've always hated my tiny hands and the fact that I have to buy child-sized gloves to accommodate them. Finally, as I took off my robe and stepped into the bath, I wondered if I shouldn't make my breasts smaller too. Although I know most girls think they'd be happier with larger breasts, trust me. If they were, most would change their minds. Ever since I passed a C cup in ninth grade, mine have caused me more negative attention than positive. Dudes always sneaked up behind me to pop my bra straps when I was younger, then creepy old men stared at them as I got older. Even some women, probably out of jealousy, would walk up to me randomly and cop a feel, asking me right to my face whether they were real. As I sank into the water, I concluded that it couldn't hurt to try out what life would be like as a member of the itty bitty committee. At least for a few hours.

Once I had everything situated and began the incantations, the glamor began to work. Almost instantly, my legs appeared six inches longer, and my hair swirled into the loose mane of cascading ringlets that I'd so long coveted. Yet, the sensations accompanying it were surreal. Patting my hair with my longer-seeming fingers, the texture still felt smooth, even though I could see curls in the mirror. My hands felt weird too. Testing them by pressing the tips of my right into the palm of my left was like that optical illusion trick about the floating finger sausage that kids do. My strangely long fingers seemed to go right through my hand, even though I could feel the actual flesh of their tips on my palm. Touching my hands to my breasts, I could feel their actual circumference, even though they looked like A cups. Getting out of the bath, my eyes struggled to adjust to the mirage of the floor being both the same distance and further away, as it would for someone six inches taller.

At first, it made me so dizzy that I almost fell. Holding onto the furniture as I waited for the vertigo to pass, I crept cautiously into the bedroom of my suite. There, I stood before the full-length mirror in my dressing area. Although I felt sick to my stomach, the visual effect produced by the glamor was stunning. I looked like a supermodel, albeit with smaller breasts.

Slipping back into my robe, I noticed that the length of it magickally extended to accommodate my new height. Part of the glamor's effect was that every item of clothing fit perfectly, as I would learn when I tried on a pair of gloves from one of my cabinets. Mary and the others hadn't noticed how tiny my hands were when they selected them along with my other clothing because they were for a normal-sized woman. Yet, when I put them on while I was in my glamor, they seemed to shrink. The gloves fit my shorter fingers exactly, even though they appeared to be the desired inch or so longer, held at arm's length. Pleased with myself, even if still a little woozy, I headed downstairs.

"Why, look at you!" Alice exclaimed as I stumbled down the stairs. "Careful, now. Walking in a taller glamor takes a bit of getting used to. I should have mentioned that before I sent everyone up. Perhaps I should post some signs or send the rooks around with messages."

No sooner had Alice said this than Hana came staggering down the deep blue carpet that led out from the Water tower hallway. We both called out unnecessarily for her to be careful. Hana clung to the banister for dear life as she descended. When she made it to the bottom, Hana still seemed a little unsteady on her feet. As she wobbled over to us at the center dais, I could see that Hana had chosen to make herself significantly taller too. Probably almost six feet, if she were able to stand up properly. To me, that made sense, but I was shocked to notice that her boobs looked like the size mine were before I'd used the glamor to shrink them. Imani emerged next from the Earth corridor. She was the same height as usual but looked vaguely like an African American version of one of the Kardashian sisters. In my opinion, Imani's appearance was okay, but I preferred the original, more athletic-looking Imani to this slim-thick, skinny-armed, highlighted, and contoured-within-an-inch-of-her-life version.

All three of us burst into a fit of giggles when we saw Elliott. He'd decided to turn himself into some kind of Channing Tatum clone. Every bit of the enhanced attraction that I'd felt for him when he'd only made the small change before was gone. I sighed when I noticed his hair, now ash blonde, straight, and trimmed short instead of his usual dark curls. "What happened to your hair?" I asked.

"Looks like you got it," Elliott replied, patting my head. "Oof! That's a weird feeling." He drew back his hand as if he'd touched something slimy. Glancing back and forth between Hana and me, he added, "The two of you seem to have swapped a few parts as well."

"Of course you'd notice that first," I said, rolling my eyes.

Hana preened. "Well, what do you think?"

"Not to hurt your feelings, because I know it's not the real you, but it's awful," Elliott said. "You were just fine before. Petite girls are cute. Why would you want to look like..." He searched for the right comparison. "Kimora Lee Simmons, maybe? You're so tall. And you," he turned to Imani. "Why would you want skinny arms? I'd kill for the muscle definition you have."

"Clearly," Imani replied, smirking at the near insult as she studied his arms. "Man, you are *not* cut out to be Magic Mike!"

"Good one!" Hana seconded, high-fiving Imani. Elliott looked crestfallen. I think he'd been hoping we'd all swoon at the sight of him.

"It didn't work!" Tayen whined as she materialized from the Fire hallway. Pouting as she descended the staircase, Tayen seemed to be the only one of us unaltered. Then, realizing the changes in the rest of us, she complained, "All the rest of you are like something straight out of TMZ. Even freaking Anne Hathaway over there," she waved in my direction. "But me, nothing."

"What did you set your intention to be?" Alice asked, with a puzzled expression. Alice was probably thinking the same thing as all the rest of us. Tayen was already a model with a perfect body and a face that could sell anything. What was there to change?

"I wanted to look like Adriana Lima," Tayen pouted.

"You already look like Adriana Lima," I said, matter-of-factly.

"No, I don't!" Tayen replied, indignantly. "I have copper eyes, and hers are blue. In the last photoshoot I went on, all the photographer could talk about was how he loved to work with Adriana because blue eyes caught the light so much better than shades of brown."

Elliott snorted. "Please! Just wear contacts. Some of us have real problems. Try having your face plastered on every gossip rag in the world because of your stupid dad everyone hates. Believe me, you'd be wanting to change everything about your appearance."

Tayen started to say something smart but was cut short by a cry for help from upstairs.

Glancing at all of us to see who was missing and realizing that it was Miranda, Alice dashed toward the Air corridor. The rest of us followed. Trying the door but finding it locked, Alice used her magick to open it. She rushed inside.

"Don't come in here!" Miranda wailed as she heard Alice's knock on the bathroom door. "I don't want you to see me. It's too ridiculous."

Relieved that Miranda wasn't hurt, Alice tried to remain calm. Though I could tell that she was exasperated. "There is nothing to worry about, Miranda. Everyone makes a mistake in casting a glamor eventually. It's nothing that can't be reversed. Just put some salt in the water and duck yourself under. You'll be put to rights again in no time. Check in your cupboard. There should be a small blue pot of salt somewhere. I can slide your wand under the door to heat the water and..."

"I can't," Miranda interrupted her. "I can't get out of the tub."

"What is going on here?" Mary asked.

Grace, Miranda's Mentor, was right behind her. Our attention was focused on Miranda's mysterious predicament. None of us had noticed them enter the room.

Moving to the front of the group, Grace called through the door. "Why can't you get out of the tub, dear? Are you injured?"

"I'm not hurt," Miranda sobbed. "I'm a... I'm a..." she stuttered, unable to say the word.

"Oh, enough of this nonsense," Mary pushed past Grace and unlocked the bathroom door with a flick of her wand. "Cover yourself, Miranda; I'm coming in there after a count of ten." Mary counted down the numbers and opened the door. Then, she gasped. One of those shocked old lady-like gasps like you hear in black-and-white movies.

"You're a mermaid!" Mary exclaimed.

The rest of us crowded close behind Mary to see. Sure enough, there was Miranda, with a long, shimmering tail flopped over the edge of the tub. Only I could tell that this was no glamor. Actual water dripped from the tip of her tail fin into a puddle on the bathroom floor. Miranda's top half was completely normal, as she propped against the back of the tub holding a towel over her chest.

"This is not the glamor spell we discussed," Alice said sharply. "What did you add to it?"

Miranda stared up at Alice, her hazel eyes clouded with guilt and rimmed red from crying. "I know I shouldn't have changed the spell. I shouldn't have taken the piece of Celine's hair at all." Miranda put one hand down in the water and pulled out a small lock of golden hair tied with a white ribbon. "But I couldn't help myself. Grace's grimoire said it would make us the same."

"You added mermaid hair to a glamor spell?" Grace asked, with a shocked expression that matched Mary's. "Oh my! We'll have to get you down to the pier right away. Regular salt solution won't be strong enough. We need the extra potency of actual ocean water." Grace took the lock of hair from Miranda's hand. "And we must give this back to Celine."

"No!" Miranda yelped, horrified at the thought. "We can't tell Celine that I took it. I cut it while we were in the water and she wasn't paying attention. She doesn't know. She'll hate me!"

Grace's expression softened. "Dear, Celine already knows *something*, I'm sure. Although she probably doesn't know why or who took it. A mermaid's strength is in her hair. When a piece of it is cut off, it weakens them until it grows back. Since it's just a small tuft, Celine might only be feeling a bit run down. As if she has a cold coming on or a headache. However, mermaids are naturally so healthy that any small ailment is noticeable. You simply must tell Celine the truth, return this, and ask for her forgiveness. It's the only way. Plus, the moment we put you into the water out there, all the Merfolk will sense your presence anyway. You would be an imposter in their midst. If you don't apologize immediately, they could interpret it as a sign of hostility. They might suspect that you intended to use Celine's hair to work some kind of dark magick spell to harm them. For centuries, bad witches have stolen mermaid hair for various spells. Thus, doing so has very serious implications of disrespect in their world."

"I will go down ahead and see if I can summon Celine to the surface," Mary said tersely. "A formal apology might help to smooth things over, rather than simply dumping Miranda into the water. At least it will prevent whatever sentinels are patrolling from sounding the alarm unnecessarily." Looking down at Miranda, Mary concluded. "Miranda, I am surprised at this act of theft and deliberate misbehavior. I would never have expected it. Tayen perhaps, but not you."

"Hey!" Tayen protested. "What did I do?"

"Nothing today," Mary replied. "But there's always tomorrow."

The rest of the evening was a spectacle. After Mary returned to say that Celine wasn't upset that Miranda had taken the lock of her hair, so long as she brought it back, Grace spirited her down to the pier. Alice followed along behind, carrying Miranda's robe and swabbing up the trail of bathwater left in the hallway with a mop that danced under the direction of her wand. Once we were all out on the pier, Miranda gave Celine back the lock of her hair and apologized profusely. Then, Miranda rolled off into the water and disappeared. Moments later, she bobbed to the surface. Alice handed Miranda her robe, which she put on while still in the water. Although Mary or any of the Mentors could have dried Miranda off immediately with a spell, they chose not to. Probably they thought that the chilly walk back to the castle in the now-frigid night air would be punishment enough to remind Miranda never to pull a stunt like that again.

Back in the Great Hall once more, the rest of us returned to our rooms for quick, salty dips in our tubs to wash away our glamors. Later, as we sat sipping warm mugs of apple cider spiced with cinnamon, Alice summed up the day's lesson.

"As we've seen today, glamors can be used to great advantage when a witch prefers to be seen under a beguiling disguise. However, one must always be careful to resist the temptation of overdoing it. Misused or overused glamors can create a sort of narcissistic ouroboros that causes a witch to lose touch with who she is, rather than who she'd prefer to be. Although glamors allow us to appear as idealized versions of ourselves, a little goes a long way. Too much can make a witch a stranger to everyone, including herself. This is why it is so dangerous to combine glamor spells with love spells. They can quickly spiral into the deception of all parties involved until the witch spoils the effect and gives herself away by acting inconsistently with the glamor she's cast. No one likes to be deceived, especially by someone they love."

Alice shot Miranda a meaningful look. Miranda nodded silently as Alice concluded. "Even though witches don't believe in sin, we do intrinsically know when an action is morally wrong. What you did today was wrong, Miranda, but I am proud of you for being brave enough to admit it and apologize. And I feel certain that Celine understood. She is quite fond of you, and such fondness opens the heart to forgiveness."

Later that night, after we'd all gone up to our rooms, Elliott knocked on my door. I'd kind of been expecting it, so I'd stayed dressed. As usual, he started talking without any introduction.

"So you didn't care for Channing Welles-Capell, huh?" he asked.

"Not particularly," I replied. I wanted to tell Elliott that he didn't need a glamor for me to find him attractive. Though, from the way he was shuffling around as if he had something else on his mind, I didn't want to confuse him by talking. I'd been hoping for some sort of discussion about his avoidance of the topic of our kiss after the Yule Ball for almost two months.

"Well, that's good then, I suppose," he began, carefully avoiding eye contact. "I think I'd make a rotten golden boy if I had to do it all the time. I'm too grumpy; I can't pull it off."

"I applaud your sense of self-awareness," I said, adding a politely quiet golf clap.

"You're not making this easy," he smirked. I returned with a look that said, *Who, me?*

Elliott sighed. "You're going to make me have to say it, aren't you? Alright, here it is. When all of this is over and we're out of this panopticon, I want us to be together. To see if we can mean something to one another. After you've had time to come to your senses and decide if you still see me not as I *appear* to be, but as who I *am*. Or if you choose to view me as everyone else does. Because things don't turn out so well for fellows like me when they fall for someone under the glamor of this place. I know Mary doesn't mean any harm. Nor do the others who are trying to give me a chance and are sort of pushing us together. But it's like a curse."

Elliott winced, becoming self-conscious of how that might have sounded. "Not that I mean you're a curse. It's that I am, or rather, I feel that I've been cursed by all that's happened with my family or..."

He looked at me in kind of a half-panic. "Oh, blast it! I've been working out what I was going to say to you ever since Yule Ball. Now that you're sitting right in front of me, I can't do it. Turn around or go in the other room or something so that I can say it. When I'm done, leave me alone, okay? I don't want to have to discuss it."

I rotated slowly in place so that I was facing the shelves of grimoires beside my desk. I knew what Elliott was going to say, and I didn't want him to have to say it alone. As I heard him begin to speak, I echoed his sentiment to the bookcases.

"I think I'm in love with you."

Turning around, I meant to elaborate. To say that he didn't need glamor to impress me or anyone else. That he was enough by himself and that all his fears about curses were rubbish. That was what I wanted to say, but I wasn't fast enough. Having expressed what he'd come across the hall for, Elliott was already out the door.

I almost followed after him. Then I thought better of it. He'd finally said what I'd waited to hear. It just wasn't how I'd expected to hear it. Instinctively, the fox in me knew that if I wanted to know anything more, there was no trick to it. I would just have to be patient.

Chapter Thirty-One

By the time the daffodils began to push their way through the spring-thawed soil, I had come to understand that the word witchcraft was truly composed of two halves. There was the half that made up a witch's awareness of their identity and sense of place within the universe, which was an ever-evolving construct, and the other half that was about the daily practice of the actual Craft, which consumed almost all our time. The originally designated days for particular Mentors to guide specific lessons began to blur, mirroring the interweaving of our strengthening bond to the Craft. When the wheel of the year spun around to Ostara, I could cast a myriad of spells and glamors, fly and transport myself magickally at will, wield some measure of control over the natural environment surrounding me, concoct healing potions and elixirs, and even utilize several means of prognostication to predict the future. However, the one thing I could not divine was what would happen to me after I left Rookes College.

The other students seemed to be of the same uneasy mindset. In our free hours, we spoke of it constantly. Everyone, even Hana, who'd walked away from an early decision summer at Harvard to follow her key to Rookes, felt that merely going back to regular college and starting a normal career of any kind seemed too mundane in light of everything. Yet, what were we to do with ourselves and all the knowledge we'd gained? No one seemed to have an answer. The matter of our futures was on our Mentors' minds as well. Around Ostara, most of our lessons seemed to shift in focus to preparations for life beyond Rookes College.

It began one evening after dinner, with Candy's announcement that she was going to teach us how to make ceramic incense burners to summon our familiar animals. Through working more closely with our familiars, Candy explained, we would gain self-awareness of our instinctual natures. That familiarity would provide a greater understanding of how to adapt our natural callings in magick to find some kind of career path in the non-magickal world.

The next morning found us bright and early out in the courtyard just outside the Earth tower. Now that the weather was turning warmer, our Mentors began holding classes outside again. The bright spring sun shone like a glowing citrine in the sky. We sat among early-blooming gardenias, inhaling their sweet essence as bees wove lazily through the air, half-drunk on nectar. Standing in front of a row of large hive-shaped brick kilns on the opposite side of the patio, Candy described the process of creating the ceramic figures to summon our familiars.

"First, you will knead all the bubbles out of the clay on your boards and form it into one solid piece about twice the size and shape of your hands," Candy said. She held up her palms with her fingers extended next to the ball of clay in front of her. "Then, you will use a stylus to begin tracing a rough shape of the animal you intend to carve onto the surface. After that, you will take up the extruder," she waved a metal loop-shaped object with a wooden handle, "to begin peeling away the portions you don't need. Take your time with this part. It creates bubbles if you attempt to replace a part mistakenly shaved off. That could cause your piece to explode in the kiln." Candy glanced back and forth between Tayen and Hana as she said this, since both were known for hurrying through the more tedious parts of Craftwork.

"Last, you will finish sculpting the piece using these carving and fluting tools." Candy motioned to the array on the table in front of her. "Make sure to keep the bottom thick, level, and solid, but incorporate openings into your design to allow smoke and heat to escape. When you're satisfied with what you've created, let me know. I will show you how to prepare it for firing. Pack sawdust beneath it. Leave room for paper and wood in between. Once everyone is finished, we will light the fires, go out to the apiary, and collect beeswax for the candles. We'll dip candles indoors after luncheon so that no particulates from the air become embedded in the wax."

Candy's gaze followed a small cloud of dandelion fluff passing in front of her, almost as if on cue. "It's important to keep the wax as pure as possible so that the essences of frankincense and myrrh with which we will infuse them retain full potency. Those resins produce the best results in meditations to gain self-awareness. As such, they are excellent for enhancing mental power to summon familiars too."

Molding my lump of cloud-colored clay into a fat little fox shape wasn't difficult. Although I'd never really thought about it before, foxes are pear-shaped when sitting down, kind of like cats. Working out the bubbles and then patiently shaving away the excess in the rough shape of a head and two large, pointed ears, I noticed as I often had before why our Mentors discouraged us from using magick for daily tasks when it wasn't necessary. The feeling of shaping something with my own hands felt so real, so viscerally grounding and comfortably warm. After several days in a row of holding raw energy in my hands during heavy spellwork, I could feel the tension ebbing out of my muscles and tendons as I kneaded the clay like a cat.

After carving out the face of my fox, complete with three holes about the size of a dime, which I hoped would make it look as if the creature were blowing smoke out of its ears and mouth, I waved Candy over. Laughing, she shook her head as she led me over to the kiln, murmuring something about fox children always needing to make a joke out of everything.

We packed the little clay fox cozily in a nest of sawdust, paper scraps, and fallen twigs. Then, Candy handed me a small, squarish block of something that looked like chalk and told me to eat it. I must have looked puzzled because she explained without my asking that the substance was called kaolin. In African cultures, people would chew bits of this type of clay as they were undergoing cleansing rituals. First in her native Ghana, and later in the American colonies, all the way down to Georgia. She stressed how it was important not to chew too much of it and to use it only in rituals because it could easily become addictive if overdone.

"The firing of pottery is a similar type of purification ritual," Candy said. "The clay must be tempered and hardened by fire, much as a human is shaped by life experience. By the end, if neither cracks under the heat of the flames, both are transformed into something more beautiful and permanent."

Candy motioned for me to hold my hands up before the kiln's opening as she continued. "Take your time," she said gently. "Visualize yourself in your fox form, meeting the fox whom you will draw as a companion, for it will be a mirror of yourself. All that you are, even though you may not know it yet. Breathe deeply and allow the fire within you to kindle gradually. If you go too fast, the heat of the flame will become too intense, and your creation could explode. As one tempers desire with rationality, so should you learn to control the animal spirit inside you. Hold it close enough to hear its heartbeat, but not too close. Absorb its essence, just as your body digests the minerals from this clay that you have shaped after it has been drawn from the Earth. The sensation when you meet its spirit should be welcoming and relaxing. That is why it is called a familiar."

Following Candy's instructions, I closed my eyes and tried to visualize myself in fox form. Worrying at the piece of kaolin between my jaw teeth helped. The unusual mouthfeel of its crumbly texture and mineral taste provided just enough distraction for me to fully concentrate, like a child with a fidget spinner. Moments later, an image came to me. I was sitting in a small forest clearing, by a moon-dark pond, staring into the water. The tip of my long, fluffy black tail twitched, and my pointed ears rotated involuntarily toward the sound of something snuffling through the underbrush. Lifting my gaze from the rippling silhouette in the water, I saw what was essentially the mirror image of my reflection, only as a living, breathing animal.

The fox tiptoed delicately around the bushes at the edge of the clearing, pausing every few steps to sniff at the tiny green teardrops that grew from the bushes. I realized they must have been unripened wild strawberries, judging from their size and shape. Desiring a taste of their sweetness, he took a cautious nip at one, then drew back, wrinkling his nose and sneezing. Feeling the tartness on my tongue, I squeaked in surprise. The fox wheeled around, ears up and eyes bright. His tail swished in anticipation as he tasted the air. Giving an excited yip, he took off running. At that moment, Candy awakened me from my daydream by tapping me lightly on the shoulder.

"Look!" she whispered, pointing into the kiln. All around my little ceramic fox, the bright embers of smoldering sawdust burned. "Your fox has heard your call and has answered, yes?" Candy asked. I nodded.

"Good. By the time the vessel has finished firing and is cooling, he will have made it to the island. At this rate..." Candy peered into the kiln. "I would look for him probably tomorrow afternoon or perhaps later in the evening. He will come when you least expect it, but you should begin to dream of him as he approaches. When my first hawk arrived, I dreamt of

him for a week, but he had a long way to go. Across an ocean. Yours..."
Candy shrugged. "Probably not so far, since your spark ignited quickly."

After we sealed up my kiln, I waited as one by one the other students
finished their animals. Elliott's horse was next. He'd barely shut his eyes
before I saw flames begin to dance in his kiln. I overheard Candy tell him
that his horse might even be there that evening. Tayen's coyote was quick
too, followed by Miranda's eagle. Theirs took about the same amount of
time to get going as mine had. However, Imani's and Hana's kilns seemed
to take forever to catch light. Hana was visibly anxious about it, and Candy
whispered something reassuring in her ear. However, the ever-calm Imani
just shrugged it off.

Once everyone finished, we headed inside to begin dipping candles.
Inside the Great Hall, Grace and Cora were preparing for us. Grace handed
each student a long double-pronged rod across which a two-ended wick
was stretched. A holey stone was tied at the end of each cord to make the
weight fall evenly. Next, Cora led us over to the cauldrons and explained
how we were to dip the wicks up and down in the molten wax as we
counted to four. Then we would hold them to drip back into the cauldron for another four-count before finally dipping them into tall, narrow
cylindrical vases of cold water. Afterward, we could continue to repeat the
process until we'd each made a pair of tapered candles. We were to light the
candles in our windows every night as signals to our familiars, who would
come in search of us.

As with the shaping of our clay incense burners, I found the candle-making comfortably satisfying. Dipping the wicks into the hot wax
and watching the excess drop back with a soft plop into the cauldron, then
watching my uncut pair of candles steam as I moved them over to dunk in
the cold water, I felt the very essence of what the Scandinavians call *hygge*.
The aroma of frankincense and myrrh filled the air of the Great Hall with
spicy perfume as each student stood before the cauldron corresponding
to their hallway. Naturally, because Elliott and I shared a hall, we found
ourselves dipping our candles together from the same cauldron in a sort of
slow, unspoken rhythm.

Ever since his midnight confession a few weeks earlier, Elliott had seemed
more at ease. Having freed himself from the burden of admitting he loved
me and hearing me echo the same sentiment, the emotions in his psyche
seemed to come back into balance with themselves, and his magick sta-

bilized. Regardless, Elliott wasn't completely the same gruff creature as before. Plus, he was still gorgeous. Perhaps even more so, because he was choosing to act like a civilized human being capable of having rational conversations, instead of an animal avoiding a snare. Still, Elliott seemed distracted by something. I noticed that he was careful to tiptoe around any other expressions of sentiment. When I accidentally brushed his arm with my candle rod, he leaped about a foot in the air.

While we were waiting for the candles to cool and set, the Mentors decided to tell stories based on a related theme. It was something they often did to pass the time while waiting for our Craftwork to finish. Since we had been shaping incense burners from clay in hopes of summoning our spirit familiars, which was in essence Firework combined with communication, they chose tales that blended the two. Cora told her story first, and Katerina followed.

"Have any of you ever heard of the Lost Colony of Roanoke?" Cora asked. "And of the message that was left behind carved into a tree?"

"Croatoan," I said. "Like the Native American tribe. Yes, I've heard of it."

"Wasn't it carved into both a post and a tree?" Imani asked.

"You are both correct," Cora replied. "The first documented English colony in America was located on an island just north of us, called Roanoke. In 1587, Virginia Dare became the first child born to its settlers there. Not long after her birth, Virginia's grandfather, the colony's governor, returned to England for supplies. Unfortunately, he was prevented from returning for three years because England was at war with Spain. When Governor Dare was finally able to get back, he found his family and the entire colony of over a hundred settlers missing. The only sign as to their whereabouts was those carvings in the tree and post. Over the years, many have correctly suspected the English settlers were taken in by a local tribe, the Croatoan."

"Buuuut..." Tayen interjected, dragging out the word after a long pause. "I feel like there's a plot twist coming."

"You are right, my dear. There are two of them. Both of which are directly relevant to the history of this college," Cora answered. "When the Croatoans welcomed the settlers, it took no one long to realize that many physical similarities indicated a common lineage. Although the Roanoke colonists believed themselves to be the area's first European settlers, stories circulated among the Croatoan and other local tribes stating that Norsemen and Anglo-Saxons were there long before. Some of these earlier settlers married into the Croatoan tribe back then, before they were called by that name."

"Isn't that part of the mystery?" Miranda asked. "That no one knows the true origins of their tribal name?"

"Yes," Cora replied. "However, I think a great bit of the confusion surrounding that name is that most people who attempt to trace its origins are using the wrong alphabet. Observe."

Waving her wand in the air, Cora made a bright series of letters spring to life above us. Although the characters spelling out the word *CROATOAN* bore some resemblance to normal English letters, they were highly stylized and angular, in a way that suggested they might be a different language entirely.

"Any guesses?" Cora challenged.

"They're Anglo-Saxon runes!" Hana exclaimed. Tracing their outlines in the air with her index finger, Hana read aloud their names. "Kanu, Raido, Ingwaz, Yr, Nydeis, Ingwaz, Yr, Hagali." She paused, considering their meaning. Then, crinkling her upturned nose with effort as she pieced their message together. "Seeking knowledge, our strongest men journeyed forth for our defense and protection. However, fate was not with us. Our seeds were not sown with... prosperity or posterity... I'm not quite sure of that one. Anyway, it ends by saying that there was a tumultuous time, and they went through Hell. In the end, they were transformed into something better."

"Very close," Cora said approvingly. "Runes are almost impossible to read with full certainty, but I applaud your efforts. Katerina told me you've been working together on different methods of prognostication." Cora glanced in Katerina's direction.

Katerina nodded as Cora continued. "Generally speaking, your translation is accurate. Hundreds of years ago, during the time of the Viking invasions of England, some Anglo-Saxons left. Searching for a place where they could be safe and free from Viking raids, they found the island that would become Roanoke. The name that they gave the native tribe who helped them to survive was spelled out in their language of runes. The name itself told the story of how they struggled and afterward were saved and welcomed into the tribe. About seven hundred years later, when English settlers attempted again to set up a colony in the Outer Banks, one of the local tribes still carried the name. When one of their elders spelled it out for Governor White, he looked at the word and pronounced it *Croatoan*. Although he was completely unaware of its runic origins, along with their magickal correspondences."

"What happened to the little girl who went missing?" Imani asked. "Virginia Dare."

"Ah, glad you asked," Cora replied. "Legend has it that Virginia Dare was changed into a white doe after her assimilation into the Croatoan tribe. Thus, making her possibly the oldest transmogrifying witch in North America. At least, through the English tradition of which records are kept. In her familiar form, young Miss Dare appears as a white doe. If you ever make it up past Hatteras' way, you might see her."

"She's still alive?" Tayen asked incredulously. "That would make her over four hundred years old! How is that even possible?"

"As we've discussed before," Cora answered, "When a witch chooses to live behind a glamor in the Otherworld, her progression of aging almost stops. All six of the Mentors at Rookes College this year are from British colonial times. Every one of us is at least three hundred, even if we don't look like it." Cora fluffed her hair to emphasize this last remark.

Any further discussion on the topic of witches aging glamorously halted with the sound of a heavy thud at the front door of the Main Hall. Several more thuds followed, but they sounded lower to the ground. As if someone were kicking the door, rather than knocking on it.

"Elliott!" Mary called out, jerking him out of the daze he had been in ever since we came in to dip candles. "Please go let your horse in before she paws the door down. I'm in no mood for mending spells tonight."

Elliott laughed, the first genuine, fully open laugh that I'd heard him utter. It shook his whole body. His eyes began to water, and he ran to open the door. When he opened it, a massive silver dappled mare clattered across the slate floor into the Great Hall. Shaking her long, ivory mane, she whinnied, rearing back onto her hind legs and pawing at the air with enormous fringed hooves. The packs of muscle at her haunches rippled like quicksilver as she snorted and continued to stamp at the ground impatiently.

"By the stars, that was quick!" Mary remarked to Elliott while they both stroked the magnificent creature's face. "You've not even had time to take your incense burner from the fire. Don't suppose you'll need to cast any summoning spells tonight. Go on then and take her outside for a run. She's ready for it. We've mostly finished up with the candles anyway."

For a moment, Elliott looked puzzled. I could tell that he was trying to figure out how to get up onto the horse's back without a saddle and not look foolish. Almost as if she were reading Elliott's thoughts, the giant horse knelt down upon her knees. As he approached, Elliott bent over to touch her face. The mare turned her head, nuzzling his ear as if she were whispering something. Climbing across the mare's broad back, Elliott gathered two fists full of her snowy mane in his hands. "Come on, Grana. Up we get," he said. The horse rose and trotted calmly back out the door of the Great Hall. Mary closed it behind them.

The rest of the students were awestruck at the communication that was completely unintelligible to us between Elliott and his horse. Silently, we pondered the same questions. *Where had the magnificent animal come from? How had the mare told Elliott her name?* We were all used to working magick by that point. However, there was something about the mythological physicality of the horse who answered Elliott's call that stunned us with wonder at the possibilities of what our own familiars might be like when they appeared.

"If you'd like to learn more about the life of Miss Virginia Dare," Mary stated, breaking our collective silence as she tried to return to the previous discussion. "Then you should have a look at a volume I wrote many years ago called *A History of Witchcraft in Early America*. There should be a copy in each of your rooms. Like all our other books, you may take as many notes as you like for your grimoires, but the originals must remain here. For now, though, I'm feeling a bit hungry. Let's have a bit of supper, shall we? Then tidy up the candle makings and retire for the evening. We have a big day planned for tomorrow. Hana will read us our rune predictions for the upcoming year, and Katerina will introduce us to another prognostication method involving eggs. It's generally best to rest up so that we have clear mental and spiritual channels through which to receive the messages. None of the kilns will be ready to open until at least morning, will they, Candy?"

Candy shook her head, *no*.

"Good," Mary nodded simply. "Anyone else in the mood for fish and chips? I'm feeling nostalgic tonight, and I know that's a favorite of Elliott's.

He'll want me to set some aside for him when he returns. I'm sure he'll have many new ideas gnawing in his mind." After taking everyone's orders, Mary whisked out baskets of batter-fried cod and fries for our tables, along with a stack of plates and bottles of malt vinegar. The fish was flaky and delicious. Being a pickle-lover, I doused the filets with plenty of briny vinegar too.

By the time we'd finished and cleaned up the candle-making with a few quick spells, Elliott was still outside. Mary directed us to take our pair of freshly made candles and light them in our bedroom windows to help guide our familiars. Passing by her on my way upstairs, I asked Mary why Elliott's mare arrived so quickly, while the rest of our animals would be at least overnight before answering our calls.

"Two reasons, my dear," Mary replied, as Gregor fluttered down to perch on her shoulder. "The first is more practical. There have been wild horses roaming the Outer Banks for centuries, ever since the first few escaped from the Spanish settlements. Elliott's horse may be one of them. If so, she wouldn't have had very far to come in answering his call. However, the other reason is more personal. Familiars often come to witches in times when they feel as if they are in distress, whether the witch summons them or not. Thus, Elliott's mare may have already been en route if she sensed Elliott was feeling emotional turmoil. Which I presume you might know something about, hmm?" Mary eyed me, hinting at the obvious.

"But I don't mean to cause him any distress at all!" I insisted defensively. It was the first time I'd ever plainly admitted to anyone other than Tayen or Elliott himself that I had feelings for him. Needless to say, I was embarrassed to be saying such things to Mary, the most austere witch there. "That's the last thing I want for him. He's already been through so much!"

"I meant no harm by it," Mary replied. She motioned for me to come closer so that she could whisper in my ear. "I was merely suggesting that Elliott is feeling the mild distress of learning that he cares for someone. Such things make any young man feel vulnerable and uncertain. However, in his case, the pressure is compounded by the weight of history. I'm sure he's told you that his parents met here at Rookes. Unfortunately, the entire magickal world knows the ending to that sad story. I'm not a specialist in prognostication, but even if I were, I wouldn't attempt to use that past to predict the possibility of your future with Elliott. You are a highly intelligent and infinitely kind young witch. That tells me all I need to know about why your story will turn out differently, even if a romantic relationship is not what fate holds for the two of you."

A panicked flurry of thoughts raced through my brain. *How much did Mary know about Elliott and me? Didn't Elliott say that he had no plans to pursue any romantic feelings for me until after we'd left Rookes because he always felt watched?*

Elliott had called Rookes College a panopticon. I knew what he meant. Even if the Mentor witches or our fellow students never intended to interfere, they were still always watching. Wondering how the only son of warlock wife-murderer Albert Capell would react to his first crush on another witch. Trying not to judge his actions but inevitably doing so anyway. The possibility of embarrassment and rejection was high. It would be a lot of pressure for anyone, but for a guy who struggled so much with self-expression anyway, it must be torture.

"Any advice?" I whispered back.

"No," Mary smiled, steering me upstairs. "You're already doing everything that I would suggest naturally. Just listen to the prognostication tomorrow and continue as you are. Whether the boy knows it or not, he's chosen the best possible girl."

"For him?" I asked, hopefully.

"For anyone," Mary said. She circled back toward her suite of rooms on the bottom floor at the end of the Spirit tower as she waved goodnight.

That evening, after I'd lit my pair of candles on the windowsill, I sat in the velvet window seat between them, watching the lawn below. Elliott was leading his horse Grana to the Rookery, doubtlessly preparing her to bed down. I thought about what Mary said. How everyone was trying to be silently supportive of the possibility that Elliott and I might become a couple. Instead of being comforted, thinking of it made me tired. I still hadn't managed the courage to tell Stephen that I wanted to officially break up with him, even though he surely must have gotten the general idea based on my absence. I'd been purposefully vague during my infrequent letters about my impromptu choice to take a gap year instead of accepting any scholarship offers. Though I'd maintained that smoke screen of excuses for over seven months, I knew the actual breakup needed to be stated. To give Stephen closure and to allow both of us the opportunity to process all the relationship-ending emotions. Yet, I couldn't bring myself to do it.

Instead, I'd simply allowed my dad to help me maintain the ruse by feeding Stephen "updates" on my alleged gap year. We'd both decided to tell Stephen that I was working with Dad out at the field station while I tried to "find myself." Oliver had given me the idea during our first visit, thinking that it was best to give Stephen a rational explanation. The story wasn't completely a lie, I *was* finding myself at Rookes, but it certainly wasn't the truth, either.

Being the generally well-mannered and non-intrusive sort of guy that he was, Stephen hadn't pressed the issue or insisted on speaking with me in person. Somehow, I hoped that he'd been so absorbed with his new life at college that thinking about us didn't bother him too much. Still, Mary's words haunted me. She'd felt good about Elliott's interest in me because I was the type of girl who could be trusted to be kind to anyone, no matter how I felt about them. Yet, was I truly being kind to Stephen by waffling over how best to break up with him when the final truth was the same regardless? Stephen had always been more like a brother to me than a boyfriend, and it was time to move on.

That night, I decided to write to Stephen directly again and to send the message out by my rook. The letter took me hours, mostly because I stopped and tossed it in the trash half a dozen times before finding the correct words to express how I felt. By the end, I'd figured out why breaking up with Stephen was so difficult. It wasn't so much that I'd miss the romantic part of our relationship. I hadn't ever experienced very strong feelings for Stephen in that way. Instead, I figured out that it was so hard for me to break up with Stephen because of what he represented. The certainty of a logical and secure pathway through life.

Stephen Thornton would finish college, start a career, marry a nice girl, and have children, always protected by the shelter of his wealthy family's connections. Although he would be quick to argue that such connections were often more smothering than comforting, Stephen had never done much to resist the organic flow of his life. Did he enjoy telling jokes, and would he make a great stand-up comedian, like he'd always claimed he wanted? Yes. However, did I believe that's what he'd actually do with his life? No.

To me, it was far more likely that cheerful, dependable Stephen Thornton would finish law school, join his father's firm, and allow himself to be pushed into life of public service and probably politics. Always doing what was expected of him, nothing unusual or unconventional. Even his hair, cut carefully feathered to fall just so over his eyebrows, never looked out of place. Where would a witch like me fit into such a life? Even a witch who was well-trained in proper behavior so that she could live among non-magickal people undetected? In my heart of hearts, I could find no place.

So, I finished the breakup letter to Stephen. Then I wrote a second letter to my dad explaining as succinctly as I could why I'd finally made my decision. I didn't think Dad would be upset. He'd never disliked Stephen, but he'd not felt any special affinity for him either. Then, I summoned Stella and instructed her on how to carry the letters to Dad and Stephen. Letting Stella out the window, I set the latch and went to bed.

Chapter Thirty-Two

T he next morning, I awoke feeling cranky and irritable. Even
though I'd slept well, almost too soundly, I had a pounding
headache. Also, there was no sign of my familiar fox. When I went
down to breakfast, the Great Hall buzzed with chatter, both anxious
for the imminent arrival of more familiars and excited about something
new that Miranda found among the books in her suite.

The eagle that Miranda summoned as her familiar flew in the night
before. The rest of us had already gone to bed. When he swooped
through the open window of Miranda's suite, the eagle was grasping
a large fish in its talons. Miranda was awake reading in her study. The
massive bird dropped the fish with a splat in the middle of the desk
in front of her as if he were a cat presenting his owner with a freshly
caught mouse. She'd just finished explaining to everyone how surprised
she was that he ate it right in front of her.

"I'm glad that he arrived quickly," Grace said, as Miranda reached
for the pot of fresh strawberry jam and spread some on her toast. "You
were so fretful last night. Of course, that's to be expected with intuitive
young witches right after their first summoning of familiars."

"I was worried," Miranda acknowledged, as she offered the bird a
jam-free bite of bread. The eagle snatched it from her hand with its
hooked yellow beak and swallowed it whole, looking quite satisfied.
"Which was why I stayed up researching. It helps calm me down."
Probably the most voracious reader among us, the normally quiet
Miranda liked to stay up late at night leafing through some obscure
volume. She could frequently be counted on for some random story of
forgotten lore told over the morning table.

"How did you say that you found it again, dear?" Grace asked as I sat down at the table. Her face still flushed with discovery over her find, Miranda explained.

"Well, I'd started out looking for more about that Virginia Dare story," she said. "You know, the one Cora was telling us about at the Ostara celebration. That's how I found it. We found it," she corrected herself. Miranda stroked the wing of her eagle absentmindedly as the bird sat perched on the arm of her chair, watching her with his golden hazel eyes. "It was almost dawn. I'd gotten up to get some more ribbons to use as markers. When I sat back down at the desk, Dylan had turned the book to that page." Miranda nodded at her familiar.

"Dylan was insistent I read the whole thing. Why, I'm not sure. It had nothing to do with the other stuff I was looking for, but it must mean something. He's a very clever bird." Miranda shook her head. "Such a sad story, though. That she was betrayed like that. Even her father left her behind. I feel so bad for her."

"What's she talking about?" I asked Elliott, who was only half paying attention.

"Some sad love story about a French woman named Karen, I think," he replied. "She's been going on about it for a while now, so I'm lost. You know how Miranda is when she gets wound up in telling a story. Like she becomes a different person." Elliott made the yapping motion with his free hand as he squeezed a slice of lemon into his tea with the other.

"Kerys, not Karen," Alice corrected, looking slightly perturbed at Elliott's dismissive air. "Kerys is the name of the city, not the woman. It was supposedly this very old city built around the time of Augustus Caesar, across the English Channel from Cornwall. The coastal land was very low and prone to flooding, so a dyke was built around it as a kind of seawall. Gradlon was the Breton king who built it, and he had a daughter named Dahut. Miranda's talking about the old Breton legend in which Dahut is alleged to have stolen the keys to the city of Kerys that belonged to her father. Depending on which version you believe, and Miranda seems to have found a version that tells all of them at once, Dahut either got drunk and mistook the city's gates for the floodgates and opened them accidentally, or she was deceived by her lover into opening them deliberately. Regardless, the city of Kerys was destroyed. Some versions of the story say everyone perished except her father, King Gradlon, who may or may not have escaped to Cornwall on a horse named Morvarch. Many claimed that Gradlon's horse Morvarch could run on water. I'm surprised you haven't heard of Morvarch, given the obvious connections to horse folklore. There are quite a few monuments dedicated to him down around the coast."

Elliott stopped stirring his tea and looked warily at Alice as if trying to detect any hint of derision. He always bristled at even the slightest mention of his father or the Capell part of his family. Sensing his tension, Alice rolled her eyes. "Oh, don't be so sensitive. You know I didn't mean it like that. I merely thought you might be interested because your familiar *is* a horse. You *are* English, and you *do* have a great deal of horse magick in you." Alice shrugged. Although she didn't voice her next thought, she might as well have. *Whether you admit it or not.*

"What happened to Dahut?" I asked, not wanting to exacerbate the headache I'd woken up with by arguing. "Did she die too?"

"That depends again on which version you read and what you consider death to be," Alice answered. "Some versions say Dahut escaped and went to Avalon, where she founded the coven of female witches that worked with King Arthur. One legend folding into another, with no evidence of either, so probably not much truth there. However, most have Dahut drowning after her father pushed her back into the ocean for her wicked behavior, thus bringing an end to her human life. Later in those versions, Dahut returns as a mermaid who haunts the seas. She combs her golden hair and sings sad songs about those who've lost their lives to the ocean."

"Ah," I said, realizing why Miranda was so captivated by the story. "A mermaid tale about a woman whose father pushes her away after a forbidden romance. That makes sense."

We all knew Miranda's crush on Celine, her mermaid tutor, persisted. Also, we were aware that even though she didn't speak of it much, she'd changed since meeting Celine. Miranda was much more in tune with both her sensuality and the fact that she wanted to study marine biology, rather than returning to work in her father's television ministry like her brothers. What no one was sure of was how Miranda would transition back into her life after Rookes.

When she'd initially picked up her key, Miranda was at a Christian wilderness retreat. After coming to Rookes College, she'd written home to say that she'd been offered an unexpected opportunity to do mission work with another organization operating in remote parts of Africa. It was a perfect excuse for a year because it meant she only had to write letters and send them by her rook messenger, Puck, to keep making up additional false reports.

As our time at Rookes was drawing closer to the end, the unanswered question of what Miranda would tell her parents hung over her like an ominous cloud. For the rest of us, our futures were more about deciding what we wanted and how not to disappoint our families with the careers we chose. However, for Miranda, the problem was twofold. Turning her back on ministry as a vocation was one thing, but coming out and risking being disowned as living a lifestyle completely inconsistent with her family's carefully constructed conservative image was another one entirely. It pained all of us to consider the criticism that gentle Miranda would have to endure. We tried not to discuss it.

Nevertheless, pondering Miranda's issues instead of my own on that particular morning helped distract me from my concern over the continued absence of my familiar fox. When she overheard me discussing the situation with Alice, Hana said she felt awful too. Her usually bright eyes were ringed with dark circles. "At least you could rest. I didn't sleep a wink last night. All I kept thinking about was my tiger in this cramped little cage. Not even enough room to turn around. Every time I almost nodded off, I'd jerk back awake, tangled up in the sheets. It was miserable. I hope he's okay."

"I've told you dear," Katerina said, over a sip of coffee. "What you were likely sensing was just your familiar's discomfort at her method of transport. Tigers can't exactly traipse across the island to you like his horse." Katerina gestured toward Elliott, who had a mouthful of waffles and syrup. He looked unusually cheerful. "Nor can they fly in of their own accord like Miranda's eagle. It would be too obvious and quite possibly put them in great danger. You'll receive word today about the circumstances of her arrival. I feel certain of it."

Sensing Imani leaning forward inquisitively to listen, Katerina continued. "Same for you too, dear. Lions can't run around free, at least in North America, without causing an uproar."

Tayen groaned at Katerina's unintentional pun, which no one else except she and I seemed to recognize. Katerina shrugged. "Regardless, we've sent your rooks out already. They should bring word of your familiars' whereabouts by dinner time."

"That's truly the best thing to do, given the circumstances," Mary added, in a reassuring voice. "Changing the subject to something a bit more positive, I believe Elliott has some insights to share with us this morning about a prospective career path. Perhaps hearing about the peace of mind brought by a familiar's calming presence might help assuage some of our concerns about the future, hmm?" Mary glanced pointedly at Elliott. He swallowed his mouthful of waffles and began explaining while holding a napkin over his syrupy lips.

"I've decided that I'm going back to the UK," Elliott announced, full of pride as if he were declaring that he'd won a Nobel Prize. "I'm going to be a botanist. The University of Edinburgh has a cracking program in plant biology. I believe it would suit me. Because..."

Elliott's extended explanation was cut short by Tayen's cackling. "Is that what your horse whispered to you last night? *Follow me, lad, and become a man of the forest.*" She rounded her arms and swung them side to side in ridiculous exaggeration. "Like Robin Hood and his Merry Men. Sounds like the path to riches and intrigue to me. Not!"

Elliott's beaming expression collapsed. Normally, I found Tayen's snarky comments pretty hilarious, but I could almost feel Elliott's rush of hope escape like air from a punctured balloon. Granted, I didn't think that becoming a botanist sounded like the most exciting career decision either. Yet, I hated seeing Tayen stomp Elliott's idea flat almost before he'd gotten the words out. He'd been so worried about what kind of life awaited him after Rookes. A choice that put him around plants and labs rather than the prying eyes of the press wasn't a bad idea. Fortunately, Grace intervened before I found the words to rip into Tayen for being a dream killer.

"Oh, Elliott, I believe that's a splendid idea!" Grace exclaimed, crossing the room to put a protective arm around his shoulders. She encouraged him to rise and follow her out of the hall. "The regenerative power of Nature is speaking to you. That's completely logical, considering, well..." Grace paused, choosing her words carefully. "How damaging the extraction and burning of fossil fuels can be to the environment. It's as Mary always says, the stars seek balance. Why don't we go up to the ecology library now that we've finished breakfast while the girls are working with Katerina on their oomancy? I have stacks upon stacks of my journals to share with you. Then, we could go out to the greenhouse. Miranda, why don't you and Dylan come with us? Together we can start showing Elliott a few of the spells we've been working on out there."

The rest of Grace's suggestions to Elliott were lost to me, as Alice leaned over to whisper in my ear. "And that's why they call her Grace. Artful, isn't it? The way that she can turn a conversation." Alice stepped into my line of sight, blocking Tayen from view, and placing a hand mockingly over her heart. "Ouch! If looks could kill, we'd have one less witch respirating in this room." Alice glanced over her shoulder at Tayen. I continued to seethe as Cora took Tayen by the elbow and led her over near the entry of the Fire corridor so that they could speak privately. Elliott, Miranda, and her eagle left in the opposite direction, following Grace down the Air hallway.

"Take a breath," Alice said. "Cora's her mentor. Let her handle it. Tayen's having a rough morning too. I'm sure she didn't mean any harm. She just expresses her concern differently. I overheard Tayen talking with Cora earlier before anyone else was awake. I think she's been up all night as well, but her visions have been more confused and muddled than Imani's or Hana's. Tayen can't seem to grasp where her coyote is or how he's attempting to communicate with her."

"How do you know her coyote is a he?" I asked.

"Because a witch's familiar is almost always the opposite gender of his or her birth," Alice answered. "It helps to maintain the balance of energy in the relationship between witch and familiar. Too much masculine or feminine power put together in one place can sometimes cause spellwork produced by the pairing to become erratic."

Although Alice's explanation made sense, and I wanted to know more about what she'd said later, at that moment I remained distracted by my own familiar fox's absence. "Well, nobody's worrying about me," I replied, crossing my arms. "I haven't had even the slightest glimpse of my fox. Unlike everyone else around here, I slept like a baby. Shouldn't that be a cause for concern? What if that means mine's not coming at all? What would that signify?"

"What it means," Alice sighed, "is that he's probably already here. Hiding somewhere on the island. He may be trying to use his absence to make you aware of your unfailingly pervasive imposter syndrome and increasingly annoying insistence on instant results." Alice put her hand to her forehead, massaging her temples. "I swear, the only thing more exasperating than the hormonal surge caused by one's first calling of familiars is having to go through it in a room full of young Americans. Everything must always happen *right now!*" Alice snapped her fingers louder with each word for emphasis.

"I'm sorry," I said, meaning it as I saw how frustrated Alice was with me. In my irritated brain fog, I truly hadn't considered the possibility that my familiar might already be prowling around the island. Even though it was certainly possible.

"It's alright," Alice sighed. "I'm just a bit frazzled too. You might have slept well last night, but I did not. Not because of the familiars being summoned, but because Mary and I..."

"Had a lot of work to do," Mary finished the sentence abruptly. The rest of Alice's unspoken explanation hung in the air. Wanting to maintain the precarious peace, I didn't pry.

"If everyone's finished with breakfast, why don't we all go up to the Water tower and allow Katerina and Hana to engage us in a little demonstration of oomancy?" Mary asked. "Perhaps some festive prognostication for Ostara might help clear our heads of all this unnecessary worry. By the time we're done, the familiars may have arrived. Then, this uncertainty will have been for naught."

Once Hana, Imani, and I were shepherded into the Water tower with Katerina, I noticed that Mary, Alice, and Candy quickly took leave of us. It made me think about what Alice almost allowed to slip into the Great Hall. I wondered what the Mentors were up to. Nevertheless, I forced such questions out of my mind when I saw a more subdued Tayen slip into the room quietly after her discussion with Cora. I tried my best to ignore her and concentrated on Katerina's introduction to a prognostication method that I'd never heard of before.

On the table set before us were four thick, clear glass mugs full of hot water and a large basket of fresh brown eggs. Steam swirled up from the mugs into the chill air of the spring morning. Beside each mug was a small empty bowl, which I supposed was for eggshells.

"Oomancy, or the art of prognostication by using egg whites dropped into hot water," Katerina began, "was a favorite method of colonial Puritans in New England. Particularly women, who wanted to know the identities of their future husbands. That's why these," Katerina motioned toward the mugs of water, "became known as Venus Glasses. In honor of Venus, the goddess of love and beauty. They predicted with whom a young girl might fall in love. Although an unconventional method of prognostication, it made use of the limited supplies available in households of the time. The shape of the egg, as it coalesced, was supposed to indicate the man's occupation."

Imani's hand shot up. "I thought the Puritans forbade divination as a tool of the Devil. Because it was considered an indication of witchcraft."

"As usual, you are correct, Imani," Katerina nodded. "However, as we've continued to learn all through our year and a day here at Rookes, just because something isn't allowed by polite society doesn't mean that witches don't do it in secret. If anything, such edicts often heightened the appeal of whatever magick they were attempting to work. The established authority of most civilizations usually forbids any method that would allow those who are oppressed to gain power and find agency to direct their lives independently."

"Now you've got my attention," Tayen said, reaching for an egg. "What do we do?"

"First, as with all spells, you have to set an intention," Katerina said. There was a hint of consternation in her voice. Tayen took the hint not to be impatient and placed the egg back into the basket. "Today, witches aren't so dependent on needing to marry a man of means as cover for her uncanny good fortune. Thus, when we use oomancy in a few moments, I want you to clear your minds. Instead of imagining the person you may marry and their occupation, I want you to allow your thoughts to drift until you see yourself ten years from now. Don't focus on what you look like, but instead on what you're doing. Try to feel the motions of your work through the exertion of your mind and your muscles. When you can sense the tiredness that comes with pushing yourself to your furthest limit, crack the egg. Use the halves of the shell to separate the yolks into these bowls to save for afterward. Then, close your eyes and try to concentrate on the tiredness you experienced as you dropped the egg white into the water. Do it quickly, in one continuous motion. Lay the empty shells on the table. We'll need those later too. Ready?"

We nodded as Katerina handed each of us an egg and told us to begin.

I shut my eyes and tried to concentrate on clearing my mind. It was surprisingly difficult. After several minutes, I could feel the headache that I'd had all morning beginning to grow worse. Sharp pains flared between my eyes as if I'd been staring into bright light for too long. My back and shoulders began to feel tired too. Leaning into the ache, I opened my eyes to the tiniest crack to get my bearings. Then, I scooted my chair closer to the table filled with glass water mugs, cracked my egg, separated the yolk into the bowl, and plopped the remaining white in. Keeping my eyes shut, I could hear the three other girls do the same. Not wanting to interrupt the flow of clarity to my prediction, I opened my eyes and focused on my glass alone.

The egg white had separated into two pieces. One was a roundish blob that settled near the bottom. The other made a sort of T-shape, like a hammer, but with a longer head pointed at both ends. I studied for a moment, trying to figure out what it meant. Beside me, Imani sighed and leaned forward to examine the formation of her egg more closely. Prognostication was always her least favorite subject. The more I practiced it myself, the more I began to agree with her. At best, it was a maddeningly imprecise science.

"What does that look like to you?" Imani asked, focusing on her glass.

The formation of Imani's egg was almost the exact opposite of mine. A large, brain-shaped blob hovered near the surface of the water, while a long tail tapered thinly down toward the bottom. Little branches feathered off it, looking like a winter-barren tree.

Leaning forward, I squinted hard. "Maybe a brain with a tail?"

"Spinal column," Hana whispered loudly over her shoulder. Being a Water witch, Hana was always leagues ahead of us in any new method of divination. "It's the brain and the nervous system. Something to signify your future career in medicine."

"How can you be sure?" Imani questioned, her nose so close now it touched the glass.

"Because she's telling a bit more than she should," Katerina intervened, tutting at Hana. "I know we've already seen the results through other media, Hana. However, please refrain from commentary except for confirmation. Let your sisters learn to draw their conclusions. It's important for helping them develop their third eyes."

Nevertheless, Hana's tip seemed to spark a realization for Imani. "Oh!" she exclaimed. "It must mean my major. I am..." Imani paused, reconsidering. "That is... I was supposed to begin at Ohio State on a full scholarship this fall. Psychology and Neurology double major first. Hopefully, graduate school in psychiatry or neuroscience will follow. I wanted to study memory and cognition. The causes of dementia and Alzheimer's, for obvious reasons."

"Why do you speak of your aspirations in the past tense, Imani?" Katerina questioned. "When has the glass just confirmed where your heart was leading you in the first place?"

Imani nodded, deep in contemplation. Katerina moved on to ask what I thought my egg's pattern signified.

I refocused my attention on my glass and replied hesitantly. "It looks sort of like a pick, or maybe an ax. And a rock or something."

Hana was sitting on her hands and rocking back and forth to stop herself from saying anything. She's the kind of person who can't talk without moving her hands, so it helped. Hana glanced up at Katerina, whose approving nod released her from silence.

"You were right the first time," Hana assured me. "It is a pick, and those are rocks that have been extracted with it." Hana's deep brown eyes locked with Katerina's for a second, as if she were concerned about being reprimanded for saying too much. Then, Hana continued. "Doesn't your father work with rocks and minerals? Don't you also collect crystals?"

"Yeah, Oliver is a geologist," I replied. "And I have collected crystals and geodes since I was very small. However, I've never thought seriously about becoming a geologist myself."

"Why not?" Katerina interceded. "You have the family background if you need guidance or assistance, and you seem to possess at least a passing interest in the topic."

"Well, because I..." I stopped short, not wanting to say that rest. I found it too painful. After what my mother Darla said, making fun of my dad and his work, which she always dismissed as mere *digging in the dirt*. How little money he made for countless hours of field and lab research. But that was before when he'd worked with the nonprofit. Now that he'd *sold out*, as Oliver once would have put it, to big oil, my dad's financial prospects seemed a heck of a lot more promising. I didn't want to open that can of worms though, right there in the middle of a prognostication lesson. "Because I didn't think it made enough money," I finished simply.

Tayen cackled again, the same derisive sound she'd made about Elliott's newly discovered calling in the Great Hall. Only this time, she followed her outburst with bitter wisdom instead of a mocking joke. "Oh, get over yourself, Willow. It's probably not millionaire stuff, but it's enough to live on, isn't it? Everyone thinks finding a career that rakes in piles of cash is the key to happiness. That it can solve all kinds of problems, but it's just wishful thinking. Believe me, a gig you don't want that makes millions can still suck if it's not what you're cut out for."

"I agree," Katerina seconded. "Now, tell us what you see in your glass, Tayen. We'll try to help interpret."

"Wings," Tayen answered, without hesitation. "And I don't need help. I know what they mean. It means I'm supposed to fly."

"But all of us can fly," Imani questioned. "What makes your flying different?"

"Because she doesn't mean flying the way we do it," Hana hinted, looking at Tayen.

Before Tayen could reply, a gentle scratching at the door to the Great Hall, followed by a low whine, echoed through the stillness of the Water tower. Tayen's face pulled into a tight-lipped smile of recognition. She rose from her ornately carved chair at the heavy wooden table and hurried down the center aisle to open the door. Through the opening trotted a large coyote, about five feet long from nose to tail. His coat turned from glistening bronze to silver as he rippled past the table and circled it once, taking in every detail with his bright copper eyes. The coyote sat down like a trained dog beside Tayen's empty chair. Tayen reseated herself next to the coyote and ran her fingertips gently up the animal's long nose and around his ears, coming to rest at his shoulder. The animal rubbed his muzzle along her cheek. Tayen whispered to him as her expression softened, "Yes, Koh, I knew. I was just... okay. I'll tell them."

Contact with her coyote seemed to refocus Tayen's thoughts as she responded.

"I want to train as a pilot. I've wanted to for several years now, but my mom always discouraged it. She said it was too dangerous and that I should use the best years of my face and body for modeling. That I needed to make my money now while I was young because beauty fades. Flying lessons would need to wait until those years were over if I still wanted to learn."

"Technically, your mom's not wrong," I said, diplomatically. "However, what if you kept at it? The modeling, I mean, and just took flight lessons on the side, a little at a time? Surely, you're not booked for photoshoots every day of the year?"

Tayen raised an eyebrow and gave me a hard look that said, *You have no idea*. Weirdly, the coyote, Koh, mimicked her expression, cocking his head to the side as if to echo.

"Okay, so clearly Willow doesn't read enough fashion sites," Hana intervened. "Because if she did, she'd see Tayen on every one of them. She does have a point though. Aren't there, like, different levels of getting your pilot's license? How long does it take for the first one?"

"Three weeks. That's just for the student's license. The next step up takes several months, and to be a real professional is about two years." Tayen said softly, tracing her long fingers gracefully along the coyote's jawline. The familiar coyote lifted his shining gaze to meet Tayen's, as I noticed for that their eyes were precisely the same shade of copper. The faint smile returned to Tayen's lips as another thought occurred to her.

"I could lie," she said, thinking aloud. "For three weeks, anyway. I could tell Bly that I was off to another shoot somewhere far away so that there wouldn't be any cell signal. Maybe in a remote part of Africa or South America. Say that it was for a charity promotion so that she wouldn't notice if she ever checked my bank account to see if anything was posted. Maybe I could even book something like that with a quick turnaround. A single-day photo op to benefit whoever might want me to be seen somewhere to help raise funds. I've got a pretty solid stash of cash I could use to pay for an actual donation. Bly might not ever have to know."

"Wait," Hana said. "One, that's a great idea. At least it's a start. But two, why does your mother have access to your bank account where your earnings are posted? You're like, twenty now. You don't have to allow it."

Tayen's hint of a smile faded. "Because I paid for Bly's house. Our house, whatever." She waved one hand dismissively in the air while she continued to pet the coyote with the other. "Bly sold our original house that she got in the divorce from Nyles a couple of years ago. I was sixteen and in Europe doing runway shows all summer. Back then, Bly had to be a co-signer on my bank account because I was required to have a guardian. When I got home in September, she'd bought us a new house—a bigger one—a few streets over. It was nicer than the other one, so I didn't complain. Since then, well... it's made sense to let her stay on the account so that she could pay all the household bills. I'm traveling so much now; it's easier that way. Plus, Bly doesn't really have any other income," Tayen shrugged. "To be honest, I've never been good at keeping up with money. It just doesn't matter much to me."

"This is starting to sound like some Britney Spears shit," Imani said. "Forget about wanting to learn to be a pilot for a second and come back down to earth. You've got to take charge of your finances. Let your mother know that she can't just make big decisions like buying a new house with your money and not telling you."

"Especially if she's going to give you hell and be unsupportive when you're there," I added, remembering how Bly had berated Tayen when she went home for her Imbolc visit. Along with everyone else in the room, I was beginning to get a better sense of Tayen's life outside of Rookes and what it might look like afterward. I'd never stopped to think that Tayen's bluntness signaled honesty to a fault. To the point that she might not comprehend why someone close to her would conceal anything. Or that it might be necessary for everyone to lie just a little bit, now and then, in order to survive.

That was when it hit me, as I watched Tayen grow wiser, absorbing our advice, with her coyote sitting at her side. The whole purpose of witches having familiars. They weren't merely companions to offer comfort in times of uncertainty. They were bringers of whatever types of energy that we lacked. Whether it was strength, confidence, or slyness, they were the purest distillation of natural self-preservation instinct. The magick was in being able to mystically touch their power. To tap into that animal viscerality of spirit was just as grounding as putting hands on Earth. Only theirs was an ever-mutable, transferable, cognizant intelligence that went beyond words, straight to the soul of the matter. The light to banish our insecurely shadowed selves.

The remainder of the lesson carried on. The star with over a dozen points that Hana's glass displayed was interpreted to mean a future in communication. That meaning came as no surprise to Hana or anyone else. She'd already declared a communication major at Harvard, much to her parents' chagrin, before coming to Rookes. Like Imani, the prediction of Hana's egg was merely a confirmation. Afterward, Katerina showed us a simple wand spell for putting our eggshells back together. Last, we worked by hand in dyeing them the colors of our respective elemental affinities, which for me meant a silvery gray.

After finishing up with the main lesson in oomancy, Katerina informed us that we would draw runes next, to provide further insights into our futures. She instructed each of us to pull one rune from a velvet bag and to allow Hana to help us interpret its meaning. If we wanted, we could add the symbol of the rune we selected to our freshly dyed eggshells to carry with us as reminders of what self-knowledge we'd gained.

Hana pulled Raido for herself first, indicating that progress toward her life's goals would involve a journey. Imani's rune was Othala, which symbolized home and heritage. Kenaz, or the torchlight of inner wisdom, was the rune that Tayen chose. I selected Berkana, or the Birch. It was the same as my wand wood, signifying renewal or rebirth. We finished using long needles to thread ribbons through holes at either end of our eggshells and marking them with our runes. Katerina said that it might also be beneficial to use the runes that had selected each of us as the basis for our first sigils, or signatures in the Otherworld of the Craft. Even though, she explained, our sigils would change and evolve as we grew further into our magick.

By the time we returned to the Great Hall, it was nearly dusk. Rather than our usual dinner spread, Candy brought in our incense burners from their kilns and placed them at each of our seats. Little dishes filled with handmade wax cones of frankincense and myrrh sat in the center of each table. Miranda was already seated at her place with her eagle on a little wooden stand beside her. Elliott was slowly feeding his horse slices of apple. Tayen's coyote yawned and stretched out on the floor, head on his paws, as she sat down. Hana and Imani's rooks perched with rolled paper notes tied to their legs on the backs of their chairs. However, when they unrolled the papers, both appeared to be blank.

"Ah, the keepers have written them in burner oil," Candy said knowingly, examining the papers. "Quite clever, the witches we have keeping watch over your familiars. You will have to burn these to receive the message. Here," she said, pulling Imani's burner closer and striking a match against the table to light the scrolls. "I will show you."

Together, we watched as the tiny flame consumed the paper. The wax cone inside began to melt, filling the hall with its sweet, spicy scent. As the smoke rose from the ceramic lion's mouth and the top of its head, a hazy image formed. It was a male lion; the silhouette of his mane was unmistakable. He was bounding through an open, grassy area. Behind him was a lake with several large cabins. While we watched, a bus filled with people trundled slowly by. Candy asked Imani if she recognized anything from the foggy tableau.

"I think so," Imani nodded. "My family back home has season tickets to The Wilds. It's a nature preserve just outside of Columbus. We used to go there all the time when I was a kid, but not so much anymore. Someone always has to stay and watch after Mom."

"That makes sense, given what was in my rook's message too," Candy replied. "I also received word while you were in your lesson that the lion who is to be your familiar was rescued, along with Hana's tiger, from the estate of a private big cat collector in Texas. The man passed away recently. Consequently, both big cats are unusually tame and would not thrive in an unsupervised habitat. Instead, they will live out their lives as ambassador animals, albeit in different facilities. I assume that, since yours resides not far from where you intend to attend college," Candy glanced from Imani to Hana. "That yours will be somewhere equally convenient. Why don't we go ahead and see?"

Candy repeated the process of lighting and burning Hana's paper, just as she had done with Imani's. Within moments, the smoke curled from the top of the head and mouth of Hana's round-bellied ceramic tiger into the shape of its real-life equivalent. Only this tiger was smaller and a younger animal, possibly still a cub.

"That looks like the Franklin Park Zoo," Hana said, peering into the smoke. "My folks used to take me there as a kid too. Their last tiger, Anala, died in 2022. I heard they were going to try to find another one because the tiger exhibit was empty. He'll probably live a long time. Anala was like seventeen when she passed."

"If he is the tiger who is your familiar," Candy replied, "perhaps even longer. Familiars are known for having very long lives. Further, we can always extend their natural lifespans by bringing them behind the glamor with us. The Otherworld slows their aging process too. Some of our magick rubs off on them, I think."

"All animals are magickal," Mary seconded, motioning for the rest of us to light the incense in our burners. "Let us now give thanks to the gods who've allowed these free and pure-spirited creatures to find their ways into our lives. May they grow like our dreams."

Although I followed along with the ritual, I couldn't help but feel a little bummed out. There I was, having watched for the last two days as all my friends' familiars appeared or at least sent word of where they could be found. Yet, I still hadn't received any sign of my fox. Even when I lit my incense burner, the smoke merely rose into a single, flattish, cube-like puff and hovered there, giving no indication of his whereabouts. I finished eating as quickly as I could. Feigning tiredness from my morning's headache, I excused myself upstairs to bed early.

As I brushed my teeth and changed into my nightgown, I felt lonely for my corgi, Luna. For the last seven years before I'd gone to Rookes, I hadn't been away from Luna for more than two days at a time. I'd always treated her like a human friend who just happened to have fur. A friend in whom I could confide my most secret thoughts and fears, finding only patient concern and, somehow, understanding. It was into Luna's fur that I cried so many times after Mom canceled plans to visit at the last minute or when I wallowed in frustration over how to tell Stephen that things were over. I had missed Luna's companionship so many times since coming to Rookes that I was sure seeing her again daily would be one of the best parts of my life after I returned home.

Slipping into bed, I snuggled down deep under the covers. As I began to drift off to sleep, I felt something fuzzy move by my feet. At first, I thought I must be dreaming of Luna because I'd gone to bed longing to see her so much. A few moments later, the little furry creature began wiggling its way to the top. In the half daze of sleep, I didn't realize what it was until his little triangular face was nose to nose with mine. A half-grown fox, its black fur speckled with silver like tiny stars.

Stretching out his small paws, the fox patted both sides of my face. He yawned so widely that I could see the pearly needle rows of his sharp teeth back to his molars. Then, as I continued to awaken, the fox began scratching beneath the pillow next to me. He squeaked and spat out something green. I jerked fully alert, wondering if the little fox had caught a frog or lizard.

Jumping out of bed, I flipped on the light. There, lying next to the little black fox, was a raw emerald roughly the size of my fist. Taking the flat, rectangular stone in hand, I examined it, noticing from its shape that it had been broken off from a larger piece by some human-made instrument. Where it came from, I had no idea. From its size and clarity, it appeared to be quite rare and probably expensive. The fox had no answers for me. He just squinted curiously with his sleepy green eyes as if to ask, *Don't you like your present? It took me ever so long to find it.*

Relieved, I climbed back into bed, setting the emerald on the nightstand. The light from the rising moon shone through the stone, creating a soothing glow. The little fox crawled up under my arm, encircling himself with his fluffy black tail. As I drifted off to sleep beside him, I could feel the throbbing headache that had lasted all day subsiding. In its place was one word that whispered itself into the furthest reaches of my consciousness. That word was *patience.*

Chapter Thirty-Three

F or the next eight weeks, we all worked on leveling up the results produced by our magick by learning how to work with our familiars. These efforts intensified when Mary announced, a few days after all our familiars arrived, that the final tests of what we'd learned during our time at Rookes would come early, around Beltane, rather than Midsummer, as was always the tradition. The reason was simple. It was intertwined with the revelation of what the secretive meeting of the Mentors was all about.

Finally, the Grand Council at Glastonbury had responded to Mary's request for assistance in protecting both the college and the Carolina coast from the hurricane that had been foreseen. However, rather than sending actual magickal intervention on their own, the Grand Council merely issued an edict allowing Mary to post officially authorized notices in *Old B* and *The Augur*, calling all alumni of Rookes to reassemble and assist in raising a Cone of Power against the storm.

In theory, it seemed to be a good idea. Using the combined energies from generations of witches, all educated at Rookes, and thus relying on their shared powers rather than the Grand Council, was just the sort of solution Mary preferred. She seemed almost giddy when she made the announcement over breakfast. Breathlessly, Mary explained she'd stayed up all night, crafting the perfect notice for the papers and sending it off immediately by way of her rook. Also, she'd written individually per-sonalized invitations to every Rookes College alumnus currently living, using magick to control several dozen quills simultaneously and employing every bird in the rookery to dispatch them immediately. Grace and Candy shared Mary's enthusiasm. However, Alice, Katerina, and Cora remained skeptical. I overheard the three Mentors gossiping about it when we walked back to the castle from outdoor lessons, on the morning after Mary's announcement.

As usual, my fox was playing his version of hide and seek, forcing me to find him by second sight instead of returning when summoned. I didn't want to look foolish by having to stand and call out *Fox! Fox!* over and over again, so I ducked into the garden to see if I could catch him in his favorite hiding place among the grape arbors. Not only was my familiar the one who most loved to play games, but he also refused to tell me his true name until I guessed it. Of course, that limited the amount of spellcraft we could work together. A familiar must tell a witch their true name to perform their best work. Believe me, if a fox ever enters your life, you'll figure out all the stereotypes exist because they're true. They love tricks. Regardless, I'd just spied him behind some rows of early berry cages in the garden when I heard the Mentors approaching. I crouched down beside him to listen.

"Mary only likes it because it fits her narrative of being an outsider among outsiders," Cora complained. "And because it gives her a chance to re-establish her sense of relevancy within the magickal community when enrollment is almost non-existent. But it's a huge risk."

"I agree that it's dangerous," Katerina seconded. "Not only for the college but also for the witches involved. I mean, what if no one else shows up? Will we be left to try to turn back the storm all by ourselves? If so, that would be a total disaster. The Cone of Power would need to be raised and maintained in shifts for days as witches grew weary. Long enough to ensure that the full threat of both the storm and its flood surge passed harmlessly back out into the ocean. Only a dozen witches, half of them young and barely trained, to work a spell of that duration and magnitude? It would be suicidal!"

"Oh, I don't think that's the problem," Alice countered. "Plenty of alumni will show up when they receive the call. When I'm outside the glamor, I'm constantly running into witches who want to reconnect with the rest of the magickal world. However, I think the real problem is that so many of those who would have the time and inclination to help have simply forgotten how to practice magick." Alice shrugged. "They've spent too many years hiding their talents in the broom closet. Trying to conform to the expectations of regular, non-magickal life as employees, spouses, and parents. I would seriously doubt that most of them would even remember how to transport themselves back here without assistance, let alone collaborate with other witches. I mean, can you imagine?"

Cora cackled at the thought, spreading her fingers wide and moving her hands in mimicry of an explosion. "That's true! It would take a lot of re-training just for the rest of us not to end up with our hair on fire!"

"We'll just have to retrain them," Grace interjected firmly as she entered the conversation. "Perhaps it's partly due to a lack of continued outreach that our numbers are down in the first place. Who knows? It might rekindle some interest with potential young witches to start looking for keys of their own if they knew some of their local elders were more active."

"I agree," Candy seconded. "There's strength in numbers. This is why I told Mary that we should send out more keys as soon as the rooks returned from carrying out the initial round of invitations. Not just to official alumni of Rookes College, but to other potential witches whom we've continued to observe through the years after they missed their initial key drop."

"You can't be serious!" Cora exclaimed. "Why would we want to waste time on anyone who didn't have the intuition to pick up their key in the first place? We'll have enough to manage as it is, what with re-training possibly hundreds of witches who haven't cast a spell since Roosevelt was in office!"

"Not to mention that it defeats the entire mission of Rookes College," Alice added. "To provide magickal education to witches who were selected based not on inheritance alone, but by curiosity, free will, and ability."

"Sisters," Grace sighed. "Let's not pretend that we don't know every witch here this year possesses some level of inherited magick. We've acknowledged Elliott's situation, but we've chosen not to address that in the cases of Imani, Miranda, and Hana; their magick came from their grandmothers. All of them declined formal training by failing to pick up keys when they were offered. That can weaken a magickal lineage so that sometimes it skips one generation and manifests in the next, as it did with their granddaughters. However, magick never truly leaves a family or an individual either. If it's there, it's there, even if they never attempted to develop it."

"But those are usually the ones who are the craziest and most difficult to educate in how to control their magick," Katerina insisted. "The ones who've waited too long to try. Magick possessed without an outlet can drive a person mad. Every witch knows that."

"All the more reason to give them a second chance," Candy stated, crossing her arms as if she felt Katerina had inadvertently proven her point. "At least, in the most obvious cases. Alice, you can't deny after Willow's visit with her mother that Darla has regretted not picking up her key every day of her life. Neither can Cora ignore that Bly would not be trying to live vicariously through Tayen if she felt that her magick wasn't irretrievably lost because she ignored her key. We wouldn't just be offering those women a second chance, sisters, but we'd be helping our students too. What young witch doesn't benefit from a more open and understanding relationship with her mother, through which goddess energy can flow more easily and uninhibited? How many more potential young witches could we be saving in future generations who haven't yet been presented with their keys? What could be gained if we offer their mothers the empowerment of hope and a challenge worth rising to one more time?"

The other Mentors fell silent, pondering Candy's questions.

At last, Cora spoke. "Well, if that's what we're going to do, then I'll support it. However, I'm not going to be the one who tells Tayen that her mother is being offered a second key. Tayen's talented, and her heart's in the right place, but that girl is like a firecracker of anger when something sets her off, even on a good day. Mary can tell her, or she can wait. You all better pretend to act surprised if Bly answers the call."

"It will only make things worse if we wait," Alice replied. "I don't relish telling Willow that Darla might be offered another key either. However, it simply must be done. Otherwise, we risk breaking the trust that we've built up all year, at a time when it's most crucial."

"I agree," Grace replied, always the peacemaker. "I think it might be best to tell them both tonight over dinner if the decision has been made. It will give them some time to adjust to the idea but not dwell on it before we announce their tasks for the end-of-year trials. If they take it badly, we can have Mary suggest that they rechannel their frustration into working extra hard to prepare so that they can be more impressive when or if their mothers arrive."

Trying to process the conversation that I'd just listened to made me feel dizzy. *Darla? Here at Rookes? After what had happened when I'd tried to visit with her at Imbolc? There's no way that could go well,* I thought. A wave of panic prickled through my body like a chill. Just then, my fox sneezed, right in my face. Unable to control it, I sneezed back, then swore.

"Willow, is that you?" Alice called, peering over toward the garden beneath a slim hand over her brow. "If so, you can come out now."

Guiltily, my fox and I slunk out from behind the berry cages. The other Mentors giggled and whispered among themselves, staring at me with amusement. Eavesdropping is like an Olympic sport for witches, whether in person or by magick. To quote Jane Austen, *'tis a fact universally acknowledged*. Their entertainment was based on the fact that I'd failed to conceal it.

"That fox is a bad influence on you," Alice joked, looking down at him. My fox looked away, like a cat on one of those home video shows who gets caught tearing up a whole pack of toilet paper. "How much did you overhear?"

"All of it," I replied, thinking silently, *and I'm not super thrilled*. Not ready to spew my insecurities all over the side lawn, I attempted deflection with a question that I'd already been wondering about, pre-revelation. "If Darla and Bly are being sent keys, will Elliott's father Albert receive one too? Or has Mary sent him a letter because he's an alumnus?"

Looking somewhat relieved that I hadn't screamed or burst into tears, Alice replied. "Willow, I think you already know the answer to that. If Albert won't respond to the request of his son, what good would it do for Mary, or any of us, to extend another invitation?" The expression on her face said the rest without words. Albert Capell's choice to cope with his banishment from the magickal world by spending the remainder of his life in exile was one of the reasons why all of this was happening in the first place. He was a man completely without reason and beyond the hope of anyone offering him refuge. If Mary could have persuaded Albert that the prognostications were accurate and that his business posed a danger, she would have already done so. His allegiance to preserving the future of Rookes remained unknown.

Over dinner, I dutifully pretended to be shocked along with all the other younger witches by the two announcements in the Great Hall. A first round of invitations would go out to alumni, followed by the second round of keys being offered to former prospective witches who'd failed to accept them before. Alice told me that this response, while slightly deceptive, would make it easier on Tayen because it would leave the opportunity open for us to commiserate about both of our mothers' imminent arrivals.

She and I agreed, along with the other mentors, that to reveal my accidental prior knowledge would only make things worse.

In truth, I was still somewhat stunned at the thought of Darla being physically present at Rookes, so my expression of bewilderment wasn't entirely disingenuous. Nevertheless, as I watched Tayen swear and storm off down the Fire hallway, slamming the door behind her in Cora's face as she followed, I felt slightly guilty once more. Even though I'd only had about half an hour's prior knowledge, that's a lot when the alternative is a revelation in front of a big room.

The feeling became worse when Hana got up from her seat and came around the table to hug me. Her sympathy started a chain reaction from everyone except Elliott. Instead, he hung back, mumbling only a cursory *I'm sorry*, in passing as he left the Great Hall for the barn to care for his horse, Grana. Sensing his discontent and my concern over it, Mary whispered, "Just give him some time," in my ear when her turn in the hug circle passed. Although I expected a late visit or at least some kind of message from one or both of them, I heard nothing all night.

The next day was one that we normally had free to ourselves. However, Mary decided that it would be better to take everyone's mind off the previous evening's unwelcome news to announce how tasks would be divided up for our final demonstrations of skills. We assembled in the Spirit tower after breakfast to listen as she explained how we were to proceed.

"To be granted welcome and full citizenship into the Otherworld," Mary began, "a new witch must prove that she has learned to control her magick enough to earn the right of choice between living in this world and our other, more consistently magickal one. All of us will pass into that world on a more permanent basis in due time. For over a thousand years, this exercise was known as the Trying of a Witch. However, since the Renaissance, the term has evolved in the common vernacular into what it is known as today, the Presentation of Powers. The rationale behind this linguistic change should be obvious to all. I would prefer not to elaborate further."

Mary's dark eyes darted sharply around the circle as we murmured in agreement. Over the year, we'd learned more than enough about the sordid history of witch trials throughout the world. Still, it was odd to think about how the phrase used to describe the process of young witches proving themselves ready to enter the Otherworld and become equals to their peers, a sacred rite of passage, had been twisted and distorted into a fight for their lives against non-magickal people who wished to condemn them. Even so, it was consistent with all that we had learned about the history of magick. Those in power sought to distort, demonize, and destroy that which they could not control.

"Good," Mary continued. "Then, let's proceed to the tasks, of which there will be three for each of you to complete over one day in the week following Beltane. First, your Mentors will devise some kind of test that will involve a magickal task with which we have witnessed you struggle in the past. To progress, you must show us how your level of skill has increased so that it is no longer a challenge. Next, you will be asked, on your own accord, to demonstrate some magickal ability that you are very proud of, but for which perhaps we have not fully recognized your aptitude. This act will provide an outlet for current self-assessment of your strengths. Last, after witnessing the results that you produced during the first two tasks, we will take a brief recess. During that time your fellow students will confer with one another and devise a third task for you. It will require you to show that you can work in concert with at least one other witch in attendance to produce some act of sympathetic magick. This final task will prove your potential for working together with other witches in the future. A capability that shall prove essential quite soon, as we are all aware."

Mary gestured toward the windows facing east, out toward the ocean. Again, we mumbled in quiet agreement, none of us wanting to call particular attention to ourselves. Having all survived twelve years of formal education before coming to Rookes, we all knew without saying what would happen next. One of us would be selected to go first.

Fortunately, we didn't have to wait long to find out. Unfortunately, it turned out to be me.

I attempted to protest on admittedly weak grounds. That it should be Tayen instead, since the sorcery lessons featuring her and her Mentor, Cora, typically began each week. Tayen shot me a look so cold that it could freeze water. However, as Tayen began to fume about my throwing her under the bus, Mary raised her hands for silence.

"There is no need for commentary, Miss Kennerly," Mary stated. "Your Mentors and I agreed last night that Miss Todd will be the first to present her powers. Tayen will go on the second day, followed by the rest. It is not a case of favoritism, I assure you, but a mere function of practicality. One's magick is typically strongest when not hampered by extraneous doubts or unexpected interferences."

Mary's sharp gaze met mine as her rook settled onto her shoulder. "I received notice late last night through our network," she nodded to Gregor, "that your mother, Darla, has at long last received and accepted her key. Stella delivered it yesterday to Brentwood. I wanted to give us a bit of time to complete your Presentation of Powers first, Willow, without distraction. Thus, I have not fully activated the spell that creates the key's pull. Having seen a key before, Darla is nevertheless instinctively aware of what it is. I do not want to hold her in suspense long enough to let uncertainty fester into fear. If all goes well, I will summon her to celebrate your passage tomorrow."

Turning to Tayen, Mary continued. "As for your mother, it will take an additional day for Darcy to convey Bly's key to Calabasas. Assuming Bly accepts it, I will initiate its drawing power as well, immediately following the completion of your presentation, Tayen. Depending on those results, we will continue one each day until all have completed their tasks. My thinking on the remainder of the order is to have Elliott next after Tayen, then Miranda, Hana, and Imani. If all goes according to plan, we should finish by the end of the week."

I must have looked worried. Alice came over and put her arm around my shoulders, whispering encouragement. My mind reeled with the news that Darla wasn't only coming to Rookes, but that she would be there most likely the very next evening. After I'd just completed what would likely be the most challenging day of spellwork I'd ever done. That is, if I passed. Mary seemed confident that I would, but I wasn't so sure.

Hadn't my worst struggles always happened when I was presented with memories of home? What if my magick simply decided to take the day off, like it had when we'd first been taught to fly? What if my condescending mother arrived, after a lifetime of predicting that I'd never amount to anything special, only to witness my total failure had proved her right? That she was the one who'd deserved to be presented with the powers of the Craft all along but had, on a whim, dismissed her chance in a moment of youthful foolishness? Wouldn't it prove that all the training I'd received at Rookes was wasted on someone as basic as me?

Staring blankly across the room as I descended into a spiral of self-doubt, I could see Tayen wasn't much better off. She lay forehead down on the table, delicate fingers interwoven in her long, tangled hair. Unwilling to look at any of us, I knew she must be struggling through the quicksand of apprehension in her mind about Bly's impending arrival.

Fortunately, Imani broke the tense silence in the room with a concern of her own. "If I'm going last, and the other witches who've been summoned will have begun to arrive, how many will there be by the time I'm supposed to present?"

"As usual, I think you already know the answer to that question, Imani," Mary replied. "It's why I chose you last. You're the best when asked to perform when all eyes are on you."

Imani beamed. I could tell she was excited by the challenge of showing off her powers to a castle full of elder witches. A star student-athlete and daughter of a college football coach, Imani was the embodiment of grace under pressure in pretty much any circumstance. Hana was almost as well off. Nobody grows up the child of overachieving college professor parents and earning a full ride to Harvard without learning to be comfortable under intense scrutiny. However, as Hana began to chatter energetically about what she might select as the spell of her choice, Mary called the room to silence again.

"There is one other rule that I forgot to mention. After we leave this room, no one is allowed to speak with anyone else about what their chosen demonstration of hidden abilities might entail. Further, Mentors will only speak with other Mentors regarding the tasks that we might set, and students shall only talk amongst themselves about potential tasks for other students. We will postpone our regular Beltane festivities until all have completed their Presentation of Powers so that even in the merriment of celebration we do not give anything away. Have I made myself abundantly clear?"

No one moved. Not even a nod. It wasn't necessary. What Mary asked wasn't a question, even though she had phrased it as such.

"Excellent," Mary answered herself. "Now, so that we are not tempted, ladies and Elliott, I think it would be best if we spent the rest of the day in preparation. Take your familiars with you for guidance. We will reconvene at dinnertime. And remember," Mary shot Hana a warning look. "Absolutely no further discussion about your individually chosen spells! We want to preserve the wonder and delight of surprise at seeing the best each of us has to offer."

If Mary had told me that I was to be expelled the next day, her words as we were dismissed couldn't have filled me with more dread. As my fox and I left the Great Hall, I wondered, how in the world was I, probably the worst witch there in terms of pure ability, supposed to come up with anything that would wow a room full of other, far more skilled witches? Nudging his smooth head under my hand, the half-grown fox switched his tail back and forth as his green eyes glowed up at me.

Don't worry, he seemed to say. *We'll think of something.*

Chapter Thirty-Four

Many people in this world practice gratitude journaling. I think it's unnecessary. Mostly because I've never been unaware when I felt genuine gratitude for anything or anyone in my life. That being said, I've rarely been more aware of my thankfulness for the presence of another creature than I was for my fox on the morning set for my Presentation of Powers. I know it sounds cliché given the circumstances, but there's no other way to describe it. The entire day was pure magick.

My familiar fox and I had spent the entire afternoon following Mary's announcement trying to come up with some magickal skill that would show me as both distinct and at least equal to my fellow students. At first, my fox was getting on my nerves, doing his thing of running off and hiding to make me find him right in the middle of every spell that I tried. Sneezing up a storm too, which made me wonder if he had a grass allergy like some sort of high-maintenance lap dog. He kept breaking the concentration that I needed to manifest my intention, which I was trying to amplify by keeping him in close contact. After scolding him for running away several times, I realized that he wasn't trying to play games. My fox was trying to communicate in little squeaks and barks. Frustrated and out of breath, I flopped down in the grass and yelled at him. *Why couldn't we communicate clearly like the other witches and their familiars?* How was I supposed to make our energies work together for spellcasting when my familiar couldn't even tell me his name?

For an answer, my fox hopped up into my lap and sneezed right in my face multiple times. An exaggerated series of sneezes, over and over, repeating the same two syllables that sounded like "fall-near." When he finished, the fox narrowed his eyes to little green slits and touched his nose right to the tip of mine. Squinting hard with his neck stretched out, his stare seemed to say, *I am telling you my name. Don't you get it, dumb human?*

"Gross!" I exclaimed, swabbing at my cheek with my sleeve and tipping the fox out of my lap. "I don't get it. Fall-Near? Is that supposed to be your name? What does it mean?"

The fox rolled over in the grass and rubbed his paws over his muzzle several times, as if he were trying to physically pull more words out of his mouth, but couldn't. He stared up at me expectantly, so I said it again. "Fall-Near. Tell me, is that your name?"

"Yes!" The fox squeaked, bouncing in the air to almost shoulder height. "It took you long enough! I've been answering for weeks!" His voice, when I finally understood it, was a cracked, high-pitched, nasal whine. Kind of sounded like the actor Pat Buttram, on those old Westerns that were always playing in the background of the vice principal's office at my high school. We had to go there for detention while we wrote sentences about whatever we needed to stop doing in class. A bizarre association, but that's exactly what my fox's voice sounded like.

"Fjolnir! Fjolnir!" The fox cried, racing around me in excited circles. Jumping back into my lap, he put his paws on my shoulders and his nose against mine once more. This time, he didn't sneeze but instead tilted his head forward so that I was looking straight into his shining eyes. As he did so, four words flashed across my mind's eye. *A Wise One Conceals.* It was then I realized that I hadn't asked him what his name meant. I'd only thought of the question, and he'd heard my thoughts.

Sensing that we were on the verge of a breakthrough in our communication, I concentrated as hard as I could on the question that had plagued me all afternoon. *What should I do for my part of the Presentation of Powers?*

Giving a huge sigh of relief mixed with exasperation at my slowness, Fjolnir pushed the answer back into my mind, clear as day. The idea was perfect.

After working out every wrinkle we could think of, Fjolnir and I returned to the Great Hall for dinner that evening, both quite pleased with ourselves. Not wanting to accidentally break the rules by sharing my excitement, I left early and went up to bed. Fjolnir snored contentedly in the crook of my arm all night, his paws quivering in the air during unseen dreams. My sleep was dreamless.

The next morning, I awoke filled with nervous energy. I hurried to get dressed and ran downstairs for breakfast. Fjolnir never left my side. I made him a plate of two soft-boiled eggs, which he gulped down happily. Little mention was made of the upcoming Beltane holiday, save for the crowns of small sunflowers set at our places as a remembrance of the celebration that would follow once we'd all passed our presentations. Everyone else seemed eager to see what was in store for me too. We rushed through breakfast and hurried out to the back lawn, beyond the Spirit tower.

The first task, devised by the Mentors, turned out to be kind of a trick that was intended to put all of us more at ease. Even so, I have to admit I panicked for the better part of an hour until I figured out what the trick was.

They'd intentionally given me a broken spell.

It was a pretty ideal task for someone like me if you think about it. I've always been plagued with imposter syndrome, both in my witchcraft and in my regular life. The kind of person who thinks they must be doing something wrong if everything in their life doesn't go according to plan, especially if they follow all the instructions to the letter. Also, one who tends to run away from problems that at first appear too intimidating or complex to solve.

This particular spell was very complex. Afterward, I learned all the Mentors had a hand in putting it together the afternoon before. Part one involved growing a lemon tree from seedling to fruit-bearing size. Easy enough, with a little combination of fast-growth spells for plants that we'd learned from Grace. In the second step, I was supposed to call lightning to strike and split the newly grown lemon tree using the summoning spell that Cora taught us. That wasn't difficult either. However, the third phase of the task was when things almost fell apart. To complete the challenge, I was supposed to use a healing balm to rebind the tree together so that it would produce lemons with a second application of the fast growth spell. Unbeknownst to me, Candy left out a key ingredient from the healing balm recipe on purpose. Without it, the spell couldn't work.

The possibility of such intentional trickery would never have crossed my mind had my fox, Fjolnir, not figured it out while I stood puzzling over my third fatally split lemon tree. The moment Fjolnir suggested it, I felt certain it must be a trick. Alice wanted to make me trust my familiar's intuition, along with my own. The key was having to question that there must be something wrong with the spell itself, rather than the way I was working it. In other words, I had to demonstrate that I believed in my own powers more than anyone else's I'd read about.

Once I'd figured that out, the rest of the solution was clear. I used a mirror scrying technique that Katerina showed us to view remotely what happened the day before in the Mentors' meeting. From that, I quickly determined that myrrh was the missing ingredient from the healing balm. Half an hour later, I had a basket of lemons from the newly healed trees. Mary whipped their juice into frozen lemonades for everyone to sip on while they watched the second phase of my Presentation of Powers. That part was the most fun.

During our practice the day before, Fjolnir and I figured out ways in which I could use glamors to impersonate every witch there simultaneously. I simply had to cast multiple glamors at once. My presentation involved sending all the Mentor witches back into the main castle building of the college while I went into a different room. Then, I cast the glamors, not only over myself but also over all the other student witches so that no one looked like who they were supposed to be. Last, I sent my glamored friends to knock on the doors of their Mentors, who would then question them to see if they could figure out who was behind which glamor.

The purpose of having the Mentors go into different rooms was to lessen the likelihood that my peers would give themselves away accidentally by acting in conformity with their true habits around certain Mentors. That way, they would avoid the risks of breaking their glamors. People tend to naturally behave more on their guard when met with a person they don't expect. I knew that first impressions when the doors opened would be crucial. Also, I was fairly certain that the Mentors would try to keep me on my toes by concealing themselves in glamors of their own. Just to see how far they could push the limits of my ability to maintain six glamors at once, by doubling the number to twelve. Although it was strenuous, I was glad that I'd chosen to glamorize myself as Elliott. Doing so concealed my sweating with what he would have produced on his own, given how nervous he gets working with glamors. Thus, I managed to pull it off.

The best part was that, just as I'd predicted, all the Mentors glamored themselves before the first doors opened. We all had a huge laugh in the mass confusion of the reveals at the end, which helped ease off the remainder of my tension for the day. Thanks to Fjolnir's help, I'd managed to fool every witch there with a challenging spell that worked a dozen times over. Everyone was properly impressed and somewhat giddy with the excitement of trying on each other's personalities, as viewed from my perspective.

After everyone finally changed back, which took a while because we were all clowning, it was time for the third and final task. The one that my fellow student witches were supposed to come up with was the biggest challenge they could think of for me. It was based on my performance in the other two challenges and lessons that we'd had together. I'd expected to have some time to cool down as they deliberated, but nope. They had already decided what my challenge was going to be the night before. Goaded by several pokes in the back from Tayen, Elliott moved forward reluctantly to act as the group spokesperson.

"Um," he began, clearing his throat and trying to avoid eye contact by staring at the paper in his hand. He'd written down what he was afraid he'd forget to say. I leaned forward in anticipation. Feeling the intensity of my gaze upon him, Elliott erupted into a fit of nervous coughing. He gulped down the rest of his lemonade and crumpled the paper into a wad that he stuffed into his pocket. Glancing at every other face in the circle gathered around him so that he could avoid mine, Elliott's words spilled out.

"We all know that prognostication, particularly with the crystal ball, is your biggest challenge. Also, it has been brought to my attention," he turned his head over his shoulder to indicate Tayen, "that your views tend to be especially obscured where I am concerned. Therefore, for your final task, they've..."

"We've," Tayen interrupted him. "It says *we've* decided, not *they've* decided. Don't put all the blame on us."

"Okay, okay," Elliott replied, resignedly. "We've decided that your final task is to scry for both our futures, using a crystal ball, for exactly one year from today. Happy now?"

"Yes," Tayen said.

"No! Mary, is this allowed?" I pleaded, hoping she'd intervene. The day had gone so smoothly I hated to end it with me becoming a nervous wreck and freezing up over the idea of looking into the possible future for Elliott and me.

"It most certainly is," she replied primly, looking amused. "I believe it's a legitimate choice. Katerina has told me that prognostication is one of the most challenging parts of the Craft for you. As such, the selection makes sense. However, there is nothing that requires every one of us to be present. Just one student and one Mentor as witnesses to the fact the task was completed satisfactorily should suffice." Mary paused and glanced around the group. "Katerina and Hana, I believe, would be the most appropriate choices, given that is their area of elemental affinity. So that you are free from distractions, you may complete the task in the Water tower. Are we all in agreement then?"

Of course, no one objected. Even though everyone else looked a little bummed, knowing that they'd miss out on witnessing firsthand what they all wished to be true.

While everyone else went off to dinner in the Great Hall, Elliott and I followed Katerina and Hana up to the main room in the Water tower. Maybe it was because Fjolnir was with me this time to help my clarity of vision, or maybe it was because I'd just had one of the greatest days of my life and I was channeling my best energy. Whatever it was, I had no problems seeing the future for Elliott and me that next year when I gazed into the crystal ball.

The vision itself was nothing extraordinary. Simple, but enough to tell both of us all we needed to know. Elliott and I were sitting outside some pub just off campus in Edinburgh, a couple of pints and a basket of chips between us. A series of open books on the table appeared as if we were studying. Our hands brushed together as we both reached to turn pages at the same time. Our fingers intertwined. I looked up from the crystal as the vision faded to see that we were holding hands across the table in real life.

"That was beautiful," Hana said, acting as if she were about to cry. "And perfect."

"Well," Katerina seconded, sniffling a little herself. "I believe that does it then. Let's go down and tell Mary and the rest that you've succeeded in meeting your last challenge. Congratulations, Willow. You're one of us now." Katerina hugged me. Then, she and Hana headed downstairs and into the Great Hall.

"So I guess that's it then, eh?" Elliott whispered as we stood alone in the atrium of the Water tower, the evening candelabra flickering above us. "You're coming to Uni with me?"

"To quote the Magic 8 Ball, signs point to yes," I replied.

"What's a Magic 8 Ball?" Elliott asked with a puzzled expression.

"Seriously?" I said. "Of all the weird, random things about magick that you've known your whole life, that I've never heard of, and you don't know what a..."

"Gotcha!" he interjected, raising an eyebrow, his gray eyes twinkling at the joke.

Fjolnir fell on the floor rolling and chattering, like it was the funniest thing in the world. And in a way, it was. This sad, beautiful boy, whom I'd hoped to cheer up every day for almost a year now, was finally made happy by something as basic as a vision of us reading and eating chips. I had become the reason for his happiness. Who knew such magick was possible?

As it turned out, I had one more surprise left for me downstairs in the Great Hall before my presentation day was over. Seated beside Alice at the white table was my mother, Darla.

In the back of my mind, I had known all day that she was coming because of what Mary had said the previous night. Still, it was impossible to believe. My mother. The one who bolted out of my high school graduation right after pictures without even offering to stay for dinner. Sitting right there, in a chair at the table in that magickal place, among all the other witches who'd become my family.

Darla was wearing the ceremonial white robe of a Spirit element witch. When I approached the table, she and Alice rose to offer their congratulations. Mary stepped forward and placed a sunflower wreath on my head. Everyone began to applaud. A thousand questions rushed through my brain. Checked by the filter of better judgment, only the least important one came out.

"How long have you been here?" I asked my mom.

"All day," Darla said. Her blue eyes were filled with a sort of girlish wonder as she studied me head to toe, lightly touching my robe and my face. "Long enough to see everything. I watched everything from up there." She pointed up to the top of the Spirit tower.

"And what did you think?"

"What did I think?" Darla repeated as she met my gaze. For once, standing there in the Great Hall of Rookes College, in the presence of pure magick, the brazen Darla Denton seemed genuinely humbled. "I think... I think I have missed out on so much. And I am sorry, Willow. Truly sorry. But I didn't know. It appears that I never knew anything. Is it too late to teach me?"

"Never," I answered, as I reached out to take my mother in my arms.

Chapter Thirty-Five

Darla and I sat up most of the night after dinner, gabbing like high school girls who hadn't seen each other in forever. The Mentors assigned her to the room adjacent to mine, second from the top of the stairs. It was wonderful, but also strange, to see my mother so happy and animated. Every little thing about Rookes College and its magick delighted her, from the avian messengers to the magnificent architecture. I mean, she was still Darla, egotistical and self-aggrandizing, but she criticized nothing. Not even me. Sure, part of it had to do with the fact that she was completely sober for probably the first time I'd seen her in about a decade. Throughout the whole evening, we drank only lemonade made from the fruits of my repaired trees. However, another part, I realized as we continued to talk, was that finding the key again had given her a new sense of hope.

When I asked her where she'd found it, Darla made me guess. Naturally, I couldn't, and I didn't feel like unwinding from the comfy chair in my sitting area to retrieve any of my prognostication tools. They were all put away, and I tended to knock stuff over onto the floor if I used a summoning spell while sitting down. So, I made her tell me.

"Do you remember a few years back when I got mad at Kurt and hired my real estate broker to pick up some vacation rentals to add to my portfolio?" Darla asked.

I admitted that I didn't, without telling her why. It would only kill the buzz of what was turning out to be one of the best conversations of our relationship. To tell my mom that it made me sick to think about how much wealth she enjoyed with Plastic Kurt when she must have known that Dad and I were struggling financially would put a damper on the evening.

"I know I must have," Mom said. "Anyway, my lawyer Cliff Tuttle wanted me to go down there and personally inspect all the mountain cabin rentals I had in my holdings over in East Tennessee. You know, to sort of get my bearings so I could guide the appraiser around better. There were six of them to be sold, and I'd bought all of them online through a broker. I hadn't seen a single one live and in person, or so I thought."

I let my mother's humble brag of owning half a dozen vacation rental cabins that she'd never seen slide and merely nodded encouragingly for her to continue.

"Well, when I got to the last one on the list, the one that my broker acquired most recently, I didn't even have to see it because I knew the address already!" From her build-up, I could tell that Darla was trying hard to fish me into guessing something that she thought was super intriguing. I refused to take the bait.

Still, her blue eyes held mine intently, so I finally indulged her attempt at a guessing game. "Okay, so what was the address?" I asked in a sing-songy, patronizing way.

"7023 White Wing Road!" she exclaimed, tipping over her empty lemonade glass. "The old cabin where we all used to live! Isn't that wild? I mean, I'd owned it since last summer, but I wouldn't even have known it if Cliff hadn't made me go out there!"

"Wow, that's some coincidence," I said, finishing off my lemonade as well. I tried not to show that I was surprised. The last person that I ever thought would buy Oliver's old cabin was the woman who'd run away from it before and never looked back. "Where did you find the key?" I asked, refusing to fall down that rabbit hole of memory.

"Do you remember that little trail that ran into the woods, out behind the pool deck?"

I nodded. On summer evenings during high school, I used to stay in our above-ground pool floating around until my fingertips were wrinkled as prunes and the fireflies came out. "Yeah, the one that ran down by the creek, where Luna used to chase squirrels and..."

"Who's Luna?" Darla asked.

At that moment I had two revelations at once. The first was that my mom, even at her best, had so absented herself from my life that she didn't even know the name of the dog I'd had for seven years. However, the second was the conclusion of the thought I'd been about to finish when she interrupted me. "And foxes," I said. "Luna is my corgi. She used to chase squirrels and foxes down that trail."

Foxes that I knew now had been watching over me. Most likely on that very trail leading into the woods from our swimming pool. They reported back to Mary so she would know to send my key. Years later, they had watched my mother too.

"But that's... just... it!" Darla exclaimed, drawing out each word individually for her dramatic conclusion. "I followed a fox down the trail to where I found the key that brought me here. A fox that looked just like..." she waved at Fjolnir, who lounged on the footstool.

"Wasn't me," the fox yawned. "I'm English. Distant cousin likely. Black fur is rare. We may be kin though."

"How can you be English with a name like Fjolnir?" I asked.

"All English foxes have Old Norse names," he replied, stretching out his paws and swishing his brushy tail. "That's where our magick comes from. East Anglia. Look it up."

Darla stared at us, amazed by our exchange. The funny thing about familiars, I'd learned, was that they could only be understood by humans who shared their familiar form. Darla was no fox. That made sense since it was Oliver's name, Todd, that meant fox. During my visit to him several months before at the field station, Oliver mentioned that we should talk more about his mother, Ursula Todd. I'd supposed that he thought she was magickal as well. However, if Darla wasn't a fox spirit too, who knew where her magick came from?

We discussed the possibilities for a while, without coming to any real conclusions. The Dentons were, despite their moonshining past, what Southerners call "deeply religious." The nearest we came to figuring it out must have meant that whatever magick Darla possessed would be hard to trace since it had been repressed into dormancy for a very long time. As the energy of our evening finally wore down, Darla had a few more revelations for me before we retired.

"I'm leaving Kurt," she said. "I'd been thinking about it for at least five years now, since his last fling with that nurse. In truth, it doesn't even make me angry. Kurt works in an industry that worships youth, and I'm getting older. Even though I'm well-maintained, it's something even I have to admit, sooner or later. However, if I left, I wanted to be smart about it. I started hiding money away from him. That's why my lawyer had me go up to check out the cabins and have them appraised. I'm planning on selling them off to buy a place of my own. It won't be much. A million and a half doesn't go very far in the Nashville real estate market these days, but I suppose that's the price of freedom." Darla shrugged nonchalantly.

Same old Mom, I thought. Even in her most difficult moments, Darla's narcissism could buoy her along. I felt bad for her, kind of, but I knew she didn't care about Plastic Kurt. She'd miss the big house in Brentwood, but she'd be okay.

"What about your guitar collection?" I asked. "If you're having to downsize to a house worth only a million and a half, it might be a good idea to think about selling some of those off as well for extra capital. They looked pretty valuable."

"Perhaps," Mom replied, yawning as she uncoiled herself from the chair and blinked slowly. "I don't need all twenty-five of them. I could make do with a half dozen or so for my writing."

"You're writing songs again?" I asked, somewhat interested, despite my sleepiness. Fjolnir had given up on us and gone to bed, burrowing himself deep under the velvet comforter. I was past ready to hit the hay myself, but I was intrigued by her revived ambition. "Planning on doing anything with them?"

"As a matter of fact, I am," Darla said, as she rose to let herself out. "A new artist approached me after a hot yoga class a few months ago and wanted to know if *he* could work with me on some new material. *He* specifically thought that an older, more experienced female co-writer's opinion would be very valuable and add a lot to his creative process."

She paused, letting the fact she'd emphasized the word *he* several times sink in. Darla always liked to drop hints about the weight of anvils. "We've been working on a lot of new things together," she added flirtatiously.

"Mmm hmm, I bet," I replied, rolling my eyes as she opened the door. Hoping she'd spare me the details, I added, "Mom, have you ever heard the saying that goes something like 'she who toots her own horn never gets tooted'?"

Darla made a face as she slipped out the door. "Oh no, I'd never do that. I've never even been attracted to side men."

As I crawled into bed beside my sleeping fox, I couldn't help but smile about my evening with Mom. At her best, my mom was very similar to the Blanche Devereaux character from old *Golden Girls* reruns that I used to watch on repeat. Spoiled and salacious, but still charming and a lot of fun when she chose to be. At worst, though, Mom could be quite cold and calculating. I thought about how she still planned on selling our old house just for her benefit, even though I'd told her why Dad had lost it. Drifting off to sleep, I wondered what kind of witch Darla Denton would be once the innocence of discovery wore off. Only time would tell.

The next morning, we were all up bright and early again for Tayen's Presentation of Powers. Hers went as smoothly as mine had the day before, with the added flourish of an elaborate fireworks display that looked like shooting stars at the end to show off her Fire witch powers. Similarly to Darla, Tayen's mother Bly was waiting in the Fire tower after it was all over. However, Bly wasn't the only one. At least a couple dozen other witches waited too. They all got up and applauded loudly as Mary placed the sunflower crown on Tayen's head, signifying both her rite of passage into the Otherworld and our Beltane sabbat.

Every day following, more witches continued to arrive. Most looked to be middle-aged and older, but a few were still in their twenties. By the end of the week, when Imani completed her last presentation, she returned to a Great Hall filled to overflowing with five hundred of us. The numbers were split evenly between alumni of Rookes, some who were still actively practicing magick and some not. The others were those who'd missed picking up their keys the first time around. The enormous room, in which the voices of only a dozen witches had echoed all year, hummed with hundreds of excited conversations, like a crowd waiting for a concert. The entire castle radiated with enthusiasm. Even Cora and Alice admitted that their initial concerns about having to tolerate hundreds of untrained and out-of-practice witches were largely unfounded. Every witch in attendance was full to bursting with excitement, eager to learn and hanging on to every word that the Mentors said as if it were a lost gospel.

On the first official morning of their training, which began the day after Imani's presentation, Mary had all the Mentors and regular year-long students distribute and explain their wands. The idea was to get them started right away on the spellwork they would need to produce collaborative magick that could raise and maintain a Cone of Power.

Their first official act of magick would be to build the Beltane bonfire out on the beach near the pier. Under our instruction, they ignited individually fallen branches using energy sourced from the cloudy sky and channeled through their wands. Then, we showed them how to redirect that energy, using only magick to pick up their branches and stack them onto the pyre. Despite their eagerness, or maybe because of it, there were more than a few singed robes getting started. However, no one was seriously injured, and nobody's hair caught on fire. Thanks be to the gods for small favors. As you might imagine, with five-hundred pieces of kindling fueling it, we had an enormous blaze going in no time.

With the flames leaping higher and voluminous clouds of smoke billowing into the gathering darkness, Mary called for all of us to join hands. Taking Darla's hand in mine, I glanced over to see her face, as well as Bly's, glowing in the firelight with sweaty exertion from their spellwork. Tayen's mother and mine had become almost instant friends, which wasn't surprising, given their similar backgrounds on the fringes of the entertainment business. Learning of her re-selection for the Craft had the same effect on Bly as it had on my mother. According to Tayen, Bly's constant criticism of her daughter dissipated once she had other more engaging thoughts to occupy her mind. Judging from Tayen's grin, I could tell that for once, she was unreservedly happy.

"Tonight, we enjoy this somewhat belated celebration of Beltane, one of the sabbats during which the veil of illusion between this world and the next is at its thinnest," Mary began. She hovered slightly above the ground, between our ring of clasped hands and the pyre.

"Our fully presented witches and our new sisters will gain their first glimpses into the Otherworld. The realm into which witches may choose to cross over and never grow old. To open the portal wide enough to see what special message awaits us, we shall dance and chant. Everyone, repeat after me."

Spirits of night, we circle and sigh,
Toiling and spinning, as flames climb high,
Cast open for us these doors from below,
Into perception's shadows from above we go.

Mary's voice took on a rhythmic quality. As she finished the verse and began another, I could feel the tension of a slow beat pulsating through both Darla's hands on my left and Alice's to my right. The circle began to sway back and forth uneasily, like the needle of an uncertain compass, as we echoed back the chant in unison. Levitating above the sandy shoreline as we repeated the rhyme, Mary prompted another quatrain:

From the heart of the ocean, dark as a tomb,
A cursed azure flower of destruction may bloom,

Give us a sign, so that all here may know,
The specter against whom our magick must flow.

As all echoed this second verse, the wavering energy of the circle caught in the air, like a tumbler clicking in a lock. We all began to run, still holding hands, but with our feet several yards above the ground. Faster and faster, we chanted and circled, until I began to notice what at first seemed to be just another point of light from a distant star growing larger. When it was directly overhead and as broad in circumference as the bonfire, it seemed to twist and open from the center, like the aperture of an analog camera.

Looking into the circle of sky above the camera, I could see the back of a very tall man in a floor-length, forest-green velvet cloak over tall black riding boots. His long, dark hair, a wild mess of curls highlighted with silver, cascaded over his broad shoulders. He was peering into a massive, old-fashioned brass telescope. His thin profile, with its slender-bridged nose pointing downward toward a chest-length beard, curled up slightly at the end, reminded me of a crescent moon. Sensing us looking over his shoulder, he pulled back from the telescope and pointed across the horizon in front of him.

"There is *a* storm, but not *the* one," he croaked, in a hoarse, strained voice that matched his face, which was lined deeply like a topographical river map. "However, I maintain a constant vigilance. As soon as I lay eyes upon it, I will send word to prepare. When the hour of landfall is near, I will come to the aid of Rookes College. Tell my son I will be there with him soon. I have left him too long alone."

As the man stepped away from his telescope and turned towards us, I could tell that he was about to say more. Then, several older witches gasped. The spinning circle, powered by our running feet in the air, stopped abruptly as I crashed into Darla's side. Immediately, the golden window of vision snapped closed and was obscured by ordinary bonfire smoke.

The spell was broken. We all fell to the ground. Hushed whispers rumbled through the group, with worry following quickly upon the heels of speculation. *Did you see him? Was it him? Who? Capell. Yes, that Capell. Albert Capell. No. It can't be. Can it? I thought he was dead. Capell. Albert Capell.* Over and over again.

His ashen face made even paler by the glowing firelight, Elliott ran around the roaring fire to Mary. "Father!" Elliott exclaimed, his voice trembling as a flood of questions poured out. "Where is he? What did he say? Is he coming? Did he ask for me? I couldn't hear!"

Making a motion with her hand as if turning the page in a book, I felt the sand of the beach beneath where I sat ripple. Pulling the sand over it like a wave, Mary extinguished the bonfire, leaving behind only a great dusty cloud of smoke. As we coughed and struggled to our feet in the salty, acrid air, Mary called for us to reassemble inside the Great Hall.

When we were all seated, Mary began to explain. "For those of you with at least passing familiarity of the magickal world and who had an unobstructed view through the aperture into our Otherworld, I confirm that the man whom you saw was indeed Albert Capell." Again, a concerned murmuring rippled through the crowd. "However, there is no need for worry. Despite the fact of his unforgivable act that resulted in the tragic death of our fellow witch, Gwendolyn Welles, rest assured Mr. Capell means none of you any harm."

"But he's a murderer!" one witch yelled.

"I thought he'd been cast out of the Otherworld!" another hissed.

"There is no denying that you are correct on both counts," Mary replied, holding up both palms open for silence. "By causing his wife's death, Albert has committed a heinous wrong, for which he has been and will continue to be severely punished, both by this community from which he is in exile and by his conscience. Since beginning construction, Mr. Capell has been completely truthful with me about his belief in the safety of his most recent offshore drilling enterprise with Albion Oil. Recently, however, his ambivalent position toward the possibility of a hurricane causing major damage to the region has changed. He swore that he would do everything in his power to keep me fully informed regarding any threats to our island that the weather or other unforeseen circumstances might pose."

"How can you trust the word of a killer?" A third voice cried from the far side of the hall.

"Because he's risking certain death himself to offer us the longest possible window of time to prepare for the coming storm," Mary answered. "Albert Capell has been banished upon punishment by execution if he is ever caught by the Grand Council Guards either setting foot in the United Kingdom or the Otherworld. However, even at this great personal risk, he has volunteered to maintain personal watch over the construction of

Albion's wells. Through the less inhibited visionary environs of the Otherworld, he can report any potential threats to me immediately. Although every precaution has been taken, it will be impossible to know how much flood surge the wells can withstand until they've been tested by a strong storm. Once this first hurricane threat is past, Mr. Capell plans to return to semi-anonymous exile in non-magickal America. Until then, Albert keeps watch over us."

Elliott looked stunned. "But... why?"

"Because there are two things here at Rookes College that Albert Capell cares more about than anything else in the world," Mary answered. "His son and his memories. After his conviction, I remained one of the few witches who would offer your father counsel, Elliott. It was I who advised Albert that leaving you with your grandparents and allowing you to work through your training in the Craft at Rookes would offer you the safest and most stable path to a normal life as a witch in control of his powers. Albert agreed. He watched from a distance until you accepted your key. It was also Albert who helped arrange for the transport of your familiar horse, Grana, so that she would be close by to answer your call. You have never been far from your father's thoughts, Elliott, even if you haven't seen him."

"If what you say is true and he cares so much, then why does he refuse to open the door when I try to visit?" Elliott asked, fighting back the tears that threatened to choke his words. "If he's been speaking with you, why does he refuse to listen to me?"

Mary's face wrinkled with pain as she answered. "Two reasons. First, because your father knows that being caught interacting with him can only cause you trouble. Albert is aware that every school in Britain refused you training simply because you were his son. You've seen what the press and court of public opinion can do. How much worse would things be, Elliott, if it were known that you and your father were on regular speaking terms? That one of the only witches of his generation to have been banished from the Otherworld for killing his wife was to suddenly take an interest in guiding the life of his son? Much worse, I assure you. Witches are a smaller and more insular community than non-magickal humans, and they never forget. Also, crossing between the Otherworld and this world is dangerous for an exile like Albert. Although he might be able to sneak between worlds miles out into the ocean, regular reappearance even over a place as sparsely populated as Rookes Island causes a disturbance in the energy field that can be detected by Grand Council Guards. Thus, if your father wishes to maintain his constant vigil from the enhanced remote viewing perspective of the Otherworld, it is much safer and easier if he does so while disappearing and reappearing from the deck of one of his oil rigs out in the Atlantic Ocean. That way, he can take advantage of the concealment offered by salt water. And without risking your safety in going back and forth out there either," Mary added.

Sensing Elliott's questions rise before he asked them, Mary continued. "Doing so could only draw further attention to his actions. The Grand Council would prefer if your father were dead, Elliott. It would be much more convenient than maintaining watch over him in permanent exile. However, that kind of punishment has been unanimously banned by the magickal world since the 19th century, and for good reason. Given time, especially over a witch's lifetime, which could span hundreds of years, people can change and redeem themselves. And that is what your father is trying to do, Elliott. To find a path to redemption for himself. If he does not make it, Albert wants to leave you with something else beneficial. His fortune, enhanced by this new drilling enterprise, only without the burden of his attachment."

Naturally, a volley of questions followed from all sides. Mary fielded them with brevity and kindness. It must have been difficult, because their tone was insulting and accusatory, at least in the beginning. It seemed everyone hated her sympathy for Albert. Although their anger at her concealment of their communication was valid, I kind of understood her reasoning. She was the only witch there who'd known Albert since he was just a student trying to distance himself from a terrible family. The fact that he'd come to be known as one of its worst, and to father a son who sought to run away from his legacy too, was cruel irony.

After a while, things died down. We enjoyed a delicious meal of rice and kabobs, which had been roasting over the many hearths in the Great Hall since before we'd even gone out to the bonfire. The fact that all the food for our Beltane feast came out cooked perfectly and on time was a marvel. It occurred to me as I lay in bed afterward that somehow, Mary must have planned every detail. From the building of the bonfire to the shocking reveal of her communication with Albert Capell and the intensely emotional round of questioning that followed, Mary was always a woman with a plan.

Whatever else history in the regular human world or the Otherworld might say about her, one thing was clear. Mary Rookes remembered everything.

Chapter Thirty-Six

In the weeks that followed, I would never in my wildest dreams have imagined that the Mentors could get all our newly recruited witches prepared in time. Yet, that was exactly what happened. By focusing only on two parts of the Craft instead of five, primarily sorcery with some specifically chosen spellwork, and taking zero days off, five hundred new witches were ready to take their places in raising and maintaining the Cone of Power by Litha, or Midsummer.

Through Mary's continued contact with Albert as he moved between the Otherworld and his Irish home, and my earthly correspondence with Oliver, who watched the weather like a hawk after I told him what we'd envisioned, the witches of Rookes College followed the storm's progress. A day after she formed near Cabo Verde, the hurricane was named Persephone. For over two weeks, the slow-moving squall churned its way across the Atlantic, gathering width before speed. By the time it passed just below Bermuda, Persephone had reached Category 2 status. It continued to be upgraded every other day. Soon, she was a Category 3 and still gaining strength. News reports afterward would blame global warming for her swift increase in size and velocity, as that hurricane season turned out to be one of the strongest on record. At her peak, Hurricane Persephone was moving about 150 miles per hour, or just shy of official status as a Category 5.

Of course, I didn't learn about any of this official meteorological news until later. We continued to exchange messages with Oliver at the field station about the storm by our rook messengers until about three days before landfall. When we received news that Oliver was being required to evacuate inland, along with most of the population along the eastern seaboard from Ocean City, Maryland, all the way down to Charleston, Mary decided that it was time to bring the rooks into the castle to ride out the storm. The Mentors summoned every land animal willing to take shelter inside. Our last couple of days before Persephone arrived felt like living in a strange sort of zoo. Every kind of native animal from deer to raccoons, dozens of species of birds, and even a couple of curiously docile bobcats prowled around the hallways.

The Mentors directed us to raise the Cone of Power around the perimeter of the college island. We began a rotating schedule of a hundred witches at a time, holding it in place. Limiting ourselves to four-hour shifts, it was still exhausting work. The original students and Mentors took turns flying close to the edge to keep watch for weak spots in the protective glamor. Half of the newer witches on each shift constantly sourced lightning from the clouds and rechanneled it to push back against the outermost edges of the glamor that concealed the island. Then, the other half stationed themselves out in small boats near the glamor's edge. They pulled energy from the waves that crashed against the outside of it, diffusing it over the surface. This action reinforced the bubble surrounding the island, rather than breaking through it. The Merfolk remained inside the bubble with us, using their sympathetic magick to sustain the glamor down to the bottom of the sea floor.

Looking up at the gray sky roiling over the glamor was surreal, as if we were inside of a washing machine looking outward through a dome of glass. All the redirected energy holding the glamor in place flashed constantly across the outside of the sphere it created in blue and magenta streaks like a giant plasma ball. The whole process left the air crackling with ozone and the air smelling slightly of sulfur. Inside the glamoured sphere held up by our Cone of Power, it was curiously calm. The air was dead still, and not a single drop of rain fell.

Our goal was to hold the energy in place until a few moments before landfall. Then, just as the eye of Hurricane Persephone reached us, to drop the glamor and release all the power that we'd maintained for days in one big push, hopefully turning the storm back out into the ocean.

Both Albert and Oliver seemed confident that the cutoff caps on Albion's oil wells would be able to withstand the storm surge left in Persephone's wake if we could succeed in either slowing the storm down to below a Category 3 or altering its course completely. Although he'd urged his staff to evacuate after shutting down, Albert Capell remained behind to monitor the storm's progress alone on the Albion rig closest to our island. From his perspective above it in the Otherworld, Albert could to report to Mary any changes in the hurricane as soon as they happened until it was almost directly over us. At that time the amount of salt water in the air would prevent communication even through magick. Then, Albert would signal Mary that it was time for the glamor to be dropped. All five hundred witches would be summoned to make the final push. Having no protection against the storm surge once the glamoured sphere supported by the Cone fell, the Merfolk would shelter in sea caves beneath the island until after this maneuver. As soon as our witch magick began to turn the storm, the Merfolk would re-emerge and back us up by combining their sympathetic magick and providing additional support from underwater. By re-establishing the Cone of Power and glamor quickly from the sea floor upward until it covered us again in its protection, the Merfolk could prevent the backwaters of the storm from flooding the island.

In terms of magickal theory, the plan was solid.

As it happened, Miranda Flanagan was the witch flying closest to the top of the glamor when Albert Capell fell from the sky.

Using his familiar form of a winged horse for extra strength against the wind, Elliott's father tried to reappear from the Otherworld right on the other side of the glamor just as the hurricane was about to make landfall. His intention was to give the signal and ride the storm straight down through the eye as the Cone dropped. Then, to remain inside and help as we raised the Cone again. As soon as she saw him approaching, the witch on top perimeter duty was instructed to relay his signal to Mary that the eye of the storm was precisely overhead. Mary would direct all other witches to work together in the final push as the Cone of Power receded.

Yet, Nature was too fast for us. At some point in the moments this relay took, the force of the hurricane's winds slammed Albert against the electrified perimeter of the glamor, penning the wings of his horse to the blazing surface. Frozen in horror at watching thousands of volts of electricity shoot through Albert's body, Miranda was unable to fly down to safety, meeting the rest of us on the ground as planned. In the confusion of our desperate attempt to organize all the witches as quickly as possible after the missed signal, no one noticed Miranda wasn't there. As a result, Miranda was still almost a mile overhead, right next to the edge of the glamored sphere when the Cone of Power collapsed.

The plan worked exactly like it was supposed to otherwise. As soon as the Cone dropped, over five hundred witches thrust their wands skyward, catching the rush of the hurricane's raging winds and towering waves. For a split second, I stared right into its eye. Then, an impenetrable wall of surging water roared above us, followed by a deafening boom as the currents of all our combined magick hit it at once. When the storm turned, it created a vacuum, pulling us off the ground and into the air. Terrified, many of the new witches lost concentration, plummeting back down to Earth. The rest of us held steady though, keeping the energy going long enough for the Merfolk to raise the Cone and close the glamor once more above, sealing us inside. With our powers severely spent on the rush, it took every bit of what little magick we had left among the witches who hadn't passed out from exertion to maintain the glamor. Yet, it was immediately noticeable the hurricane had turned. The wind whipping rain against the perimeter of the sphere was coming from the opposite direction.

Taking a count as soon as the ear-splitting din above us softened enough to hear names being called, it was apparent that two witches were missing. Miranda Flanagan and Albert Capell. Although none of us had seen it because it happened so fast, the reason for their absence was clear. Hurricane Persephone had taken them both with her into the churning ocean.

In the evening that followed, those of us trained in healing tended to the minor injuries, mostly sprained wrists and ankles, of the witches who'd fallen. Even though I was exhausted, it was good to mix salves and wrap bandages. Having something to do with my hands kept me from crying. The other witches of our year felt it too, I could tell. None of us were able to look at each other. Gentle Miranda was gone.

Still, in our grief, we had each other. Although they hadn't known Miranda as long as we had, her sweet nature made an impression on many of the newer witches too. As we finished up with the initial round of triage, I realized Elliott had left. Alice told me he'd asked if it were okay for him to go back to his room once he'd finished working with the witches who needed care. She agreed and added that I should go up to speak with him when I was done. There were enough witches still strong enough to hold the glamor without me until we resumed rotating shifts again in a few hours.

I found Elliott in his room, sitting at his writing desk with pen in hand, in front of a mound of wadded-up paper. Freyja, his grandmother's falcon, was beside him. Nan Welles had insisted on the bird staying with us so that Elliott could write to her as soon as the storm passed. Like many witches, Elliott's grandparents didn't trust either the non-magickal news or the official magickal papers to tell them the truth about almost any story. Even though Elliott was sworn to secrecy like the rest of us at Rookes not to breathe a word of his father Albert's efforts in trying to help us, Nan Welles must have figured it out.

"What should I tell them?" Elliott asked, looking up from the desk when he sensed my presence. His eyes were bloodshot from holding back tears. I could tell that he was frustrated and angry. "What can I say to my grandparents, about the man who killed their daughter? Or to the thousands of witches who despised him? That the world is finally rid of the menace that was my father? That by dying, he finally did something right?"

Carefully, I knelt beside Elliott and took the pen from his hand. "You might say that he died helping to save us," I offered quietly. "And that you're sorry to not have the opportunity to get to know him as a man who wanted to change for the better."

Elliott grimaced. "I'll have to deal with them too. His people, the Capells. All my life, I've avoided them, but now..." He trailed off.

"For the memorial maybe," I tried to reassure him. "But that's just a few days. You won't have to live in the shadow of your father and his family forever."

"No! Don't you see?" Elliott yelled, slamming his fists down on the desktop. "That's just it. I do! Albion and his castle in Shanagolden with that goddamned demon woman living there who corrupted my mother. All of it!" His eyes were wild with fear. "I'm his only heir. Those are my burdens. They belong to me now!"

What could I say in answer to that? Everything Elliott said was true. Before he'd even be able to think about going to university in Edinburgh or living any part of his life as he wished, he'd have to figure out what to do with his father's oil company. Although Albion was only one of the smaller independent oil and gas companies, it was among the world's most hated. Primarily because Albert Capell had been known for pushing to drill in areas where others wouldn't go, in hopes of staying competitive. Anyone who inherited it would have to make a choice. Keep up the web of shady inside deals that Albert had going with dozens of politicians or go out of business. Selling wasn't an option, at least for most of their operations. I knew because Elliott had told me before. None of the more reputable energy companies would touch Albion's holdings with a ten-foot pole.

As for Albert Capell's estate at Shanagolden, the castle was covered in a glamor. It was a ruin, as far as anyone in the non-magickal world could see. Not only that, but it would be irresponsible to sell it to anyone unaware of its propensities for dark magick. From everything I'd heard about it, Elliott was right when he claimed the inevitable burden of its ownership. The Capell family had given birth to the Black Hag, and her legacy was theirs to bear. Her castle was ungodly ground.

Up to that point, all of my instincts in life had been to run from confrontations like the ones I knew Elliott would have to face. To be the bolter. Yet, my year at Rookes College had taught me two things. First, when faced with a problem that your instincts couldn't immediately solve, sometimes you just had to stand your ground and be patient. And second, if you trusted Nature and followed the Craft, somehow magick could help you outfox any situation in the end.

"I wish more than anything that I had answers for you," I said softly. "Right now, I don't. But that doesn't mean I never will, or that I won't sometime soon. Remember the vision from my presentation. One year from now, we'll be sitting outside a pub in Edinburgh, studying for a bunch of silly tests like a couple of basic college kids. And I'm not sure if all of this will be over by then, but even if it isn't, it still looks like we've found one small reason to be happy, doesn't it?"

Elliott took a deep breath and massaged his forehead. He brought his hands down to cover his eyes. Lost in the darkness of his thoughts he whispered. "Promise that whatever happens, you won't leave me. I can't do this alone."

Reaching up to move his hands gently away from his face so that I could look into his eyes, I swore with one word. "Never."

We were sitting there silently, just looking at each other when Hana burst into the room.

"Willow, Elliott, come quick! It's Miranda. She's alive!"

The three of us rushed down the stairs. Following Hana across the back lawn toward the pier, I saw a group of Merfolk gathered around something. As we got closer, I could see it was a cocoon of seaweed. It was similar to the one in which Miranda had been wrapped before, on that day in which she nearly drowned. Only her face, ghostly pale, shone out of the viridian shroud.

"I found her in the surge that followed when we closed the glamor," Celine said, her large, bright eyes red from crying. "She wasn't breathing, and I knew there wasn't much time left, if any, to save her. So, I covered Miranda's mouth with mine and willed her to breathe as I dove for help."

"When Celine brought her to my cave, I could see that it was already too late," said Arnaud, a merman with a long gray beard that trailed down past his waist. I remembered him as the one who'd helped rescue Miranda before. "There was no way for me to bring her back to the human way of living. Miranda had simply been without oxygen for too long, even though her soul had not left her body. So, I had to do the only thing that was possible to save her life. What the Merfolk have done since time immemorial to preserve the lives of humans caught too long in the sea." The elderly merman reached both hands to touch the sides of Miranda's neck, carefully pushing back the tightly woven strands of seaweed. "I made her one of us."

Leaning down over where Miranda lay, I saw two sets of pink scars, three on each side, scored into her neck. As she inhaled and exhaled, moving the flaps of skin that covered them, I could tell that they weren't just ordinary cuts. The merman had surgically carved a set of gills into Miranda's neck. Glancing down toward where her feet should have been, I wasn't surprised to see that instead of legs, the bottom half of Miranda's seaweed-encased body fanned out in the shape of a tail. Then, I understood what Arnaud meant. To save Miranda from drowning, they had turned her into a mermaid.

"She'll need to stay like this with us for several days," the old merman explained, patting the seaweed back into place around Miranda's neck. "Until the changes have fully integrated and she's used to respirating both above and below. Once she's healed enough to swim on her own, we should notify her human family. I will leave it to your judgment, Mary, as to what would be the best method to go about it. My apologies that I had to act without notice beforehand, but there was simply no other way. If I hadn't..."

"Miranda would have died," Mary completed his thought. "Yes, I understand completely. You did the right thing Arnaud, and for that, I am certainly grateful. The outside world will come for all of us soon enough."

Mary stared up at the pitch-black sky, where the rain continued to fall steadily and heavily, obscuring any hope of starlight. The only illumination in the eerily quiet darkness emanated from the torches carried by the dozens of witches encircling Miranda's body on the pier.

From this ring of concerned onlookers, Grace, Miranda's Mentor, stepped forward. "When she is able again, I will help Miranda decide how best to tell her parents."

"As will I," Celine seconded. "Miranda need never feel that she has lost one life without gaining another."

Hearing familiar voices close by, Miranda's eyes fluttered open. I noticed that their color, always an unusual shade of hazel, had become even more striking after her transformation. The irises glowed with brilliant incandescence that reflected the torch flames around her like the facets in a pair of emeralds. Unable to speak yet, I could see Miranda's lips forming the names of the two who stood closest to her, *Celine* and *Grace*. Tears slid down Miranda's cheeks as her confusion upon waking into her new body became apparent.

Kneeling on either side of Miranda, both whispered gently.

"You're alive, dear heart. That's all that matters. We're here for you."

Epilogue

S o mote it be. And so it was, for all of us.

Hurricane Persephone, or the Midsummer Hurricane, as it came
to be known in the twenty years since, was recorded by weather histo-
rians as perhaps the strangest anomaly documented in the history of
storms in the North Atlantic. No official determination was ever made
by NOAA regarding why the over one hundred miles per hour winds
of a Category 4 storm suddenly reversed direction just after making
landfall on the most far-flung islands of the Outer Banks.

The leading theory was that a deep-water earthquake had been the
reason. Claiming the earthquake was caused by new offshore drilling
that destabilized the continental shelf surrounding the East Coast,
environmental activist groups were able to successfully lobby for the
President to issue an emergency executive order shutting down all operations of Albion Oil in the area. In the months that followed, panels
of geologic experts, including former Albion Oil employee Dr. Oliver
Todd, testified in a series of Congressional hearings that although
Albion's wells were built strong enough to withstand such storms initially, there was a high possibility that over time, that natural wear and
tear on the equipment by subsequent hurricanes made a future disaster
inevitable. That expert testimony was enough to convince the Bureau
of Ocean Energy Management to issue a permanent injunction for
the immediate cessation of all oil drilling operations off the Carolina
coast because such practices were inherently unsafe. By the following
summer, Albion Oil's East Coast operation was bankrupt. After its
Gulf Coast assets were sold off to larger energy conglomerates both
to satisfy the debts and to ensure the safe deconstruction of the wells,
investors walked away with a wash.

Rookes College changed drastically too, in short order. Although we'd managed to save the castle itself, the Grand Council of Witches at Glastonbury revoked its official educational charter the following fall, when Mary Rookes was forced to report that not a single new witch had picked up a key, thereby resulting in an enrollment of zero. Nevertheless, among the five hundred witches who'd responded to Mary's call before the storm, there was a tremendous outcry.

A petition was drawn up to allow Rookes College to continue with a new mission: to re-educate older witches whose magick had fallen into disuse in proper methods of re-entering regular practice. Feeling that short refresher courses might prove to make the magickal world a safer place because out-of-practice witches who attempted literal homebrew spellcraft at random intervals were considered to constitute a general menace, the Grand Council granted Rookes College a new charter the following year specifically for that purpose. Today, Rookes remains the only place in the world where adult witches can seek out a second chance, once they're past the usual age considered appropriate for training.

As for the members of Rookes College's last class of traditional graduates, we're all still out here living our lives, both magickal and mundane.

When Miranda recovered and her transformation into a mermaid was complete, she sent word to her parents through her eagle about all that had happened. Unwilling to believe a word of what they considered a trick concocted by their missing daughter, whom they just knew must certainly be under the influence of drugs, the Reverend Flanagan and his wife chose not to write back. Instead, they told their congregation that Miranda was on an extended scouting trip to the most remote parts of Africa, actively seeking those in need. Fueling the narrative with false news reports generated by the public relations department at LifeSpark, the Flanagans announced on their official television show that their youngest daughter Miranda was going to lead a new branch of their mission program overseas on a permanent basis. Hundreds of thousands of dollars in support poured in for their LifeSpark Africa campaign, and the Flanagans quickly began a new branch of ministry.

To their credit, the LifeSpark Africa campaign actually did a lot of good in helping fund hospitals in rural areas of the continent. It's just that Miranda Flanagan, former televangelist's daughter turned first witch then mermaid, had nothing to do with it. She was otherwise quietly occupied, building a new life with her aquatic girlfriend, Celine.

Dr. Imani Griffin, although kept well-informed by Miranda during subsequent visits back to the island for our annual Rookes College alumni reunions, chose not to tell her grandmother that LifeSpark Church's new Africa mission was founded under somewhat false pretenses. She had too many other things on her mind.

After finishing medical school, Imani completed a residency at the Cleveland Clinic's Alzheimer's Disease Research Center. Over the years, she was eventually promoted to Director. Although Imani hasn't yet found a cure for the disease, her team has made great progress in new treatments that can almost completely arrest its progression if caught early enough. Her husband, Maestro Moses Tembo, is currently in his tenth year as conductor of the Cleveland Orchestra. When we gather, Imani never fails to mention it's the number one-ranked classical music organization in America and the seventh-ranked in the world. Together, Imani and Moses share three almost annoyingly talented sons, who are all honors students. They each play several different instruments perfectly. None of them play football.

Speaking of spouses, I'm sure that Hana would be quick to point out that even though Imani's husband Moses leads one of the most esteemed orchestras in the world, he's never been on *Saturday Night Live.* Turns out, I never had to introduce my ex-boyfriend Stephen Thornton to my former classmate, Hana Atwater. They found each other all on their own the summer after they both graduated from college and moved to New York. Hana and Stephen have the cheesiest meet-cute story you've ever heard. I'll spare you the details, which I'm sure you can look up on YouTube if for some reason you're into all that fairy-tale, meant-to-be celebrity romance stuff. They've both given several versions of the story in various interviews over the years.

After Harvard, and much to her parents' chagrin, Hana chose to intern at a big-name talent agency in New York that represented a bunch of famous comedians. While she was working there, Hana met Stephen. He'd recently finished with Vanderbilt and was desperate to land an agent so that he could avoid getting roped into moving back to Tennessee for law school and joining his father's firm. Somehow, Stephen convinced Hana, who was working the front desk, to talk one of the senior agents into going and seeing his standup routine at an open mic. The agent loved Stephen's act and signed him immediately. From there, Stephen was picked up as a new cast member on *SNL*. He and Hana carried on the stereotypically awkward will-they-or-won't-they type of relationship you see in all the rom-coms for about five years before getting married and having a daughter. You've probably heard of her too. She's the voice of the main fish in that children's cartoon, *TigerBarb*. Hana owns her own public relations firm, which handles both entertainment clients and local politicians. She says people keep trying to convince Stephen to run for office. He says he's more interested in performing comedy than becoming a clown in real life.

Tayen's been on television too, of course, both for her modeling and to promote her family's enterprises. Turns out, the reason that Bly got so upset when Tayen popped into her house party was that Bly had some very important guests over that night. Bly was afraid that Tayen's introduction of some impossible tale into the evening's polite discussion would crash her credibility after she'd gone to the trouble of buying a whole new house and decorating it with prototypes to create what she called a livable showroom concept. Some of those first party guests went on to become investors in Bly's sustainable furniture company. Their specialty is mid-century modern replica sofas made entirely out of recycled plastic water bottles and bamboo fibers. Tayen appears in a lot of their ads.

She's also the spokesperson for her father's space tourism company. As Tayen neared forty and her runway career slowed down, she finally took the time to earn not only her commercial pilot's license but also her commercial spacecraft license as well. Tayen gets a real kick out of randomly showing up as a transport pilot for Nyles's moon colony vacation company. People don't know what to think, she says, when they see her in the cockpit and recognize her from her other life. The YouTube videos of passenger reactions that people post from time to time about it are hilarious.

My mom Darla's career has taken some pretty unexpected turns too. After her divorce from Plastic Kurt was finalized, Bly invited my mom to move to Calabasas and live in her guest house. The change of scenery from Tennessee to California, without a doubt, made Mom's songwriting creativity take off. I think she's always been more suited to writing pop than country. Darla's never been able to fake enough interest in pickup trucks and small-town Saturday nights to convince anyone. Humble, she will never be. However, give her free rein to name-check designer brands and rehash high-class relationship drama, and she can instantly morph from hick to Hollywood. It was no surprise to either of us that when Darla was able to summon her animal familiar at last, it turned out to be a chameleon.

As for Elliott and me, we did make it to the University of Edinburgh. The story of what happened during our years together after Rookes College could fill many books. I may get around to writing them someday, but publishing the truth is complicated. As John Wayne said in *The Man Who Shot Liberty Valance*, "When the legend becomes truth print the legend."

Suffice it to say that Elliott finished his program in botany and went into hydroponic agriculture, which turned out to be a very financially successful venture. Tayen's father, Nyles Kennerly, selected Elliott's company to be the official provider of locally sourced produce for his lunar vacation company, which gave it plenty of positive press while still a startup. The corporate branch of Hana's public relations firm handled the media promotion. I do some contract work for Kennerly Aerospace too, mostly geological surveys. Tayen keeps trying to convince me to join one of their lunar research colonies as a mineralogist, which is technically my research specialty.

I'm thinking about it.

Although she'd never admit it, I think that Tayen's whole purpose in calling us to work with her is that she misses all of us. Someday, we may be together again. Who knows? As Mary Rookes says, the tree of any witch's life has infinite branches of possibility.

Every branch symbolizes a new path that starts the same way.

A witch sees a silver key in the dust, and she picks it up.

Acknowledgements

Every writer is a product of the world that supported her creation, and I am no exception. First, I would like to thank my mother Linda for introducing me to the fact that real magic exists, if you just know where to look. Next, I appreciate my grandmother Roberta for taking me to the library every summer and encouraging me to read all the "big girl" books, beginning with Charles Dickens's Great Expectations. Third, I want to recognize the emotional support of my partner Andrew, who patiently listened and offered suggestions through many lengthy discussions of my manuscript, and who helped me with digital formatting. Also, I was fortunate to find a very talented cover designer, Marta Obucina and an insightful editor, Raigan Nickle, who helped me prepare the witches of Rookes College for their public debut. Fifth, I must acknowledge the encouragement I received from my fellow authors at the Midwest Writers Workshop and the Killer Nashville Conference, who selected the manuscript of this novel as a Top Pick for the 2024 Claymore Award in Fantasy. Last, I am grateful to Ray Bradbury, a legend who took the time to visit a small literary conference at Birmingham Southern College in Alabama that convinced a ninth-grade girl she could be a writer too.

What Bradbury said was true.
The magic of imagination can make you live forever.

About the Author

Vivian Catfield is the pen name of Dr. Candace Ursula Grissom. She holds a PhD in English from Middle Tennessee State University and an MFA in Creative Writing from Sewanee: The University of the South, among other degrees. Born in North Alabama, she lived in Murfreesboro, Tennessee for many years.

Currently, she resides in Cincinnati, Ohio with her partner Andrew and her cat Jim Nightshade. Outside of literature, her interests include acting, exploring haunted history, and spending time outdoors. Keys in the Dust is her first novel.

If you enjoyed this book, please check out www.viviancatfield.com and www.catfieldpress.com for the latest news and updates on upcoming titles.

Also by Vivian Catfield

What would you change if you could live your life over again?

Following her husband's death, Nora Hewitt seeks a new beginning by opening an interior design firm in Wilmington, North Carolina.However, Nora's entrepreneurial dreams are shattered after she acquires a set of haunted mirrors. Eerie, inexplicable events lead her to befriend a ghost hunter, revealing a forgotten world beyond the glass. When her sister vanishes,Nora must confront her family's tragic history: secret paranormal experiments, her father's alleged suicide, and her husband's mysterious death. Guided byrestless spirits, including a past-life lover, Nora races to save her sister, while embracing her power as a woman alone.

Also by Vivian Catfield

Who can you trust after finding out that your beloved was a liar?

Grieving her husband Ethan's murder, private detective Shiloh Foley finds two dead women in Eden Park. The investigation reveals a shocking secret: Ethan, a Cincinnati police officer, knew about the cover-up of a horrific sexual abuse scandal at his elite local prep school. Now, the victim seeks revenge as the Prophet ofEden Park, building a cult in the city's abandoned subway tunnels to systematically terrorize and eliminate his attackers. With a team of unlikely allies, including a nun, a teacher, a social worker, and her assistant, Shiloh struggles against family betrayal and fights political corruption to uncover the truth and she races to stop the Prophet's deadly plan before it's too late.

Also by Vivian Catfield

Which wolf will win the battle raging inside of you?

On the eve of the Colorado Gold Rush, Mae Ulrich, a strong-willed, progressive heiress from Maine, leaves her home with dreams of starting a frontier school.Plagued by prophetic nightmares of vicious beasts, Mae's idealism is destroyed when she uncovers a ruthless plot to steal Native American lands and gold.Traveling west with a saloon keeper and a fur trader, Mae bonds with a mysterious cowboy and a gifted student. When a violent attack forces Mae to confront her fears, her shocking connection to the beasts is revealed. Embracing her inner darkness, Mae fights for justice in a gold-hungry nation, questioning the costs of change in a brutal pre-Civil War America.

www.ingramcontent.com/pod-product-compliance
Lightning Source LLC
Chambersburg PA
CBHW051950240626
47153CB00005B/1699